# Puck, MARRY, Kill

OTHER TITLES BY LAUREN LANDISH

## Stand-Alone Novels

*It's Just Business*

## Dirty Puckers

*The Diamond Puck-Up*

## Maple Creek

*I Do With You*
*The Pucking Proposal*

## Cold Springs

*The Wrong Bridesmaid*
*The Wrong Guy*

## Never Say Never

*Never Marry Your Brother's Best Friend*
*Never Give Your Heart to a Hookup*
*Never Fall for the Fake Boyfriend*

*Never Kiss the Bad Boy*
*Never Bargain with the Boss*
*Never Dance with the Devils*

## The Truth or Dare Series

*The Dare*
*The Truth*

## The Big, Fat, Fake Series

*My Big, Fat, Fake Wedding*
*My Big, Fat, Fake Engagement*
*My Big, Fat, Fake Honeymoon*

## Bennett Boys Ranch

*Buck Wild*
*Riding Hard*
*Racing Hearts*

## Tannen Boys

*Rough Love*
*Rough Edge*
*Rough Country*

# PRAISE FOR LAUREN LANDISH

## *The Pucking Proposal*

"A total treat to read from start to end. I loved all the lighthearted drama and humor."

—*Harlequin Junkie*

## *I Do With You*

"[A] playful small-town romance and series opener . . . Readers will be eager to return to Maple Creek."

—*Publishers Weekly*

"Some authors just seem to have a natural knack for penning original stories of romance with all the highs and lows and ultimately happy endings that make the genre so popular. With the publication of *I Do With You*, author Lauren Landish demonstrates herself to be just such a novelist."

—*Midwest Book Review*

"This small-town good girl falls for the bad boy romance was cute, sweet, and a bit spicy. A total must-read."

—*Harlequin Junkie*

## *The Wrong Guy*

"Loaded with spice, heart, and drama, this is sure to win over readers."

—*Publishers Weekly*

## *The Wrong Bridesmaid*

"Landish's steamy novel begins as a standard wedding-fling romance but develops into an exploration of small-town life, the rising costs of real estate, and navigating family responsibility and personal ethics, all of which anchor a sexy love story featuring a bold heroine who loves a good innuendo and a decent hero who knows that the wrong bridesmaid is the right woman for him."

—*Library Journal*

# Puck, MARRY, Kill

LAUREN LANDISH

Montlake

This is a work of fiction. Names, characters, organizations, places, events, and incidents are either products of the author's imagination or are used fictitiously. Otherwise, any resemblance to actual persons, living or dead, is purely coincidental.



Published by Montlake, Seattle

www.apub.com



EU product safety contact:
Amazon Media EU S. à r.l.
38, avenue John F. Kennedy, L-1855 Luxembourg
amazonpublishing-gpsr@amazon.com

ISBN-13: 9781662532023 (paperback)
ISBN-13: 9781662532016 (digital)

Cover design by Hang Le
Cover image: © FTAPE LIMITED; © Weera Travel / Shutterstock

Printed in the United States of America

# *Puck,* MARRY, *Kill*

# Prologue

## Dominic

"What the fuck did you just say to me?" I spit the words out so quickly that there's no chance to stop them. Not that I would've, even if I could've.

My heart is racing too fast, pounding against my ribs. My hearing is down a long hallway, hollow and echoey. And my eyes are wide open, which is why I see the instant Coach Leverson registers both my rude tone and my disrespectful cussing.

"Now, look here, son . . ." he starts, sounding like he's placating a too-willful-for-his-own-good, stubborn asshole of a child. Which I might be. I'm not arguing that possibility.

"Don't 'son' me after telling me I'm getting traded, when I helped this team win the fucking Cup last season. A few very short months ago." Did he forget? How could he have forgotten? I sure haven't. It was the biggest, brightest, best moment of my life. The culmination of a dream I've had since I was a kid.

Coach closes his mouth, the clack of his yellowed veneers making a sound of finality that matches the steely look in his tired eyes.

"Why?" I hiss.

It's starting to sink in—I, Dominic Lee, am getting traded from the best team in the league, the one where I've played for years, to one of the league cellar dwellers. Okay, that's not fair. Coach said I've been traded to the Blizzard, who we played against in the finals last season, but there's no argument to be made about it, they're lower on the hockey stick than we are.

Not *we*. Because I'm no longer an Ice Hawk. I'm a Blizzard.

Me, fucking traded? What upside-down, topsy-turvy world is this? If this is a nightmare, I'm ready to wake up. Now. I curl my toes in my boots, digging them in and hoping the slight pain will raise me from sleep, but other than a cramp in my big toe, nothing happens.

"Dom, I know this comes as a shock to you," Coach says placatingly. "It was a shock to me too. Definitely a decision made above my head, and I tried to keep you. Know that, son." He pins me with an earnest look, but it only slightly eases the sense of betrayal starting to take root in my gut. "The Blizzard are having some turnover this year and they need you to do for Kipson what you did for Mahoney."

My brows draw together sharply. "What?"

I've done a lot of things for Griffin Mahoney, the right defenseman for the Ice Hawks, but more importantly my brother from another mother. Most recently, that has included only *attempting* to kill him after I found out he was fucking my sister. I say *attempt* not because *I* stopped, but because my sister, Penny, stopped me with an announcement that they're dating, in love, and blah, blah, blah. Not my best moment, but now that we're all good, we can laugh about it. As long as they don't talk about their sex life.

"What do you mean do for Kipson what I did for Griffin? I don't have another sister and I'm pretty sure Griffin doesn't share," I say flatly. It's a joke, but also . . . not. Unsurprisingly, Griffin is head over heels for my sister, which translates to protective as hell.

Coach leans back in his chair, steepling his fingers in front of his chest. "What do you know about the Blizzard?"

"They're not the Ice Hawks," I declare flatly. "They're not the current champs. That's enough."

Coach tilts his head, staring at me in disappointment, before he carefully says, "That's true. They're not like the Hawks in a lot of ways." I don't know what that means and he doesn't explain further. Instead, he shares, "Kipson got divorced right before the finals last year. He's not doing well. Some might say he's spiraling, and that's putting it mildly." Coach frowns hard like that's a generously kind description of Kipson's current state.

Realization dawns.

"Shiiiit. Kipson is thinking of quitting?"

Mike Kipson is good at two things—popping nifty wrist shots that seem to curve around goalie pads in midair, and staying out of the spotlight. The man's a wizard with the puck when he's on. All I know about him is how to go up against him in a game. But peripherally, I know he's in the prime of his career, with years of ice time left. Unless injury or mental shit, which is surprisingly a big part of success in hockey, takes him out.

"Not if you can stop him," Coach declares. "He's down bad. Thinking of running off to Nebraska or somewhere to chase after his girl." Coach makes it sound like the most ridiculous thing he's ever heard of.

"That sucks for him. Really, it does. But it's not my problem. I saved Griffin because he's my brother."

Coach shrugs. "Looks like your family's growing. Congrats, it's a boy."

Coach has jokes? Now? When he's telling me that my dream of back-to-back league championships is dead in the water?

"Fuck." The curse isn't directed at Coach this time. I've got my wits about me enough to know that's unacceptable. But directing it at the ceiling isn't much better.

"I'm sorry, Dominic. But if you want to keep playing—which we both know you do—this is happening."

I take a measured breath and slowly exhale as resignation sinks in. Meeting Coach's eye, I admit, "I don't want to go. This is home for me."

He nods in understanding. "I know, kid. But this is the name of the game in pro hockey. You go where they pay for you to be." Admittedly, a bit of a cynical outlook, but he's not wrong. "Just don't do *too good* of a job saving Kipson. I plan on the Hawks winning again this season, with or without you."

The subtle jab makes me smile tightly, back on confident ground. "Good luck with that, Coach. You know the only reason we won last year was because of me," I brag, aiming for my trademark cockiness but coming up short.

"I know," he agrees, smiling warmly. We both know it was a team effort that required every Hawk doing their part, but I appreciate him letting me save face a little bit because this feels like I'm being dismissed as the weak link, the one they don't need. "It won't be the same here without you, Lee. The Blizzard is damn lucky to get you."

He stands and holds his hand out. I rise, taking his hand in mine and shaking it firmly. "It's been an honor, Coach."

"The honor's all mine. Now go kick some sense into Kipson and I'll see if I can getcha back next season."

It's nothing more than a polite pleasantry, but it does keep a tiny light of hope lit in my soul. Maybe I can get back home—to my team, to my family, to my life—soon.

# Chapter 1

## Dominic

Sitting in my truck in the parking lot, I stare at the pair of double doors like they've offended my entire family line, and snarl at the garish neon-green sign above them proclaiming "O'Neal's" as though the double apostrophes are bullets straight to my brain. To be fair, neither the sign nor the doors have done anything to me. It's what they represent.

They're the portal to this new phase of suckage that is my life. My life, which was going stellar until a few weeks ago, when I suddenly had to sublet my place, pack up my truck with most of my shit, and move to a short-term rental in a city where I don't know anyone or anything.

And yeah, the generic cc on a "welcome back" email from a team I don't even know is pretty much the cherry on top of this shit sundae. No assistance on moving, no star treatment, nothing. Since it's not a mid-season trade and I'm not a hot young draft pick, I'm ignored to the point that I don't even want to get to know these assholes.

Fuck this. I'm only going to be here for a season, and then I'm going home.

But I am a man who enjoys a mission, so I studied up and did my homework like a good little soldier. Mission: Yank Mike Kipson's head out of his ass, slap him stupid, and get myself traded back to the Hawks as soon as possible.

With that in mind, I stride across the parking lot, sling open the door, and enter O'Neal's, switching out my grim-set mouth for the fakest of fake smiles. "Let's do this shit," I grumble to myself.

The bar is surprisingly welcoming, with dark wood floors, green-globed chandeliers, and a dozen small round tables surrounded by guys. I don't head there. Instead, I go straight for the bar along the wall. I need a drink for this.

"Whiskey, beer back. Whatever you have is fine," I tell the bartender. She sets a shot glass in front of me and I swallow it in one go, welcoming the burn. Taking a sip from the beer so it won't spill, I approach my doom, otherwise known as the Blizzard players.

Amazingly, I'm greeted well, considering the beatings I put on a lot of these guys during the playoffs. "Dom!"

"Hey, man! Heard you were joining us!"

"Welcome to the best team in the league."

The guys seem friendly enough, a bit rowdy even if I'm being honest, but that last one I can't let slide. "You mean the second-best team. Hawks won the Cup last season," I boast, proud of the accomplishment.

Anderson, the Blizzard goalie, grins like he was poking at me intentionally. "A toast to it being us this year! Welcome to the shit show." He throws an arm around my shoulders like we're best buds and holds up his beer.

"Welcome to the shit show!" the chorus echoes.

"Thanks," I tell them. Then I tilt my head and tease, "I think."

Initial awkwardness handled, I work my way around the room, mingling and meeting a bunch of players and various team staff, including my new coach. I hold my hand out in greeting as I say, "Coach Boothe, nice to meet you."

The Blizzard coach is in his late fifties, could probably bench press as much as some of the team guys, and has a suntan line around his eyes that tells me he spends a lot of time outdoors wearing sunglasses, probably golfing. But he's no armchair analyst, I know his playing stats and he's earned his reputation.

"Good to have you here, Lee. You were impressive last season. Hope to make good use of those skills this year too." He flashes a smile, but it's gone too quickly to be friendly. He's a businessman at heart, and his business is hockey.

"Same," I reply because agreeing seems to be the safest answer. I mean, I do want to play. Otherwise, I would've told both teams to fuck off. But hockey is my life. There's nothing like flying across the ice, slipping through holes that no one else sees, and keeping our goalie from having to be target practice.

Coach Boothe lowers his voice, his chin dropping too. "I trust Leverson told you the deal?" I nod subtly, and Coach looks pointedly toward a man sitting alone at one of the tables. "Hope you've got some magic. Otherwise, this team is fucked and so are you."

"No pressure, though, right?" I joke.

"Oh, make no mistake, there's pressure." With that, Coach drifts away, finding a group of what appears to be interns to talk to.

I sigh, my anger at the situation reigniting in my gut. But I might as well get this shit started.

It's not the type of situation where I can walk right up to Kipson and lay my cards out with an "I hear your life sucks ass and I'm here to save you from yourself, so nice to meet you" type deal. I have to play it smarter than that. Instead, I work the room, getting closer and closer to my target. I'm not overly friendly with anyone, which isn't that hard to do since I'm not happy to be here and a lot of these guys know it after my situation last season. But eventually, I'm in front of Kipson.

Mike Kipson is a monster of a hockey player, whose stats put him at six foot three and 225 to my six foot and 200 pounds of lean muscle. Those few inches and pounds make a world of difference, both on and off the ice. But right now, the man in front of me looks so hollow that I could probably knock him down with a playful slap to the shoulder.

"Hey, man," I say, starting this rescue mission.

He barely lifts his eyes from where they're locked on to his beer. "Lee."

We're not instantly trading friendship bracelets and braiding each other's hair, but it's a decent start for two assholes who are reasonably pissed at their lot in life at the moment.

"Looking forward to hitting the ice with you this season." A white lie, but I think God will forgive me given the circumstances.

He sighs heavily, his lips settling into a deep frown. "Look, I know you and Mahoney are all buddy-buddy, but it's not like that here. We're not gonna be bros."

Griffin Mahoney and I have been friends for years, and other than the pesky matter of gestation, we're brothers, so of course Kipson and I aren't going to suddenly have the same level of connection. "I don't need another brother, so no worries there," I inform him, eyes narrowed to watch every microexpression that crosses his face. What I see most is surprise, as if he fully expected me to want to be his new bestie. "All I need is for you to keep your off-ice shit *off the ice*. Think you can do that?"

Okay, so maybe I'm throwing my cards out a bit prematurely, but it happens to the best of us. Or so I hear. Besides, some people need a velvet glove, some need a swift kick in the ass. Hopefully Kipson's the latter.

He huffs out a dry, humorless laugh. "Yeah, I can do that."

I don't believe him any more than he believes himself. "Good. Then we'll be fine."

Kipson picks up his beer, downs the whole thing in one swallow, and slams the empty glass back to the table. "Gonna hit the head."

"Make sure you shake it off before you come back out." I don't mean his dick, but rather his mood, and he knows it.

"Fuck you, Lee."

"Fuck you, Kipson."

It'd seem like we're already sworn enemies, but in the ways of guys, we're about two weeks out from an after-practice beer and a month out from those friendship bracelets. But if he needs help moving into his postdivorce bachelor apartment, he can fuck off. I'm not letting him borrow my truck.

An hour and one beer later, I've avoided Kipson in favor of getting to know some of the other guys. Mostly because I figure they can give me a bit of recon insight, plus I do have to play with them this season.

But mostly what I've learned is that these guys are annoying as hell. On the Hawks, we had a guy we called Brody, not because it was his name but because he was such a *bro*, like the most stereotypical frat dude you've ever met. The rest of us were *professional* athletes, and conducted ourselves that way.

The entirety of the Blizzard team seems to be cut from the Brody cloth, however, which is to say immature, annoying, and obnoxious.

"Hey, Dom, pick three . . . fuck, marry, kill," Anderson tells me. He raises his beer to the bar at large, which is filled with people coming in for a quick after-work drink or to meet friends. Or strangers.

I furrow my brow and shake my head. "I don't do that sort of juvenile bullshit."

Sabine, a left winger, and Pacholek, a center forward, join in with Anderson's teasing. "Come on, it's just for fun. Look around." Anderson points at a few women scattered throughout the bar.

I have half a mind to point at Tweedlefuck (Sabine) and Tweedlefucker (Pacholek) as at least two of the three options just to get them to shut up. But in the end, I point at two women. "Fuck. Marry." Then I point a finger gun to my temple. "Kill."

They laugh, but honestly, *kill me now* sounds about right. How did I go from dinners with my best friend and sister to this? How did I end up traded from a winning team to this group of assholes?

"Go talk to her. See if you can score. Work that Dominic Lee magic we've all heard about," Sabine taunts, pointing at the woman I deemed fuckable.

Three words, and I talked myself into a corner. I have less than zero interest in women right now. What does interest me is getting the hell away from these bozos for a minute, so I swallow my beer and head over to the bar under the guise of getting another one.

"Draft, please," I tell the bartender, pretending to ignore the beautiful blonde perched on a barstool two feet away. Although to be honest, it's hard to ignore her.

She's stunning, in skintight jeans, a simple white tank top, and tan boots with a floral design on the sides. Her eyes are bright as she looks around, but there's something about her that makes her seem uncomfortable, like this isn't her scene. Whether that's the bar or its occupants tonight, I don't know.

"Hi," I say.

"Hello." Her tone is friendly, but the quick return of her attention to the room is not.

I scoot a little closer. "I'm Dominic."

She drags her eyes back to mine, humor in their blue depths now. "Dominic Lee, All-Star left defenseman for the Hawks last season, now for the Blizzard. Led all defensemen in the league in points last season with"—she pauses, her eyes slipping closed as she thinks—"ninety points." She opens her eyes, pinning me with a triumphant look as her lips slowly tilt up. "Not bad for a defenseman."

"Ninety-two actually," I correct with a smile. "You seem to have me at a disadvantage . . ." I trail off, waiting for her to fill in her name.

"Briar."

"Like a briar patch?"

She rolls her eyes like she's heard that at least a million times in her life. "My mom said I was a thorn in her ass from the moment I was conceived."

"You don't seem that prickly to me," I say, giving her a once-over.

"You don't know me well enough to make that assumption." Flipping her hair over her shoulder haughtily, she adds, "Nor will you."

"Fair enough," I say with a shrug, taking a sip of the fresh beer the bartender set in front of me. "You're right. Maybe you're a bitch. What do I know?"

Her mouth drops open, a little "uh" of shock escaping unbidden as she returns her full attention to me. I grin at her reaction. This woman doesn't have a bitchy bone in her body. In fact, I'm pretty sure the yellow beaded bracelet on her wrist says "good vibes only."

"Obviously not as much as you think if you're over here flirting with me," she murmurs as a hint of confusion flashes through her eyes, gone so fast I would've missed it if I wasn't watching her as closely as I am. But as though she's remembered herself, she straightens her back and squares her shoulders. "Especially given everyone in this place knows the team's reputation."

"Not the champs? Which is better known as the league losers?" I suggest helpfully.

I can sense the laughter she's trying to suppress, but what she says is, "I don't think the other players would take too kindly to that label."

"Not sure I give a fuck what they think," I reply a bit too honestly. I look over my shoulder at Anderson, Sabine, and Pacholek, who are watching me with eager grins on their stupid faces. "Though I am curious about what you think."

"Sure. I've heard that before," Briar says, turning her whole body back to the bar. I can feel the dismissal in the move. "Nice meeting you, Dominic."

My jaw tightens. I hate the way she says my name like she's already written me off. No one's ever written me off that easily, and I'm not sure I'm going to let her either.

"You'll remember me, even if you don't want to. My friends call me Dom."

"Dominic," she repeats emphatically, not even looking my way.

Never one to stay somewhere I'm not wanted, I pick up my beer and return to Tweedlefuck, Tweedlefucker, and Tweedlefuckest. They laugh and grin as they console me. "Don't worry about it. Briar was never gonna give you the time of day."

I don't like her name on Anderson's lips. It pisses me off for some reason I can't explain. Except . . . "How did you know her name?"

They laugh harder. "That's Coach Boothe's daughter."

These motherfuckers. They set me up. "You sent me over to talk to Coach's daughter with zero warning? Real great welcome wagon you've got here. Fuck all of you."

They try to sober up, mostly unsuccessfully, but Sabine manages to share, "No worries, man. We knew you weren't gonna get anywhere with her. She's anti-man, anti-player, and basically anti–anyone who isn't her son. Truth be told, I don't think she even likes Coach."

"You still set me up," I reiterate. "That's some bullshit." Even as I argue with them, I file away the information about Briar . . . no, about *Coach's daughter*, I correct as I scold myself for getting caught in their tomfuckery.

"Just a little welcome-to-the-team fun. No harm, no foul," Pacholek claims, seeming slightly more apologetic than his brethren. "Half of us have been through the same."

I grit my teeth, not liking it but also well aware that guys do that sort of thing. Or at least some do. Apparently, the Blizzard being the *some*.

"She said something about the team's reputation? What's that about?"

The three guys look from one to another, but it's Anderson that answers. "You don't know?"

I shake my head. "Would I be asking if I did? I know what I saw on tape, and what I saw on the ice against you assholes, but I get the feeling that's not what she meant."

Anderson looks over both shoulders—which is never a good sign—and lowers his voice as he says, "Wanna know the one thing the Blizzard doesn't have that all the other teams in the league do?" I stare at him, the answer obvious—of course I want to know, so spill it. "A WAG coordinator."

I glance at Sabine and Pacholek in confusion, hoping they understand what the hell Anderson is talking about, but they don't offer up any insight.

A WAG coordinator is the unlucky intern who shows up with stars in their eyes, thinking they're going to get a behind-the-scenes look at sports for whatever their degree is in, but gets assigned to dealing with the players' wives, girlfriends, and families. It's an often thankless job—making sure they have parking passes, travel arrangements, security escorts, and more, and all for the big result of zero gratitude. Just an asterisked line item on their résumé they're supposed to be grateful for.

"Who takes care of the WAGs then?" I ask. I shouldn't be surprised, considering my lazy reception by the team.

"We don't have any," Anderson says. "Kipson's wife was the closest thing anyone had, and now she's gone. Thank fuck." He lifts his eyes to the ceiling like that's an answered prayer. "Right now every man on the Blizzard is single and unattached."

"Clean house, baby!" Sabine brags, holding up his hand for a high five that Anderson returns, both of them grinning.

Pacholek takes pity on me and explains, "Our Blizzard motto is: 'Women are a distraction. Keep your focus on the ice.'"

I look at the crowd of players, some of whom have women at their sides . . . or on their laps, I realize, but it's clear that they're all Miss Right Now rather than Miss Right. Well, ain't that *friendly*. "You don't date?" I ask, wanting to clarify exactly what they're saying. After all, we're all hockey players, not dating experts.

"Flowers and dinners? Nah. I don't have time for that," Anderson says with a laugh, as though the very idea is preposterous. "I stick with dicking around. Speaking of . . ." He trails off as he steps away, toward a passing woman with a margarita in her hand and a tight skirt around her hips.

Sabine basically does the same, a redhead instead of Anderson's brunette, leaving me alone with Pacholek.

"It's not as bad as it sounds." I'm not sure if he's trying to convince me or himself. "Sex is biological, but we need to stay focused. This is our year for the Cup." Even as he says it, he glances toward Kipson, their supposed weak link.

"And everyone feels this way?" I question, sure there must be one man with some damn sense.

Pacholek shrugs. "Look at Coach," he instructs, and I glance over my shoulder to find my new boss with a young brunette glued to his hip. "He's married to a woman half his age and she isn't with him for his dick or for love. It's for the bank account and they both know it, even though she puts on a good show of being the queen at Coach's side." As I watch, Coach leans into the waitress with a little too much familiarity to simply order a beer and his wife intentionally turns her head away as though she didn't see it. "She's wife number four, I think."

I am not a man who's looking for love and I don't have time for some romantic fantasy story, but I've been in a relationship or two in my lifetime and I understand the value they hold. Especially after seeing my parents, who are ridiculously, adorably in love after decades together. And of course there's Penny and Griffin, who, despite my early reservations about their relationship, prove one simple truth. Love exists, it's real, and it makes you better. It doesn't distract you from what matters, it brings it into sharper focus.

So the Blizzard being a whole team of dick slingers? No wonder they fell apart when it was put up or shut up time in the playoffs. And no wonder Kipson's wife bailed on him. It must've been hell to withstand this type of constant barrage, for both Kipson and his ex.

I scan the room . . . from Coach and his sugar baby wife, to Anderson, who does in fact have a woman hanging on his every word like she's ready to suck his dick in the bathroom, to all the other players in the bar, who are grinning, chatting, and mingling. I look at every woman too. Of course, not all women are looking for love, either, certainly not in a bar and not with a professional athlete, but they deserve more than to be a hole on rotation for guys who probably won't remember their names tomorrow. I've never believed in so-called puck bunnies.

Yet *this* is my team now? The one I'm supposed to help?

A wave of nausea overtakes me, bile trying to rise up my throat. I need to get out of here. I knew this was going to be an awful year, but things just got so much worse. A whole season of locker room stories and one-upmanship? I can't do it.

I slam my beer and leave the empty glass on the table, stepping away. Pacholek calls after me, "Dom? You good?"

I ignore him. I ignore all of them, heading for the door.

The only thing that stops me is . . . her.

# Chapter 2

## Briar

I watch him out of the corner of my eye. I don't know why. I don't have time for a simple conversation, much less dating.

All I wanted tonight was the free drinks and appetizers-for-dinner my dad promised. This bar's got a pretty decent kitchen. And honestly, sitting home alone while my son, Harley, is with his sperm donor gets boring. I always miss him when he's gone . . . and worry the whole time too.

But Dominic did grab my attention for some reason. Maybe in the way our conversation ended.

He walked away easy enough, not upset at my dismissal, and the guys he went back to pretty obviously laughed at him, yet he didn't grit his teeth or look angry. That's . . . unusual.

Except now, as he strides across the room, heading for the door, he looks downright furious. Until he sees me.

I watch as he pulls that anger in, tucking it under a facade of calm, cool, and collected as he approaches once more. "Look, I'm sorry about before. I didn't know you were Coach's daughter. They told me to do some shitty fuck, marry, kill thing and I just pointed you out because you're beautiful and honestly, were the closest woman to me. When they told me to come talk to you, I just wanted to get away from those fucksticks, but apparently it was all some sort of hazing thing. I'm sorry. I didn't mean any offense, to you or to Coach."

The way the words roll off his tongue—fast and impulsive, like a stream of consciousness he doesn't even try to control—makes him seem genuine, and I can definitely see the guys pulling that sort of prank on a newbie so I choose to believe him. Mostly. "They're assholes, the whole lot of them. Anderson especially." I cut my eyes across the room to the slick-talking goalie who never wants for female company. Puck bunnies basically line up to hop on his dick, which I don't understand.

"They said you don't do guys or players or whatever. It's none of my business, but you're right. You should stay away from them." He gives me the warning as if I'm not wholly aware of that, his eyes dark and his jaw set in stone beneath a slight scruff.

"Away from you, you mean?" I correct.

"I'm not one of *them*," he snaps, tossing a thumb behind him to point at the other players.

Stating the obvious, I remind him, "You're wearing a team shirt."

He glances down at himself, seeming surprised to find the baby-blue shirt with the team logo on the chest. "I keep forgetting I have the damn thing on. It feels weird, like it's the wrong color, the wrong size, the wrong everything. It doesn't belong on me and I don't belong here." He fidgets and squirms like the T-shirt is irritating his skin as he glances at the sea of baby-blue shirts in the bar, looking like he wants nothing more than to rip his shirt over his head and toss it, along with everyone else's, into a big bonfire. Shoving his hands through his dark hair, he drops to the stool beside me and grumbles, "Fuck my life."

"Welcome to the team," I say dryly, and he glares at me coldly. At least I'm not the only one who thinks this franchise is a mess. Dominic obviously agrees wholeheartedly, and he doesn't know the half of it. On the ice, off the ice, it's a small miracle the Blizzard got to the Cup finals last season. "So what'd you label me?"

"Huh?"

"Fuck, marry, or kill?" I lift a finger for each option and then wiggle them at him.

And I swear to God, the man blushes. He ducks his head, but I can see the touch of redness rising on his cheeks above his scruff. "I'm embarrassed to say *fuck*. In my defense, I said *marry* the bartender because I think I'm going to need to take up drinking as a hobby to make it through this season here."

"That a problem for you? Drinking, I mean?"

He recoils as though I slapped him. "No. I had one shot of whiskey when I got here, then sipped on two beers and two Jack-free Cokes so I could keep my wits about me tonight. That's probably more than I've had in the last month, and that includes the going-away dinner my sister threw me."

Unneeded details usually mean the guy is lying. I know that down to my soul. But there's something about the way he says it, and again, I believe him . . . for now. Foolhearted? Probably. But what else is new?

"Who'd you say kill?"

He huffs a dry laugh, and taps his chest. "Me."

"Aw, poor, pitiful Dominic. Playing professional hockey on a team that tons of guys would kill to be on. Your life is so tough, isn't it?"

I know what I'm doing—teasing and taunting and poking and prodding, but mostly testing his reactions, his limits, his edges. The guys are right about me. I don't fuck around and I don't date (especially hockey players), but Dominic is surprisingly fun to talk to. Or maybe I'm just desperate for conversation with an actual adult, given most of my daily chats are either with my nine-year-old son, or a monkey. Being a zookeeper severely limits your conversation options sometimes.

Dominic flashes me a shit-eating grin. "I know I sound like a whiny baby. And I am thankful for the opportunity." That's the first lie he's said. I can see it clear as day, like the polite, professional response caused a visceral reaction inside him because it's patently untrue.

"What was so great about the Hawks?" I ask curiously. "They couldn't have been that different. Hockey is hockey, after all."

"The Cup," he says reverently, his eyes closed and hands in front of him like he's holding a ghost trophy. Shaking it off, he says, "It's home, you know? I've been there so long, my whole NHL career in fact. And it's a great group of guys. We give each other a hard time, but it's all done in love. They're the first to show up if you need something. They even came over to help me pack, though they did more shit-talking about the Blizzard than putting stuff in boxes." He chuckles at the memory and I realize he talks about the Hawks like he's still one of them. I think in his heart, he is.

"And I got to play with my best friend, Griffin." He leans my way, revealing, "We've always called ourselves brothers, and now we actually are. He's married to my little sister." His wide smile shows true happiness, but I remember there being something in the news last season about the two of them going at it on the ice mid-game.

"The sister who threw you a going-away dinner?"

"The one and only Penny Lee, the badass who's able to trip over her own feet when she's sitting down, create art from her own hands, and somehow get my asshole bestie to wax poetic." He shakes his head in disbelief, though he speaks about her in clear admiration. "She's either a miracle worker or a freak of nature, one or the other for sure." He weighs the two options in his hands, neither coming out the sole winner.

"She sounds awesome. I'm sorry you had to leave her, your friends, and your team behind."

"Me too," he says as the bartender stops in front of us. "Another Coke, please. No sugar this time. You want anything?" he asks me. "Another—" He glances at the cocktail in front of me. Like him, I don't drink much, so when I get the chance, I do it right, with all the creamy, fruity goodness I can swallow. "Piña colada?"

"No, I'll take a water with a splash of grenadine, please. Oh, and a lemon." To Dominic, I explain, "It looks fancy and tastes good, but keeps my head clear." I give him a narrow-eyed warning, expecting him to scoff at my girly, boring drink, but he nods and mouths *smart* like he understands.

Like he's well aware of the effect he has on people . . . on women. Even, and I hate to admit this, me. Because I'd be lying if I said I hadn't noticed his broad shoulders, scruff-covered jawline, and dark eyes that seem to take in everything around him. I'd also have to pretend that my heart hasn't been pitter-pattering in my chest and my dust-bunny-covered center hasn't been suddenly awakened from a too-long slumber by the smell of his cologne.

The bartender sets our drinks in front of us in seconds and disappears. "What brings you to . . . here?" Dominic asks, waving a hand vaguely. He doesn't mean the bar, but this town, this area, this . . . here.

"My ex," I answer as I take a sip of my drink. *Poke, poke, poke.*

He doesn't flinch, not a single muscle tightens in his face or body. Huh, weird. One thing guys don't like to hear about is the ones who came before them. Not that Dominic is coming anywhere near me, but it's true in general. Or at least that's my experience.

"He got a job, so we moved. Bonus that my dad was here." It was not a bonus at all. At that point, I wasn't even talking to my dad, who divorced my mom when I was seven and only occasionally came around after that. But when I'd finally worked up the courage to leave Tyler, Dad was the only resource I had here. Swallowing the last dregs of my dignity and asking him for help had taken all I'd had. In fact, if it hadn't been for Harley, I wouldn't have bothered. I would've been fine eventually, but I would never let my son pay the price for my pride.

"Did the job not work out? Or the guy? Or both?" He's matter-of-fact about it, like he's just making conversation, or at most, mildly curious.

"All of the above," I answer. "Turns out the job was only a thing until he got caught screwing a secretary in the office."

He hisses. "Shiiiit."

"By his boss, who was married to the secretary."

Dominic's eyes go wide and he mutters, "The fuck?"

I laugh, the sense of betrayal long ago burned to ash. "Yeah, that was when I found out he'd run up our credit cards and was four months behind on the mortgage. It was a really great time in my life."

"You seem to be doing alright now," he says, giving me a look of pride.

"Oh yeah," I say, nodding, "single mother, working a job I love but that barely pays the bills, living in a house with questionable electricity that makes my son truly believe I'm magic because I can flip a breaker when it pops, and whose exciting night out consists of free drinks and food because my dad lets me crash team events gratis. I'm expecting the Person of the Year award ceremony in my honor to happen any day. They should be showing up with the cameras right about now." I glance around, knowing I sound silly, but what else am I supposed to do? Wallow in misery over the rough years I made it through and never appreciate the amazing life I do have?

"Look out, here they come." Dominic points past me and I have to fight the urge to turn around and peek. There's no *Time* magazine crew entering the bar, I know that. But the teasing grin lifting his lips makes me want to play along.

"How's my hair?" I ask instead.

His eyes trace over my blond hair, which I took extra time to both blow dry and curl tonight in honor of going out, even if it was to Dad's team thing. "Gorgeous."

His tone just changed. Like a light bulb turning on and he's flirting now.

With me, Briar Johns. A woman who usually rocks out in cargo shorts, knee socks, and Crocs with animal Jibbitz on them while giving lectures on the various types of animals on display at the zoo to school kids on field trips. A woman who washed her face, put on makeup, checked her reflection, and decided it looked stupid, and washed her face again, only to put on the same blush, mascara, and pink lip gloss I always wear. A woman who's regretting the two piña coladas and the cheese- and bacon-covered fries I consumed like a dumpster-raiding raccoon who's hit the jackpot.

A woman who hasn't had sex with another human in four long years and is suddenly struck by how hot Dominic Lee actually is, even if he is wearing a baby-blue Blizzard T-shirt.

"I have a son," I blurt out. "He's nine . . . and amazing . . . and my heart walking around outside my body . . . and he's all I have time for." The words tumble out, one right after the other, putting up barricades between Dominic and me with every syllable.

"I heard," Dominic says, not repulsed at all. Quietly, he asks, "What's his name?"

*What? He knows I have a son? How?*

"Harley. How did you know that?" Wariness blooms in my belly, extinguishing any long-ago embers that might've been trying to ignite.

"Sabine," he explains. "His exact words were that you're 'anti-man, anti-player, and anti–anyone that isn't your son.' He didn't mean it as a compliment, but to be fair, I completely understand your position. Kids first, always."

"Do you have a kid? Or kids?" It's a reasonable question. He wouldn't be the only professional athlete, or man, with a string of kids with various women from his past.

He shakes his head, frowning. "No. Not yet. One day, though. I love kids. My favorite part of the off-season is the camps we do for them." His frown deepens. "The Hawks do, I mean."

I lift an eyebrow. "Most guys run screaming at the mere mention of kids."

It's the truth. I've even been known to use that convenient little factoid to run off a few men who were too aggressive with their flirting. Nothing turns most guys off like hearing that a nine-pound baby wrecked your vagina, leaving tiger-striped skin in his wake.

Dominic laughs, his smile not the least bit dimmed. "That what you're trying to do? Make me run away?"

*Yes. Absolutely.*

*But also, no? Because looking at you, part of me wonders what it'd feel like to have your hands in my hair, holding me close while pinning me to a bed.*

Before I can analyze that too closely, he adds, "Being divorced, having an asshole ex, and a son isn't exactly the usual first date conversation."

I take a sip of my water, the sweet and sour bite a bit too reminiscent of me tonight. "Guess it's a good thing this isn't a date then, huh?"

"Yet you're trying to warn me off all the same," he says, clearly calling me out with pinpoint accuracy.

"I don't date," I declare, trying to protect myself. "I don't flirt. I don't fuck around. I'm not looking for a relationship or anything remotely close to that. Me and Harley, that's it. That's all I have time for. Just want that to be clear."

I'm telling him, but also reminding myself. I know this game and I don't play, no matter how surprisingly attractive Dominic is proving to be.

He doesn't get up and leave, which is what I fully expected. Instead, he nods. "Heard. I get it . . . he should be your first priority. I respect the hell out of that." With a smile, he asks, "One very important question, though."

I arch a brow, certain I already know what it's going to be. Something like, *Do you have to get home to him right this minute, or do you have time for a quickie in the parking lot?*

"Does he like hockey?"

A laugh bursts out at the unexpected question, and I feel a wide smile grow across my face. "He does actually. He plays Squirt this year."

"Good times," he replies, a wistful look taking over his face. "My Squirt team was the Otters. We were 15, 8, and 10, which were pretty good stats for our area. Didn't matter then about championships, just the game. So if you ever want a little extra coaching time, hit me up. I'd be glad to do drills with Harley."

Being able to pull stats out of his head like that doesn't surprise me. Dad can do that, too, about dozens of players and decades of play. What does shock me is Dominic's offer. He doesn't know me and definitely doesn't know Harley. "Why?"

He shrugs. "Why not? I don't know anyone here, and the few people I have met seem like assholes. Other than you, obviously."

Not giving up so easily, I pry, "What's in it for you?"

He cocks his head, his dark eyes peering at me from beneath furrowed brows. "Damn, he fucked you up good, didn't he?"

Does he mean Tyler or my dad? Either way, the answer is an unequivocal yes. I lift my chin haughtily, unimpressed with his too-astute assessment, and silently refuse to answer.

"I love hockey," he finally explains. "Love kids. Love kids who play hockey. Loved the camp we did back home. That's it, no ulterior motive."

So he says, but something else caught my attention. "Isn't this home?"

He huffs a dry laugh, no humor to be found in the sound. "Fuck no. I'm going to sleep in a place that I rented for three months to give me time to figure shit out. I'm on a contract year, and my roots are somewhere else. Hell, my stuff is still packed, the suitcase just sitting on top of the dresser. Not exactly what I'd call home."

He glances over his shoulder at the Blizzard, who are celebrating as per usual, which is to say, loudly, obnoxiously, and full of entitlement, like O'Neal's is their bar. Dominic's loneliness is palpable, surrounding him like a heavy cloak.

I do something even I don't expect. "Maybe we could do a trial run and see how it goes? Harley would be over the moon," I admit. "Want my number so we can arrange it?"

"No."

I deflate instantly. He offered to help and I thought he actually meant it. I should've known better. I *do* know better. All those red flags I waved must've done their job and warned Dominic off, but instead of feeling victorious, I feel disappointed. There was a tiny sliver of me that hoped he might be different.

*Stupid. All men are the same.*

"Take mine instead," he says, sensing my mood shift. Holding his phone out with his number displayed, I type it into my phone, making his contact name *Hockey Coach* with a stick and puck emoji.

While I type, he tells me, "Think it over, check your gut when there's no rum in it. Be sure that you trust me to be a nice guy, not just nice in comparison to those assholes over there, especially when there's twangy music setting the tone for this to be some sort of meet-cute. If you want me to help your son then, call or text me. No pressure, though. I get it."

A loud chorus of *"whoaaaaa"* sounds out behind us, something obviously happening that's excited the team. Dominic closes his eyes as his chest expands with a deep breath. I wonder if he knows that there's an obvious look of distaste and disapproval on his face, like the team is working his last nerve and he's annoyed at their very existence.

Suddenly, he stands. "I'm gonna go."

Shocked at the declaration, I stammer, "Aren't you supposed to stay for the whole thing?" The team will be here for another couple of hours at least, drinking and eating and talking. And taking over the bar.

"My mission left twenty minutes ago, sober and alone. I'm calling that a job well done for the night." He makes a checkmark in the air, marking it for his mental to-do list.

"Mission?" I echo in confusion.

"Yeah, Mission: Don't Let Kipson Fuck Himself Up Too Badly," he says wryly. "It's why I was traded here in the first place. Your dad, or the owners, clearly expect me to fix their star player's shit." He pats his chest, right over his heart.

About a hundred puzzle pieces click into place, namely why Dominic is so grumpy about being here. Nobody would appreciate being called in to babysit another grown adult. But it sounds like Mike might need it. I know enough about him to understand why too. "He's not handling his divorce well."

"So I hear."

"It's hard—divorce, I mean," I reply softly. "Even when it's the right thing to do."

"Speaking from experience?"

I hold my chin high, unashamed. "Absolutely. I knew I had to leave Tyler for a while before I managed to actually do it. Some of that was me needing to save money and make an escape plan, but also, I had to steel my spine and build some walls around my heart. That took longer than it should've. Even so, it was painful for a while after. Kipson is hurting."

"He'll be okay. You are."

I laugh brightly. I am so *not* okay. I haven't been okay since the day I met Tyler. I thought I was, I even truly believed I was, but from the moment he saw me as his, I haven't been okay a single day. "I'm four years out, and still dealing with his manipulation tactics on a near-daily basis, so I'd beg to differ."

All humor and flirtiness evaporate from Dominic as his eyes sharpen warily. "Call me if you need any help there too. I don't like the idea of you dealing with anyone's bullshit."

"Not even yours?" I challenge.

The attempt to lighten the mood falls flat, with Dominic's face staying stony. "Especially mine," he agrees.

"You don't even know me."

He nods slightly. "Fair. But I don't like anyone being subjected to that. Especially a woman, and especially you, when you seem to be sweet and kind, and just want the best for your boy."

I drop my chin, staring unseeingly at my half-empty drink. That sounds . . . nice? Like Dominic isn't playing some game or scheming to get into my jeans or into Dad's good graces by being nice to his daughter, though little does he know that would have the opposite effect. Still, I don't know what to do with his generosity. I'm too used to fighting my own way, making my own magic out of nothing, and figuring things out for myself.

Like he can sense my struggle, Dominic doesn't pressure me, saying, "Just let me know if I can help with anything—hockey, exes, or I don't know, light bulbs that need to be changed or whatever. So far, you're the only friend I've made here, which means my schedule's wide open."

I lift my eyes to meet his. "Thank you."

"Whether I hear from you or not, it was really good to meet you, Briar. You made tonight a billion times better than I thought it'd be."

He smiles but it doesn't quite reach his eyes. "To be fair, my expectations were in the gutter. Maybe lower."

"It was good to meet you, too, Dominic," I concede. "Piña coladas, loaded fries, and a conversation including actual words with more than one syllable? Winner-winner, chicken dinner, in my book. Not sure what that says about my expectations."

As he walks away, I watch him . . . His shoulders wide and sturdy looking, tapering to his waist, his long legs eating up the wood floor on his way to the door. He doesn't spare a single glance toward the team he's supposed to be a part of, and when he disappears through the door, I look over at them. Too busy raucously playing pool and darts, not a one of them notices their new top defenseman leaving either. They really are awful.

I look down at my phone, seeing Dominic's info still on the screen. Before I can second-guess myself, I type out a message and hit send.

Thank you.

That's it, just two little words, but it means that he has my number now too. Wait . . .

This is Briar.

Okay, three more words and now he has my number and knows who it belongs to.

I wonder if he realizes that this was the first date I've had in over ten years. Because despite my argument, that was as close as I've gotten, and it wasn't as bad as I thought it'd be.

# Chapter 3

## Dominic

Preseason camp is important . . . for newbies and rookies. I'm neither, yet Coach Boothe made it clear that I was expected to attend in the email he sent the day after our bar get-together. It's basically Blizzard onboarding, meeting their behind-the-scenes crew, getting checked out by the team doctor, and then doing drills until exhaustion.

Which I hit twenty minutes ago. Not physically, because I stay ready so I don't have to get ready, but mentally. This is bordering on torture, with Coach red-faced yelling at us after each round, saying the last attempt wasn't good enough and we have to do better if we're hoping for any time on the ice. I've played for coaches with a variety of leadership styles over the years, and Boothe is my least favorite—death by a thousand cuts that are supposed to make you stronger. Newsflash: It rarely works, and it definitely doesn't nurture the camaraderie and support that create a team.

"Again." Coach's order echoes through the arena and we dutifully line up.

"Can't believe I'm playing with *the* Dominic Lee," the guy next to me says. He's in position, his skates in perpetual motion, his stick tapping on the ice in preparation for the signal.

"I'm just a player, same as you." That's not remotely true. Rodney—I think that's what he said his last name is—was drafted to the Blizzard as a late-round pick, and he looks like he turned eighteen yesterday. I drop my eyes to his stick. "Relax your lower hand. It's not your dick."

He laughs, but does as I advised. *He's coachable,* I think.

A loud whistle sounds out and we take off, skating across the ice like our lives depend on it, our sticks slapping our pucks with each stride. Rodney gets to the farthest goal line a split second faster than I do. "Holy shit, I beat you," he pants, his hands on his knees and cheeks flushed red.

I chuckle at his wide-eyed excitement. "None of us are going full out for drills. Especially this late in the day." He deflates, his pride evaporating at the hard truth. "But you're fast as hell, so keep at it."

His smile returns. "Yeah? Thanks, Dom." He frowns and clarifies, "Can I call you Dom? Seeing as we're teammates and all, ya know?"

I nod. Give him his props for now. "Sure, kid."

If he sees NHL gametime ice this season, I'll be surprised, but if he's smart, he'll soak up everything around him and put it to use.

Coach makes us do a few more drills before sending us into the locker rooms for postpractice checks with the trainers. I've perfected my own routine over years, so my plan is to skip out on that and get the hell out of here, but I hear my name and turn around to see Coach waving me over from the bench.

I take a steadying breath and dutifully skate over to him, praying he doesn't want to talk about his daughter, or our friendly conversation at the bar. And definitely not about the text she sent me or my careful response of "anytime," an invitation she hasn't taken me up on.

"Looking good today. What do you think of the guys?" Coach asks.

Is he serious? He wants my input on the rookies after a few days of drills? I should probably play it cool and figure out what he wants to hear and spoon-feed it back to him, but I'm too grumpy about being here to strategize that clearly, so my gut instincts spill without filter.

"Rodney's fast as fuck," I start, "but greener than a pasture. He's gonna beat everyone to the puck, only to get eaten alive before he can do anything with it due to his lack of situational awareness. He needs to learn how to see the ice in order to be a center, but he's probably the best rookie you've got. Bill is clunky with his back foot on pivots. Tomville needs to gain about ten pounds of muscle without losing his speed." I should stop there. I know I should, especially given the way Coach's eyes are glazing over with disinterest, but my mouth keeps going. "Anderson is a PR nightmare waiting to happen, which makes him dangerous for the team. What's worse is that Sabine is a follower, so anything Anderson does, he'll do, too, which increases their volatility and puts the team at risk. This team's going to be known as the Paternity Suits, not the Blizzards. Pacholek might be okay, though he keeps bad company, which brings his judgment into question."

There's more I could say—about the Blizzard's reputation and the way Coach fosters it, unknowingly or not; about how steady home lives create a steady team while drama-seeking, lust-fueled players who fuck around, literally and metaphorically, also tend to not take their work seriously; about his daughter and how he should've never let her be in a situation that she had to escape from. Thankfully, I do manage to force that back down my throat . . . for now.

He nods along with my assessments, but mostly doesn't seem to give a shit. "And Kipson?"

"Still undecided if he's salvageable," I declare flatly. "He's angry, and if he can use that fire, it could work. If he goes self-destructive, he'll take the whole team with him."

"Don't let that happen." Coach points a finger at me like that's an order, but if it's as easy as that, then why the fuck do they need me? Clenching my jaw, I grunt in acknowledgment.

I've had plenty of orders in my career, but this one sits wrong. The main thing I want to save lately isn't the team, it's the woman who looked at me like I was really worth something.

"Hustle up," I tell the two guys drag-assing behind me as I check my watch. "You've got just over an hour before you need to be in bed. That gives us thirty minutes to eat, so that you can get home to shit, relax, and jack off before lights out."

"Living the dream," Rodney proclaims through a blissful smile, but he does pick up the pace to get to the door first.

He holds it open for me and Tomville to walk through first.

"I haven't found my new usual yet, but this place will do in the interim," I tell the guys as we get in line at a Chipotle close to the team's practice facility. Because once again, unlike the Hawks, the Blizzard is cheaping us out. For the Hawks, preseason camp meant buffet meals catered with good food. For the Blizzard? A tub of weight gain powder and free milk. The farts alone can drive a man across the ice.

Back home, Griffin and I have a place we go to regularly for protein bowls. But in a pinch, or when we travel, any basic rice and meat place will work. I've even gone into sit-down restaurants and asked them to pile rice and whatever protein they serve on a plate and charge me however they need to. The point is food, and food is fuel for our bodies to withstand the hell we put them through.

"What's your usual? I'm a cheese burrito man myself," Rodney says as he pats his flat stomach. At his age, he's got the metabolism to handle that shit, but it won't always be that way, so he might as well start better habits now.

"Not tonight you're not," I correct. "We need calories, protein, vitamins, and fat to replace what we've lost today. You can't waste stomach space on a huge tortilla with no extra benefit."

The worker behind the counter calls next and Tomville steps up. "Bowl, please. Rice, beans, and chicken." He's a fast learner, but still glances at me for approval.

"Double chicken. No queso. Guacamole. Salsa. Fajita veggies, heavy on the bell peppers. Lettuce."

Tomville turns back to the worker. "What he said."

Rodney pipes up, "Make it two."

The worker looks at me and I hold up three fingers.

Once we've got our bowls and waters, we find a table. There's no talking, not at first. We're starving and our focus is shoveling in as much food as we can, as fast as possible. But as we start to quell the growls in our bellies, conversation starts to flow.

"What do you think so far?" Rodney asks me.

"About what?"

He chuckles. "All of it, man. I'm freaking out about everything, mostly that I'm having dinner with Dominic Lee." He cuts his eyes to Tomville, sharing a look of disbelief with his new teammate.

"I'm just a guy."

"Yeah, one I've watched play since I was a kid."

I scoff, letting the old man allusion slide. "You are a kid."

His smile, which seems pretty constant, fades a few degrees. "Which means I'm probably not going to get much playtime, right?"

He wants reassurance that he'll get his turn on the ice. It's what we all want—our time to shine, with the crowd shouting our name as we finally get the chance to turn the dream we've had since we picked up a stick for the first time into a reality. "Probably not," I tell him honestly. "Might even end up doing some time in the minors again this season. But keep working. You'll get there."

He brightens again. "Hey, I beat you to the goal line . . . once." It's a joke, poking fun at himself and his earlier earnest belief that he'd truly outskated me. "I'd appreciate any tips you're offering, though. You know a helluva lot more than I do." He lifts a plastic forkful of chicken in the air, silently thanking me for the advice I already gave.

I look from Rodney to Tomville, both of their eager faces bright with hope. They want direction, need it like air, and I have no faith that Coach Boothe is going to give it to them. Or if he does, it'll come with a degradation and humiliation chaser.

I set my fork down. "No holds barred," I warn them, and they nod in agreement, their faces going serious. "Rodney, you're fast. You know that." He starts to smile, but I continue, "You depend on that too much. You get to the puck first, and in your mind, that's a win. But it's barely step one."

His brows furrow as he listens closely, taking in what I'm saying. "You're a center, which means you need to read the ice. Sometimes you're able to skate away from trouble, but you also have to be prepared to fight off a pack and then have your eyes up to get the pass off to the open man. Don't focus on developing speed you already have. Focus on attacking the other team the way you attack the ice. Hard. Create opportunities, and then exploit them."

He nods firmly. "Heard."

"Do me. Do me next," Tomville pleads around his mouthful of food. He's holding his hand in the air like he's in a classroom back in school.

"Where Rodney has physical skill and needs to work on his mental game," I point at the kid, then swing my finger toward Tomville, who is only slightly older, but shorter and lighter, "you're the opposite. You can predict the plays before they happen, you see the holes, and you have that 'balls to the wall' mentality that you need."

"But?"

I grin, glad he heard that coming. "But you need the brawn to back it up. You said you were an enforcer on your last team, but that was in the minors. The batshit crazy terrier act won't cut it up here, this is a whole different league. Guys with six inches and nearly a hundred pounds on you are going to be coming at you full-force, and while you've got the mindset to not flinch, they're gonna mow you down. It's simple physics. You need muscle and power, like yesterday. But don't pack it on too quick, or it'll make you slower than shit. You need to grow steadily so your body can adjust to moving more mass each day."

Tomville blinks several times, and for a second, I think he's going to argue with me. Instead, he comes back with, "You got a workout plan I can follow, or should I hit the strength coach up for that?"

"Try Coach first, but I'll take a look at your plan if you want," I reply, having no reason to trust the Blizzard's strength and conditioning team so far. "Basically, make sure you pick up heavy weights every day, no excuses and no skips. Low reps only, none of that 'sets of twenty' toning crap."

"Will do. Thanks, Dom."

Two coachable rookies? The odds of this season being a complete clusterfuck are decreasing. Though they'll be years in development to fully reach their potential. But we all start somewhere.

We finish the rest of our dinner with the two kids talking about their past hockey experience. I don't bother sharing mine, because they could probably recite it as well as I could. By the time we leave, I think they feel a bit better about themselves and their new positions on the Blizzard.

I wish I could say the same.

Hanging out with those guys was a fun, momentary distraction that I greatly appreciate, but as I open the door to my home away from home, all I feel is empty inside, just like the house. I didn't even decorate any of this shit, it's as soulless as a hotel room.

I flop onto the couch, one foot on the coffee table and one on the floor as I look around. My suggestion to the guys was to handle their business and go to bed before tomorrow's camp, but all I want to do is punch the closest wall.

# Chapter 4

## Briar

"How're you holding up, honey?"

I can see that my son's been crying, with tell-tale pink around his eyes and faint tear tracks on his freckled cheeks. If I could squash the other kids on his hockey team like bugs, I would . . . not that you should do that to our wonderful insect friends. They're an important part of our ecosystem, even if they are weird and creepy sometimes.

His sniffle breaks my heart. "I'm fine. Connor's right, I should've passed to him."

Holding a hand up to cup my ear, I scrunch my nose in confusion. "What? It sounded like you said Connor was right, but"—I shake my head dramatically—"that can't be, because you know better than to second-guess your own instincts based on what someone else tells you." I keep my voice light and playful, but it's a hard truth about Harley's teammate, who acts like everyone's boss and seeks to have the spotlight shine only on him.

"Mooom." That single syllable has gotten longer and longer over the years. Soon, it's gonna be more like a Siberian husky's howl, except hopefully lower pitched.

"Harleyyyy," I drawl out, mimicking his tone and turning it into a full-blown ambulance siren situation. He's not amused and continues to stare blankly at me. More seriously, I remind him, "You had the puck. It was your responsibility to get it to the goal in the way you saw fit. That means working with your teammates if they have a better shot, but it also means trusting yourself to take the shot when it's available."

He frowns deeper than a little boy should be capable of. "I know, but I missed and Connor wouldn't have."

"Connor's stats are better than yours by the teensiest, tiniest sliver of a margin." I hold my finger and thumb up, no space between them. "He might've made it. You might've made it. Either of you could've missed. But he's not the coach. He doesn't decide what you should do. You do." I tap his temple, reminding him of the supersmart brain beneath the mop of blond hair we really should get trimmed.

"Deciding's hard."

"Doesn't get much easier as you get older," I confide. "Sometimes I flip a coin, and in that flash of a moment when it's in the air, I can feel what I hope it lands on, and by the time it does land, I already know what I should do. Maybe we could put a quarter in your pocket?"

He giggles the little boy laugh I will miss when it turns to a deep rumble one day. "I don't have pockets in my uniform, Mom."

"Oh, right. Maybe behind your ear?"

"Noooo."

"Ooh, I got it! In your sock? But then we have to decide, left or right?" I grab his feet, which are still covered in stinky, sweaty hockey socks, lifting them as I examine each one for insight on which might be the better piggy bank for a coin.

"That tickles," Harley laughs, squirming to get his feet free from my grasp. "No coins in my socks either."

"Huh, guess you'll have to make the decisions on your own then." I give him a pointed look and he starts to smile. "Good. Let's practice . . . chicken or beef for dinner?"

"Dino nuggets!"

"Long chicken nuggets," I suggest, though it's not a suggestion. We don't even have dinosaur-shaped chicken nuggets in the freezer, but I do have an entire bag of frozen chicken strips, a.k.a. long nuggets. If there's one thing moms are good at, it's reframing the unacceptable into the acceptable by any means necessary, and obviously chicken strips are disgusting while long nuggets are the best things ever.

"With honey mustard?" he asks hopefully. My son's half hockey player, half debate champion.

"Deal." I hold my fist out for a bump, but as Harley reaches out to bump me, I quickly switch to an open hand, wiggling my fingers. "Turkey feathers."

He groans and rolls his eyes. "You've already done that one, Mom."

I shrug, unbothered. "Still got a grin so I'm calling that a win for me, and the game was a win for you, no matter what the scoreboard said." To be fair, the score was 4–1, with Harley's team taking the *L*. But I'm focusing on the positives, staying in the sweet spots, and enjoying the good stuff the day has brought. "Go hop in the shower, and dinner will be ready by the time you're out."

"Okay!"

Just like that, my smiling, happy little boy is back. He's just trapped in an ever-growing doubt-filled shell. In the few minutes it takes me to toss those long nuggets on a pan, a very questionable idea hits me. I should second- and maybe even third-guess myself, but I don't. Like Harley needs to do, I trust my instincts.

Were you serious about helping Harley?

I half expect an instantaneous response as though Dominic was staring at his phone, waiting for me to text. When that doesn't happen, I begin to stress clean the kitchen, taking out my doubts on crumbs that spilled out of the toaster this morning.

I'd all but written off Dominic's offer to help my son. He hadn't been all that responsive after my initial thank-you text, and I didn't hear from him after that, so I decided it'd been 1) a polite, albeit meaningless, gesture or 2) a failed attempt at getting in my pants.

Either had me moving on to one of the other dozen things on my always too-full to-do list.

But desperate times call for desperate measures, and I'll make a fool out of myself anytime for my son. Still, I can't believe I'm doing this. Texting Dominic Lee for hockey help? What world am I living in?

Ding.

Absolutely.

The single-word response is glaringly similar to his previous text, the bubble on the left side of the screen barely a blip.

Great! He could use some help. When are you available?

That sounds like I'm scheduling a haircut, but this isn't too far off from that. It's not like it's a date or anything.

Tomorrow at 6pm?

Perfect. I'll make us a reservation at the rink.

"If this is a joke, I'm never gonna forgive you," Harley informs me as he throws his gear bag over his shoulder. It's nearly as big as he is, so it makes him wobbly on his feet as he looks from me to the rink door with the hope he's scared to have blooming in his eyes.

He knows disappointment. Unfortunately, he's learned it firsthand . . . from his father.

I've done my best to never say a single negative word about Tyler, but he is who he is, and he's disappointed Harley enough on his own over the years to make our son not trust something good until it's actually happening.

I send a silent prayer up to the sunshine-filled, blue sky, *Please let Dominic be behind those rink doors. Please.*

"Let's go see," I tell Harley with a plastered-on smile.

There's only a handful of people on the ice, so it doesn't take me long to find Dominic skating a slow loop around the boards. And though his back is to us, it's like he's watching the door for our arrival because his eyes find mine within seconds of our entry. The smile that steals across his face should be illegal considering it makes my heart race in my chest, pounding on my ribs.

"He's here, Mom! He's really here!" Harley shouts. His eyes are wide, his smile even wider as he looks at Dominic as though he's a fictional character magically come to life.

"I told you he was coming," I say with an implied sigh of *no biggie*, even though I had my own doubts. Tyler left scars on me, too, emotional not physical, though sometimes they feel equally deep.

Dominic exits the ice and immediately squats on the rubber mats outside the boards, holding his hand out. "Hey there. You must be Harley. I'm Dominic. Nice to meet you."

My son, the one who huffs and puffs about the most minor of big boy responsibilities, stands taller, pulls his shoulders back, and shakes Dominic's hand like he's a full-grown man meeting another man. "My name is Harley Johns. It's nice to meet you too. Thank you for helping me."

Tears of pride spring to my eyes. He's on that cusp between childhood and tweenhood, where I tend to think he's still a baby and he thinks he's older than he is, but in this moment, all I see is the hard work we've put in on having manners and being respectful.

"Hi, Briar. I'm really glad you texted." There's nothing inherently flirty in the words, or even the tone, but I don't miss the sparkle in Dominic's eyes. He thinks I'm using my son to get closer to him. He couldn't be more wrong. This is for Harley, nothing more, nothing less.

If only the butterflies flopping around in my belly believed that too.

"Thanks for helping. He's really excited in case you can't tell." I drop my eyes to the floor, where Harley has plopped down to trade tennis shoes for skates.

"Me too." Dominic's words are to me, but he makes sure his new student hears them too. "What're we working on today?"

Lacing his skates, Harley offers, "Connor says I'm not good at scoring, so . . ." His voice trails off uncertainly.

"Alright, we'll do some target work then. Skate a few laps and get warmed up while I talk to your mom."

"Yes, sir." And with that, Harley hits the ice and Dominic's eyes track his progress for a few seconds before he turns to me.

"Hi." He already greeted me, but this one feels more intimate, less child-friendly for sure even though it's barely a syllable.

I blush instantly, and when Dominic's smile grows as he clocks the rising heat on my cheeks, I lower my chin, hating my body's overreaction to his nearness and focused attention. Trying to stick to the reason we're here, I say, "Connor isn't his coach. He's Harley's teammate, one he needs to learn not to listen to." I let the smallest edge enter my tone, not wanting to speak ill of a child, but also, not particularly caring for Connor.

Dominic's expression changes in a blink, Mr. All Business as his ears fully open.

I give him the quick rundown of Harley's team and how Connor is a bit of an ice bully and tell him that while I appreciate the help with drills, what I really want is for Harley to trust his own instincts and stand up for himself.

Nodding, he says, "Okay, we can work on that for sure. But one question . . . Is Connor right about the scoring shots? Objectively."

"Well, he's not laser-precise if that's what you mean. But he's okay compared to the rest of the players."

Dominic glances out at Harley. "Gotcha. Let me see what he's got."

As Dominic joins Harley on the ice, I stand back, simply watching their interaction. They start with skating skills, doing simple footwork that Harley nails, and then moving on to stick drills. Dominic watches thoughtfully, analyzing and gently making corrections here and there.

To my surprise, Dominic is actually really great with Harley. Though I can't hear their conversations, I can see my son's confidence growing with every passing minute as they work together. Eventually I relax enough to take a seat on one of the benches, but I keep my eyes locked on the two guys who have my full attention. One always has that. The other? It feels strange to be this locked in on a man.

I don't do that. Not anymore. I learned that lesson the hard way and refuse to have a repeat experience of that hell.

Harley, first. Me, second. My work, third. And that leaves no time, energy, or desire for anything else, and definitely not for *anyone* else.

The reminder is automatic, yet my eyes keep finding Dominic again and again. His easy smile, his broad shoulders, his grace on the ice, and fine . . . his round butt in the black sweatpants he's wearing. All make him a feast for the eyes.

Before I know it, an hour has passed and Harley speeds over to the boards, his face full of excitement. "Did you see me, Mom? I got a shot past Dom!"

Noticing the nickname, I glance at Dominic as he comes up behind my son, but he's smiling proudly. "Sure did. Great job, man. Just gotta trust yourself to see those pockets and act on them the instant you do."

Suddenly an apt student, Harley nods emphatically. "Trust the puck to be where I left it. Let my eyes look for where to put it. Act fast." He says it like he's quoting the advice Dominic gave him.

"You got it," Dominic says as he holds a hand out for a fist bump that my son happily returns. "We've got the space for a few more minutes. You want to skate it out?"

Harley checks in with me and I nod, giving permission, and he's off. Dominic leans down, planting his elbows on the board, to get closer to my level. "The kid's good. Age appropriately speaking. He's not a prodigy, but he's got heart, and that's more important than skills that can be developed with practice."

"He's really great, right?" I say wistfully, watching my son do the footwork drill Dominic taught him.

"I didn't want to ask in front of him because that wouldn't be fair, but I'd love to take you two for dinner if you have time?" The question hangs in the air between us, both of us knowing that he's not asking as a coach wanting to take his new student out, but rather that he's asking me out on a date.

And again, I don't do that.

"As friends?" The question is for my clarity as much as for his.

There is no hint of disappointment on his face, not a single flicker of it in his dark eyes as he agrees. "Sure. Friends get food together."

He accepts the semi-yes easily, which is exactly what I want, so why do I feel disappointed?

# Chapter 5

## Dominic

"Are you saying he's a sweet potato hog?"

Briar freezes, her fry halfway to her mouth, and then starts laughing. "Yes, I guess I am. Though technically Snuffles is part of the rodent family, not the Suidae one."

Somehow, I'm enchanted as Briar tells us a story about a capybara from work that likes to hoard his sweet potato treats, hiding them from the rest of the herd. I didn't even know what a capybara was until five minutes ago, but apparently, they're huge rodents that break the norm of "the bigger the rat, the scarier they are." With these guys, they get so big, they're suddenly somehow cute enough that people want to pet them and curl up with them in their laps like puppies.

I've been learning a lot from Briar. Like that she works at the zoo, which is where she met Snuffles. She hates pickles on her burgers, but will eat one by itself, and she draws a ketchup happy face on the top bun before smooshing her burger together because it makes her smile. Her favorite hobby is kitchen dance parties while she waits for the microwave timer to beep, especially when she's cooking popcorn because it gives the microwave noise an extra beat. Oh, and socks make the best dance shoes for this activity.

"Technical or not, these fries are mine." I grab a bundle of four big sweet potato fries from the basket in the middle of the table and shove them into my mouth all at once.

Like a mini-mimic, Harley follows suit, though he doesn't do it quite as neatly and one falls into his lap. Thankfully, Briar is pressing her lips together, fighting to hold back a giggle at our antics. "Manners at the table, please."

"Mooom," Harley grumbles, looking embarrassed, not about his mild misbehavior but at Briar calling the two of us out.

I swallow the wad of mostly chewed spud, and back Briar's parental limit. "Sorry. Didn't mean to be a bad example. I'll behave appropriately." I wipe my mouth with my napkin and then set it in my lap, an epitome of etiquette my mother would be proud of.

Harley watches me closely, scrubs the back of his hand across his mouth, and then sheepishly says, "Sorry, Mom."

"Thank you. There's a time and place for properness, and a time and place for more relaxed dining." Briar daintily reaches for a fry as though eating with royalty, then pointedly grabs three and chows down on them T. rex–style, growl and all. Grinning around her mouthful, she mumbles, "I'm not really a five-star restaurant kinda girl anyway."

Harley and I both laugh, but what I'm really thinking is that she's a great mother. She's obviously taught the kid how to behave, but she's fun and silly with him, too, not making anything too serious.

"Could've fooled me," I tease. "Everything about you says fancy-schmancy."

She strikes a pose, her hand placed beneath her chin as she bats her lashes. "It's the unwashed hair, bare face, and sloth shirt, isn't it?"

I choke on my tea as a laugh bursts out. "It's definitely the shirt. Who's your tailor?"

She's kidding, but the truth is, Briar might not be red-carpet ready, but she does look hot. Her hair is pulled up into some sort of floppy style that makes me want to run my fingers through it and make it a bit messier, her face being bare lets me see the frequent blushes that sweep across her cheeks every time I look at her a little too long or a bit too directly, and her shirt, which proclaims "Hang In There" with a sleeping sloth barely gripping the letters, hugs her chest and stops just shy of the waist of her jeans. When she walked into the arena earlier, I'd had to recite old game stats—in reverse order, mind you—to get my dick to settle down. Even then, I'd had to sternly remind myself that she's Coach's daughter, and while I don't care too much about what he says, giving his daughter sexy eyes is probably a no-no I should mind.

Briar chuckles. "My entire wardrobe consists of shirts from the gift shop that I bought with my employee discount and the occasional animal-themed gift."

"So what I'm hearing is that you sleep in one of those oversize T-shirts with a giraffe body on it where your head sits at the top of the giraffe's neck."

Briar gasps in shock. "How did you know that?" I'm truly not sure if she's kidding or if I hit the nail on the head. In a stage whisper, she adds, "Do you know about the matching giraffe knee socks too? *Très chic.*"

"She's so weird," Harley declares, but I'm picturing Briar fresh from bed with sleep-drunk, soft eyes, in what amounts to a giraffe costume, and instead of looking strange, it's doing unexpected things to my face. I think I'm smiling . . . a lot.

"Says Mr. Spider-Man pj's," Briar teases Harley, and then she turns to me. "And you probably sleep in team gear, right?"

I arch a brow and deadpan, "I sleep naked."

"Oh!" Briar squeaks as that pretty pink blush colors her cheeks once more. I'm 99.4 percent certain she's imagining me, bare-assed and hopefully hard. But she quickly points at Harley and says, "Don't even think about it, mister."

The boy instantly slumps in disappointment, and I can't help but chuckle. "I bet Snuffles gets to sleep naked," I stage-whisper to him.

Briar's mom voice returns as she declares, "Snuffles is responsible for an entire herd. He gets to do whatever he wants. You have to be reminded to brush your teeth every day and pick up your dirty clothes from the floor."

I pull a face, cringing, and say to Harley, "Your mom's got a fair point. Definitely need to brush morning and night. And clean up after yourself. Morning breath and dirty drawers are a big no-go."

"But if I slept naked, I wouldn't have laundry to pick up," Harley counters, but he's joking with his mother. She gives him one of those trademarked mom looks, silently saying so much, and he shrugs. "It was worth a try."

I like how comfortable they are with each other. It reminds me of my parents, who are amazing. If you looked up *mom* and *dad* in the dictionary, their pictures would be there. Loving and supportive, they are the foundation on which my success is built, and I'm grateful for them every day, especially after seeing how fortunate I am to have them in my corner. Not everyone is so lucky. Harley's lucky, too, at least with his mother.

"How'd you end up taking care of animals?" I ask curiously. "It's not exactly the usual nine-to-five."

"And hockey is?" she challenges. But she explains, "I loved science as a kid. Every animal show I could watch, I did . . . on repeat. The plan was to go to college for a zoology degree, but plans changed." Her eyes drop to Harley for a split second, but there's only affection in their depths, no regret over her changed course. "When Harley was little, I would take him to the zoo in his stroller every chance I could. I'd walk him around all day, teaching him about the animals, and eventually, I got to know the keepers. That grew into volunteering, and when we moved here, I applied for an entry-level job, mostly cleaning habitats and helping with the education programs like I'd done before. I did finally get my degree, just an associate, but because the zoo is so small here, that's been enough to let me move up the food chain so to speak. Now, I get to work directly with the animals, which is exactly where I belong."

"Dream come true, I guess," I summarize, and she smiles happily as though she truly believes that.

Caretaking seems to be her nature, something I can relate to. I took care of my sister, mostly protecting her from herself, for my whole life, then added on taking care of Griffin through his rough patch, and now, I've been tasked with taking care of Kipson the same way. It might not be my career choice the way it is for Briar, but I understand what it takes.

"Was hockey always your plan?" she asks.

Nodding, I say, "Plan A, B, C, and every letter to Z. There was no alternative. It's all I ever wanted. Dreamed about it as a kid, focused on it through high school and the minors, and now that I'm living it, I still have to put in the work every day to keep the dream alive. The guys coming up are younger, hungrier, and sometimes stronger. I used to be like that—on that side of the team equation," I say wistfully. "But now, I'm on the other side, as the grizzled veteran, which means I have to be smarter." I tap my temple, emphasizing that so much of hockey is mental, not only physical—a lesson I've seen play out in front of me too many times. "Things can go sideways in a blink, and you end up somewhere you never expected to be."

I'm referring to my detour to the Blizzard team, but I see Briar's smile fade slightly as she unconsciously leans toward Harley. "Unexpected can be good, though. It's the surprises that life throws at you that make it fun. When things get too boring, I always try to sprinkle a little 'unexpected' in on my own. Like we'll head out on a road trip with no destination in mind, and every once in a while, we'll stop and decide 'left, right, or straight' and see where we end up."

"Last time, we ended up lost and Mom had to go into a sketchy gas station to ask for directions because there was no phone signal," Harley informs me.

Briar laughs. "And we got the most delicious saltwater taffy we've ever had at that gas station, didn't we? So it wasn't all bad."

I think that's how she sees the world. Nothing is bad, it's just good that hasn't happened yet. Even the way she talks about being a single parent, which can't be easy, is kindhearted.

*"Mmm,"* I groan dramatically, patting my stomach. "I love salt-water taffy. I don't think I've had that in ages. Where'd you say that gas station was?"

Harley looks at Briar, who laughs. "Sorry, I have no idea. We were so lost I couldn't even tell you what part of the state we were in. It was just a one-and-done experience to be appreciated for what it was."

"Then, to the unexpected," I conclude, raising my tea in the air.

Briar and Harley pick up their sodas and clink the plastic glasses to mine. "To the unexpected," Briar echoes.

She gives me a questioning look, like she hasn't quite figured me out yet, but is definitely trying. Unfortunately, she's looking for schemes and strategies where there are none. I'm a "what you see is what you get" type of guy, with no dark depths to plunge into and explore. I'm a simple man—I want to play hockey, spend time with people I love, and make the best of the life I've been given. I think Briar wants that last one, too, but she's got infinitely more layers than I do. Her glowy, bright exterior and quick smiles make it seem like she's had it easy, but there's so much hurt inside her. She's covered it up with big mom energy and magic, but it's there. I see it. I see her.

"Like getting to practice with my favorite nine-year-old," I tell Harley, and his eyes almost pop out of his skull. I tilt my head, adding out of the side of my mouth, "To be fair, you're the only nine-year-old I know personally."

"The guys are going to be so jealous," he whispers in disbelief. "Especially Connor."

"Just a bit of ice time between friends," I say with a shrug. It's no big deal to me. I had fun with the kid (and his mother), but I can remember being his age and know how much it would've meant to have the opportunity to play with a professional that I looked up to. "And who cares what Connor thinks? Not you." I plant that little seed in the kid's mind, hoping to get the chance to water it and see it grow.

Harley grabs Briar's hand, shaking it, and therefore her, wildly. "Mom, did you hear that? Dom says we're friends!"

She smiles at him, but her eyes cut my way for a split second. I swear she can see right through me, so it's a good thing there's nothing but good intentions in my heart. "I heard. That's really nice of Dom, isn't it?"

*Fuck.*

She pointedly refused to call me Dom at the bar, and now that she has, I like it. A lot. Especially with that little glint in her eye that says she knows it's an intimacy she declined before and is giving me now.

She might be the only friendly face I've met since getting to town, but I'm not feeling particularly friendly right this second. I clear my throat, telling myself again that she's not looking for something romantic, and she's especially not wanting anything like the dirty thoughts running through my mind—of my hands threaded into her messy hair as she sucks my cock or her giraffe sock–covered feet on my shoulders while I lick her pussy. Or even a sweet little kiss where I can taste the spicy ranch she's been dipping her fries into.

*Be cool, Dom. Be chill. Breathe. Don't be one of the assholes she's dealt with before.*

"Yeah, kid. We're all friends. You, your mom, and me." The words are sawdust on my tongue, but a necessary reminder. Mostly for me, considering Briar seems to be laughing behind her blue-eyed stare, all too aware of the effect she has on me.

"Unexpected friends," Briar declares as she reaches for another sweet potato fry. "Much like capybaras and crocodiles, who get along surprisingly well considering one is the prey and one is the predator." Briar meets my gaze directly, a question hiding in the science lecture–toned words. "Capybaras will even ride on the crocodiles' backs, floating along on the most dangerous paddleboard in existence." She moves the fry through the air like the swimming crocodile and then snatches it between her teeth.

Does she think I'm the predator? If anything, I'm her fucking prey, embarrassingly at her mercy. I even skipped out on postcamp dinner with Rodney and Tomville to meet her and Harley tonight. I would've skipped out on a hell of a lot more, too, without her even asking me to. I wanted to see her, wanted to meet the son that is the center of her universe, and wanted to find out if the spark I felt at O'Neal's was as real as it felt to me.

It is. It absolutely is.

"How does that work? Do the crocodiles just not like the taste of capybara? I'd think it'd be like chicken," I surmise thoughtfully. I'm only half talking about the actual animals. The rest of me is drawing some straight-line similarities to the woman across the table from me.

"Probably saltier," she quips with a raised brow.

Grudgingly, I admit, "And tougher."

# Chapter 6

## Briar

"Bye! Have a good weekend," I call out to the last after-school program employee as she locks the school's door and walks across the parking lot. She gives me one of those forced, professional smiles, the kind that doesn't reach her eyes, and then glances at Harley with a knowing look. This isn't the first time this has happened. It's not even the tenth time. More like the fiftieth in the four years that Harley's been at this school.

Tyler is supposed to pick Harley up from school every other Friday for his weekend visitation, and he does . . . mostly. Just on his own schedule, not the school's. Or mine. Because no one else matters in Tyler's worldview. It serves him or it doesn't happen.

So like too many times before, we're sitting on the bench out front, waiting on Tyler. Technically, he should've been here thirty minutes ago at the designated pickup time—one I have never been late for, not even when one of our petting zoo sheep was giving birth. Unfortunately, he still has fifteen more minutes before being considered a no-show according to our divorce decree.

Do I have a plan for that? Of course I do. That's what mothers do—plan for every possible contingency, both good and bad. If Tyler no-shows, I'll surprise Harley with a movie night at the discount theater in the next town over to see the most recently released superhero movie.

I don't remember what it is, but it seems like there's always one, and it'd be a decent distraction for a disappointed son.

"Think he's actually coming?" Harley asks. He's not even scanning the street hopefully anymore. Instead, he's sprawled out with his head in my lap, staring at the seemingly endless flocks of birds flying overhead. It's only September, but they seem hellbent on getting out of Dodge.

I hate this. With every bone . . . every muscle . . . every cell in my body. I hate that my son is the one who pays the biggest, most painful price for Tyler's actions, again and again. Once upon a time, I covered for him, saying he got hung up at work or we must've gotten dates or times confused. Those days are long gone. Not because I want to degrade Tyler to our son, but because I learned that lying on Tyler's behalf only made Harley not trust me either. So I'm honest, to a point. "I don't know, honey. I haven't heard from him."

Harley closes his eyes, and I search his face for some sign of what he's thinking. What he's feeling. But he's perfectly blank, no tears escaping or frown turning his lips downward. Just empty. I hate that too. At his tender age, he should still think the world is filled with kindness and good people. He shouldn't be jaded by the true reality of it, especially when that cynicism is the result of his own father's actions and inactions.

Harley's buried pain makes me angry all over again. Tyler fucking up my head is one thing, but Harley's? That's an entirely different issue, one I take much more seriously.

Just as I'm about to give up, the obnoxious growl of an engine revving too high comes around the corner. Harley sits up instantly, the dawning shock on his face replaced by happiness in a blink. "Dad's here!"

I don't curse. Out loud. But I was starting to look forward to a movie night with a popcorn dinner.

Tyler's white pickup truck pulls into the school lot and he stops at the curb, right in the middle of the carpool lane. That'd be a cardinal sin, except no one is here to care at this hour. As he comes around the hood, he says, "Hey, Harley! Who's ready for ice cream?"

He's got a cosmetically enhanced white smile on his tanned face, sunglasses still covering his eyes, and is wearing jeans and a polo shirt emblazoned with the logo of the construction company he works for. I used to think he was so handsome, and maybe objectively he still is, but all I see is the devil inside him. The one I saw too up close and personal to deny any longer.

He holds his arms out wide for a hug, which Harley readily gives him.

There's no apology. No explanation. Nothing. Not that any excuse he could give would make his tardiness acceptable. The urge to pull Harley back to my side and protect him from Tyler rides me hard, but I fight it back. That would only make things worse . . . for my son and for me.

"What're you doing here?" Tyler asks me, somehow looking confused at my existence.

"When you weren't here at pickup time, the school called me. I was close by"—I give him a pointed look, silently communicating that I do that because he is wholly unreliable, and his jaw clenches at the rebuff—"so I came over to check Harley out. I didn't want to pay the one dollar per minute fee for"—I glance down at my watch—"thirty-six minutes."

"I had to pick up Amber from work first."

As far as explanations go, it's as good as any, but it's most definitely telling. Amber is Tyler's girlfriend, and choosing to pick her up before Harley shows his priorities clearly.

I glance at the woman sitting in the passenger seat of the truck, and she gives me a narrow-eyed scowl. Thanks to Tyler's version of our divorce, in her mind, I'm the enemy, the evil ex who keeps trying to get her claws back into Tyler, who left me because I'm a crazy bitch. Girl code rules state that I should tell her to watch her back because she's sleeping with the actual enemy, but she's not ready to hear that. She's too deeply under his spell, enthralled with the charming man he at least on the surface can be.

And if I'm honest, she's a stabilizing force in Tyler's life, or at least as much of one as he'll allow, and selfishly, I can appreciate that. It means that he's more consistent with his obligations than he used to be. Plus, she is nice to Harley, which is the main thing I care about, so I just offer her a hint of a smile, hoping that by not pressing her buttons, she can manage Tyler's emotions when they leave with my son.

"Pickup time is six o'clock. Drop-off is four o'clock on Sunday. I'll meet you at the park then." Straightforward, factual, and emotionless is the goal, and I hit every point.

Tyler takes his sunglasses off, hooking them in the neck of his shirt. "Aw, Briar, don't be like that. I appreciate you coming to sit with my boy till I could get here." He places a hand on Harley's shoulder, pulling our son into his side for a moment, and flashes me one of those *aw-shucks* grins that used to fool me.

This is his game.

For all his faults, stupidity isn't one of them. He's strategic. And this whole picture reframes in my mind. This is how he wanted it—me waiting for him, him heroically showing up to rescue Harley like the good-times-only dad, flaunting Amber in my face and me in hers. Every piece a pawn, but he's the only one playing.

I ignore him. The gray rock method has become my way of taking back power, especially when all Tyler wants is to find some little way to still control me. Every time he tries to throw toxicity my way, I don't react and just do my thing. I hug Harley tightly, pressing a kiss to the top of his head. "I'll see you Sunday, honey. I love you."

"You act like you're never gonna see him again. It's not even forty-eight hours, babe. He'll be fine."

The fact that he thinks I want forty-eight hours—hell, *an* hour—away from my son pisses me off. The last thing I want is to send him away, with his dad or anyone else. But I don't react, knowing he's baiting me with that and the endearment he used to call me. I haven't been his "babe" in a very long time.

"Call me anytime." I pointedly say the words to Harley and Harley only, nearly nose to nose with him so that there is no misconstruing my intention.

When Tyler doesn't get the reaction from me that he's looking for—whether that's anger or affection, he tries another tactic. "Why don't we do handover at my house on Sunday? I can grill out and we can eat dinner like the old days."

The old days.

Sunday cookouts were our routine. I'd clean the house, top to bottom, making sure every nook and cranny was spotless, wash, dry, fold, and put away all the laundry, go to the grocery store, haul it all inside and put everything away, prep snacks and lunches for the week, and generally, do all the work, taking care of an into-everything toddler along the way, while Tyler played a round of golf with his buddies and drank too much beer. Then, he'd waltz in, disappear into the bathroom for an hour, reappear to throw the meat I'd trimmed and marinated onto the grill while I made side dishes and set the table, and then remind me to thank him for taking care of dinner as though he'd done me a favor.

And also, his house used to be *our* house. He kept it in the divorce because I couldn't pay the mortgage on my salary. I have no desire to go back to the place where I was the unhappiest version of myself.

I don't give him that truth, though. He'll only hold it against me, delighting in any remaining echoes of the pain he caused. "The park is fine."

He shrugs as if completely unbothered, but I see the muscle twitch beneath his eye, a telltale tick he can't control when he's angry. "Suit yourself. We'll meet you there at five o'clock."

"Four," I correct before I can stop myself. Habits are hard to break, even after all this time, even when I know better. He intentionally said the wrong time to make me say the right one. It's an example of "his cause, his desired effect." Tyler's every word is a bullet looking for a target, and I let him hit one. It's not a center mass hit, but his grin says he still recognizes the win. The smallest, stupidest one, but a win nonetheless.

"Right, four."

Why do I feel like he's going to be an hour late for drop-off? Because he will be, especially now that I reminded him. Just to be ornery, to irritate me, to make me sit on a park bench and wait for him the way I sat on a school bench today.

"Dad, did you mean it about getting ice cream?" Harley asks.

I want to tell him to at least eat dinner first, but I swallow those words down. Still, Tyler knows I'm thinking them. Any responsible parent would be. Which is why he tells Harley, "Of course I did. Who would joke about ice cream? Get in. Amber can tell you all about the Fall Festival we're going to tomorrow."

"Festival?" Harley's grin is nearly ear-to-ear as he runs toward the truck and climbs inside without giving me a second glance. "What festival are we going to?" I hear him ask Amber before closing the door.

I pray it's actually fall themed, with pumpkins and leaves, and not Halloween, with zombies and monsters. Harley likes to fancy himself a brave, big kid, but scary stuff can still give him nightmares. I want to ask. I want to tell Tyler to be thoughtful about what he's exposing our son to, but I don't have any control over what they do on their visitation and have to trust that a haunted house isn't going to let elementary-aged kids in if it's too scary.

It's ridiculous that I trust a haunted house to be more responsible for my son's well-being than his father, but that's where we are.

"Let me know if you change your mind about dinner Sunday," Tyler tells me, his voice gone husky and his smile filling with heat. "Or anytime." He lets his eyes drop over me from head to toe, making sure I feel every unwelcome caress of his weighted look and that Amber doesn't see any of it.

"Four o'clock at the park."

"Sure, babe. Whatever you say," Tyler tells me with a chuckle. He walks away, and I swear he's trying to strut around the truck with a little more pep in his step, as though he actually did something with our exchange.

As he climbs in, the back window of the truck rolls down. "Bye, Mom! I love you!" Harley calls out. He didn't forget. He got distracted by the dangling carrot his dad threw out, but he remembered me in the end.

"Love you too," I yell, but I'm not sure he hears me over the too-loud engine of Tyler's truck as he pulls away. So I wave the *ILU* fingers, hoping it's enough.

Alone in the school parking lot, I wrap my arms around myself. Almost forty-eight hours until Harley comes back. These weekends are the worst. I don't know what to do with myself and too often end up stress cleaning, doomscrolling, or forcing myself to do something fun and feeling ungrateful the whole time as I wonder what Harley is doing while I'm goofing off.

That night, I'm eating a bowl of popcorn for dinner, the remaining vestige of my movie plan, when my phone dings. It's a text from *Hockey Coach.*

I'm free all weekend if Harley wants to practice?

It seems pretty straightforward, and I'd like to believe that's true and Dominic is exactly what he says he is—a new-to-town guy who wants to share the sport he loves.

But he's also Dominic Lee, a professional athlete with a whole life that doesn't involve elementary-level hockey drills with a nine-year-old kid. I might've done a bit of googling to see what his story is, and while nothing damning showed up, surely he has better things to do.

That alone makes me question his motives.

Truthfully, Dominic has been nothing but nice, but I used to know another nice guy, and he turned out to be a monster. Masks are easy to keep in place at first, and while I'm not sure Dominic's wearing a mask,

I also don't trust that he isn't. Nor do I have the time or inclination to figure it out.

Especially when I'm feeling too raw and vulnerable after the forced interaction with Tyler today and I'm worried if Harley is going to be okay all weekend. Tyler will make sure he's safe and fed, stuff like that, but emotionally? He's always a bit of a wreck after spending so much time in Tyler's toxic cesspool of influence.

He's busy. Sorry.

I leave it at that and so does Dominic. And I only glare at my phone a few dozen times after that, wishing it would ding again and his *Hockey Coach* label would flash on my screen.

I'm a mess of inconsistencies, both wanting him to leave me alone and contrarily wanting him to ask if I'm busy too. But he annoyingly respects my no.

# Chapter 7

## Dominic

Practice sucks. It's familiar in that it's the same drills and plays I've done thousands of times since I was a kid, but it's also unfamiliar in that I don't have the same trust in my teammates that I did with the Hawks. I'm not opposed to newness—as a pro there's fresh faces on the team every year. I'm just annoyed with assholes, and the Blizzard has more than its fair share as far as I can tell, especially now that we're all practicing together. Not just rookies and newbies, but the entire bench.

To be fair, I think they feel the same way about me—that I'm an asshole, that I'm annoying, and that they'd be better off without me. I know Kipson does. We're still in the stage where he's ignoring my existence and in denial that there's a problem, despite there being a very obvious one. The man plays angry, but in a self-destructive way that's going to fuck us come the season starting.

The only thing that doesn't suck about this new gig is Briar. And Harley.

She blew me off over the weekend, which only made me more surprised when she reached out today, saying Harley was talking about me nonstop and asking if there was any way I might have a few more minutes for him. Obviously, I said yes immediately.

Practice with him is an entirely different thing. I enjoy the time with the kid, who listens and works hard, and I especially enjoy the time with his mom, getting to know more about the woman who smiles at everything and makes me laugh at seemingly nothing. And who is also currently watching us on the ice so I should get back to it.

"Alright, touchpoint one," I say, pointing at a cone, "then two, three, four." I indicate each spot as Harley follows the path I'm setting. "In the net, right corner." I'm working with Harley on scoring today, specifically aiming for small targets inside the net. It'll increase the spaces he sees during games, so he won't only search for center shots, which get rarer the older the players get.

"Got it," Harley tells me with a nod of certainty.

I move back, keeping a close eye on him. The first pass is a bit slow, but as he gets more confident in the pattern, his speed increases, as does his aim. I let him run it ten times before skating back over. "Now, reverse," I say with a diabolical grin. "Your body's using muscle memory, so we challenge it in a new way. One, two, three, four, left corner."

He looks unsure again, but goes for it without question. I let him run the drill that direction ten times too.

"Let's put them together. First drill, right corner. When you skate back to start, the puck will be waiting for you to do the second drill to the left corner. Keep track," I tell him, tapping my temple with the butt of my stick. "There's no autopilot here."

I expect him to be hesitant at first. It's not a complicated pattern, but it requires thinking and then moving. Slowly but surely, he gets faster and faster. His aim falters a bit as his speed increases, but after quite a few runs, he's both fast and accurate . . . and entirely out of breath.

"Great job. Quick water break."

He nods and beelines to Briar, who is holding his water bottle out. I pick up the cones before following. "That was rough, but you handled it like a pro," I tell Harley and he beams. "Let me know when you're ready for more."

"Let's go," Harley says excitedly, shoving the bottle back to his mother and fixing his helmet, which had gone a little off-center with the gulps he was swallowing.

Briar's brows lift. "We don't want to take up your whole evening. It's okay if you need to go."

"Mooom."

We've been here for almost an hour and it's a school night, but there's one last piece to this drill I'd like Harley to do. "We'll make it fast," I promise, giving the kid a chin nod of *get out there before she stops us*. Thankfully, he gets the message and skates away, heading back to center ice as Briar gives me a trademarked mom glare of disappointment for encouraging him to semidisobey. But I can also see the smile trying to lift her lips.

"Bad influence?" I say, skating backward as I shoot Briar a cocky grin. I point at myself. "Who, me?"

Her smile breaks free, lighting up her face. Shaking her head good-naturedly, she sits down, but calls out, "Ten more minutes."

I meet Harley's eyes and in sync, we answer, "Yes, ma'am."

I give Harley his instructions and he takes his place. From off-side, I hit pucks his way, calling *right* or *left* as I send them. His job is to react quickly, shooting to the corresponding corner. The goal is to get ten in a row in the correct corner. It's harder than it sounds.

The first attempt, Harley makes it to three before missing. The second, seven. The third, fourth, fifth, and sixth, he still doesn't make ten.

"Eight, right." *Thwak.*

"Nine, right." *Thwak.*

"Ten, left." I hold my breath, wanting this for him probably as badly as he wants it for himself. *Thwak.*

"I did it!" he shouts. Behind his helmet, I can see his face light up with surprise, and as he flies to me with his hand up for a high five, his pride grows.

"Way to go, man! That was some awesome work."

He whirls to find Briar, making sure that she saw. Of course she did, her eyes have been locked on Harley the entire practice. Not once has she started scrolling on her phone or looked bored. She's watched, rapt with what's been happening, so she saw exactly how much work that took and is standing up, clapping proudly.

"Great job!" She starts waving her hands in the air like a pom-pom-less cheerleader, "Woo-hoo!"

The reality hits Harley and he starts jumping around. "I did it! I really did it!"

I'm grinning, watching his celebration with some pride of my own, when he wobbles on a landing. "Ow!" he shouts, instantly lifting that foot up from the ice.

"Honey? Are you okay?" Briar hollers. She's got that *oh no, not my baby* horrified look that I've seen on my mom's face when I've gotten hurt over the years.

"I got him," I tell her, skating to Harley at full speed. "What happened?"

He looks up at me with tears starting to pool in his eyes. "I landed funny. My ankle kinda twisted. It hurts . . . a lot."

I nod. "Did you feel a pop or anything?"

He shakes his head and I breathe again. "Good. Let's get you off the ice." I grab under his armpits, tell him to hold that foot up, and steer him toward the exit gate. I could pick him up easily, but there's an honor to leaving the ice yourself, even if it's with help, and I want to give Harley that dignity and respect. But once we're clear, I scoop him up and carry him to the closest bench before squatting down. "We need to take off your skate. Laces won't hurt, pulling it off might hurt a little." I'm as matter-of-fact and honest about it as I can be, not wanting him to be surprised by the pain.

He nods bravely and I get to it. I'm as careful as possible, fully unlacing the skate, but he still whimpers a little as I remove it. Briar comforts him, shushing him softly as she looks at me with *fix it* eyes.

Under his sock, his ankle looks . . . fine? It's not swollen or purple thankfully, but as I press gently, he winces.

"I think we should get it checked out, just to be safe," I tell them both. Like she was already thinking the same thing, Briar is nodding before I get the words out and starts grabbing their stuff. I make quick work of taking Harley's other skate off and changing into tennis shoes myself.

"Can you carry him to the car?"

"Yep." Harley is light in my arms, but my gut is churning. The kid got hurt on my watch. It might not have been an injury at my hand, or even because of a drill I had him doing, but I still feel responsible. Which is why I head to my truck. "There's room for him to stretch his leg out on the back seat," I explain to Briar, who looks ready to argue with me. Thankfully, that makes sense to her and she nods in acceptance.

I set him down and move out of the way so she can fuss over him for a second. Once she's sure Harley is situated safely, she comes to stand in the open passenger door and meets my eyes. I'm expecting blame, accusation, and a fair amount of anger. What I get is, "Thank you."

The adrenaline has worn off for Harley and it's late for his little boy body, so after a delicate exam by the doctor and an X-ray we don't have the results for yet, he's crashed out on the hospital gurney. He looks tiny amid the white blankets and pillows Briar piled around him to keep him comfortable. She's sitting in a chair, her eyes locked on her son.

"He'll be okay," I tell her quietly, laying a comforting hand on her shoulder.

Slowly, her eyes find mine, as if she'd forgotten that I've been standing here for the last three hours. "I know. I just wish I could take the pain away."

I sigh, wishing the same. I'd take the kid's pain myself if there were a way to do it. But there's not, there never is. "My mom has sat vigil by my bed more times than she'd like to remember. When I was a kid, she even tried to get me to play something less physical, like golf." I laugh at the memory. "Dad told her that if I wasn't attacking the ice full throttle, I'd probably get kicked out of school for fighting. He was right."

"You were aggressive? Even as a kid?"

"I wasn't aggressive, then or now. I was *active*." That's putting it mildly. I was a wild child that constantly climbed, ran, and roughhoused, and according to Mom, gave her the first gray hairs of her life. "Plus all my friends played hockey. Some of them still do, though not professionally. Now, it's my job. One I love, but I don't go around getting violent off the ice." I'm admittedly a bit offended. I know the hockey stereotype, especially for defensemen, that we're all big lunks of brainless muscle looking for any opportunity to beat the shit out of someone. But that's not how I play and definitely not how I live.

"Sorry, I didn't mean—" Briar waves her hand by way of explanation, and I decide to give her a break. She's a mama bear whose cub is injured. The doctor is lucky Briar didn't bite his hand when he pressed on Harley's ankle. I nod, accepting the apology, and she sighs. Her eyes locked on her sleeping son's face, she says, "Harley used to like watching hockey with Tyler, but he was so young that he never asked to play. I was thankful for that. Then, a few years ago, seemingly out of nowhere, he got angry . . . at Tyler, at me, at everyone. He was only six, but he was so mad."

She swallows thickly, like she can still feel her son's pain. Not the ankle, but his heartbreak. "We talked, and basically, it boiled down to him realizing that other boys in his class had fathers who showed up for Donuts with Daddy, practices and games, and even just for dinner. It was the first time he saw that our family was different. His best friend played hockey and I talked to the coach, who said a sport can be good for kids. Not only for the usual 'learn discipline' and 'wear them out' stuff, but to express their emotions in different ways. *Healthy ways.* So he started playing and he loves it so much."

"I'm glad you didn't talk to your dad then," I note, and Briar scoffs in agreement. There's no way she'd get a healthy outlook on hockey from him.

"True. But I was convinced, so I let Harley play. I'm glad I did." Her eyes lift to mine, something in their depths I can't quite pinpoint.

"And you?"

She runs a finger over Harley's hand, tracing his tiny fingers. "I'm glad he loves it."

"But?" I prompt, hearing it even if she didn't say it.

After checking that Harley's still asleep, and keeping her voice low, she says, "But honestly, it pisses me off that Tyler does this whole 'chip off the old block' thing when it has nothing to do with him. He never comes to practices, rarely makes appearances at games, and doesn't even listen to Harley talk about his team. He wants Harley to sit quietly while he watches the game. It's not even *together*, Harley is just there. And it's not fair that Harley's doing this big thing to make a connection with Tyler, and he doesn't care. Every time Harley skates out there, I feel . . . bitter. And not just because of Tyler, but . . . growing up as Robert Boothe's daughter wasn't easy." She releases a deep breath as though it might be the first time she's ever said those words. Maybe the first time she's acknowledged that feeling.

I move closer, crouching down beside her and moving my hand to her knee. "Feel better?" I ask gently.

She turns glittery eyes to me, our noses nearly touching. I want to take her in my arms and soothe all her pain away. I want to tell her that it's going to be okay. I want to kiss the fuck out of her and make her forget everything else, especially that her son is injured. But I don't. As much as I want to, she needs the friend I keep telling her I can be. So I don't move, not closer nor farther away. I stay exactly as I am, waiting for her answer.

"Not especially. I had that pushed down and locked away. I wasn't planning on airing my deepest, darkest baggage tonight. What was in that coffee? Truth serum?" She glances toward the now-cold cup of coffee I got her shortly after we arrived at the ER. It's been a roller coaster of a night, and the coffee had been my most minor of attempts at caring for her given she's been a bit raw and vulnerable with her son laid up in a hospital bed.

"No, I just tend to have that effect on people," I tease, letting her retreat from the truth of her words as I swipe an errant tear from her cheek. As she scrubs at her own eyes and sniffles a bit, putting her calm, cool, collected mask back in place, I have one more question. "Why doesn't your dad help Harley with hockey stuff?"

Her mouth opens like she's about to explain why the kid's grandfather, an actual NHL coach, isn't helping him with skills, showing up for his games, or taking him to professional ones. But before she can, the curtain jerks open. "Harley? Daddy's here."

The man standing here looks relatively unremarkable. He's wearing jeans and a T-shirt with dust-covered brown work boots. His blond hair is sticking out from underneath a ballcap with a machinery company logo and his thin lips are turned down into a frown. The only remarkable thing about him is his blue eyes. They're vacant, cold, and emotionless, despite his urgent tone. And that disconnect would be enough for me to hate the guy, even if I didn't know how he'd hurt Briar and Harley.

But I do know. So I hate this asshole even more. Every protective instinct I possess surges to the forefront. But there's someone else who's just as protective, of Harley at least.

"Shh," Briar snaps, a finger in front of her pursed lips. "What're you doing here?"

"What am I doing here?" he echoes. "You texted that Harley was hurt. Where the hell else am I supposed to be? He's my son, Briar."

He's being loud—*too loud*—when Harley is resting and doesn't need to witness his parents fighting. So I do what I do best . . . step forward to take the hit. Holding out my hand and modeling a quieter and more appropriate volume, I say, "You must be Tyler. I'm Dominic. Nice to meet you."

"You're Dominic Lee," he says as he shakes my hand, staring at me dumbfounded. His confusion only lasts a split second before he cuts hard eyes back to Briar. "Is this who you're fucking now? A hockey player? Guess you changed your mind there, too, huh?" The sarcastic accusation is caustic, meant to dig into Briar's scars.

"Whoa," I warn, physically stepping in front of them as I move to block her from his verbal attack. The fact that she doesn't even flinch is telling, putting my already-raised guard on extra high alert. "I'm helping Harley with some skills and drills, and he turned his ankle a little. Kid's tough, though. He'll be okay." I'm intentionally turning Tyler's attention back to Harley so he'll leave Briar alone. She's been through enough—both with this asshole and tonight.

"You didn't need to come down here," Briar tells her ex, leaning out from behind me. "I'm required to notify you in the app of any emergencies. Consider yourself notified. But Harley is fine. We're just waiting on the X-ray results."

"X-ray? He broke his leg?" Tyler barks.

Is he even listening? I clearly said he turned his ankle.

"His ankle," Briar corrects. "And no, not broken. Possibly sprained or strained at the worst, more likely a tweak that'll be fine tomorrow."

The doctor hasn't officially said that, but he didn't seem too concerned after the exam. His actual words were, "Kids are bendy so joints go loosey-goosey sometimes." It'd been intended to settle Briar's nerves, but it'd made Harley laugh, which was almost as good.

"So this is your fault?" Tyler says, turning his vitriol on me. He's puffing up his chest, trying to seem larger, which is laughable. I easily have a couple of inches on him, at least fifteen pounds of muscle, and fight on the ice for a living. Ten to one odds he usually berates people he perceives to be weaker than he is. Too bad he miscalculated with Briar. She's strong as hell.

I smirk, unbothered by his posturing, until he takes a step forward. Into me? I don't give a shit about that. He can bring it if he's so inclined.

But Briar is right behind me, and I don't want him any closer to her. "Look, man—"

"Dad?" a weak voice says, immediately drawing everyone's attention.

Tyler gives me a hard look, but rushes to the other side of the bed to get closer to Harley. "Yeah, buddy. I'm here."

"Why are you yelling at Dom? He was helping me. You should've seen the shots I made tonight. I did so good. Right, Dom?" Harley glances at me for assurance, and my heart melts for the kid. Fucking trooper, this one is.

Nodding, I confirm, "You did great, kid."

"You should've been there, Dad. I missed over and over, but Dom told me to keep trying because practice makes progress, and he was right. I did it!"

I can't help but smile at Harley. His pride in himself is a beautiful sight.

Tyler, however, looks like he wants to kick my ass. Well, he can try if he wants. I know his game. I'm better at it than he is, mostly because I'm not playing. I don't read people to manipulate them. I get to know people so I can be a good friend, a good brother, a good teammate. So I hold my fist out to Harley, initiating a fist bump that I know will reinforce his confidence, while simultaneously pissing his father off. It's a win-win in my book.

"Sounds like you practiced a bit too much," Tyler suggests sourly. "Maybe if Dominic had stopped before you were too tired, you wouldn't have gotten hurt."

He means it to be a dig on my coaching skills, but Harley's proud smile falters and that makes me want to punch this fucker in his smug, smirking mouth.

"Can I talk to you in the hallway, please?" Briar asks Tyler through a forced, fake smile, her teeth clenched tightly.

As they step out, Tyler gives me a shit-eating grin. "Sure, babe. Let's talk." He makes it sound like they're stepping into the hallway to fuck.

I take a steadying breath, reminding myself that punching him won't do any of us any good. Especially Briar and Harley.

"Did I take too long to make the shots?" Harley's question grabs my attention, and when I turn back, he looks uncertain.

"It took however long it took. You were still slamming those shots full-strength and hadn't slowed down the pace, so you didn't seem tired in the slightest. To me, you were putting in good effort, which is all you can ask of yourself and all a coach should ask of you." I let that sink in for a moment before adding, "Hockey's a tough sport. You get hurt, you get better, you play again. This is nothing more than an asterisk on your season and a cool story to tell at school."

Harley dips his chin, thinking that over.

In the moment of silence, we hear raised voices, and he looks to me for help. Standing up, I say, "Gimme a second, Harley. Need to blow my nose."

He gives me a wary look, but I use the excuse to step outside, where Tyler's leaning into Briar, his tone harsh and bullying. "What the hell are you doing, bringing that motherfucker—"

"Excuse me," I growl, stepping in between them. I'm trying to play it cool, but if this asshole takes one more step toward Briar, I'll forget this isn't the ice, and show him what it feels like to get boarded . . . right through the fucking wall behind him.

Keeping my voice low and calm, I tell him, "Harley can hear you. And you don't raise your voice to Briar. Not while I'm around." I correct myself, "Not ever. Understand?"

Tyler, for a second, looks like he's about to bow up, but instead, he smartly backs up a step. Briar lays a hand on my back. "He can hear us?"

"Not any longer," I assure her, but I'm glaring warningly at the man everyone, not only Harley, heard speaking to her that way. Turning, I look into her eyes, making the whole world just the two of us. "Are you okay? What can I do?"

I have a few ideas of my own. Most relate to teaching her ex some fucking manners, but he's not my focus here. Briar is. Harley is.

She nods jerkily and cuts her eyes to the curtain. "I'm fine. Can you watch Harley?"

My message has been delivered, so I dip my chin slightly, and go back inside the room, leaving the curtain a bit more open, needing to see and hear Briar and Tyler better.

Harley peers at me uneasily. After a long minute of silence, he whispers, "Can I tell you something?"

His tone has me immediately locking in. "You can tell me anything, kid. Anything."

He glances toward the curtain, smartly checking for feet beneath it, but there are none. Wherever Briar and Tyler went to continue their conversation is far enough away to give Harley and me a moment of privacy. Honestly, there's a big piece of me that wants to track Briar down and fight that battle for her, but she's been doing it on her own for a long while, so I have to trust she's strong enough to continue it. Plus, she asked me to stay here with her son, a responsibility I take seriously.

"I hate it when they're together. My mom and dad, I mean." He acts like that's full-blown blasphemy to say aloud.

"Why?" I come back over and sit down in the chair next to his bed. "Do they fight a lot?"

"I wish," he huffs. "But no. Dad says mean things to Mom. She tries to correct him sometimes; other times, she ignores him. She calls it gray rock." He shrugs a tiny shoulder. "Either way, he gets mad and gets loud. The louder he gets, the quieter Mom gets."

He risks glancing up at me, gauging my reaction to his revelation, and I have to work to school my face into something less murderous than I'm feeling. Tyler is mean to Briar? Yells at her? At all is bad enough, but in front of their kid? That's even worse.

"And then what?" I ask carefully, my fingers gripping the arm of my chair.

"She used to cry after seeing him. She doesn't know that I know that, so don't tell her, okay?" he pleads. I nod, silently agreeing, even though Briar and I are going to have a chat about this. But I'll make sure to do it without betraying Harley's confidence. "She thinks the crying makes her look weak, but I think it means she's strong enough to not unleash on Dad. I wish he was that strong because all he does is take stuff out on her that she doesn't deserve. Like him always being late or no-showing. He says she should've reminded him, but he's a grown-up. He should know, right?" he implores me. Under his breath, he grumbles, "Mom doesn't have to remind me about my homework and I'm nine."

The things I want to say about Tyler aren't suitable for little ears. Instead, I concentrate on Harley. "You're pretty smart, you know that?"

He smiles weakly. "Thanks to Mom." He starts fidgeting with the blanket, pulling at a loose string. "Dom? Can I ask you a favor?"

"Anything," I vow.

"Don't treat Mom like Dad does, okay? She shouldn't cry. She should smile all the time."

Fuck, if only it were that easy. We should all smile all the time, be happy and joyful at the blessings we've been given. But life isn't easy like that. "I would never treat your mom or anyone else poorly. It's not who I am. But you know that your mom and I . . . we're friends. That's all."

It stings a bit to say that, but it's the truth. She's a complete smokeshow, with a flair for weirdly interesting animal facts, a healthy sprinkle of silly fun, and a plateful of heavy responsibilities and trauma, but we are just friends. I think she needs that. Hell, I do too.

"Friends can be jerks too. Just be nice to her," Harley tells me. "She does so much for me, even putting up with Dad because she thinks I need a male role model." The kid rolls his eyes hard. "As if he's one."

Damn. That's harsh. But true.

I sigh, giving the boy a heavy look. "Sometimes the role modeling isn't in what to do, but rather, in what *not* to do. Who not to be."

"Like opposites? So if I do the opposite of what Dad would do, I'll be okay?"

That is a nuclear bomb of a question. But I tell him the truth. "The fact that you see how he behaves, and you asked that question? You are already more than okay, Harley."

"Thanks, Dom."

"Anytime."

"Can we still practice again?" he asks hopefully.

Laughing, I nod. "Absolutely." I hold up one finger. "After both the doctor and your mom clear you."

He sags. "So, like never."

A short time later, Briar comes back in, and sure enough, Harley was right—her eyes are a bit bloodshot and red-rimmed, something they weren't earlier. Clearly, the conversation in the hallway wasn't polite. But more importantly, she's also alone.

"Where's Dad?"

"He left," Briar tells him with no further commentary and no explanation.

I wonder if she asked him to leave. Or told him to. Or if he wasn't getting his way, so he stomped out like a tantrum-throwing child. And though I'm glad he's gone, I worry what he said to Briar before leaving. What buttons did he push? What thoughts did he plant?

Briar places a gentle kiss on Harley's head before turning to me. "You should go too. It's getting late and we're fine. We'll wait for the discharge paperwork and go home."

I'm not going anywhere. If Briar doesn't want me in here, I'll go sit in the waiting room, but I'm not leaving her. I don't have to argue with her, though. Harley does it for me.

"No! Stay, please. Mom never has anyone to help her and you're already here," he tells me, bypassing his mother's orders. "You could get her a candy bar or something? So she doesn't get hangry. We didn't have dinner," he reminds us.

Briar looks uncertain, like she's worried Harley's pressuring me into doing something I don't want to. As if that's even possible. "I wasn't leaving anyway. I was going to sit outside and wait for you," I declare, quietly but 100 percent serious. The look of surprise on her face is beautiful. I don't think Briar has had people in her corner before. Lucky for her, I have, and I know what to do. "I'll check the vending machines and see what we're working with. Maybe some chips—potatoes are a vegetable, some peanut butter crackers—that's a protein and fat, and some Starburst? Fruit flavoring is probably the closest thing to a fruit we'll get."

"Sounds good," Briar admits, looking relieved. "They might have Hostess pies too."

"Get Mom a Snickers," Harley instructs. "She likes that they're named after a horse."

I glance at Briar in confusion. "A horse?"

She shrugs and half smiles, seemingly embarrassed. "They named it after the beloved family horse."

Grinning at learning another random animal fact from her arsenal, I promise, "Definitely getting a Snickers. Back in a minute."

As I leave them, I glance up and down the hallway, checking to see if Tyler is still lurking around. I would be, and I don't expect any different of him. But I don't spot him anywhere—not in the ER, or the nearby hallways I make a quick loop through, and not in the vending machine area. I grab us some snacks—especially a Snickers—and get back to the ER as fast as I can, where I find the doctor talking to Briar.

"No fracture. You'll want to let it rest for a couple of days, so no skating. But by the weekend, he should be okay. Tape it up the first few times he laces up and he should be good. Here's a printout of how to do it."

Briar is nodding along like she's memorizing every word and takes the paper from the doctor, looking it over. From here, I can see that they're telling her to do a basic figure-eight taping job, something I've done and had done to me a thousand times.

The doctor finishes his spiel. "Any questions? Mom? Dad? Harley?" He looks around the room at us.

Briar's eyes pop open wide as she points at me. "Oh, he's not—"

The realization hits me like a wrecking ball—the doctor thinks I'm Harley's father. Rather than bristling at the mistake, it strangely feels . . . good? The kid deserves a better dad than the one he has. I'm not saying it's me, but I'm not mad at the logical assumption, either, given Briar and I are the ones that brought Harley in.

"Thanks, Doc," I say, holding a hand out.

When he leaves, Briar turns on me, hissing quietly, "He's going to think you have some secret love child you've kept away from the press for the last nine years. You're going to end up on ESPN tomorrow now."

*She's worried about my reputation? At a time like this?*

I laugh, shaking my head. "That guy has no idea who I am. Probably doesn't know a puck from a paperweight." To Harley, I say, "You ready to get out of here?"

"Yeah," he says with a heavy nod. "Mom says I get to skip school tomorrow and go to work with her. Caprice has a new baby."

"Caprice?" I repeat questioningly.

"One of our siamang gibbons had a baby a couple of months ago. It's our first on-site birth in years, and we're monitoring mom, baby, and the whole family unit closely," Briar explains.

"And Mom says I can sit and watch her tomorrow so I stay off my ankle since it's so late on a school night," Harley says excitedly.

"I could watch a gibbon tomorrow too," I suggest casually. "I don't have practice and you two are like the only people I know here."

"Shouldn't you be reaching out to Kipson?" Briar asks, her tone taking on a scolding edge.

"Forget Kipson. There's a baby . . ." I trail off, leaning toward Harley for my cue.

"Sia. Mang. Gibbon," he supplies, slowly sounding it out for me through the conspiratorial grin he's wearing.

"Sia-manga gibbon to observe," I finish, intentionally mispronouncing it slightly to get a laugh out of Harley. It works perfectly.

Briar shakes her head. "You two are something else."

Harley whispers to me, "That means yes."

I grin and hold a fist to him. When he bumps it, I wink at Briar, who looks amused by our antics. And confused by me. "You don't have to do that," she argues.

"I know. I want to. Friends go to the zoo. It's a thing, I think," I shrug like it's not a big deal. But we both know it is.

"So this is . . . what? A friendly outing?"

"Call it whatever helps you sleep tonight."

I'm weaving myself deeper and deeper into her life and into Harley's life, and that's scary to her. But I'm not Tyler. I'm me, and if I can help tomorrow go a little better for her and Harley, that's what I'm going to do.

It doesn't hurt that the smile stealing across Briar's face right now feels like sunshine filling this cold, sterile room.

"Can a friend get a ride home then too?" she asks.

"Absolutely. It'll only cost you one bite of Snickers." I glance at the candy I haven't even given her yet.

She laughs, and after a night like tonight, that feels like a big win. "If I give you half, can I add a stop at whatever drive-through is open?"

I grab at my stomach. "As long as you don't judge me for getting a triple meat, triple cheese, lettuce-wrap burger. I didn't eat dinner, either, and I'm a growing boy." I wink with the double entendre and she scrunches her face up. Reaching over to smooth the delicate wrinkles between her eyes, I whisper, "You're judging."

"No. I don't care how many greasy, artery-clogging patties—"

Leaning in extraclose, I rumble, "I like the way you look when you pretend not to care."

A smile grows on her face. "Fine, you can eat whatever monstrosity of cheeseburger you want. Just gimme that Snickers."

I hold it up, teasingly high, but I only make her reach for it once before handing it over. I want her to eat, to take care of herself, and maybe, let me take care of her a little too. It's what I'm good at, and I don't think she's had anyone do that for her in a long time. Maybe ever.

"Uh-oh, Harley. I think we're too late. She's getting hangry."

# Chapter 8

## Briar

"Who is that?" Trina purrs. Literally. She sounds like one of the cougars housed here at the Berkshire Zoo. She's also peering across the walkway with quite the hungry look . . . at Dominic presumably, who is sitting on the ground outside the gibbon habitat with Harley.

"A friend," I answer vaguely. I'm not trying to be coy, I just don't know how to phrase this situation. And a lifetime of experience has taught me, even a single stray comment about Dom could end up splashed across the sports pages. I don't want to cause him, or myself, any unintended drama.

Dominic's clearly wise to the game too. He isn't exactly famous in that paparazzi-chasing sort of way, but since there's a chance someone might recognize him, he's wearing a ballcap pulled down low and sunglasses. Paired with his khaki T-shirt and black jeans, he blends into the zoo personnel quite well, and no one should identify the professional hockey player in their midst. Or at least, that's the hope, and so far, nobody seems to be giving him a second glance.

Except Trina and me, and neither of us are the least bit concerned with Dominic's job as an athlete.

"Can I be his *friend* too? Girl, look at the chest muscles stretching the hell outta that shirt. Those nipples are downright bitable." She takes a snarling bite out of the air.

"Trina!" I scold, but when she *rawrs*, complete with clawed fingers like a big cat, I can't hold back the giggles.

Despite my declaration that Dominic is a friend, that's getting harder to argue. He picked us up early this morning, with a bag full of bacon, egg, and cheese sandwiches and a cup of coffee for me already on the console. It's a small gesture, but it means something, like he wants to take care of us. And the more it happens, the more I'm starting to like it.

He drove us to the zoo while switching between his own coffee and a gross-looking green protein smoothie, asking questions about my job the whole time. Once we arrived, he opened my door, helped me out of the jacked-up truck, then made sure Harley wasn't overdoing it on his still slightly tender ankle. I gave him a quick tour of the gibbon area, basically pointing out the viewing windows and the closest bathrooms, and then I had to get to work. But dragging myself away from them was hard, and I've spent most of the day wondering what they're up to.

The answer seems to be . . . happily watching Caprice and her baby.

Dominic is not what I expected, nor what I thought . . . about hockey players or about men in general. I didn't think men like him existed in real life. Men who are kind, generous, and supportive, and who don't expect to be revered by the mere right of having been born with a penis. At least in my experience, he's a complete anomaly.

And fine, I'll admit that his chest looks pretty nice too. So does the cocky yet not arrogant smile, the gentlemanly manners, and the way he stood up to Tyler without escalating things. It was nice to have someone on my side for once.

And while he keeps calling us friends, I can feel the way he looks at me. He wants me, but he's not going to force things. He's not going to make me do anything that I'm going to regret. Instead, he seems to be rock solid, strong enough to silently say, *Here I am. When you're ready*—if *you're ready—I'm still going to be here.*

It's reassuring, but the truth is, all that strength, all that restrained intensity, also feels overwhelming. I've spent a lifetime having men in my life tell me I'm not good enough. Dominic's dark gaze not only says I'm good enough, but that I'm a queen.

It might make a good fairy tale, but jumping from Cinderella to princess is scary, especially when I already made that leap once and ended up so much worse off, in many ways.

"I think I'll go check on him," I tell Trina, and she gives me a knowing look. "Them! I mean, them! Harley and my . . . friend."

Trina isn't convinced in the slightest. Despite our twenty-year age gap, she's one of my best friends at work, and she knows the basic gist of my history, though I haven't told anyone the worst of it. But she's been around the block enough times to know that I don't usually get blushy and weird about guys, nor do I let my son hang out with random strangers.

"You do that. Go check on him." She does not mean Harley, but rather than argue, I start to head their way. "Oh, Briar?" I pause, turning back at her questioning tone. "If it matters, your friend has been talking with Harley literally all day. They've been thick as thieves over there, just watching the gibbons and having a grand old time. And if Harley likes him, and he makes you smile like a quokka does, that's a good man in my experience. You deserve some good."

I take a slow breath, her words touching me deeply. I do deserve some good, but Harley is the good in my life. Everything is centered on him, not me and definitely not a man. I learned that lesson. It's just gotten harder to remember it lately.

"Thanks, Trina."

Her words have the opposite effect than she intended, making me slow my pace as I walk toward Dominic and Harley. With each step, I remind myself . . . friends, friends, friends. But the two of them, sitting side by side, looking comfortable and chummy, make quite the cute picture.

"That's a personal question there, kid," I hear Dominic say.

I shouldn't eavesdrop, but I slow even more, listening to see what my son has asked. With him, especially at this age, there's no telling.

Harley grins, unrepentant. "You avoiding the question? Chicken."

Dominic laughs loudly, completely unbothered by the callout from a child. "Definitely. But alright, you want the truth?" Harley nods wildly and I freeze, not even breathing with how much I want to hear this answer to a question I don't even know. "I don't think the knee socks are cringe at all. In fact, I think they're pretty cute on some people."

I glance down at my legs, which are in fact covered by khaki knee socks. I also have on knee-high muck boots because I've been cleaning out the flamingo pond, which means I smell like mud and dried shrimp.

*Definitely sooo cute,* I think. But I'm trying not to feel flattered because it's pretty obvious I'm the "some people" Dominic is referring to. Unless he thinks Gary, the volunteer who specializes in primate education, is looking extra good today as he wanders the area, answering questions in, you guessed it . . . knee socks. Though I happen to know his are compression socks to help with his arthritis.

I clear my throat, getting both Dom's and Harley's attention. "Mom!" Harley yells, "Come look at the baby!"

My son seems completely oblivious that I might've overheard his conversation, or that I would care if I did hear, but Dom is smirking. He knows I heard, and to prove that point, he intentionally drops his gaze to my legs. When his eyes travel back up my body to meet mine, the look on his face has my cheeks feeling hot. Cargo shorts, knee socks, and muck boots have never felt like lingerie before, but under Dom's appreciative eyes, they definitely do.

"What's she doing?" I ask Dom instead of what I really want to ask, which is *Want to see me without the socks on?* or maybe, *With* only *the socks on?*

"Sitting beside Caprice," Harley explains, sounding thrilled by what would seem to be a pretty boring day.

Dominic chuckles. "He seems really excited that she's sitting?" He looks confused by my son's exuberance.

"The baby is only three months old, so she spends almost the entire day and night clinging to her mother. Sitting beside her is a major milestone in her growth and development." I get closer to the plexiglass, peering through it to see my favorite animal in the entire zoo . . . Caprice. "Did you tell him about the trick?" I ask my son, and he shakes his head.

"Trick?" Dominic echoes. His eyes bounce from me to Harley questioningly.

Instead of answering directly, I tilt my head back slightly and let out a loud, high-pitched whooping noise that sounds vaguely like a car alarm going off. Harley grins. Dominic looks surprised and horrified in equal measures. "What the—"

I don't have to explain, though. Caprice does it for me, answering with a car alarm sound of her own. *Whoop whoop whoop whooooop.*

I close my eyes for a moment to listen to her song, feeling the happiness in it. She's proud of her baby and wants to show off her progress. "I see her, Mama," I tell Caprice, even though she can't hear me through the viewing window. But her eyes stay on me, like she knows I'm talking to her.

Caprice has been here for the entirety of her twelve years, born at the zoo just like her offspring. When I started here four years ago, we became fast friends. Mostly because I bring food, but there are other workers who do that, yet they don't have the same bond with her that I do. Somehow, our connection is different. She talks to me, watches and follows me around in the backstage area of their habitat, and has even protected me when one of the younger male gibbons tried throwing his nutritional biscuit at me in protest. Suffice it to say that after her intervention, that male never did anything like that again. It might sound silly to some people, but I consider Caprice a friend.

"You can talk to monkeys?" Dominic teases.

"Gibbons aren't monkeys. Technically, they're lesser apes," I say automatically, ready to launch into my speech about the origins and differences. But then I see Dominic fighting not to smile and realize the truth. "Which you already knew because either Harley or Gary has told you everything there is to know about gibbons today."

He chuckles. "Both actually, and Gary knows a *lot*. But I would love to hear it from you too."

The way he says it, with his dark gaze dropping to my lips and the slightest heat in his tone, I think he truly would listen to me ramble on my favorite subject for hours. Not that I'm going to test that theory.

My walkie-talkie crackles at my waist, Jonah calling for me. I grab it and lift it to my mouth. "This is Briar. Go ahead."

"You were just over here at Flamingo Fountain, right? It's flooding again," Jonah answers.

Under my breath, I whisper, "Shit." The drain in the flamingo area has been clogging too often, which creates stress on the sensitive birds. "I'm coming," I tell Jonah on the walkie-talkie. To Dominic and Harley, I say, "I'll be back. I've got to go unclog the drain again."

I start to jog toward the flamingos but realize there's another thud sounding out along with my boots' clomping noise. I glance over my shoulder to find Dominic jogging along with me and I stop. "What are you doing?"

"Helping. A flood sounds serious. Let's go," he answers.

He doesn't wait for me to say anything—not *thank you*, or *I don't need you*. He just starts jogging in the same direction we were going. Apparently, he's helping? I look back at Harley, checking in, and when he catches my eye, he flashes me a thumbs-up that he's okay and then points at Gary, who also gives me a thumbs-up. My son is here a lot, knows how to behave himself, and every employee recognizes him. Trusting that he'll be fine with both Gary and Trina watching from nearby, I continue after Dominic.

He's made some headway on me, apparently using the signs to direct his path, and I catch up right as he reaches Flamingo Fountain.

"Where's the issue?" he asks, annoyingly not even breathing hard. Unlike me.

"Drain. Clogged," I pant, pointing. The drain itself is under the murky, muddy water and not visible, but I've dealt with it enough to find it blindly. "Jonah will help take care of it."

Dominic frowns, worried eyes swinging from me to the flamingos, who have water nearly up to their knees now. But they're fine. Not in danger or anything serious, they just don't like changes in their environment, like rapidly rising water.

"I've got it."

And before I can stop him, Dominic wades into the water, tennis shoes and jeans and all, like it's nothing. He tries not to splash, kinda skating forward instead of stepping, so as not to scare the flamingos.

"Tell me where," he says, looking over his shoulder at me, but keeping a close eye on the birds. Even in the wild, they're not aggressive, and in captivity, the most they might do is approach in hopes of getting a shrimp pellet, but he's acting like he's been cast as the hapless victim on *When Flamingos Attack*. To be fair, they're watching him with bald curiosity, but that's about it.

"Two feet to your left." He moves accordingly. "Right there," I say. "You should be able to feel it with your right foot. There's usually grass and dirt covering the grate."

He looks thoughtful as he tries to find it under the water. "Got it."

I expect him to kick the debris out of the way. Maybe swipe it with his foot. But nope. Dominic bends down, reaching under the dirty water with his hand to clear the clog. He angles his head to keep his face out of the water, but it's still up to his chin as he works.

The flamingos, now especially interested in the unusual specimen in their midst, move closer. "Marion, leave him alone," I warn one of the more curious and territorial males.

Dominic sends a wary glance their way, and mockingly assumes a decent *Karate Kid*-esque crane kick stance. "Back it up, Marion. You don't want this smoke."

As if he understands the challenge in Dominic's words, the flamingo starts honking loudly at the invader in his pond. *Kaa-hooonk, kaa-hooonk.* He adds in a few beak clacks and wing flaps too.

"Probably should've asked this sooner," Dominic grits out as he lowers his leg and goes back to rooting around, trying not to swallow any of the gross water, "but are flamingos mean? I'd rather not get an eye pecked out, if possible." Dominic sputters as he throws a few handfuls of weeds far away from the drain and the flamingos.

"I don't think he's trying to attack you," I say, pressing my lips together to hide my laughter.

Dominic glances from me to Marion, realization dawning. "Oh no, not interested in your mating dance, either, birdie."

I do laugh then. I can't help it. Dominic looks ridiculous, neck deep in the water with a pink flamingo inching closer with those high-knee steps like he's sneaking up on the big behemoth of a man.

"Look out, he's gonna getcha!" I taunt.

Dominic tosses a few more handfuls of sludge away, and after a moment, the water starts to drop to normal levels. Standing up tall to survey his handiwork, he grins. "I did it," he says proudly.

He is covered in mud, his wet clothes clinging to him, and when he threw the debris, some of it landed on him, so he has a few blades of grass on his hat and a streak of questionable origin on his cheek. He looks adorably, boyishly dirty. "Yes, you did," I agree, nodding.

"Why are you laughing?" he asks, growing suspicious. Looking behind him, he grunts, "Where's Marion?"

Right then, Jonah returns. With the extralong-handled rake that we typically use to clear the clogs, which we use from the platform on the edge of the pond, where the process is relatively no muss and no fuss. I usually only get my boots muddy and that's it. I've definitely never gone full-dive into the habitat. I don't think anyone has.

Wind taken out of his sails, Dominic sags. "Oh."

"It's okay," I tell him as he starts to wade back out of the water. "Your way worked. And the flamingos will be talking about you for months. Listen."

I point to where Marion has rejoined the flock and is honking like, *You're never gonna believe the shit I saw.*

"I just wanted to help," he grumbles.

"Recent events notwithstanding, I don't always need help. But thank you for wanting to." I am grateful for his assistance. I don't like needing it, or being seen as someone who needs to be rescued, but I do appreciate that his instinct is to be a helper. That's a rare and special trait in my book.

"Well, at least I made you laugh," he says, the self-deprecation out of character given his usual cockiness.

"Laugh?" I ask, and he nods.

"I'd wrestle that damn bird every day if it means making you laugh again," he says softly, and my heart races in my chest. The way he looks at me, he knows it too. He's proud of what he did, like my laughter belongs just to him.

Maybe it does.

"Come on, I'll buy you a change of clothes from the gift shop as a thank-you. If they have something to fit you." I take his measure visually, reminded again how muscled he is. I doubt they'll have anything properly in his size, but there's not really any other option. Dominic is covered in stinky mud, and as it dries, it's going to begin to flake off, making a mess in his truck.

In the end, we scour the gift shop's stockroom for anything remotely his size and we're able to get him a pair of orange swim trunks, a neon-green T-shirt with the zoo's logo emblazoned on it, and a pair of flip-flops left over from the Fourth of July sale. None of it is ideal, but beggars can't be choosers, or at least they shouldn't be when the alternative is going naked.

Although it might be interesting . . . in a purely scientific way, of course . . . to see Dominic nude. All those muscles would be a textbook study of anatomy and physiology, a class I'm suddenly remembering with new appreciation.

"Here," I say, handing Dominic a beach towel, also with the zoo's logo. "You can wipe off with that. It won't help with the smell, but at least it won't be seeping into your pores anymore."

His brows knit together, and he sounds worried. "This smell is seeping into me? Like I'm always gonna smell like shrimp and shit?" He rubs the towel furiously over his face and then along his arms as I laugh.

My laughter dies in my throat when Dominic reaches down and pulls his ruined shirt over his head in one fell swoop, revealing a body that will haunt my dreams for the rest of my life. I swear to God the man is built like a brick shithouse, as my dad used to say. Or probably still does. I wouldn't know since we barely talk.

Dominic doesn't have those bumpy ridges of abs like the models on romance books. No, his stomach is just one big, solid sheet of muscle, the individual abs delineated by slight lines more than deep ridges. His pecs are topped with flat, brown nipples that are currently puckered up from the cold water in a way that I know would have Trina panting. And his biceps? Now that I can see them in their full glory, I want to wrap my hands around them to measure them. I have no idea why, but I do.

It's not until I realize that Dominic has gone still that I drag my eyes up. His dark eyes are locked on me, watching me watch him, and filled with fiery heat that could probably burn me up quicker than a blink.

Oh shit! He totally caught me staring like a sex-starved lunatic.

"Sorry!" I rush to say, dropping my gaze to stare at the toes of my muck boots. There's a glob of mud already drying on the left one. "I usually only see animals naked, not men. I mean, people. I mean . . ."

"It's okay, Briar. I don't mind if you look at me," he says, his voice low and rough, like a beard across the inside of my thighs, and just as arousing.

Slowly, I let my eyes climb his legs, linger for a heartbeat on the ridge I can see in his jeans, and then back up to his bare chest. I'm not brave enough to meet his gaze. But I watch rapt as he drops his hands to his waist, unbuttons his jeans, and then unzips them. As he starts to shove them down, I finally come to my senses and whirl around, giving him my back. "Let me know if you need another towel or anything. I can go grab it for you."

I turn my eyes to the ceiling, irritated with myself. Yes, Dominic is hotter than Hades on a summer day. But I'm not doing that. Not doing *him*. Sure, sometimes I'd like a dick with a pulse, and not just a pulse mode, but I need my life to be as unmessy as possible. And if there's one thing Dominic Lee is, it's messy.

# Chapter 9

## DOMINIC

"It's starting to feel cold in here," the announcer booms over the sound system, and the crowd starts to cheer. "Entering the arena, welcome the . . . *Blizzard*!"

We hit the ice one right after another, immediately skating in loops and swirl patterns around our half of the ice to warm up. It's a preseason game, but the routine is the same every time. Athletes thrive on routine—it helps balance out the chaos of the game itself. So everything should be normal.

Except I'm wearing a fucking baby-blue jersey and the team around me isn't family the way the Hawks have always been. They're a bunch of dipshits who act like life is a frat party.

"Ready for this?" I ask Kipson as I stretch beside him.

"Born fucking ready."

Liar. He is not ready in the slightest. His eyes are jumping all over the place, he's bouncy as hell, and I don't think he pissed before we hit the ice, which means he's starting at a hydration deficit. Or he's going to piss his pants.

I've been watching him at practices. I've been watching everyone, plus spending all my free time watching old games to get a better feel for each and every Blizzard player. If this is gonna be my temporary home, I refuse to let them take me down.

*Not that these guys could do anything in a blaze of glory. It'd be more like a weak-assed puff of YouTube infamy and fuckup memes,* I think bitterly.

*That's not fair and you know it.*

Internally, I sigh at my own woe-is-me bullshit. Truth be told, I wish I could write this whole team off as lost causes, but despite me not liking them personally, most of the guys are solid on the ice. That's what got them to the Finals last year.

Except Kipson.

He used to be one of the stars of their highlight reels, but now, he really is their weak link. But my observations have revealed more about him than he would probably suspect, and tonight, in a preseason game where it doesn't necessarily count, is the time to test my theory.

I skate up to him until we're nearly chest to chest. "Born ready or not, get your shit together so we don't lose this fucking game because you're butthurt."

"The hell'd you say to me?" he snarls, pushing me in an attempt to put inches between us.

That's what I'm looking for—that fire, that anger, that zeroed-in focus. It'd be better if he was angry against our opponents, but giving him fuck-you energy against me might work too.

I don't relent. If anything, I lean back in even closer. "You heard me. All that pain, all that anger, all that emptiness you're feeling?" I spit the words at him, watching his eyes narrow as each one hits its intended bull's-eye. "Take it out on the ice. Take it out on those assholes that're gonna be gunning for you because they know you're fucked in the head. Show them that the fucked-up version of you is scarier than the lovesick asshole you used to be."

"I'm gonna kick your ass, Lee." It's a vow he means wholeheartedly.

"Maybe later," I reply with a cocky smirk, inviting him to try. "For now, let's win this damn game."

"Fuck you."

"Aw, love you, too, man." I skate away backward, holding up my finger and thumb in a tiny heart shape.

Hard truths followed by annoying bullshit. It's not exactly rocket science, but it's surprisingly effective on a testosterone-addled mind, resulting in anger that's particularly useful in a physically demanding sport.

Taking my place on the left side of the ice, Anderson whistles at me from his spot in the net. When I glance back, he asks, "You got a death wish I need to know about?"

"We'll see," I answer before putting my own focus solidly where it needs to be . . . the drop of the puck, and the incoming attack from the Vortex's center.

Midway through the second period, I'm perched on the bench but my body is reacting to every movement on the ice as if I'm the one out there.

"Get in there, Rodney!" I shout. "Help him, Sabine!"

These guys are not my guys. This team is not my team. But if I'm stuck with them, I'm gonna be supportive. Especially of the rookies who might still be worth something and are just glad to get some ice time since if they show out in tonight's meaningless game, they might not be sent down to the minors.

As though my cheers, or the small crowd's, actually helped, Rodney makes a slick move toward the Vortex's goal and takes a quick snap shot. It's blocked, but it was a solid attempt that I can respect.

"I know what you're doing," Kipson growls from beside me. We rotated out together this time and thankfully, he's been drinking the water he should've had before the game started.

I don't give him my full attention, just merely cut my eyes his way. "Good. You've got another period to go still to earn your place on this team."

"Asshole." He takes another healthy swig from his water bottle.

I lean over the slightest bit, inclining my head. "If you've forgotten, the key to winning is that little black thing out there."

He bumps his shoulder into mine, the hard impact jostling me on the bench. I don't fight back, not now. It's not the time. Instead, I chuckle. It'll set him off more. I know it will, but I've gotta hurt him to help him.

Coach must have eyes in the back of his head because, though his never left the action on the ice, he snaps, "Do we have a problem, boys?"

"Nah," I fake-drawl, "just doing my job, Coach."

"Put that fight into the game. Fight them, not each other," he advises. "Get your asses back out there."

Kipson and I stand, wait for our chance, and on the signal, vault the boards and hit the ice once more.

If I had to choose when to fight, while I'm standing in my underwear in a locker room full of guys would not be my first choice. Hell, it wouldn't be my tenth choice, but here I am.

*Bam!*

Kipson's fist slams against the metal locker, mere inches from my head.

"Missed me," I deadpan.

He earned this go at me, I'll dance with him. Not that I'm going to let him get his satisfaction that easily. If anything, I might turn the tables on him. A good ass-kicking might do him some good and give him something new to whine about.

*Same could be said about you.*

"Leave me the fuck alone, Lee."

"No," I clap back. "You might not like it, but you play better angry. That's why we won out there tonight."

Anderson makes a half-assed "hey!" noise, mumbling to Pacholek about having something to do with us coming out ahead 3–1 against the Vortex.

"I'm always fucking angry!" Kipson roars.

"Not about the right thing!" I roar right back, pointing at him and then the ice. "Not in the right way! I'm trying to help you, motherfucker."

"I don't need your help."

His rage is like a flash fire, igniting with the slightest spark, but dying quickly as the darkness he's living in snuffs it out. The fight in him is waning, his voice going quieter when even he doesn't believe his own lies.

I snort a humorless laugh. "If you think that's true, you really do need help. And I can tell you one thing for damn sure . . ." I wait for his fury-filled eyes to lock on to me. He can't help it, he wants to know what's on the stick I'm dangling in front of him. "These guys don't have your best interest at heart. Shockingly, I do." I point around the room at the team, who are loudly hooting and hollering as they celebrate tonight's win, already making plans to hit the club for a nightcap.

"What the hell are you talking about? You don't know shit, and you sure don't know me." He gives me a scathing up-and-down that would send a weaker man away with his tail between his legs.

I throw it right back at him. "I know that what they did to you was wrong, and neither you nor Sofia deserved that."

That too-touchy target I should avoid tap-dancing on top of? Yeah, that was it.

"Keep my wife's name out of your fucking mouth or so help me, I will—"

"What? Kick my ass?" I interrupt him to suggest, leaning in close so only he can hear me. "So you keep saying. And do you think anyone in here would help you? Or help me? Or would they stand back and cheer us on while we destroyed each other?" We both know the answer. This group would probably start taking bets on who would win, but none of them would actually care. Not about me, which is understandable since we've just met. But Kipson has been on this team for years and they should care about him. But they don't. "You think that makes a good team? You think they give a shit about you? I don't even know you and I care more than these motherfuckers do."

He doesn't want me to be right and spins on a heel, heading for his locker and trying to hide from the truth.

This team is rotten. Not from the ground up, but from the top down. Coach sets the tone, but the rest of the team has gone along with it for so long that the foundation of what a team should be has never properly developed.

I yank a pair of sweats over my underwear and pull a T-shirt over my head, letting Kipson pretend I'm not right. But as I throw my bag over my shoulder, I offer, "If you want to get a beer, let me know. If you need a fight to get your head straight, I'll put that shit on my calendar too."

He doesn't glance up to state, "No."

"We don't have to be friends, but I'm stuck here for at least the season, and as far as I can tell, you might be the only decent human being on this team."

At that, he does lift his chin, and I pointedly look around the locker room. He follows my gaze and I know what he sees . . .

Anderson is holding up his phone to show Sabine a close-up picture of someone's cleavage while making a jacking-off motion with his other hand. Pacholek is laughing along with them. There are other guys all around the room getting cleaned up and dressed, but each and every one of them is goofing off. Not a single one of them is checked in to the drama between Kipson and me, his ongoing distress, or even rehashing the game we just drained ourselves to play.

It's all shits and giggles playtime around here.

"This isn't what a team is supposed to be like," I state flatly. Before he can answer, I walk out of the locker room and to my truck. I don't know if Kipson is salvageable. At this point, I don't know if I am. Or at least my hockey career, which is basically the same thing.

# Chapter 10

## Briar

Weekends alone are always hard. I use the time as best I can because it seems like there are never enough minutes in the day to get everything done that I need and want to, like deep cleaning the refrigerator, painting my toenails, and filling up my online shopping cart with an astronomical number of goodies only to close it out without buying anything because the browsing is the fun part.

But even while I'm scrubbing baseboards with my hands encased in moisturizing gloves, my mind is on Harley. Do I wish that he didn't have to see Tyler at all? Absolutely. And my lawyer did the best he could to limit Tyler's access, but my ex can put on the charm when it benefits him and he got the judge to believe that he was a caring, attentive, involved father. Hence, every other weekend visits.

At least he was on time for pickup yesterday, rolling in at six o'clock on the dot.

The stress of Harley being with Tyler never lessens, though. In fact, I think it might be worse this time after his stunt at the hospital. He was furious, not at Harley's accidental and minor injury, but at me for bringing a "boyfriend" to the hospital. I knew better than to argue with him, since that's what he wants, so I stuck to discussing Harley's exam in short, emotionless statements. Tyler didn't really care about that, but did call me some choice names before stomping out, promising that I'd regret *everything*.

As if. The only thing I regret is him.

Though if there'd been no Tyler, there'd be no Harley, and I would never undo the gift my son is to me.

I just can't shake this feeling that something's wrong. I'm worried if Harley is okay, and hoping that Tyler isn't filling his mind with his twisted version of whatever truth he's decided serves him.

By ten o'clock Saturday night, I've stress cleaned the whole house, baked Harley's favorite cake, and taken an extralong shower. Still, my belly is churning with this sense that I need to be doing *something* . . . *somewhere* . . . I'm not sure what, but it's definitely not lying in bed, mindlessly watching reruns.

*Riiing.*

My phone's ringtone is intentionally loud and attention-grabbing, a choice for when Harley is gone because I do not want to ever miss a call from him.

Unfortunately, it's not my son's name on the caller ID. It's Tyler's. And it's not just a regular call. He's FaceTiming me.

I wish I could not answer it, but what if he's calling about Harley? Or if Harley wants to tell me good night? Those possibilities are enough to force my hand.

But first, I make sure my nightgown is covering everything it should and also tuck the blankets around my chest. I take a deep breath to settle my gut, and only then do I hit answer. "Hello?"

"Hey, babe."

"Is Harley okay?" I rush to ask, worry about his already-better ankle popping into my mind.

Tyler sighs, his brows furrowing in annoyance. "He's fine. Went to bed about an hour ago. Probably crashed out asleep by now."

He doesn't know? He didn't check?

Of course he didn't. I was always the one to do that. Still am.

"What's wrong then?"

"Nothing's wrong. Can't I just call to see what you're up to?"

He's checking to see if Dominic is here. I know that with complete certainty. "Unless it pertains to Harley, what I'm doing is none of your concern."

"Don't be like that, babe. You know that what you do will always be my business. I miss you." His lips lift into the flirty smile that used to give me butterflies. Now, it just makes me nauseous.

*Why did I used to think his possessiveness was sweet?*

I'm ashamed to admit it, but the answer is daddy issues. After having a father who left not only my mother, but me, regularly and without a second thought, meeting a man who was obsessed with me felt like the biggest salve to my traumatized soul. It took a long time to recognize that Tyler's possessiveness was more akin to ownership, and his desire for complete enmeshment between us was just as harmful as my dad's absence had been.

"I don't miss you. Now if there's nothing else we need to discuss about Harley . . ."

I'm about to hang up, my finger hovering over the X-filled red circle on the screen, but I'm too slow. Tyler pulls his phone back, revealing more of himself. "I know one thing you're missing."

He has his dick out. His erect penis, with his free hand wrapped around it, leisurely jacking himself to my face on his screen.

I remember the first time I saw him naked. We'd both been barely eighteen, and in my completely unexperienced immaturity, I'd laughed nervously, which had hurt his feelings. But over time, I learned not to laugh anymore. He always wanted me to tell him how big he was (as if I had anything to compare to), would groan in my ear that I felt good wrapped around him, and liked to brag about the veining along his shaft, which he thought made his penis look powerful and was supposed to feel good to me, though I could never actually feel it inside me.

It's a penis I haven't seen in years and did not want to see tonight. Or ever again.

I recoil instantly with a sound of shocked horror, and he chuckles at my reaction. "We had our problems, but one thing we were always good at was making up after a fight. You know you want it, Briar. You wanna suck me off to show how sorry you are, don'tcha?"

Every word is accompanied by an up and down stroke.

I gag, not because I want to service him, but at the disgusting thought of doing that again. Belatedly, I push the red circle and end the call. The feeling of violation is immediate, followed by the shoulda, coulda, woulda self-lecture.

I should've . . . not answered his call.

I could've . . . hung up sooner.

I would've . . . preempted what was obviously a planned maneuver on Tyler's part.

My phone rings again. Tyler's name appears on the screen and I hit decline.

It rings again. Decline.

He's getting off on this, probably literally. Harassing me, seeing my name on his screen even if I don't answer, and knowing that I can't help but think of what I just saw . . . all turn-ons for him.

He calls again and again. Four times, five, then six and seven. I don't even hit decline, and start ignoring the calls instead, leaving the phone face down on the bed.

But my skin crawls as my irritation grows.

On the eighth ring, I decide enough is enough. I answer with a curt, "Leave me alone unless you're calling about Harley."

"Shit. I'm sorry."

The line goes quiet and it takes me a heartbeat to realize that it wasn't Tyler's voice. "Dominic?" I pull the phone away to glance at the screen and see the *Hockey Coach* label I gave Dom. *Whoops.*

"Yeah? Is Harley okay? His ankle feeling better?" He sounds apologetic and concerned for my son. And maybe me too.

Sighing, I tell him, "I'm sorry. I thought you were Tyler. He's been calling over and over again after I hung up on his attempt at dick-dialing."

"Excuse me?" Dom says, his voice rising in disgust and shock. "His what?"

"Dick-dialing? He called, acting like he wanted to talk, but had it out, showing off like his penis was supposed to be some sort of temptation."

"Are you okay?" I can't see him through the phone, but I can hear the anger in his clipped words. He wants to murder my ex-husband, but somehow, his focus is still on me.

"Okay is relative," I answer. "Did I want that to happen? No. Am I going to fall apart over it? Also no. It's a dick. One I've seen. One I have no desire to see again. But I'm stronger than whatever penile power move he thinks he's pulling."

Dom snorts like he's trying not to laugh. "Penile power move? Was it doing MMA or something? *Hiii-yah!*"

I smile at his attempt at humor. I wouldn't have thought I could after Tyler's stunt. But I can feel my lips stretching as Dom makes more karate-esque sounds. Only when I eventually succumb to a weak laugh does he stop. "I swear to God my penis is locked away in my shorts, but can we switch to FaceTime? I need to see you."

"Uh . . ." I didn't care what I looked like when I answered for what I thought was going to Harley or Tyler talking about Harley, but Dom? I try to smooth my flyaway hairs into the messy updo on top of my head and illogically check my breath by breathing into my palm. "Yeah, that's fine."

The call switches over instantly and I answer.

Dominic is sitting on a couch, a white wall behind him. He's wearing a black T-shirt, and his eyes scour my face through the screen. "Are you okay?" he asks again.

Another call comes in, the preview bubble popping up on the screen, and I shake my head. Dominic sits forward on his couch, the phone angle going lower and his expression going dark and dangerous. "Briar?"

My name is more rumble than word, and I realize that he thinks I'm shaking my head in answer to his question. That I'm not okay. "No, sorry. I'm fine. Tyler's just calling again."

He grits his teeth, his jaw muscles popping with the work. "I really hate your ex."

"Me too."

"What the fuck did you ever see in him?" Dom asks, curious. "Motherfucker's got serial killer eyes. Don't you watch true crime documentaries?"

I laugh a little at his quick assessment of my ex. Okay, so he's not going to make an appearance on any news shows, but I do wish I'd had a touch more self-preservation instinct where he's concerned.

"My standards weren't exactly high back then," I say in the understatement of the century. "He showed up to dates, told me I was beautiful, and acted like I was important to him. That was pretty much enough to have me fawning all over him. You can overlook a lot of red flags when you need someone to love you, and I truly thought he did." The admission irritates me, but now that I have some distance from my relationship with Tyler, I can see the reality of us.

What did I get out of it? Finally feeling valued and special after a lifetime of being forgotten and dismissed.

What did he get out of it? My adoration made him feel powerful.

"You were young," Dom says sagely. "We're all stupid then."

Is Dominic giving me an out by excusing the poor choice I made or talking about his own poor choices? I'm not sure.

"Have some skeletons in your closet, too, do we?" I pry, trying to keep my voice light but sounding like a Nosy Nellie. "Girls whose hearts you broke? A trail of tearstained letters filled with promises to wait for you?"

Giving me a cocky smirk that says he knows why I'm asking, he sits back on his couch, packing away his anger like it never existed, which is fascinating. There's no explosion, not a single expletive, it just turns off like a light switch. Poof, gone. Is this what emotional regularity looks like? I'm not sure I'd know. Especially since I'm still feeling woozy from my own up and down roller coaster of an evening.

"Not really. I had a girlfriend in high school. We broke up after graduation because she went to school out of state. Dated a couple of women later on. It never panned out. Wasn't the right time. I was too consumed with getting to the pros or staying in the pros. After that, I've kept things casual."

"You're a fuckboy after all," I tease. "You should fit right in with the Blizzard."

"Hell no," he laughs, shaking his head. "But I understand that sometimes people have needs that aren't being met, and as long as expectations are clearly communicated by all parties, there's no harm in being what the other person needs you to be."

That is a very fancy way of saying he's had friends with benefits, but I don't think we're actually talking about his past relationships anymore. He's offering to be whatever I want him to be and give me whatever I want. Whether that's friendship or . . . more.

"I don't . . ." The words I've said countless times before stall out in my throat.

"Date," he finishes for me. "Especially hockey players. I know." He winks, not taking my rejection personally.

Winking is ridiculous, completely comical as far as moves go, but on Dom, it looked sexy in a cute sorta way. Like he's not taking things too seriously or pushing me into the deep end when I can barely tread water, much less swim.

Usually, I'm the type of woman who needs someone to literally say *I'm flirting with you* if they want me to catch on. Otherwise, I tend to think, *Wow, they're nice,* or more often, *What do they want?* But I'm certain that Dominic is flirting with me. What's more, I'm also pretty sure I'm enjoying it. And that is a shock.

"They're the worst," I agree, though I don't mean it quite as vehemently as I once did.

I stare at him through the screen for a long moment, reevaluating everything I've ever thought about hockey and hockey players. Dominic doesn't seem to fit any of those stereotypes. If anything, he's the antithesis of the stupid, violent, fuckboy image. He's smart and observant, kind and thoughtful, and respectful of my boundaries. Why hasn't someone snatched him up already?

Why aren't I taking him up on his offer to help me . . . *any way* I'd like him to?

"Why the hockey hatred?" he asks, seeing my thoughts and at the same time giving me a chance to make up my own mind. "Especially when you have a coach as your dad."

That is a story. One I'm not sure I should share with one of Dad's players. But I find myself confiding in Dominic anyway. It seems a safer option than addressing those potential benefits he might be offering.

"Because of my father," I say succinctly.

Dominic winces. "Ouch. Pacholek said he's on his fourth marriage. Was your mom number one?"

"Two, actually. He was freshly retired from his playing days, an assistant coach then, and Mom thought she'd met the man of her dreams."

I close my eyes, remembering the pictures of Mom and Dad I saw as a child—of them happy, together, smiling with their arms wrapped around each other. But it was only for pictures. I also remember the tears, the fighting, and Mom pleading with Dad to come home, but there was always another game, another player to see, and later I realized, another woman to sleep with.

"They got divorced when I was seven. I'm not sure if Mom was tired of him cheating on her or tired of him being gone. After that, he'd come and go randomly. A few times, he picked me up for a couple of weeks during the summer, but when I was around fourteen, I realized that those occasional trips were to scout players, not to spend time with me. It was always hockey, hockey, hockey, to the detriment of everything else." I give

Dominic a pointed look, silently reminding both of us that he admitted to the same thing a mere few moments ago with his failed relationships.

"Still, I had friends with no dads, so his minor efforts to see me and the child support money he faithfully sent Mom were appreciated for a lot longer than they should've been. Long enough that it made the bare minimum seem exceptional. I accepted his scraps and learned to accept scraps in my other relationships for longer than I should've too." I'm talking about Tyler and we both know it. "I refuse to do that now."

"You looking for the full-blown princess treatment?" There's no judgment in the question, but rather, it's like he's trying to figure me out.

I shake my head. "No. I want peace. And I have it, so I'm fine on my own."

"Do you, though?" Dominic asks skeptically. "With Tyler pulling shit like what he did tonight? Is that peace?"

He's right. Tonight has not been peaceful. It's been challenging and scary and thought-provoking in new ways that I'm not sure I like.

"Tyler will usually say out of pocket stuff, but he's never done anything like this dick-dialing stunt before," I argue.

"What changed?"

I suspect he already knows the answer and is asking to see if I've figured it out. I most definitely have. "You. You being at the hospital with me and Harley. It was the first time he's ever seen me with anyone else. I didn't realize it, but I think me being alone was giving him some sort of twisted pleasure, like he still had that control over my life because I hadn't moved on."

He looks thoughtful for a moment, then nods, agreeing with my analysis. "Have you moved on? Or are you still waiting on him to finally give you more than scraps?"

"Ouch. Not pulling any punches, are you?"

"Do you want me to? We can talk about stupid shit if you'd rather?" He pauses, letting me decide, and when I stay quiet, glaring at him, he says, "We won tonight's preseason game. Kipson and I got into it a bit.

Oh, and I found a protein bowl place online that I want to check out tomorrow. You wanna go with me?"

I made the connection between how Dad treated me and the way Tyler treated me a long time ago, but to have it so plainly spelled out for me by someone I've barely met is painful. Especially when we met mere weeks ago when I was semihappily accepting more of my dad's scraps in the form of a free night out and some gastropub apps. I'd like to pretend that it was nothing more than taking what I'm owed by the man who has never been much of a father, but deep down, I know the truth. I long for a father-daughter relationship, not with the dad I have, but with the dad I wished I'd had but never did. His priorities have always been hockey first, himself second, and anything else, including his daughter, far down the list after that.

Tyler is another matter, though. As much as Dad and Tyler have both hurt me, they are not the same.

And I don't want to talk about hockey or protein bowls. I like getting to know Dominic more deeply, even if it's picking at some uncomfortable scars from my past.

"Tyler isn't capable of giving me what I need. He's a narcissist to his core. Our entire relationship was about what I *could* do for him . . . what I *would* do for him. Every kindness he ever gave me was with an underlying intention of isolating me, making me see him in a favorable light, or some other manipulation that only he could understand. I don't want him, now or ever." I want to make sure that is crystal clear, both to my mind and Dom's. "But for Harley, I play along and don't rock the boat, trying to make sure he isn't hurt by Tyler the way I was because I have no doubt that Tyler would use our son against me if he felt like he was losing control. He'd do anything to maintain his sense of power."

Dominic leans forward, his elbows on his knees as he listens intently. "Is that your plan until Harley is grown? To let Tyler destroy whatever sense of peace you're able to string together, anytime he gets pissed that he's not the one providing it?"

"No," I snap automatically.

Dominic lowers his chin, staring at me through his stupidly dark and infuriatingly long lashes. "Isn't that what you've been doing?"

I want to say no. I want so badly to tell Dominic that he's 100 percent wrong. But is he?

The question raises prickles all over my skin. I am proud of how far I've come since getting the courage to walk away from Tyler, and to be called out on it not being enough is infuriating. Especially when it might be true. Reluctantly, I answer, "I don't like that you can see me so easily."

"Easy?" he laughs. "Briar, nothing about you is easy except your smiles. But you're worth the work."

The compliment, given after a deep and at times painful conversation, soothes the irritation that's making me feel vulnerable.

"Thank you," I say softly. When Dominic smiles back, I ask, "What time for protein bowls?"

# Chapter 11

## Dominic

Briar didn't clarify if this is a date or just two friends grabbing food, so I'm trying to manage my own expectations as we park, because Briar is deeper than I ever imagined and I'm drawn to that dark, ooey gooey center inside her as much as I am the brightness she shows to the world.

I wasn't sure which version of her I'd get today—the silly, whimsical side who spits out animal facts or the layered, hidden treasure trove of emotions. And when she opened her door, looking like sunshine and smiles, wrapped up in skintight jeans, a cropped tank top, and an oversize cardigan that makes me want to crawl inside it and snuggle with her (or more), I didn't care. I just wanted Briar, however she was coming.

"How'd you find this place? I've never heard of it." She's looking around the strip center parking lot as I help her from my truck, and every flick of her head sends her dangling earrings swinging. One is a monkey, the other a banana, and both make me smile.

"I searched for protein bowl places and voilà." I hold a hand out like a car show model, gesturing to the glowing neon proclaiming "Big Boy Bowls," with a *3* and a *B* fashioned into a logo. "This type of place is my favorite back home. Griffin and I have a pregame, postgame, and any other time habit of hitting them up. I wanted to check this one out before the season officially starts."

The season opener is next weekend and I want to ask Briar if she and Harley will come watch. But I'm waiting to see how today goes.

"Have you talked to him since you got here?" she asks while we wait in line to create our lunches.

"Yeah, several times, but I think he's getting tired of my bitching and whining about the Blizzard. He told me to fix Kipson's shit and get traded back or he'd have to fly out here and kick both of our asses himself." I laugh, remembering the conversation.

We're like most guys, I guess, communicating that we care by giving each other a hard time, and as much as I complained about being here, he was doing the same thing—grumbling that my replacement is so new, he bleeds green. In guy speak, that translates to *I miss you* and *Wish you were hitting the ice with me.*

"How's that going? You said the two of you got into it?" She looks me over, searching for any signs of a fight gone wrong.

"We're both still alive and kicking, so there's that." I'm resigned to the fact that it's not going to be a quick fix, but I also wish he'd get to the part where he realizes I'm right and starts telling off his teammates for the toxic environment they help foster.

As we sit down with our bowls—mine chicken, hers steak—I say, "Can I ask you a question about Coach Boothe? Hockey related."

It's a gamble to use Briar for intel. I don't want her to feel like this is why I want to spend time with her, but I also want to see if things can be improved for the whole team.

"That depends. Are you going to use it against him or to help him?" she asks, one blond brow arched delicately and her fork poised in the air above her bowl.

I tilt my head, thinking. "Both?"

"Hit me with it," she says, taking a bite. She pauses, chewing slowly and nodding, her eyes slipping closed as she savors her food. "Uhm, this is delicious."

I stab a piece of chicken myself and chew it thoughtfully. It is good, a definite upgrade from Chipotle . . . *if* the guacamole is good too. Another bite and . . . yep, new favorite protein bowl place. At least here. Nothing tops Pro-Bowl back home.

I remind myself to tell Rodney and Tomville about Big Boy Bowls. Maybe I'll even invite them out for a pregame meal like Griffin and I used to do. I can't automatically reset the whole team's dynamics, but I can keep the newbies from going rotten.

"Is he close to retirement?"

She laughs loudly, nearly choking on the forkful of rice she just swallowed. "No! Why?" she asks, covering her mouth.

Sighing, I tell her, "I think the only way to fix Kipson is to fix the whole damn team. If Coach was close to retirement, I could do it without worrying about him. If not, I don't think your dear old daddy is gonna like the new guy coming in and moving his cheese."

She props her chin on her palm, looking at me with eager eyes. "Tell me everything."

I do. I tell her how the guys are the hockey equivalent of finance bros, with too much focus on fucking and fun, and not enough attention on being mentally and physically sound both on and off the ice. I tell her that Coach has created an environment where relationships are discouraged with some bullshit about them being a distraction. I tell her about practices with the new rookies and the way they're already being brainwashed into the Blizzard's way of thinking.

"And you want to fix alllll of that?" she asks, doubt written in the lines around her frown as she waves her fork in a circle, indicating everything I've listed out. "How?"

"I don't know yet," I admit. "But I've got to try."

"Why? You keep saying you're only here for the short term. Play your best, have a few conversations with Kipson, and move on. Dad will trade you back if you're not the fix he thinks you are, right?"

I could do that. I'm not a magic pill to be prescribed when someone else is sick or a bandage when someone's bleeding out. I'm a person. But

I'm not a half asser. And I do think there's an opportunity here. Room I could shove my way into and improve.

"Knowing that better is possible is a privilege I don't take lightly. These guys? They don't know any different than the team they've been on, but if I can show them what a team can be . . . *should* be . . . maybe we could all be better for it. Because the truth is, this team's insanely talented. Just think, if things are this bad and they made it to Finals last year, what could happen if they were actually a team. We could win the whole damn thing."

Briar is smiling at me, her eyes filled with some combination of happiness and respect. "You said *we*, not *them*. You, my friend, are a *fixer*." She bestows the label upon me like she's figured out my deepest, darkest secret, as though I hide that I'm a mostly decent guy and not a shitstain on society.

I shrug, my passionate speech feeling a bit overzealous now. "Not everyone has what I've had—good family, good team, good teammates. It's hard to want something you don't know exists. But if they see how it could be, maybe they'll want it for themselves too."

"You need a team-building exercise for your team," she suggests, clapping her hands and nearly stabbing herself with her fork in the process. "Oops!" She sets the fork down in favor of the much safer glass of soda, which she grips with two hands in giddy excitement.

Inspired by her enthusiasm, I point a finger at her. "Exactly!"

"I might have an idea. But my dad isn't going to like it." She dances in her seat like she can't contain the happy wiggles. Like she doesn't even try, which is downright adorable.

"Honestly, whatever it is, that makes me like it more. Your dad really is kind of an asshole." I know she agrees with that sentiment, but I still watch for any flinch. I can say all sorts of things about my own family, but if someone else said one sideways word about my parents or sister, I'd annihilate them before they could finish the last syllable. I protect what's mine, and knowing if Briar feels the same way about her father, despite their messy history, is important given what I'm planning.

She doesn't react in the slightest. Unless you count a sparkle in her eyes. "Neither are the guys," she says, glossing right over the paternal insult.

The warning makes me chuckle. "Even better."

Our eyes lock, both of us grinning like idiots. Not that Briar is an idiot, but the grin on her face is huge and joy filled, and I feel like we're conspiring to steal the Declaration of Independence or some other wild adventure.

A coup of sorts. The idea sounds fun.

I like this. Like her. There's this pure lightness filling up my chest, even in this dark time. It's her . . . she's the light.

"Will you come to the season opener?" The words fall out of my mouth before I can stop them. I don't regret them at all, but I probably should've built up to them a bit smoother. Clearing my throat, I clarify, "You and Harley, I mean. I got tickets for you."

"You want us to come to the game?" Her expression softens, like she's surprised I thought of them for something so important.

I shake my head. "I want you to come watch me play." The difference is slight but significant. I don't want them there as Coach Boothe's family. I want them to come as my guests, for me.

Briar swallows thickly, her voice taking on a shaky uncertainty as she says, "Harley would love that."

"And you?" I'm pushing, being clear about my intentions. It can still be as friends if that's what she needs, but I don't want to pretend that I'm not affected by her, when I am. She deserves honesty, complete and raw.

And the truth is . . . I want to be a lot more than Briar's friend.

The same way I want to help my new teammates realize that this isn't how it has to be, I want to show Briar that not all men are like her dad and Tyler. That some men, me especially, recognize the value in having a partnership built on communication, support, and attraction. That I'm willing to sit with her, for however long it takes for her to feel comfortable, outside the walls she's been forced to put up for her own safety and sanity. And maybe, as I learn how to seep through the cracks in her walls, I can seal them over, like that fancy Japanese stuff Penny showed me once, where they fill the breaks with gold, not to hide them but to celebrate that the trauma she's been through made her into the strong, beautiful woman across from me. Tyler's manipulations didn't steal away her light, they made her shine that much more brightly in the dark he tried to surround her with.

Slowly, I reach across the table until the tips of my fingers are touching the tips of hers. It's the barest of connections, but I feel it through my entire body like a small electrical current, from my tingling fingertips to my growing cock.

I watch closely as her eyes jerk to our hands, staring at them in surprise as though they're not ours. She moves her fingers slightly, not away, but rather touching me in return. I stop breathing, afraid to break whatever spell is being woven around us.

Her gaze lifts to my face, going from one eye to the other, to my mouth, and back to my eyes, as she thinks and thinks some more. "Nothing has changed," she warns, "but yeah, I'd like that too. We'll come to the game."

Neither of us move our hands, but it feels like huge progress has been made between us. At least to me it does.

After lunch, we're walking across the parking lot and her hand brushes mine. I feel like a scared teenager that's not sure if it's an invitation or accident. But as much as I want to grab her hand, pull her against me, and taste the sweetness of her lips, I don't. Afraid of going too fast for a woman who isn't sure she wants to go down this path at all, I hesitate.

As I reach for the door handle, Briar spins and puts her back against my truck, trapping her hands behind herself. "Did you know that albatrosses mate for life?"

Is this her version of flirting? Spitting out random animal facts while looking up at me through her lashes? I think it might be.

We're only a foot apart, but I lean in a little, curious to see where this is going. "I did, actually."

"They're not the only birds that do that either. Certain swans, eagles, and cranes do too." She licks her lips. "But when one partner dies or disappears, the living albatross will eventually find another mate."

"You don't say." I move closer, my nose nearly touching hers. I tilt her chin up with a gentle touch.

"It takes years sometimes, so potential new mates have to be patient."

"So patient," I agree, nodding.

"The most patient-est."

I want to kiss this woman more than I want to breathe. Hell, I want to kiss her more than I want to play hockey, and that's my entire purpose for living. But this needs to be her move. She hasn't had the chance to be in charge of her life in a long time, maybe ever. And she should. She deserves that opportunity.

I don't want to fuck this up. Not for me, but for her. I'm almost scared to ruin the progress she's making toward her own freedom. I'm not a man who usually sits back and lets things happen to me. But in this, I need to be. For her.

So I slow the internal drum of my heartbeat that chants *kiss her, kiss her, kiss her* and instead, enjoy the close-up view of her eyes, noting that they're not simply blue, but there are flecks of brown at the centers. I let my body burn with the need to touch her, and focus on the way her breathing has sped up. I wait for her, soaking up her nearness and staying present in the moment, as if there's anywhere else I'd rather be than this close to Briar.

*Closer?*

Okay, that's fair. I'd love to be even closer to her, curled around her, protecting her from everything bad in the world until all she knows is good, and I'd love to be inside her, both her body and beyond her walls. I tell my aching cock that the delayed gratification will be worth the pain and pray that I'm right.

"Should I start flapping my wings or making bird noises to court you?" I say lowly.

She presses her lips together, fighting back a laugh. "You'd do that?"

"*Ca-cawww,*" I say with the utmost sincerity.

Her eyes twinkle. Her lips part. And slower than a sloth, she lifts her lips to mine.

I don't dive into her the way I'd like to, which is completely and passionately. I let her set the pace, willing myself to give her what she needs, not take what I want. And her lack of urgency feeds something unexpected in me too. I relish the softness of her lips, savor the press of her freed hands on my chest, cherish the moment she opens her mouth to deepen the kiss.

I celebrate Briar Johns finding herself again and feel like the luckiest fucker in the world for getting to not only witness this moment, but be a part of it.

# Chapter 12

## BRIAR

"What can I help you with?"

My nose crinkles at Dad's tone. "Can't a girl just call her father without wanting something?"

"Some girls, yes. You, no." He says it so matter-of-factly that there's no sense in arguing. He's right. We don't have the type of relationship where I call him for fun catch-up chat sessions. Of course, I don't call to ask for favors, either, but here we are. "Plus, it's season opener week, Briar. So again, what can I do for you?"

I knew it wasn't going to be easy. I warned Dominic as much. Dad's singular focus on hockey still pricks, though. But this isn't about me. It's about Dominic and the team.

*Don't lie to yourself! You know dang good and well it's mostly about Dominic.*

It is and there's no sense in pretending it's not. I'd already decided to help him, but after that kiss? I was ready to plead with my father to let Dominic be the new captain, coach, boss, or whatever else he wants to be. Reason did eventually return . . . slightly . . . but I still feel like Dominic's desire to enact some positive change for the Blizzard is a good cause.

"I have an idea, but I need your help."

"There it is," he chuckles as I prove his point.

"It'll be good for the team too," I rush to add, knowing that it's the only way to pique his interest.

"I'm listening." He probably is, but I can also hear him typing in the background, multitasking something hockey related I'm sure and unable to give his only daughter a few minutes of his precious time.

"We have an event coming up at the zoo next month. It's a party of sorts to celebrate the birth of the new gibbon and raise funds for—"

"How much?"

"What?" I say in confusion. But then I sigh, not surprised he instantly latched on to the financial aspect. "I don't want a donation. I want a few players."

It's his turn to be confused. "What?"

"I want a few Blizzard players to make an appearance at the party as a way of drawing interest to the event. They don't have to do anything other than be social and take a few pictures with attendees. It'd be great PR for the team too."

"We're a little busy with games," he says, making it sound like I'm unaware of the time commitment being a hockey player (or coach) requires. Believe me, I know how much time it takes. And what that time costs in relationships.

"I already checked the schedule. The party is on October 25, which happens to be a no-game weekend for you. And you're at home the next game, so no travel schedule either. I've thought of everything."

"Have you now?" Dad says. The typing stops, and I hear squeaking as though he's leaning back in his chair to give me his full attention. "You never want anything to do with hockey. Why now?"

It's a fair point. I never go to games, am standoffish to players, and only show up when there's free food and drinks to be had. "The baby gibbon? It was born to Caprice, my favorite animal in the entire zoo. We're raising funds by holding a naming contest for her. The highest bid gets to name the baby, within reason. No Gibbon McGibbonface or Harambaby or corporate names. I want her to have an appropriate name, something that reflects the importance of her birth. If we have a big turnout for the party, we'll raise more funds, and it's more likely she'll get a good name."

Dad is quiet for a moment and I honestly think he's going to laugh at me. He doesn't care about the zoo, or animals, or their names. He cares about me, to a point, but I'm not sure if his love runs deep enough for an ask like this.

"Do you have anyone in particular in mind?"

"Really?" I shout in surprise. My feet take me on a happy dance tour around the break area where zoo employees can have lunch without being interrupted by guests.

"Tell me quickly before I change my mind. Who do you want?"

This feels like a trap. But I do have a few people I'd like to come to the party. For a multitude of different reasons.

"I'd love for the team favorites to come—Mike Kipson, Wayne Anderson, Paulie Pacholek, Lynn Sabine. And Dominic Lee since he's new to Blizzard but has a fanbase from the Hawks. Maybe one or two of the rookies?" I inhale and add, "And you, of course."

I don't think Dad will come. But I tack him on at the last minute as an olive branch since he's even considering this idea. If he comes, great. If he just sends a check, that's good for the zoo. And if he agrees to send the rest of the players, Dominic can start to improve their team dynamics.

"Huh," Dad scoffs. "I wouldn't have thought you even knew the players' names."

"They're popular players, Dad. And I've met most of them." I intentionally don't mention that I met Dominic at this year's preseason get-together, and definitely don't mention that we've had some further contact since then, knowing Dad would not approve. For all his faults, Dad wouldn't want me to date a hockey player. He knows how they are, after all.

"I don't know if those guys are gonna want to spend their free time doing charity work for the zoo."

I laugh lightly. "Maybe not, but they'll do whatever their coach tells them to do."

"I can *ask* them," he says. "But I can't make any promises. Union bargaining agreement, you know."

It'll have to be enough. "Thanks, Dad."

"Are you a witch?"

Seeing Dominic's name—well, technically it's still *Hockey Coach*—pop up on my phone screen already had me smiling. His teasing words add a bit of giddiness to the warmth blooming in my chest. I'm pretty sure I know why he's calling. Or at least I think I do.

I smile, twisting and wiggling in delight as I stir tonight's gourmet dinner of spaghetti and meat sauce. "Mayyyybe," I singsong.

"Coach called me and a bunch of other guys into his office today. I thought I was going to get shipped off to Canada. Or cussed out, at a minimum. But do you know what he said?"

A laugh pops out. "Good job?" I guess. Dominic makes a *nuh-uh* sound. "Thank you?" Not it either. "You're all fired?" Okay, that one might actually happen so I don't laugh too hard at that possibility.

"It seems there's a very special appearance he wants us to make. Guess where?"

"Hmm, I'm sure I have no idea," I tease.

"Your zoo, you damn witch," Dominic exclaims, making it sound like the highest praise. Raising his voice into a fair estimation of a truck stop diner waitress, he says, "Ding! One team-building exercise, coming right up." Then he laughs, sounding genuinely light and happy. "Thank you."

I preen, knowing he can't see me. Probably *because* he can't see the effect his words have on me. I'm glad to be able to help him, and it will actually help the zoo too.

"So you're all coming?"

"Apparently," he laughs. "Anderson and Kipson were pretty pissed off about it. Coach didn't give them a choice, though. Told Kipson to quit moping and told Anderson that he could stand to give his dick the day off and press some palms to earn some money and goodwill for his girl."

*His girl? Me?*

The smile stealing across my face now is for an entirely different reason. Surprisingly, it's for my father. I asked for this favor because of Dominic, never dreaming it might actually improve things between me and Dad. But maybe this team-building thing can build more than one team.

"No mention of union bargaining agreements?" I ask, and Dom laughs.

"No, why?"

"No reason. Thanks, Dominic."

# Chapter 13

## Dominic

I'm not surprised. Well, not about who didn't show up to my open invitation for a pre–opening game dinner at Big Boy Bowls. But maybe about who did—Mike Kipson.

He looks from me to Rodney to Tomville and then to the door behind him. He's thinking of bailing. It's written in every tense muscle, his downturned mouth, and the way he's fidgeting with the car keys that are still in his hand.

Thankfully, that's the moment Pacholek opens the door behind him, boxing him in. "Hey, fellas! We eating or not?"

"You guys know what to do," I tell Rodney and Tomville. They instantly queue up to order, remembering the advice I gave them last time.

"You want your usual?" Rodney calls back to me and I nod.

Kipson looks at me questioningly.

"We went out to eat during training camp. Figured we were all new in town and might as well get to know each other."

His brow furrows as he stares at me. "You just invited them out?" I nod. "And invited everyone out tonight?"

"You're buying your own," I clarify with a shit-eating grin. "This ain't a date and I'm no gentleman."

"Fuck off," he growls. But as he pushes past me to get in line, he's fighting a teeny-tiny hint of a smile. He'd disagree, but I see it . . . right there at the corners of his mouth. They're approximately 3 percent less frowny than they were when he came in.

"You like playing with fire?" Pacholek asks wonderingly, watching the interaction between me and Kipson.

"Only thing I like better is playing with my dick," I joke. More seriously, I tell him, "Glad you came, man," as I clap him on the back and let him go in front of me in line.

We get our food and find a table, no small feat for five large-framed athletes. And we dig in. I even steal a bite of Pacholek's carnitas, grinning at him when he tries to stab my hand, but he snaps the tines on his plastic fork before breaking my skin.

"I . . . am . . . Iron Man," I taunt before doing the classic guitar riff.

Pacholek rolls his eyes. "I literally got you, it's just a weak-ass fork," he complains, staring at the new gap in the utensil.

"I gotchu." I hop up, grab him a new one, and make a quick stop at the register to ask for a side of the carnitas for the table. As I sit back down, I groan, "That shit's delicious."

"Yeah, I know. That's why I got it," Pacholek quips.

He quits complaining when a worker drops off a bowl with a big scoop of guacamole along with the pork, definitely more than a side, on our table. "Truce?"

"Fucker."

But all is forgiven when the rest of the guys try it. It even turns into a taste test competition—chicken versus carnitas versus steak. Personally, I think they're all winners.

Even as we all goof off, Kipson stays mostly quiet, watching it all play out in front of him like we're a show he's tuned in to but not a part of. But eventually, narrowed eyes locked on me, he spits out, "What are you doing?"

Shoveling another bite—of my own chicken this time—into my mouth, I ask, "What?"

He tilts his head, glare going even colder. "Don't act innocent. What game are you playing?"

*Okay, we're doing this, I guess.*

I set my fork down, wipe my mouth with a napkin, and turn off my Good-Natured Guy persona in favor of coldly glaring right back. "Eating dinner with my teammates before a game." He's not buying it. Not that I'm doing much to sell the idea that this is a no-big-deal meal out between friends. "Tell me, what do you usually do the night before a game, especially the season opener? Where do you think the rest of the team is tonight? What are they doing?"

"Not singing 'Kumbaya' with assholes they barely know," he answers.

Rodney sits back in his chair, hurt. Tomville takes a too-big bite, angry. Pacholek sighs.

This fight doesn't involve them. Well, it does in a larger way, but they have enough sense to let Kipson and me do our dick-measuring without interference.

"That's the bullshit I'm talking about," I tell him. "The Hawks aren't perfect by any means. We'd fight and give each other shit like it was our jobs. We even had a guy who helicoptered his dick in the locker room so many times we started calling him Chopper. But any one of those guys? I'd show up for them in a heartbeat and they'd do the same for me. I don't get the sense that's how the Blizzard operates." I pause for a moment, giving him a chance to argue, but I'm right and we both know it. "But it could be."

Taking a deep breath, I launch into my spiel, not just for Kipson but for everyone. "Look, player for player, I see y'all on the ice. This is the most skilled team, individually, that I've ever played on. I saw that last year, too, in the Cup Finals. But that's the problem. You play as six individuals out there. We beat your ass because we played as a *team*. A team needs a leader, a fucking captain. You're the one with a *C* on your shoulder, Mike. So act like one."

I'm basically throwing not only my hand on the table, but the whole fifty-two-card deck.

"Fuck you," he snarls. He crosses his arms over his chest in classic defensive posturing.

I keep my attention locked on Kipson as I say, "Rodney, anybody on the team asked you shit about where you came from, what your experience is, if you got a place to stay, or anything else?"

He huffs out a mirthless laugh. "No. Well, you, but other than that, no."

Kipson rolls his eyes.

"How about you, Tomville? Anybody but Coach know you were an enforcer that took out four players in a single game and were the reason your team won your conference championship and got them to the Frozen Four?"

"Nope," he answers, shaking his head.

"Damn, kid," Pacholek says, impressed. He holds a fist up and Tomville bumps it with a dawning grin.

"That right there is why I'm doing this," I inform Kipson. "What happened to you sucks. So yeah, *Captain*, being thrown off your rocker is understandable. But it isn't a singular issue. This whole team needs to learn how to be a fucking team."

"And you think you're gonna teach us?" he snaps.

"I don't want to be captain," I say preemptively, cutting that concern off at the knees. "But are you gonna do it? Be my guest," I invite, throwing an arm wide. "Maybe it'd give you something to do other than cry into your pillow at night."

"Fuck you."

He says that every time I make a valid point that he can't counter. Still, I'm right on the edge of going too far, but that's where I need to go if I want Kipson to wake up to what's happening around him.

"Do you want to know what Anderson told me that night at O'Neal's?"

He presses his lips together, refusing to say yes.

"He was celebrating that your wife left you. His exact words were 'thank fuck' that she's gone, and Sabine declared the Blizzard a 'clean house.' Apparently, the team likes to keep things casual only. Anything else is a distraction. Sound familiar?"

It's the first time Kipson doesn't only hear me, but actually listens. Furious, he turns to Pacholek and demands, "Anderson and Sabine said that shit?"

"Uh—"

He squeezes his fork so hard, the plastic snaps in half between his fingers. "I'm gonna kill them."

I nod, agreeing. "Good plan. In the meantime, we have a game tomorrow night and a whole damn season to play. It'd be cool if we could do it as an actual team that gives a shit about each other. What do you say?"

I hold my hand out. Kipson's glare jumps from my eyes to my hand and back again. "Fuck you, Lee. I'm outta here."

With that, he pushes back from the table and stomps to the door.

"That went well," I say, deadpan.

"What the hell, man?" Pacholek gripes. "You trying to implode the whole damn team? Are you that pissed you got traded?"

*Yes. But also, maybe no.*

"Maybe it needs to implode," I suggest. I lean his way, eyes hard. "So we can build it back *better*."

He shakes his head, unconvinced. "I get that the Hawks won the Cup last year, but it's not like we're some bottom of the barrel team. We're not just good, we're great, and don't need the Great Dominic Lee to fix us."

"Except that's literally why I was brought here, isn't it?" I counter.

"No. Fix Kipson. Leave the rest of us out of it." With that, he gets up, too, heading for the door.

"You two got something to say?" I ask Rodney and Tomville, staying composed.

"Nope," Rodney replies.

"Can I have the carnitas?" Tomville asks. "Somebody told me I need to pack on a few pounds and that shit's delicious."

"Yeah," I say with a small huff of laughter. "Have at it, man."

Tomville grabs the bowl and eats the remaining pork in a few bites.

"I see it," Rodney tells me. "What you're talking about." I realize I've been staring at the door like Kipson or Pacholek might walk back through it, but at Rodney's statement, I look his way. "I moved my senior year of high school. Left a school with a great record, for another that only had a good one. You wanna know why?"

I raise my brows curiously.

"Vibes. If I'd stayed, I don't think I would've made it through the year." He drops his chin, "Not only playing hockey."

And that's it. This sport is our life. As athletes and as men. We give our time, blood, sweat, and tears to it. It becomes who we are at our core. And being surrounded by good people creates an environment where everyone thrives.

"Hit me up anytime, man. *Any. Time.* For anything. To shoot the shit or go eat or grab a beer. Whatever. I gotchu," I vow.

He nods. "Thanks."

"Me too," Tomville tells Rodney.

That's the start. The thread of connection starting to wind through players. I hope I can grow it to include the whole team, but even if I fail there, this tiny spark is enough for tonight.

"Alright, guys. You know the drill for tonight. Shit, relax, jack off, and then hit the bed."

"Yes, sir," they reply.

# Chapter 14

## Briar

I've been to hundreds of hockey games in my life, which basically qualifies me as an expert on them. An odd label perhaps for someone who doesn't particularly care for the sport, but here I am. I've watched from every vantage point in the arena—right behind the bench, where you feel like a part of the team; in suites, with all-you-can-drink sodas and endless snacks; and from the cheap seats, though Mom vetoed that after I got a bit turned around on a solo bathroom trip once and got lost. Of course, Dad didn't notice because he was enthralled in the game we were there to watch. Well, technically not the game, but a player.

At every one, the booming announcers, chilly air, and crowds hungry for violence are always the same.

Despite my usual dislike for hockey, the atmosphere in the arena tonight is filled with an infectious hum that's working its way through me, leaving sizzling excitement in its wake. It definitely helps that Harley is bouncing in his seat, watching for Dominic to take the ice.

"Do you think he knows we're here?"

"Yeah, honey," I assure him. At least I know he's going to sleep hard tonight—he's buzzing like a bee and the postgame crash is going to be epic. "He arranged everything. He knows."

I try to not be impressed by that, and maybe if it truly had only been tickets, I could blow it off as no-big-deal. But Dominic doesn't do anything small. We have lower tier, center ice tickets, right on the glass, across from the benches so our view is totally unimpeded. Our parking pass was included. So was a gift card for the concession stand and two jerseys with the Blizzard's newest defenseman's name on the back—one in Harley's size and one in mine.

*Is wearing a guy's number like putting on a cowboy's hat? Does it mean you're going home with him?*

Surely not.

But would that be so bad? The idea makes me ridiculously overheated considering the cold ice is literally *right there.*

I haven't gone home with a guy in a long time. Like ever. Not since Tyler. And I don't think that qualifies when I had dinner with his parents and then we went to the basement to watch a movie. I'd ended up late for both my curfew and my period. We got married shortly after that, and then home was our little apartment.

Point being, after the divorce, dating and sex haven't been on my to-do list. The concept has felt foreign and wrong for so long, but after that kiss? They're starting to sound much more intriguing.

*Not tonight,* I tell the butterflies flapping around in my belly.

For one, I cannot have sex for the first time since Tyler with my son asleep in the next room. What if I'm loud? What if Dominic is? The image of a grunting, orgasming Dominic with his face scrunched up in pleasure pops into my mind unbidden. Are hot flashes a thing at twenty-eight? Because I think I'm having one.

Second, Dominic will probably have postgame things to do and we won't even have the chance to see him off the ice.

Also, what if I don't know what I'm doing? A man like Dominic will be good in bed. I have zero doubt of that. If I was unsure, the way he kissed me quickly removed any uncertainty there. He was tender but sure, exploring not only my mouth but my body as well. Honestly, I was surprised he didn't shove me up against the side of his truck and take what he wanted. I could feel that he wanted to—*wanted me!*—but he'd held himself back, and that restraint was oh so sexy, making me wonder what an unleashed Dominic would be like. On the other hand, I have little to no experience with men. Tyler and I didn't exactly have a rip-roaring love life, and sex has always been kind of a meh experience for me.

Oh God, what if I have sex with Dominic and it's still just *okay*? I've read all sorts of books and watched my fair share of romance movies. Is the knock your socks off, make you scream sex in those entirely fictional? Or could it actually exist?

I want it to be real. And I want it to be real with Dominic, which is massive progress in itself. *Go me!* If I could afford a therapist, she'd be so proud of me. But I don't have one of those, so I give myself a hearty pat on the back and a private attagirl.

"Look, Mom! There's Dom!" Harley shouts, yanking me from the whirlwind of thoughts tumbling through my head.

The Blizzard have taken to the ice, doing sweeping loops around one end to warm up. Even with the whole lot of them dressed in baby blue, my eyes find Dominic easily. He's not particularly taller or wider than any of the other guys, but he draws my attention like a magnet.

"Dom!" Harley shouts, banging on the glass as he skates closer. "Dominic!"

I see the instant he hears the familiar voice, watch him perk up and try to find us, which means I get a front-row seat to the smile that lifts his lips when he locks in on Harley . . . and then me.

The whole world seems to drop away, and in an instant, I feel the impact of his heavy gaze. His eyes drop over me, flaring when he sees the jersey I'm wearing. The look on his face says that, as important as this game is, I'm the focus. That if we were to change seats, he could find me anywhere in the arena, picking my voice out from fifteen thousand others.

It's a look that says that I *mean something* to him. It's a look that my body responds to naturally even before my brain catches up. It's a look that says, *You're mine. Game over.*

Because no other person in this entire arena is getting a look from Dominic like I am right now.

As he skates by us, he touches the glass with his gloved hand, right where Harley has placed his hand. Literally an inch of plexiglass and his glove separate them, but Harley acts like it's a direct high five. Weird as it sounds, I understand because I'd swear that I can feel Dom's heat through the glass too.

"Did you see that, Mom?" Harley asks, his eyes filled with awe.

It's like he's discovered that a celebrity is a real person, but it's just Dominic, the man who practiced drills with him, discussed proper cheese to burger to bun ratios while they stuffed their faces, and helped with both an injury and a jerk of a father.

But now, he's dressed in full gear and looks like the guy from the games on television. Still, Dominic is more than a famous athlete. He's a friend . . . to my son. And maybe to me.

Dominic is halfway across the rink when I find him again, but when I do, his eyes are already locked on me. Or did they ever leave me? I give him a big smile and two thumbs-up. Instantly, I decide the thumbs-up is weird and switch to clapping, but that must look odd, too, because Dominic grins before turning his attention to the teammates around him.

Hockey has never fully held my attention unless Harley was on the ice. I watch my baby like a hawk. But pro games? I find myself scanning the crowd, watching the mascots, dancing in my chair to the snippets of music between plays, and basically entertaining myself with random stuff until the game is over.

Not tonight.

I'm laser focused on what's happening.

I notice a few things pretty quickly. Dad is starting Dominic tonight, rare for a new player, but with Dom's playing history, nobody is surprised. Mike Kipson's been chirping at Wayne Anderson since they hit the ice, while Anderson keeps silently waving Kipson off. I get the feeling that behind his goalie's arm shield, Anderson is giving Kipson the bird. I don't know what that's about, but Kipson came out mad and only seems to be getting angrier. And Sabine and Pacholek seem to be keeping one eye on the puck and one on Kipson, a hard task when he's behind them for the most part. Or he should be, but as soon as the puck drops, the Devils are playing hot and heavy, putting pressure on Anderson again and again.

"Score!"

Shit.

The crowd's sound of disappointment matches the one I feel. "It's okay," I say, clapping my hands a little more normally now that Dominic's not watching. "Keep at it."

I'm cheering for the Blizzard the way I cheer for Harley, with positive affirmations and support, as if they care nearly as much as my nine-year-old does.

From what I can tell, it works. And I actually enjoy watching. Granted, I mostly keep my attention locked on Dominic, and though he does his fair share of roughhousing, the hallmark skillset of a defenseman, I can't help but note his surprising grace and finesse. But it's hard to ignore the action crisscrossing the ice and I find myself following along with the plays, cheering the Blizzard on with growing intensity as the game progresses.

Despite the early score by the Devils, the second period levels things, and in the third we eke out a hard-fought 2–1 victory.

"That was so awesome!" Harley yells. His hands are clenched by his face and his eyes look a bit maniacal. Someone overdid it on the sugary sodas, cotton candy, and popcorn tonight, and it's not me.

"It was a great game," I agree.

"Dom killed it. Did you see him with that body check on Paulson? Or the way he broke up Medvedev's fake out and just yoinked the puck from him like it was nothing?"

"Of course I did. I'm literally right here," I say, pointing at the seat next to his. We saw the exact same things.

"Do you think we can see the players?"

After games, players have an entire routine to go through. For some, it's a quick shower and go. For others, it might be an hour-long process with sports medicine, cold plunge soaks, and then showering and getting dressed. I don't know where Dominic falls in that spectrum.

Plus, I don't know if it's such a good idea for the other players to see me. In the crowd during the game, I blend in and am relatively anonymous. But standing in a fan line for up-close pictures and autographs? They'd recognize me and probably tell Dad that I was here. If I was a good liar, I could say I came to support him. But I've never been able to lie without some kind of tell giving me away, and that would lead to more questions. Ones I'm not prepared to answer.

"I don't think so, honey. It's late. We can send Dominic a text to thank him again."

I don't get the chance to send a politely worded thank-you that Miss Manners would be proud of, though. Before I do, my phone dings.

I have to deal with some shit, but can I come over after? I know it's late, so it's okay if not. But I'd like to see you.

He wants to see me?

I try not to squeal like a teenage girl whose crush just sent her a *WYD, girl?* text. Mostly because Harley is looking at me weirdly. So maybe I did make a noise? Oops! But also, because I'm a full-grown adult who is *not* freaking out over a man wanting to come over after dark.

That's fine. Let me know when you're on your way.

I stare at the message, making sure I didn't misspell anything and that it sounds as nonchalant as I want it to, as opposed to the ohmygod-ohmygod-ohmygod chaotic energy I actually feel. I add my address and hit send.

"He's coming over?" Harley asks. He was reading over my shoulder and knows exactly who I just invited to our home. Postgame crash, my ass. My odds of getting him to bed just dropped to less than 1 percent, especially hopped up on caffeine and sugar.

"Yes, but not for a bit. You should have time to shower and get to bed first," I tell him.

"Mooom!" he whines.

I can't help it, I laugh. "I'm kidding. You can stay up to say thank you in person." I switch into the mom inflection that I've perfected to add, "And then go to bed without argument."

He's quick to accept. "Deal."

On the drive home, Harley rambles about the game, reliving each play in detail, and though I nod along and offer occasional commentary, mostly I'm reminding myself that I am not having sex tonight. Or maybe ever again.

But definitely not tonight.

Too bad my vajayjay doesn't quite get the memo and is pulsing with a reminder that a little extra attention from a man who kisses like Dominic would be nice. Real nice.

# Chapter 15

## Dominic

I want to speed-demon rush through my postgame routine and get to Briar's as soon as possible. But I can't. On top of the typical media bullshit, I have work to do here. Especially since the fuse I lit inside a particularly troubled defenseman is starting to pop and fizzle in warning. We're going to have dynamite-level destruction in three, two, one . . .

Right on time, Kipson roars at Anderson, "You son of a bitch! You know what you did!"

They are nearly nose to nose and on the cusp of throwing hands, but more shocking than that is Anderson's unusually grim expression. For a good-time guy, he's got an impressive "don't fuck with me" face. "You'll have to be more specific. I've done a lot of things."

"Sofia." Kipson giving his ex-wife's name breath steals all the air in the locker room.

"Oh, that? *Her?*" Anderson scoffs. "You're welcome, man. Better off without that anchor weighing you down, huh? Now you can put your focus where it should be, without the whining and pouting every time you travel for games." He moves his hand like a mouth talking, right in his ear, his face the picture of annoyance, painting an image of what Kipson and Sofia's relationship was like. Or at least what Anderson thinks it was like.

Seeming to think that's explanation enough, Anderson slaps Kipson's shoulder like they're buddies again, but Kipson reflexively swats his arm away. "Better off?" he snaps. "She was the only thing keeping me out of hell and thanks to you, she's gone."

"Nuh-uh," Anderson tuts, waving a hand. "Don't put that on me. You're the one who fucked up what you had. Though why you'd want *that*, I do not understand." He shakes his head, confused. "Especially when this is the alternative. I'm just showing you what your life could be." Anderson pats his own chest like he's the ultimate example of happiness.

And maybe he thinks he is. But I can see through the shallowness in which he lives his life. I hope others on the team are starting to see through it too.

Kipson looks like Anderson just slapped him with his words. His mouth opens and closes like a fish ripped out of the water. I'd put odds at fifty-fifty on whether Kipson's going to punch Anderson or collapse from the weight of the regret he's been carrying.

"Your life is shit. Empty, hollow, meaningless shit," he says quietly, intensely, instead. Kipson means every word of it, no holds barred. I happen to agree with him, but for the moment, I stay quiet, watching this play out, along with the rest of the team.

Anderson laughs. "But it sure is fun," he brags, looking around for support. There are a few awkward chuckles, but nobody rushes to fully agree. Anderson doesn't care, though. "Whatever. You know the drill. Hockey first, yourself second, women . . . well, they're like item ten on the priority list. Right, Coach?"

I follow Anderson's line of sight to see Coach Boothe standing in the doorway of his office. How much did he hear of Kipson and Anderson's *discussion*? Judging by the stern set of his jaw? Enough.

Coach probably doesn't think so, but I'm doing exactly what he brought me here to do—fix Kipson. I just might break a few other things in the process. What's that saying? You've got to break a few eggs to make a cake? Well, I'm breaking egos to make a team.

Hopefully.

Briar's neighborhood is filled with small homes. Some are more rundown than others, but all in all, it seems safe. As I count down the numbers to the address she sent, I already know which house is hers. It's got to be the one with potted flowers on either side of the front door. There's a level of care and warmth that makes the little yellow-and-white house stand out.

Yep, unless she has neighbors who also happen to love animals a lot, the one with a wreath on the door made out of every animal print ribbon in existence and proclaiming *Welcome! It's basically a zoo here* must be Briar's.

I knock, my nerves already settling as if they know we're close to her.

"Hey!" she says, swinging open the door.

She looks gorgeous. Still in my jersey—which does things to me I should probably deny—with her hair down around her shoulders, fresh gloss on her smiling lips, and a sparkle in her blue eyes.

"Hey. Like the wreath." I flick one of the zebra-print ribbons.

"Thanks. I won it in a raffle at work." She looks at the wreath fondly. "Only cost me fifty bucks in tickets. And we do not discuss that I could've bought the ribbon and made it myself for half that." She gives me a warning glare, probably thinking it looks threatening, but it's too cute to actually intimidate anyone. Especially me.

"What I'm hearing is that you donated money to a great cause."

"Ooh, yeah. I like that," she says, appreciating my point of view. "Come on in."

I step immediately into her living room, which is small but cozy, with a couch and a TV on a wood cabinet right next to the door. Beyond that, I can see her kitchen, and there's a hallway off to the left. Everything is in shades of green with tan and white accents and obviously cared for, with little touches like throw pillows on the furniture and pictures on the walls. It feels . . . alive. Like she and Harley don't just exist in these walls, they've created a home here.

I'm struck with a sense of homesickness.

I grew up like this. With a mother who cared enough to put my crappy art on the fridge, start Crock-Pot dinners in the morning so we'd have a warm meal after practices that always ran late, and made sure I felt loved every day without fail.

Briar is that type of mother too. Harley is a lucky kid.

I really need to call my mom tomorrow.

"Thanks for letting me come over. Tonight was a surreal experience."

I don't get a chance to explain because a voice down the hall says, "Dom?" A split second later, a torpedo hits me full force in the chest and a vise wraps around my waist. Damn, even the Devils didn't hit this hard.

"Hey, kid," I say, patting Harley on the head. The hug feels like a huge leap forward in our friendship. And also, his hair is sopping wet. "Did you have fun at the game?"

"So much fun!" he informs me at approximately one hundred decibels. "It was awesome! And we won!"

I laugh, nodding. "We did."

"We?" Briar echoes quietly, giving me a *told you so* look.

She's right. There's no sense in denying that the Blizzard is my team now. I might not like it, or like all of my teammates, but it's where I'm at, so I might as well roll with it.

"Blizzard Blast!" Harley shouts, mimicking the animation that plays on the jumbotron of the team's polar bear mascot throwing snowballs. Basically, he's wildly waving his arms through the air like a windmill.

"Whoa. Alright, say thank you and good night to Dominic, and then it's bedtime for anyone under ten years old. Whoops! Looks like that's"—Briar looks around the room dramatically, then points at Harley—"you."

"Mom!"

She tilts her head, her eyes unyielding.

"Fine. Thank you for the game. Good night." I hold up a fist for him to bump on his way back toward the hallway, but he pauses and looks back at me. "Can you tuck me in?"

Other than the flip-flop my belly does, I freeze. I have never tucked someone in before. I'm not sure I even know how to do it right.

Briar looks at me questioningly and then starts to say, "Oh, he doesn't—"

But I interrupt her, not able to disappoint Harley, who's looking at me hopefully. "Uh, yeah. Sure. I can do that." I scrub a hand over my jaw, not sure at all. Is there rocking involved? Or books to read? I try to think back to my parents tucking me into bed, but those memories are lost to time and youth.

"Yeah!" Harley grabs my hand, virtually dragging me down the hall.

Harley's room is navy and gray, with a plaid comforter on his tiny twin-size bed. Then again, he's not all that large himself. There's a nightstand and a wall-mounted desk, and those small pieces fill the space completely.

He climbs into bed and I lay the comforter over him, figuring that's tucked in. "Thanks for coming to the game. I appreciate the friendly faces in the crowd tonight."

"You're welcome," he answers, but as I go to the door, he adds, "Wait! Where are you going? We have to cricket."

"We have to what?" I ask, certain I must've misheard him.

Cricket is a game. One I don't play.

Cricket is an animal. One I don't hear.

Cricket is definitely a noun, though Harley seems to be using it as a verb.

"Cricket," he repeats as if I'm stupid. Maybe I am? Is this part of tucking in that I've forgotten? "Lie down."

"Uhm . . ."

"Take your shoes off. Mom says no shoes on the bed."

I nod. "She's right." I don't lie down, though. Instead, I sit at the foot of Harley's bed and toe my tennis shoes off. "Now what?"

"We cricket. Close your eyes, rub your feet together like a cricket, and slow count to ten while you think about your day. Then you tell me the best part of your day and I'll tell you the best part of mine."

Of course. Cricket. Doesn't everyone do this?

Assuming I've understood what is obvious to him and foreign to me, he closes his eyes and takes a deep breath. Slowly, I let my eyes fall closed, though I peek once—okay, twice—to make sure he's not fucking with me. But his eyes are closed and his lips are moving as he silently counts to ten, so I breathe and count too.

"You go first," Harley tells me.

"The best part of my day was skating around the ice before the game, hearing you call my name, and seeing you and your mom sitting in the crowd. I was nervous tonight, something I haven't been in a long time. But you two being there made me feel like everything was going to be okay, win or lose."

He smiles softly. "The best part of my day was—"

I already know what he's going to say—the game. Front row seats at a league game is a pretty special experience, so it's completely warranted.

"How many times Mom smiled at the game. She did it a lot, like *a lot, a lot.*" The emphasis he places on that tells me how many times Briar must've grinned while watching the game. Or was she watching me?

"Hockey makes me smile too," I tease. Am I pumping the kid for information? Absolutely, and I feel no guilt over it because the woman waiting in the living room makes me smile a ridiculously crazy number of times too. No small feat on a typical day, and when I've been traded away from home, almost impossible. But she makes the impossible, possible.

"She should do that more," he says seriously. He's fidgeting with the comforter and won't meet my eyes.

"I think everyone could do with a few more smiles, but I know one thing that always makes your mom happy." He glances up questioningly. "You."

"Yeah?"

"Yeah, kid," I assure him. "Now, get some shut-eye."

We say our good nights, and he hugs a new-looking polar bear in a Blizzard jersey to his chest. He must've gotten it as a souvenir. I pause at the door, glancing back at Harley. He really is a sweet kid, which is a testament to Briar.

My plan is to tell her that, but when I go back to the living room, I find her lying on the couch, fast asleep. A smile steals across my face. Yes, another one. I can't help it. Even though I truly wanted to talk to her about the game and more, she deserves to rest. She does so much, for so many people. So I'm quiet as I grab a blanket from a basket and lay it over her, tucking her in too.

I should go. Just let myself out the front door, but I can't do it. I want to stay by her side, just soak in her presence, and protect her while she sleeps. From what? I don't know, but I can't leave. I'm nearly silent as I sit down in a chair across from her, sprawling out and simply watching her. She looks peaceful, relaxed, and comfortable. And slowly, I relax too. Until . . .

The gasp yanks me from sleep, putting me on high alert instantly, although I'm confused as to where I am at first.

"Harley?" Briar's sleep-scratchy voice orients me quickly.

I blink to focus, finding her sitting upright on the couch, hair tousled and eyes wild. "It's okay. I tucked him in hours ago," I say, glancing at the time on the microwave in the kitchen.

"I fell asleep?" she asks. "What're you doing here?"

"Watching you sleep like a creeper," I joke as I stretch my arms overhead. "Until I fell asleep too."

"Guess I'm not great company after ten p.m." She reaches up to smooth her hair. I should tell her that there's a bump right at the top that's sticking up wildly, but I don't. It's adorable, making her look freshly fucked more than freshly woken up. "You want a drink or something? I have soda, juice, water . . ." She trails off, listing out drinks like this is a kid's playdate.

I want to drink her, swallow down her goodness so that I don't feel like such an asshole. "I'm okay."

The air in the room feels thick with "now what?" energy. We could talk. We could kiss. We could fuck.

"I should go," I offer.

At the same time, Briar says, "Want to sit with me?" She's thrown off the blanket I covered her with, creating a spot for me beside her on the couch.

I take her up on the invite, moving to her side. "Thank you for coming tonight. It meant more to me than you could possibly realize."

"Thank you for inviting us."

All manners and polite civility. Except our eyes are filled with desire. Gazes dancing from lips to chest to eyes.

I should hold back, let her lead again. I know I should. If I touch her, right here and now, I may not be able to stop. I'll claim her, mark her, make her mine until her eyes, heart, and soul proclaim it with every breath she takes. But fuck . . . I want her so damn badly. And I've been holding back for so long, forever it seems.

With a groan signaling the last tenuous grip on restraint I possess, I reach for her. Threading my hands into her hair, I cradle her head, bringing her mouth to mine as I go to her, desperately meeting her halfway.

I don't sip at her. I don't drink her slowly. No, I devour her like the starving man that I've become. Starved for her, for her kindness and pure heart. Her lips part, or maybe I force my way in, but in seconds, our tongues touch, igniting my hunger even more.

Thankfully, she's with me, meeting my passion with an unexpected fire of her own. She shifts, trying to get a better angle, and I grab for her hips, pulling her into my lap. The heat of her pussy right over the thick ridge of my dick is heaven and hell at the same time. I want to feel more of it, but I also want to explore the rest of Briar and save that for a final prize.

So I kiss her. And keep kissing her. I let my hands trace over her face, her back, down to squeeze her ass. I make out with Briar like I'm a teenage virgin who doesn't know the pleasures that await beyond merely merging our mouths. And it's amazing. The new best part of my day for sure.

Do we make out for minutes or hours? I don't even know, but at one point, she presses her forehead to mine. Panting for breath, she whispers, "We can't."

I try to rein myself in, slow my own racing heartbeat. "We can."

She takes a measured inhale. "I can't. Harley . . ."

Okay. It's clicking together. We definitely can't have sex for the first time on the couch when Harley is asleep down the hall. Definitely not. I groan as she shifts over me again and grip her hips, stilling her. "I understand, but if you keeping moving like that, I'm gonna come anyway."

She pulls back, staring at me with shock-filled wide eyes. "You're about to come? I'm just sitting here."

I look at her incredulously. "Briar, I could come just thinking about you, so feeling your sweet heat has me right on the edge of making a fool of myself."

Pink rises in her cheeks. "Really?"

"Really," I assure her as I push her hair back from her face. "I think I've been on edge since that night at O'Neal's."

She huffs out a tiny laugh, not believing me. This woman truly has no idea what she does to me, and even less about the things I want to do to her.

My patience is a battle I'm losing by the second. Sitting this way, every breath we share drags me closer to claiming her. Her smile is pure magic, bewitching me even further. I can see that she's having second thoughts about stopping, but I know her heart, so I do it for us. One last painfully pleasurable grind against her for us both, and then I pick her up, setting her back on the couch.

"When it's right," I tell her firmly. "Because it's not gonna be a quick fuck on the couch. I want to take my time with you. All night, maybe all weekend if we can."

"Yeah, right," she says, "that's some big talk only to be done in a few minutes."

She has a point given I just told her I'm about to come in my underwear like a two-pump chump. But more importantly, I think she's hinting at what it's been like for her—all talk, not enough action. I catch her jaw, turning her attention back to me. "All night," I emphasize. "All weekend. I want to worship every inch of you."

"Oh!" she squeaks, and that pink blush deepens to red.

I think she believes me now.

# Chapter 16

## Briar

"Someone looks a bit extra glowy today."

Trina's appraisal includes about a thousand insinuated questions as to why I've been literally singing to the animals all day. I've usually got a bit of the Snow White thing going on, with animals flocking to me like . . . well, animals. But, even by my standards, today has been unique. Our grumpy old koala, who growls at everyone, even came right to me for his morning checkup before going out to his exhibit space.

"Must be my new face cream," I reply, though we both know I'm a wash-n-go girl and the only thing on my skin is sunscreen.

"Yeah, cream de Dominic." She grins like that's the funniest thing she's ever said and then cups her ear. "Tell me all about it. Don't leave out a single. Filthy. Dirty. Detail."

"Trina!" I scold. I look around to make sure nobody heard her, though we're the only people in the kitchen, her chopping carrots and me pulling lettuce leaves apart for the morning food prep. We've got dozens of animals to feed and not a lot of time to do it. "It's not like that. We're—"

She interrupts to declare, "If you say *friends* one more time, I'm going to lecture you about the birds and the bees. And I'm not talking about pollination." She gives me a warning glare, signaling that she'll do it if necessary.

I press my lips into a thin line, trying to hide it, but a smile breaks through my resolve and steals across my face. "We kissed."

"Aaand . . ." she prompts.

Wind knocked out of my sails by her lackluster reaction, I blink. "And that's it. We kissed." A bit more reluctantly, I admit, "Well, I was straddling him when we were doing it, but all we did was kiss."

All we did? Kissing Dominic felt like a huge leap into the unknown, one that has me confused, sexually frustrated, and giddy. I swear my lips have been tingling all day, like they remember what Dominic's mouth pressing against mine felt like, and all the while, the hard ridge I felt pressing against my core growing thicker and larger. And him saying he was on edge just from me sitting on him? I was at first shocked by his admission . . . and then, flattered? Maybe that's an odd thing to feel about his response to me, but I've never been the sexy vixen that makes men go wild. It felt strangely powerful to be that with Dominic.

"Ooh, girl! Look at that blush. That's not a 'we kissed' pink. That look is more 'I want that man to lick me from head to toe and then have his babies.'" She makes a smacking noise as her tongue appears and disappears.

"It is not!" I hiss. But I press my cold fingers to my cheeks, trying to cool myself off because I am suddenly feeling a bit overheated. "I'm not having any more kids."

"It's an expression, Briar. I don't mean literally. Unless you mean it literally?" Her brows climb up her forehead and she tilts her head in question.

"Not that. It's just that . . . I'm still trying to figure out how I feel about the kiss." That's true, but what I'm really trying to figure out is . . . "Do you think a man like Dominic could actually like someone like me?"

I slept for approximately zero hours after Dominic left last night. But while I tossed and turned, I kept coming back to one thing . . . Why in the world would Dominic, an objectively gorgeous, smart, kind, sexy man, want to hang out with a weird, broken single mom? He says he wants friends, but I'm pretty sure he could find quite a few of those that wouldn't come with a kid and the constant, faint smell of fur, not to mention the strange obsession with animal trivia that has never once come in handy for anything beyond a game of twenty questions.

Trina narrows her eyes, staring at me like she's trying to choose her next words carefully. "Someone like what exactly?"

I sigh, dropping my eyes to the lettuce in my hands and ripping it a little more roughly. My nails are short and scrubbed clean, though the faint crescent scratches on my wrist are a leftover from Caprice this morning, our first interaction since her baby was born.

"You know . . . just a regular woman. A mom." I swallow as the reality of my life and Dominic's comes into clearer focus. "I'm not one of those pretty girls who's into makeup and clothes and all that stuff. Once upon a time maybe, but now? I'm just not." I shake my head woefully, not exactly regretting my beauty product–free bathroom cabinet and lack of designer clothes, but for the first time, feeling like it's odd compared to most women. Or at least compared to the puck bunnies Dominic is probably used to.

Trina comes over and turns me to face her. Looking into my eyes, she asks, "You're gorgeous, Briar. Now where's this coming from?"

I shrug, but slowly say, "I've seen the women that flock to the players, and the women they choose to . . . ahem . . . see."

"Sleep with," Trina corrects. "Or fuck, if we're being perfectly blunt."

"Yeah. And I'm not remotely like that. I don't flirt and have casual sex and date." That's putting it mildly. I'm not a man-hater exactly, but I'm a man-don't-need-er since, in my experience, they come with more problems than I have time for.

But what if I want him? The idea is foreign. Want . . . a man?

"You could, if you wanted to." Trina's suggestion is casual as can be, as if she's not reading my mind.

My insecurities spill forth, unbidden and unfiltered. "I've spent years putting everyone else first, existing on the half-eaten sandwiches that Harley leaves behind on his plate, and making do so he can have what he needs. I'm the type of woman who carries bandages on my person at any given time, in case someone has a boo-boo, for God's sakes, not the type who dates a professional athlete." There's a multitude of reasons for that beyond my lack of self-prioritization and cute wardrobe, but I don't go into that. Trina knows.

"So? Maybe Dominic likes that you're caring and well prepared. Like a Girl Scout!" she exclaims, trying to make it sound like a desirable trait.

"And if that's not enough, I've got so much baggage in my head and heart that I need a dump truck to help haul it."

"Dominic seems pretty capable of carrying some of that," she offers, flexing her biceps to remind me of Dominic's strong arms. "And who doesn't have a history?" Trina rolls her eyes dismissively, as though all my arguments are ridiculous. "Goodness knows I did and Frank didn't seem to mind."

Frank is Trina's husband. They met at the gas station where she was a clerk when he stopped to fill up his semitruck. He proposed within literal hours of their first conversation despite her previous stint in jail and one year of sobriety at the time, and oddly enough, she'd been game, climbing into his rig and into his heart that very day. Their meet-cute is more like a meet-crazy. Of course, that was twenty-five years ago, so I'm not sure her advice is particularly timely. Or trustworthy.

"But—"

This time, Trina doesn't let me argue. She cuts me off. "Enough. Quit with the pity party."

That brings me up short. I do not throw pity parties, not even with confetti and streamers. Though that does sound on-brand given I'm the sort that makes life fun, even when it's swirling down the toilet drain. "I—"

Trina's not done reading me the riot act, though, and holds up a hand. "And stop with the 'not enough' or 'too much' bullshit. I know you, and know how awesome you are. What's more, you know it too. Yeah, so what if Dominic's some famous athlete and you're a regular mortal? You deserve some fun too. Some carefree happiness." She dips her chin, daring me to disagree with her when she adds, "And some *diiiiiiick.*"

I don't know about "deserve," but wanting some fun (and yes . . . sex) is definitely true. Still . . .

"Okay, not arguing with the rest of it, but what if he goes back home after the season?"

It's a ridiculous concern. She's suggesting casual fun and I've gone straight to the far end of the realm of possibilities, skipping over steps two through two hundred, and roughly a hundred hockey games including playoffs. But that's what mothers do, plan for any and every eventuality just in case, and in a way, I think that's what I'm most scared of. What if I break my own rules for Dominic and it ends up backfiring the way I've always feared it would? He's not only a man, which in my mind translates to manipulative and self-serving, he's a hockey player, which means he's a leaver. It took me a long time to be okay on my own, and I don't know if I can go through that process again, which I inevitably will have to do with a man like Dominic.

It'll be worse when Dominic is gone because he's already set the bar infinitely higher than Dad or Tyler ever did.

The whisper in my mind echoes through my heart. The truth is, I already like Dominic more than I should.

"What if you get hit by a bus tomorrow? Or the sky falls, Chicken Little?" Trina counters. "You've got to live. Every single day is a gift. Use them. Use *him.*" She clamps her hands on my shoulders, nearly hitting me with a carrot in the process. "Maybe you have some fun for a while. Or maybe you fall in love and see what happens. Or maybe a million other things."

"That's terrifying," I admit. I'm not sure which is worse, the idea of having a casual fling with Dominic and then going back to my humdrum life when he moves on, or letting myself take that big leap and falling into a void of nothingness when he's gone. On the other hand, I could just . . . not. Stay alone, keep my heart protected, and stay steady for Harley. That definitely sounds like the safer option and I like safe. It settles my scarred soul.

"You think this is what I thought my life would end up like?" Shaking her head, Trina says, "No way. Hell no. I thought I'd end up dead before twenty-five, and there was a better than fifty-fifty chance that's exactly how it was gonna play out. But look at me now. My son is about to be twenty-five years old himself, and that's some wild shit. Comparatively, this thing with you and Dominic seems pretty normal. Pretty girl, hot guy, meet at a bar and end up falling in love. There's like a million songs about it."

She makes it sound reasonable. She makes it sound possible. She makes this little hope inside my heart start to glow a bit brighter.

"You really don't think this is crazy?"

"I think you'd be crazy if you let this opportunity pass you by," she sasses. More earnestly, she says, "Don't let the life you had or the one you have keep you from discovering a completely new and unexpected one that might be everything you've ever dreamed of. I could've stayed stuck in my addiction and been six feet under years ago. I could've told Frank no when he asked me for a cigarette, and I'd still be working at that gas station. But I risked it all . . . on me, on him, and on us. And look at me now." Her smile is bracketed by lines that show the hard life she lived in her younger days as well as the easy one she's enjoyed since then.

"You do look great," I tell her honestly. "Happy, which is what matters."

"Exactly." She peers at me like she's reading my mind. "What else is holding you back? Hit me with it." She waves her hand in a gimme motion.

"I'm scared." The confession is ripped from my soul, a weakness I'd rather not have at all, but definitely don't want to admit.

"Of what?"

"Everything." I sigh. "Myself, him, Tyler. All of it. Of getting my heart broken again."

Trina presses her lips together, disappointment written in the smoker's lines around her mouth. "You survived," she says. Then she repeats it. "You survived."

I shake my head because she makes it sound like I went through something awful with Tyler, and while yes, he messed up my head, it wasn't that bad. It could've been worse. I've always been thankful it wasn't because getting out of the crap he put me through was hard enough.

"You didn't deserve any of Tyler's bullshittery, but you survived," she says again, not letting me step away from that. "And since then, you've done well for yourself, living in the 'after' of everything, the pocket of time where you shut down, protect yourself, and try to process what you've been through." She dips down, forcing me to meet her eyes. "It's time to leave that mental fortress, babe. It's time to live. Not in the after, just in your life. Taking a chance on Dominic is gonna bring up all that hurt, like bubbles in your belly that make you feel like it's all happening again even though it's not. You've got to push past that fear. Your life is on the other side of the reflexive panic. Maybe with Dominic, maybe with someone else, maybe just on your own, but the risk is worth it. For your own growth."

I stare at the lettuce in my hands, letting her words soak into my brain. I don't know if I'm strong enough to listen to her, much less to actually do what she's suggesting. Finally I ask, "How'd you get to be so smart?"

She huffs out a humorless laugh. "Therapy. Loads of it in rehab. It was actually really helpful then, and sometimes, it comes back to me when I need it."

Trina is quiet, letting me process, waiting to see what other roadblocks I can come up with to stop what's inevitable. Because the truth is, I do want to try with Dominic. As fear-filled as I am, I think I'm at a point to at least one pinkie-toe, baby step try.

"You're right. I'm gonna go for it. I'm gonna do it." I'm not sure who said that, but given the way Trina is staring open-mouthed at me, I think it was . . . me?

"Do him, you mean," she teases, instantly lightening the mood from the heaviness of our conversation so I don't fall back into the abyss that's always there, ready to take me into the dark.

"Trina!"

"What? I'm old, not dead."

"You are neither of those things." I lean her way, resting my head on her shoulder for a moment. "Thank you."

"Aww, any time, girl. Just remember, I want the whole story. Every dirty detail."

I don't have to look at her to know she's grinning. The funny thing is, so am I.

# Chapter 17

## Dominic

I have a proven daily routine that I stick to during hockey season—green smoothies every morning, lean protein for lunch and dinner, stretching, strength and speed training on the opposite side of lunch on practice days, sauna and cold plunge time. Except for game days, of course.

But one of the pluses of being a professional athlete is that my day-to-day schedule can be relatively flexible unless there's a mandatory practice or a game. For example, if I want to play golf at noon on a Thursday, I can. Chalk it up to "stretching."

I'm looking for Briar right now of course, but also, I want to get to know her world a bit better. Which is why I'm reading every plaque and sign around every exhibit, learning about the animals she cares about so much.

When I find myself in front of the gibbons, knowing they're Briar's favorites, I watch them a bit closer. They're sitting, almost seeming bored despite the plethora of toys surrounding them. No, not toys. Briar calls them enrichments. But Caprice and the other gibbons aren't engaging with the ropes, trees, balls, and tires in the enclosure.

I look left and right, seeing that there's no one around given it's midday, midweek. Gary's not even at the little wooden hut-table combo he calls his *post*, ready to dispense education like the teacher he told me he used to be.

I throw my head back and . . . *"Whoop whoop whoop whoop!"* I screech, just like Briar did. The gibbons' response is instant, their attention locking on me before one calls back, then another and another, until they're a chorus of car alarm–sounding singing. I laugh and sing along with them, feeling like we've made each other's day a little brighter.

"I thought something was wrong," a breathless voice says behind me. I turn to find Briar bent over, hands on her knees. Her cheeks are flushed and she's panting like she ran here.

"Oh, uh . . . sorry," I stammer. "I was trying to play with them the way you did."

Her brows furrow. "You were playing with them?" she echoes. "Why?"

"They looked bored?" It'd seemed perfectly logical a minute ago, but I'm doubting myself now. What do I know about gibbons? Not much, I realize.

Slowly, a smile starts to lift Briar's lips, and then she starts laughing. "When I heard them, I thought a hawk had flown into the enclosure again. It only happened once, but I'll never forget the sound they made." She shakes her head, looking haunted, and I'm honestly not sure if the hawk won or the gibbons did, or if they were equally freaked out by the others' existence. "And with Caprice's baby getting more comfortable on her own, the whole group is extra protective right now."

"Sorry," I say, understanding why she looked so panicked.

She waves me off, no longer upset. "They're usually calm this time of day. They're not hungry, it's after morning playtime, so they chill in the sun." Her eyes are on the gibbons, checking each one out from afar, and then she glances back to me, equally analytical. "What are you doing here?"

I could be coy, but why bother? This woman has me by the short hairs and we both know it. "I came to see you."

"Me?" She looks genuinely surprised, like being with her is somehow akin to a visit to the dentist.

"I have away games coming up and am already missing you, so like a complete sap, I thought I'd come to the place I knew you'd be, and walk around, hoping for a glimpse of you. Maybe get the chance to say hello. So . . . hello?" I pause, hearing myself for the first time. Some people would be calling me a simp at this point, but fuck them. For Briar? Simptown, population: me. "As I say it now, I realize how stalkerish that sounds. I can go—" I point behind me, willing to walk away but hoping she doesn't want me to.

"No!" she says brightly. "It's okay."

I step into her, cutting the space between us in half. "It is?" I ask, my voice low and husky. She looks up at me, her eyes filled with something that seems like shyness. But this woman isn't shy. She's brave and bold, not in a loud, in your face way, but in her own quiet way.

Her hands fidget like she's stopping them from doing what they'd actually like to do. Touch me, maybe? Fuck, I hope so. I reach out, taking one to weave our fingers together. Her hand is warm in mine and her lips instantly lift.

"Do you get a lunch break or something?" I ask. "Maybe I could eat with you?"

*Or eat you out. Whichever.*

I have spent days, and quite a few nights, thinking about this woman, fantasizing about her, and the urge to taste Briar's mouth, her skin, and—fuck me—her pussy is riding me hard. I won't lie, either, I've been waking up most mornings harder than a hockey stick, images of her still in my mind as I untangle myself from my sticky, precum-dampened sheets, only to finish the job with her name on my lips. Still, I try to maintain some semblance of public decency despite the images running through my mind.

"I have a better idea," she says with an arch of one brow. "Want to help me with the animals? Like behind the scenes?"

I'm well aware of my savior complex, not that I've done a damn thing about it. In fact, right this minute, I want to help her any way she'll let me. But yeah, we can start with the animals. "Let me guess, the fountain needs clearing out again?" I tease, already resigned to the loss of my tennis shoes, which will end up in the trash like the other pair did. There's just no washing bird shit out of Nikes.

"No," she says, laughing along. "But this might be just as messy and smell just as bad."

"You're really selling me on this idea," I deadpan. But the truth is, she is. I'd do damn near anything to spend a few more minutes with her.

Apparently, that includes shoveling elephant shit, because that's exactly what we do. And let me tell you, Earl the ten-year-old Asiatic bull elephant might be a spa-day prince, but he is not particular about where he relieves himself. There's not one pile that's easy to clean up. There are mounds throughout his inside enclosure that have to be scooped, scrubbed away, and then washed out. With a fire hose.

And then we do the same thing to the rhinoceros area. And then the giraffes, cheetahs, and hippos.

And that's just the Wilds of Africa section of the zoo. Apparently, this is a daily quick clean, too, not the deeper scrub-down each enclosure routinely requires. That involves brushes with plastic bristles that look like they could pierce flesh.

"Is this what you do all day?" I ask as we finish the hippo enclosure.

Briar swipes her hair back from her forehead with her arm, making sure she doesn't touch anything with her gloved hands. "Pretty much. Feed, clean, care for the animals. Why? Is it not as glamorous as you thought it'd be?" She strikes a pose, one hand on her apron-covered hip and the other flicked into the air like she's a model, which might be believable with her good looks, except I'm reasonably certain the latest fashion trend isn't dust-covered polo shirts, cargo shorts, and knee-high muck boots. Or maybe it is? I wouldn't know. All I know is that on Briar, it looks good. So does the faux pout she's trying to maintain, but her naturally infectious smile keeps busting through. "Glamour is my middle name, ya know?"

She thinks I'm judging her, but I'm not. Not at all. Smiling in surprised awe, I tell her, "You've been working your ass off all day, but I don't think you've said one bad thing the whole time. No whining, no frowning, nothing. You love this."

Her real smile slowly appears on her face, like she's not sure she can trust my words. "I do. This is what I always dreamed of doing."

From anyone else, it'd sound sarcastic. I mean, who dreams of sweating in the afternoon heat, covered in rubberized protective gear, getting misted by what's likely some sketchy splashback, while picking up actual shit, for what I'd argue is most definitely not enough money? But looking at the happy glow on Briar's face, she's completely genuine.

The truth is, Briar hasn't been just *not complaining*. She's working her magic, leaving pixie dust behind with every step. It's like everything she touches—with her hands, her attention, her heart—is better for her presence. Each area we enter, the animals scurry over to greet her as soon as she calls out to them. If there's a guest who looks interested, she happily shares her vast knowledge with them. She waves at children, makes smoochie noises at animals, and romanticizes even hard labor into whimsical fun with songs and some pretty interesting dance moves with a shovel.

And I feel like a bastard who accidentally lucked into the best day ever, all because of her.

Leaning into her, I smack her on the lips. Just a quick kiss that's over nearly before it starts, but I need to feel the happiness that bubbles out of her. "You are so beautiful." She blinks, surprise in her eyes. I move to her ear to add, "And sexy."

I'm close enough to hear her breath hitch, and fuck, that makes me want her that much more. I want to make her lose her breath completely, steal it away into my own lungs so I can share it back with her. Her body leans into mine, and I'm at least 50 percent sure it's unconscious. I'm not sure she's even aware of how her chest presses against mine, but I am acutely aware of the soft fullness behind the creak of her plastic apron.

And while I realize how unsexy that should be, I am utterly and completely gone for this woman. Unexpected and inconvenient as it may be, it's true. I'm seeing life with her at my side, listening to random animal facts, watching her spread sunshine everywhere she goes, and reassuring her when her demons try to whisper in her ear.

But her protective walls are still up, tall as ever around her heart. I have to be patient. That hasn't changed. At least not for her.

"Here, let me get the rest of this." I pick up the shovel and scoop a few more piles of hippo poop into the wheelbarrow. It's the easiest way to relieve some of the physical need inside me right now.

I'm putting my energies into manual labor and trying my best to hold myself back from her, like the gentleman I'd like her to think I am. Don't get me wrong, I have manners. My parents made sure of that. But the things I want to do to Briar are not gentlemanly in the slightest.

This is how you romance a woman like Briar. Not with poetry and sonnets, but by hauling a heavy wheelbarrow full of dung with her.

Briar has started singing will.i.am's "Big and Chunky" into her shovel handle again, making hippo cleanup my new favorite part of today because this song comes with some butt shaking that she probably thinks is silly, but looks damn sexy to me.

Briar leans the shovel handle my way and, on cue, I chime in with my part of the song.

When she smiles, I feel like I could do this forever.

"Dom?" I see my name on Harley's lips as Briar walks out of the school's front doors with him. And then he's running toward the car, all school rules temporarily forgotten.

I open the door, getting out to greet him and crossing onto the sidewalk just to make sure he doesn't plow into someone in his excitement. "Hey, kid. How was school?"

"Who cares? What're you doing here? Do we have practice?" In his excitement, the words rush out as one long, run-on sentence.

"No, Dominic helped me at the zoo today, so I promised him dinner as a thank-you," Briar explains.

"Pizza?" he asks, peering at Briar hopefully.

Instead of answering, she gives him one of the head-tilty mom looks that silently says *absolutely not and you know better than to ask so why did you*. I can't help but grin.

"I was thinking spaghetti and meatball tacos," Briar tells Harley.

Obviously, I know what spaghetti and meatballs are. I know what tacos are too. But the word combination Briar just said does not make sense in the slightest. "Huh?"

Harley has all but forgotten his pizza idea as he rushes to explain that Briar's going to put noodles and meatballs inside a French bread shell that they eat like a taco, hence spaghetti and meatball tacos.

"That sounds . . . interesting?" I say, not sure if it's extra efficient or extra messy, but figuring I'll find out.

In the end, it's actually both in equal measure.

Harley has sauce spread across his face in an approximation of the Joker's smile, and I'd bet there's some up his nose too. I had a meatball fall into my lap, leaving a red smear on my pants that Briar had automatically tried to wipe up, but then she'd squeaked in embarrassment when she realized just how close to my meatballs she was. And now, Briar is grinning at us both like we're ridiculous. But dinner is delicious. I'm more carbed up than I'd typically be prior to a game, but it's all good.

"Shower time," she tells Harley, motioning to her face in a reminder that he needs to do an extra thorough cleaning. "It's a school night."

Harley starts to leave the kitchen, but pauses to look back at me uncertainly. "You'll be here when I get out, right?"

Nodding, I assure him easily. "Of course."

I'm still staring at the doorway where he left when Briar says, "It's good for him to see that." I turn my attention to her, my brows lifted. She licks her lips before hesitantly explaining, "Tyler always says he'll do something and then doesn't. I know how much that hurts, so I make sure to always keep my promises to him. No matter how big or small. You saying you'll be here and then actually staying might seem like no big deal, but it's important to Harley."

It's important to Briar, too, but she doesn't say that. She doesn't have to. I can see it on her face, can feel it in the set of her shoulders.

"I'm not going anywhere, unless you tell me to. And even then"—I put a doubtful look on my face—"I'm a bit harder to get rid of than that. My family calls me persistent. Pretty sure it's pure pigheadedness, though." I say it as though it's the compliment that I consider it to be. My refusal to be put off easily is what made me the athlete I am, and also, what's made me the man I am.

I get up from the table, taking my plate and grabbing hers and Harley's too. I dump the bread end that Harley left into the trash and then start rinsing the dishes for the dishwasher.

"What are you doing?"

I glance over my shoulder, realizing that Briar has stood up from the table and is staring at me like I'm an alien. "Washing the dishes?" I say, confused by her confusion.

"Why?"

I blink, looking around for some context clues about why she's asking why I'm doing dishes when they obviously need to be done. "Because we ate on them?" I say hesitantly.

"You're just doing the dishes," she replies, making it sound like I'm doing something remarkable.

"Yeah, you cooked, I'm cleaning up. It's the least I can do."

My words register in my own head as I say them and I realize why she's reacting so oddly. She does everything. She does it all on her own, and she always has. I'd bet that even when she was married, Tyler never lifted a finger.

Giving her a pointed look, I say plainly, "This is literally the bare minimum." The reminder of our previous conversation is clear. "This isn't special and I don't need you to mother me. Save that for Harley. I cook for myself, clean my own place, and am an entirely functional adult." I chuckle as I say it, surprised those are actual points in my favor.

"You have no idea how attractive that is," she admits, letting out a tiny laugh as she props her chin on her hand and stares at me in awe.

"You can say it . . . you think I'm sexy," I tease, shooting her an exaggerated wink. To prove my point, I dramatically scrub the plate in my hand, making *ooh* and *aah* faces to make it seem downright sexual. She laughs at my antics, but that adorable pink rushes to her cheeks.

As she gets up, bringing our glasses to the sink, I tell her, "I also remember birthdays, will buy you flowers, and open every door for you. Though that's not because I'm nice, it's because I want to see your ass as often as possible." I grin wolfishly as I lean back from the sink to peer at said curves. "Who knew those damn khaki shorts would do it for me. Give me a spin."

She laughs nervously, but with her eyes locked on me, she does a slow turn, giving me a better view. I groan in appreciation. "Fuck, Briar."

"You're ridiculous," she says, pushing on my arm. Her touch sears me, and I want to kill the asshole who ever made her doubt her beauty, her sexiness, her spirit, her amazingness. She thinks I'm kidding, and maybe cargo shorts wouldn't be hot on anyone else, but on Briar, anything she wears, anything she does, everything she says, it's all catnip to me. And I'm addicted.

As I scrub the spaghetti pot, she watches me. "I used to want Tyler to do the dishes—I'd even flat-out ask him to—but he never did. It was all me. And now you're doing things like helping me at work, eating dinner with us, and cleaning up like it's nothing. You don't even think it matters, but it does. So much."

"If it means more time with you, a smile on your face, a lighter load on your shoulders," I tell her honestly, my sponge swirling to get out a stubborn spot of stuck-on tomato, "I'm happy to help."

"It's hard to let you," she blurts out.

"Let me do the dishes?" I set the scrubber down in the sink and turn off the water. Drying my hands on a towel, I turn to lean against the counter, giving her my full attention. Her eyes fall to the floor, where the toe of her boot is sweeping back and forth nervously. "Can you explain that?"

She's quiet for a long minute. So long that I think she's not going to answer, but I wait. I stand there, still as a statue, putting no pressure on her, but hopefully, reassuring her with my presence. She's skittish—a by-product of her ex, I'm sure—and I don't want to do anything that'll trigger her, especially when we've had such a great day and I feel like I can see daylight through the tiny crack she's peeking through.

And slowly, her breathing settles. Her foot stops moving. Her shoulders drop. Her chin lifts. And finally, her eyes find mine and I feel like time stops existing. The only thing that matters is the haunted look in her pretty blue eyes.

"I've never had anyone do these things with me, much less do them for me. So when you do, I worry that I'm going to fall into the ease of it and forget how to do it all on my own."

"What if you don't have to do it on your own?" I ask gently.

She shakes her head. I think it's an entirely unconscious rejection of my words. "Eventually, I will. I'll cook dinner, clean, get groceries, tuck Harley in, pick up the living room, mop the kitchen, turn off the lights, and go to bed . . . alone."

She waves her hand around as she lists out her nightly routine. To her, it's just a Thursday evening, same as Monday, Tuesday, Wednesday, and every other day. To me, I'm taking notes of where I can insert myself to give her a moment of existence where she's not checking something off a perpetual to-do list.

"And I'm used to that," she says. "Doing it on my own. So letting you do the dishes is hard because what if I forget how, and when I have to do it alone again, it's even harder because it's a reminder of when I didn't have to." Her eyes lift to the ceiling before finding me again. "It feels like you're chipping away my foundation, showing me that maybe I built it wrong. That maybe it was built wrong for me and I just kept building on those misplaced stones. But if I take it all back to the ground, let it all crumble around me, I'll have to rebuild everything and that's terrifying."

"Because what if I leave then too?" I finish the thought she doesn't and her eyes go glittery with tears that gut me.

I wrap my arms around her, not only holding her but holding her broken pieces together. I feel the wetness of her tears through my shirt where her face is smushed against me. Running my hand over her hair, I say quietly, "There's another option, though. What if I stay and it doesn't have to be so hard, so heavy? What if you don't have to do it alone because I want to do it with you? Dishes, groceries, laundry, taking care of Harley, taking care of you. All of it."

"Why?" Her voice is muffled by my chest.

I could give her platitudes about it being how I was raised, because my dad has never once sat in the living room recliner, expecting my mother to wait on him hand and foot. I could say it's because she's beautiful and interesting and deserves it. And all that's true. But I don't, because that's not the heart of why I'm here right now. She's being intimately vulnerable with me, so I return the gift.

"Because I need to be needed," I say simply. "Protecting people isn't what I do. It's who I am. On the ice, with teammates, and in my family, with my parents, my sister, my friends. I see people so easily, sometimes in ways they don't want me to—" I huff out a laugh at what feels like a complete understatement. I know how Griffin responded to me dragging him out of his comfort zone (poorly), how Kipson is reacting (angrily), and even how Briar is trying to pull away from me now (scared). "I see the things they need so clearly, and I want to help. Helping feeds something in me, makes me feel like I'm worth something, like I have value because of what I can do for them."

She looks up at me, her eyes wide. "You don't have to—"

I don't let her tell me I don't have to do these things because she's wrong. I do. I see myself clearly, too, and I do need to help. It's what makes my existence feel meaningful. I'm not some genius who's going to change the world. I'm not going to be a person in any history book. Even with hockey, the one thing I'm really good at, I'll be a trivia question at best, a line item on a team roster at worst. I don't have a Hall of Fame–level career, but that doesn't matter.

Briar does.

I can have an impact on the people around me. For good or for bad, and I try to choose for good every single time.

So I shake my head and say, "Yes, I do. And now, I find myself wanting to protect the little drop of sunshine in your center more than I want to breathe because it is so damn stunning when you let it shine. It makes me feel like I had some small part in making you feel safe enough to share that with the world. With me."

Her eyes are peering into mine, jumping left and right like she's looking for the trick or the lie or trying to figure out the manipulation, but there's only honesty here. I press a kiss to her lips, and then I whisper, "Let me do the dishes so you can shine."

Her smile is my new favorite. It's full of hope and, for the first time since I met her, relief.

"I'm going to start a load of laundry," she says quietly. It's not quite the shine I was hoping for, but it's a start.

And by the time Harley's shower water turns off, the kitchen is clean, the washer is running, the living room is picked up, and Briar and I are sitting on the couch, kissing. Luckily, Harley has heavy footsteps so we stop before he comes in, but his eyes still bounce from Briar to me, and he seems pretty aware of what he interrupted. "Dom, can you tuck me in again?"

"Absolutely," I tell him, getting up.

Are we playing house? Yes. Am I loving every bit of it? Also yes. Briar and Harley are a set, one I'm falling for more and more with each passing minute.

# Chapter 18

## Dominic

"What's the plan?" Rodney asks, launching himself at the bed in my hotel room. He bounces three times before coming to a stop with his feet hanging off the side and his head propped up on a hand.

"First, get off my bed," I snap. But I'm grinning, glad he's comfortable with me, but truly not wanting his germs where I'm going to sleep tonight. "Group meeting in the lobby in fifteen, then dinner." I hold up my phone where I just texted the team group chat tonight's agenda.

He nods respectfully, climbing up from the bed and even dusting it off. "On it." But he pauses at the door, glancing over his shoulder, "Think Kipson will come?"

I don't know.

Kipson and Anderson have had it out since the season opener, with some pushing and shoving in the locker room, but also a lot of harsh words, and I'm not sure whatever friendship—and I'm using the word loosely—they had will ever be repaired.

"Hope so. He's gotta eat, so there's a chance."

Rodney holds up his crossed fingers as he steps into the hall, and I swing the door closed behind him.

With a sigh, I look to the ceiling for divine intervention, telling myself, "Keep at it, Lee." I'm doing my best to create some camaraderie in this team, but it feels like using a plastic spoon to dig up concrete with how set in their ways these guys are.

I pull on jeans and a button-down and head downstairs, hoping to not have dinner alone. When the elevator doors open, I'm shocked at the gathering waiting there—Rodney, Tomville, Bill, Sabine, Pacholek, Anderson, Kipson, plus several other players. At least half the team is sprawled across the couches and chairs and sitting on the coffee tables and end tables. I scan the group, shocked to my core.

"Hey . . . everyone," I say haltingly.

"Hope you made reservations," Kipson tells me. The *dumbass* on the end is silent, but there all the same in his tone.

Considering I was reasonably sure only a few guys might come, I most definitely did not make reservations. Still, I nod cockily, feigning confidence I don't have. "Yeah, let's check out the hotel restaurant."

Surely they can get us in?

Thankfully, they do, leading us to a table in the out-of-sight back corner since we're not dressed to fit their jackets-required dress code. The waiter's face stays perfectly stoic, giving no reaction to having this many large, already too-loud guys at his table.

"Chicken breast, seasonal vegetables, light sauce," I order. I notice that Rodney, Tomville, and Bill are all listening to me and then repeat the same order, though Tomville requests a double serving of chicken. Afterward, they glance at me and I reward them with a small dip of my chin, acknowledging their good choices.

"They just do whatever you tell them to, don't they?" Anderson sneers. "Like little puppies on a chain, following the big dog around."

My face hard and jaw set to stone, I cut cold eyes his way. "Woof. Woof," I say flatly, letting my voice go low and dark.

The air charges between us and I take the measure from me to him on the other side of the white tablecloth–covered surface. He knows I'm the one who told Kipson what he said about Sofia, and since he has less than zero chances of winning against a brokenhearted beast with nothing to lose like Kipson, Anderson has decided that redirecting his anger toward the messenger—yours truly—is the next best thing. Only problem with that plan is, he can try to start shit with me, but I'm more than ready to dish it back out to him.

As far as I'm concerned, if Coach is problem number one, setting the tone for the team, Anderson is problem number two, enacting Coach's missives.

"I'll have the chicken too," Pacholek says, holding up a hand to get the waiter's attention. He's trying to insert himself and slow this runaway freight train. But this standoff has been coming since that first night at O'Neal's. It's not about Kipson. It's about the whole team.

I'm changing things around here, which means I now hold a power Anderson mistakenly thinks I took from him. Newsflash: He never had real power because he treats this team like a frat, never taking anything seriously until it's time to hit the ice. His influence has existed in a vacuum, a vacuum that I'm filling. I take it all seriously—practices, games, on the ice, off the ice, and most importantly, every single man sitting around this table.

I send text messages in the group chat, have conversations that go beyond "good game, bro," and offer some guidance about our beloved sport, especially to the new guys who are acclimating to a whole different level of hockey. And the mere fact that this many teammates showed up tonight speaks to how well it's working.

Unless they're here to watch Anderson kick my ass. Admittedly, that's a possibility too.

The waiter clears his throat and Anderson grunts in annoyance, breaking our staredown to order, "Steak, rare. Fries on the side." The waiter arches a brow, as much of a tell as he can probably give in fine dining, before disappearing.

The momentary reprieve lets me do a quick check of the table. Most everyone is watching Anderson with wariness, like he's the loose cannon they're worried about. I don't think they would jump to my defense if push came to shove, he's been here too long for that, but they're starting to see what I see in our goalie—immaturity, unpredictability, volatility. He's the poster child for what's wrong with the Blizzard.

Food ordered, Anderson returns his narrowed eyes to me, glaring angrily. He feels the change, too, both in the team and at the table. Unbothered, I let an evil smirk lift my lips, and give voice to the situation. "Feel that shift? Come over to the dark side, man. We've got snacks and braid each other's hair on Sundays." I shake my head a bit, letting my hair rise and fall back into place.

Should I poke him this way? Probably not. But it's so easy and he takes the bait so readily, which only highlights his inability to emotionally regulate better than a toddler.

"You're supposed to fix Kipson, not fuck the whole team up," he bites out.

"I don't need fixing," Kipson snarls, sounding on the verge of grabbing Anderson by the neck and tossing him to the ground, *Mortal Kombat* style.

*Finish him.*

There's a small piece of me that wants Kipson to do it. It would definitely make things easier without Anderson. Might even help Kipson get out of this mental state he's in. I won't deny that, but he's a product of the team's rotten roots, too, living up to the standards Coach sets. Which means, in theory, I should try to save him too. But maybe I could let Kipson at him first? Nothing serious, a few punches resulting in a little blood, ideally internal, or an unimportant bone break that won't affect the season, like a couple of toes that could be buddy taped, but would be an annoying reminder with every step?

"You've been moping around for months, ruining the playoffs last season and barely holding it together this year. For what?" Anderson shoots back at Kipson, thumping his fist on the table. "Some bitch left you. Boo fucking hoo, man. And if the depression wasn't bad enough, now this prick"—he points a thick finger at me—"has you wanting to fight everyone. If you'd kept your shit together like you were supposed to, he wouldn't even be here!"

"I don't want to fight everyone," Kipson corrects, leaning forward. "Just you."

His cold glare is locked on Anderson. I'd bet he can't even see the rest of the guys at the table. He's definitely not aware of the three guys between them who have scooted their chairs back to be at the ready if they actually go after one another. Only three because I'm on Kipson's other side and I will not be stopping a damn thing if he goes after Anderson. I consider it well deserved.

"You know the rules—no distractions."

"Sofia wasn't a distraction. She was my WIFE!" Kipson roars as he slams his palms to the table, making the water glasses and cutlery bounce. And oh, we've got the attention of everyone in the place now, from the staff to the well-dressed diners.

"*Was* being the operative word, there," Anderson taunts, playing Russian roulette with his life.

"My *wife*. Do you have any idea what that means?" he demands. "Of course you don't. How could you? You can't even remember the name of the last woman you fucked." Judgment drips through his tone, the words harshly spit out with an up and down sneering glare.

"Daphne." Anderson flashes an arrogant smirk of victory. But is he even telling the truth? Who knows.

"Congratulations. Another empty, meaningless fuck in your empty, meaningless life." Kipson rolls his eyes and Anderson chuckles, unaffected by the accusation, until Kipson coldly spits out, "If I gave a shit about you at all, I'd pity you."

Anderson balks. That one stung. I think Kipson plainly stating his complete indifference to him might be the straw to break the camel's back and actually cause Anderson's bravado to drop a few notches. "I don't need your pity. I'm doing just fine. Better than you, for damn sure."

"Keep telling yourself that." The fire is dying in Kipson, replaced with his too familiar detachment. "But I'm empty right now because I knew love and lost it. You're empty because no one has ever loved you. We're not the same."

Well, daaaamn. Kipson's got some self-awareness in that thick skull of his. Who knew? Not me.

"I don't need this bullshit," Anderson announces, shoving back from the table. "Fix your shit or bench yourself so you don't fuck the rest of us over," he orders Kipson. Turning toward me, he points accusingly, clearly hurt but disguising it with anger. "And you, leave me the fuck alone."

"So that's a maybe for the hair braiding on Sunday?" I taunt.

"Fuck all of you," Anderson hisses and then stomps away. At the host stand, I hear him tell the maître d' to send his steak up to his room. At least he'll eat well tonight. We do have a game tomorrow, and I'd rather him not play at a calorie deficit.

"That went well," I declare, stroking my day's worth of stubble as I nod approvingly. "Could've done with a bit more bromance and a touch less blowup, but not bad overall. It's a solid start."

Almost a dozen sets of eyes turn to me, some with humor, others with shock, a few with concerns about my sanity.

Pacholek is first to make fresh steps on the groundwork I've laid. "I'm sorry about you and Sofia," he tells Kipson. "If I can do anything to help . . ." He trails off, but the offer is an important one.

Kipson blinks, staring blankly at Pacholek for a long moment, where I wonder if he's going to tell Pacholek to keep his wife's name out of his mouth too. But after a deep breath, he says, "Do you know that's the first time any of you have told me that?"

He scans the group of guys sitting around the table, several of them ducking their heads and unable to meet his eyes. The pall of that hangs in the air, a pain that predates my arrival, but the past needs to be dealt with so that we can move forward as a team with a future worth a damn.

"I didn't know what to say," Pacholek explains, "but I should've at least said 'I'm sorry.' I apologize for not doing that."

Holy shit! I'm a fucking genius!

I should take up sports psychology once I retire from the ice because I'm fucking good at this shit. We're having group therapy, right here in the restaurant. I'm tempted to ask, *And how did that make you feel?* just to see what happens.

"Yeah, you fucking should've. Or maybe not been such a dick to her in the first place," Kipson snarls.

Okay, maybe my next career consideration was a bit premature. But progress is a good thing, even if it's slow.

"We weren't trying to be dicks. It's just how it is," Sabine says resolutely.

This is an important step that I don't want to mess up. Pacholek is on my side and doing better, but Sabine has been Anderson's bro for a long time. I lean forward, getting Sabine's attention. "How it *was*. Just because it's always been that way, doesn't mean it was right. Look at the fallout." I gesture to Kipson. "Nor does it mean it has to keep being like that. Change can be good, like scratching that itch you can't quite reach." I mime trying to scratch my spine and when I can't reach, I tilt toward Kipson with a grunted, "Little help here?"

He smacks my back, hard. Coughing, I grin at him, taking the win.

"So what, you're saying we all need to find WAGs, like yesterday?" Lavoie asks, seeming confused at the concept of a committed relationship.

I roll my eyes, inhaling for patience. "No, fuckwit. I'm saying that having a life off the ice that's fulfilling makes you a better player, not a distracted one."

"Where's your girlfriend then, Lee?" Lavoie quips back.

Ooh, that's dangerous territory that I'm not ready to explore with these guys yet. I give him my trademark cocky grin, "I just got here. What's your excuse?"

Bill clears his throat. "I have a confession to make." That instantly draws all attention his way. "I'm married."

All the air is sucked out of the space around us as we stare at him incredulously. I've done extensive homework on every teammate and nowhere have I seen a single mention of him being married. Yet, he apparently has a whole, entire wife that he's been hiding?

"What the fuck?"

"Is she real? Dolls don't count, man."

Bill grins. "She's real. Been married just over two years. She kept her name because she's a doctor."

Another shoe drops.

"A doctor?"

Pacholek hoots. "Ooh, Bill got himself a sugar mama!"

The teasing doesn't stop, but Bill takes it all in stride, bragging proudly about his wife before finally pulling up a picture on his phone. His wife is gorgeous, which means the teasing starts all over again about how a guy like Bill pulled a woman like that.

I'm grinning, feeling like I've done some real good here, when Kipson leans my way and rumbles, "I still hate you."

I whisper back, "Aww, love you too."

And the best part is . . . he doesn't say "fuck you." And that is true progress.

"Dinner the same time tomorrow?" Sabine asks as we head back upstairs after dinner.

"Yep, I'll even make reservations this time." I think we'll need them because given tonight's success, I'm hoping even more of the team shows up tomorrow.

# Chapter 19

## Briar

"I feel like a penguin. Waddle, waddle, waddle," Dominic grumbles, yanking on his tie, which actually makes it more crooked than it was before he messed with it.

"It could be worse. We have an actual penguin costume if you'd prefer?" I offer, straightening it for him. "It's only had a dozen or so people sweat in it before, so I'm sure it's fine. Definitely better than a suit. Want me to grab it for you?" I blink innocently, as though it's a genuine offer.

He arches a dark brow, not pleased with me, nor his current attire. "Just not much of a suit type." He's shifting his shoulders, pulling on his cuffs, and smoothing his tie, obviously uncomfortable.

"Well, it's for a good cause," I say airily, glancing around to check on the rest of the Blizzard players.

They're all here and I can't believe I pulled this off. Dominic, Anderson, Sabine, Pacholek, Kipson, Rodney, and Tomville are all hiding in a too-small concession stand kitchen with me and Trina, waiting for the announcement of our special guests at tonight's event.

Some zoos hold big, spectacular galas with black-tie tuxedos and gowns, flowing champagne, and catered appetizers invisibly passed by waitstaff. We're not that kind of place. The Berkshire Zoo runs on a shoestring budget and can't afford that type of event, so instead, tonight's fundraiser will be in our outdoor picnic area, where we've hung strands of twinkly Christmas lights, set out pumpkin-focused centerpieces (which will be chopped up for animal treats tomorrow), and created several areas of fall-themed fun, like a small-scale hay maze, apple toss, and scarecrow photo ops.

Lucky for me, zoo employees are wearing our nicest uniforms because we're to mingle with the guests, talk about the animals housed here, and highlight how donated funds will be used to improve things. So I'm comfortably rocking out in my khaki pants and logo'd button-down shirt. Très chic.

"I don't know, Lee," Anderson says, "I make this look good." Anderson is standing at attention, ready to step out into the crowd, and from the neck down, he's right. His suit is perfectly tailored and pristine, and he does look dapper. But his face? The sneer he shoots at Dominic is pure antagonism. Dom could say the sky is blue and grass is green and Anderson would argue just to be contrary.

I'm not sure what Dad told them about tonight, but I appreciate that they're here, as long as they don't ruin the whole thing with their infighting, which seems like a pretty distinct possibility. Of course, Dad didn't come. I knew he wouldn't. But there was a little piece of me that hoped anyway.

"Actually, you do," Dominic agrees with him. "You look slick as elephant shit."

He cuts his eyes to me, a tiny smirk on his lips. Elephant dung isn't slick at all. It's thick, filled with hay pieces, and actually really useful as fuel for campfires out on the savannah. Not that Anderson would know that, but Dominic does. He listened to me give a whole educational lecture on it while we cleaned.

Was that only a week ago?

Time has flown by. After leaving that night, Dominic had games that weekend so he was focused on team activities. But Harley and I watched the games on television, cheering the Blizzard—and Dominic—on. Dominic practiced with Harley once on Monday, but flew out for midweek games in New York. True to his word, though, he didn't bail on me. He called, video chatting as he celebrated two successful pregame dinners that hadn't sounded all that successful to me, but I'm not great at understanding the male psyche, and one winning game along with a tie, which means points in hockey. He also sent me a bouquet of yellow daisies with a card stating *simply Thinking of you—D*, and he's taking me home tonight after the zoo event.

And Harley is at Tyler's this weekend.

Dominic's words about spending a whole weekend worshipping me float back into my mind. This is the weekend. I've already decided. I'm nervous, but ready.

The guys rustle around, shoulder bumping each other in the tight space. "Watch it," Anderson snarls.

"You're standing on my toe," someone says, though I'm not sure who.

"Whoever's dick is touching my butt needs to back the fuck off." Given his smirk, that was definitely Dominic, but his back is to the wall and no one is behind him at all.

Trina stage-whispers, "Be ready, boys. In three, two, one . . . go, go, go!" She waves at them to follow her, and dutifully, they do, though Anderson and Kipson throw elbows a bit, jockeying for position. I'm not sure what to think about them. Dominic says they're slightly closer to possibly beginning to not hate each other completely, but I don't see it. The thirty minutes in the claustrophobic kitchen with them felt like someone lit a stick of dynamite and we were standing around twiddling our thumbs while the fuse burned. But so far, no explosions.

Dominic hangs back, stepping into line right in front of me. The look he shoots me is filled with heat, making me think he might've been reading my mind about what's happening later.

Blush heating my cheeks, we enter the party to applause. It's not the roaring claps they're used to when they hit the ice, but rather the polite claps of the wealthy who've come to donate their dollars for the tax write-off. Though there are quite a few true fans it seems, holding baby-blue Blizzard jerseys and posters in preparation for the players' autographs.

The guys wave at the crowd as they come in, staying behind Trina as she leads them to a table set off to one side. "Line up," she tells people who start to move toward her. "This isn't a feeding frenzy. That comes later." She winks at a family who's made sure they're first in line. "During the scavenger hunt."

The meet and greet lasts for nearly an hour, and to my surprise, the guys are pretty good sports about the whole thing. They're friendly and charming, smiling for pictures, signing autographs, and thanking people for coming out to support the Blizzard and the zoo.

It feels like the first part of my plan is working—the fundraising aspect. But I haven't forgotten the reason I came up with this idea in the first place—Dominic's need for team-building.

"If I could have everyone's attention, please," Carl, our CEO and president, says into a microphone. Once he's sure he has all eyes on him, he announces, "While I am so happy to have the Blizzard here, I must announce that it's time for our scavenger hunt. For every completed list, our corporate sponsor, SET Grocery, has agreed to donate one hundred dollars." He looks over to a woman on his left, who nods with a serene smile. I think she's the CEO of the sponsoring grocery chain. Or somebody on the board, at least.

"I will pay the hundred bucks myself to not do that," Kipson grumbles under his breath.

"We're participating," Dominic says firmly, standing from his chair. "We're gonna crush this scavenger hunt. Let's go. Hands in."

Dominic puts his hand out, waiting for the other guys to lay theirs on top, and to my surprise, the other guys stand with Dom, stacking their hands on his. Pacholek even taunts Kipson, "Come on, man. Behind the scenes, all over the zoo, at night? When are you gonna get a chance to do that again?"

With a beleaguered sigh, Kipson puts his hand in, though he doesn't stand.

"Blizzard on three," Dom prompts. "One, two . . . BLIZZARD!"

The guys chant together as they throw their hands in the air. Quick as I can, so as not to squash their enthusiasm, I grab scavenger hunt papers and hand them out. Reluctantly, Kipson takes one, and still grumbling, he leaves with the rest of his teammates.

At least he kept his, though.

Not everyone does the hunt, and there are several people milling around the picnic area, chatting about this and that. I talk to a few groups, sharing how important Caprice's baby is for our zoo and encouraging them to donate.

"Looks like you might get your wish," a voice says behind me. I turn and to my surprise, see my dad standing there. His wife, Vanessa, is at his side, smiling warmly.

"Dad? What are you doing here?" I say, completely shocked.

"You invited me." He says it matter-of-factly, as though I haven't invited him to dozens of school plays, graduations, and birthday parties that he's never once bothered to come to.

Vanessa weaves her arm through Dad's. "When Robbie told me about the fundraiser, I knew we had to come. He's been so excited to see where you work."

Robbie? I will never get used to that. Vanessa is the only person I've ever heard call my dad—Robert Boothe—by that nickname. But also? In what universe does Dad care where I work? Or about me at all?

I've worked at the Berkshire Zoo for four years, and I'd bet my right foot that Dad couldn't have named the specific zoo before walking under the archway bearing its name tonight. He's never asked me about my job, nor specifics of what I do or why I like it.

"Well, I'm glad you could make it," I say haltingly.

"It seems like a great turnout. Hope the guys being here helped," Dad replies, looking around.

Simply having a conversation with him, something that should be easy, is awkward. Like neither of us know what to say. Should we discuss the past? Leave it alone and move forward? Some combination of the two? I have no idea.

"It did," I say instead. "I even heard a couple of people say they came for the players, not the zoo. But we'll benefit either way."

He nods, both of us falling silent as the course of that conversational thread ends.

Vanessa is the one to save us. "Robbie said this is all to name a monkey?"

I look from her to Dad. He was listening to me? He shared what I told him? He's here? As I realize the answer to all of those questions is yes, the little girl inside me feels seen and heard in a way she never did before, which is very confusing for adult me, who still hasn't forgiven Dad for the years of near abandonment.

Giving Vanessa the same speech I've been repeating all evening, I say, "Yeah, Caprice is one of our siamang gibbons. This is her first offspring, which is a very big deal, not only for our zoo, but for all siamangs in captivity. We're raising funds to name her."

"Aw, that's so sweet," she coos. "What would you name her?"

"Oh, that honor will go to the highest bidder," I rush to explain. "Not me, or any of the zoo employees."

"Yeah, but what would you name her . . . if you could?" Vanessa pries.

This has been an ongoing discussion among the zoo staff since we discovered Caprice's pregnancy. Many suggestions have been made, some good, some great, and some downright strange, which is to be expected when you get a bunch of science-minded people together. I mean, we cannot actually name her Symsyn because it's short for her scientific name of *Symphalangus syndactylus*.

"Hadiah. Hadi for short. It means *gift* in Malay, and siamang gibbons are from the forests of Malaysia, Indonesia, and Thailand."

"Hadi? That's cute," Vanessa says.

Dad is quiet, just watching us make small talk. How is this easier than talking to him? Is it the topic or Vanessa? I'm not sure, but it is infinitely more comfortable than talking to Dad. Maybe because, for all her faults, I don't have a bad history with Vanessa, and since I'm not close to Dad, I've never been particularly close to her either. She's Dad's wife, nothing more and nothing less. Plus Caprice, and by extension, her daughter, is one of my favorite topics.

"Hurry! Get there!" a voice shouts amid the pounding footsteps of what sounds like a herd of buffalo.

Suddenly, two groups of people—one, the Blizzard players, and the other, a family with three teenage boys—comes barreling into the area, and very nearly into a picnic table. Thankfully, Rodney dives off to the side and does a front roll instead, coming up covered in dirt and grass. As he dusts his shirt off, the whole group celebrates.

"*Whoo*, that was close!" Anderson cheers. "But we got here first!" He thumps his chest, looking more like a posturing silverback gorilla than he'd probably appreciate hearing. For unexplainable reasons, his tie is now wrapped around his head Rambo-style, with the tail of it hanging over his right shoulder. I have no idea where his jacket went.

Actually, all of the guys are missing their jackets now, and their shirts are largely untucked. They all look quite a bit worse for wear considering it was a quick and easy scavenger hunt, not a *Lord of the Flies* campout. Though maybe their group dynamics were a bit more "every man for himself" than the average scavenger hunter.

There's a round of high fives, between the players and the family, who are all grinning widely. "That was iconic," one of the teenagers yells. Another is holding up his phone, videoing the whole thing, proclaiming he got the whole thing and they'll definitely be viral by tomorrow.

"They look like they're having fun," Dad says, deadpan.

Fun is putting it mildly. For all their protestations about being here today, the Blizzard players are happily roughhousing and seem to be having a great time now. I meet Dominic's eyes and send him a meaningful smile. He's doing it . . . fixing the team. And maybe, fixing me a little, too, I think as I cut my eyes over to Dad, making sure Dom sees him as well.

# Chapter 20

## Dominic

"What in the world did you do during that scavenger hunt?" Briar asks as we pull away from the zoo late that night.

"We're competitive," I say, as if that's explanation enough. And in a way, it is.

We'd gone out with our checklists, not a team but a bunch of individual assholes arguing and fighting with each other about where to go first and who should be in charge. But as soon as we started to see other groups with more checkmarks than we had, our competitive natures had kicked in and we'd needed to not only finish, but finish first.

With my knowledge of where things were in the zoo from my visits there, we'd made quick work of getting from one area to the next, and by the time we had only a few items left on our list, we'd run into the Parker family. The teenagers—Hudson, Maddox, and Trey—had been excited to hunt along with us until we'd all spotted the finish line. And then, the race had been on.

Luckily, Rodney was okay after that winning front roll parkour move.

"Do you think it worked? The team building?"

I shrug. "It's a start. Not majorly different from the competitiveness we have on the ice, but the whole thing—bitching about wearing suits and skipping weekend plans, sitting together and making chitchat about things that aren't hockey, doing something fun like the scavenger hunt—all play a part in creating something different. Something better between us. Or at least I hope it will."

"What about Kipson and Anderson?" Briar asks. "Were they about to kill each other the whole time?"

"Pretty much," I admit, frowning hard. "They kept it together when people were around, but there was enough shit-talking under their breath to put the rest of us on edge. But no punches were thrown, no blood was shed, and no players were harmed during the course of today's events." I throw my voice low and flat like a narrator before one of those crazy stunt videos.

"Good. Dad probably would've killed me if his players got hurt at the start of the season," she jokes.

"Speaking of dear old Dad, how do you feel about that?"

Briar wasn't the only one shocked that her father made the winning donation bid.

Carl had stood up at the microphone later in the evening to announce the winner and I'd expected it to be the lady from SET Grocery or one of the other corporations represented there, but he announced Robert Boothe as the winner and Briar had been stunned into silence. Not the team—her father himself had donated his own money. And when he went up on the stage, with Vanessa smiling at his side, he'd looked out in the audience, found Briar, and said he'd like the baby gibbon to be named Hadiah, Hadi for short. That hadn't meant anything to me, but Briar had gasped, so it definitely did to her.

"I don't understand why he did that," she says a little nervously, still digesting it all. "Like, am I supposed to be okay with everything now? That feels like he's buying my forgiveness. But also, what he did was actually really kind and meaningful to me. So I'm torn."

I nod, agreeing with her. "It's complicated. Forgiving him isn't a one and done thing, for either of you. You have a whole lifetime of hurts to heal. That'll take time."

That feels true. I haven't been hurt the way Briar has, but even lesser pains aren't healed with one act. No matter how grand.

"Baby steps," she says, but I think she's talking to herself.

As we pull into Briar's driveway, she's gone quiet. I can feel the weight of her swirling thoughts like they're floating around the truck's cab with us. But are they about what happened with her dad or what we planned for tonight when we got back to her place? I'm honestly not sure.

"You're thinking loud," I tell her as I put the truck in park and look over. "Care to share with the class?"

"I'm scared." She meets my eyes boldly, despite her words.

"Of?"

She swallows thickly, admitting, "Of . . . me, not being enough." At that, her gaze drops to the console between us.

"Jesus fuck, come here," I spit out.

I yank up the console and reach across the space I've created, pulling her over and settling her in my lap sideways. "Do you feel that?" I demand, grinding my already hard and thick dick against her thigh. "That's what you do to me."

"Oh."

She seems shocked by that. How in the hell does this woman not understand how sexy she is? How beautiful? How fucking downright radiant she is, inside and out?

My voice low and gravelly with desire, I ask, "Do you have any idea the things I want to do to you? With you? Have you do to me?"

She shakes her head, looking innocent. But I see the spark in her eyes, the hope hiding there. But her demons are loud. Too loud, working in her mind to create doubt.

"I fucking fantasize about you dancing with a shovel, for fuck's sake. I'm gonna need therapy for sure."

A tiny smile tries to lift her lips, but it disappears as fast as it came. "I have stretch marks, from being pregnant. Tyler always said they were ugly."

"Tyler's an idiot. I bet your tiger stripes are hot," I assure her with a cocky smirk. "What else you got whispering in that head of yours?"

"My boobs are saggy."

"I'll hold 'em up." I mime cupping her breasts, supporting them in each hand.

"What if I'm not good at sex?" she blurts out. "Or don't know what to do?"

I chuckle at the absurdity of that. "You know what to do, Briar. And if you're not sure, I know what I want to do. Do you want me to tell you?"

Her eyes jump from my lips to my eyes, hunger building but doubt still lurking.

I don't wait for her to say yes. She needs the reassurance, needs to know that I have a plan because she doesn't think she does. "I want to kiss you until you're completely breathless and your body is craving mine so badly that you're begging for more." My breath skates over her cheeks with every word, all humor gone, replaced with hunger. I lift a finger to her shoulder, tracing the soft curve there. "I want to finally discover if your tits fit in my hands and what color your nipples are, because I've imagined them so many times and I want to rewrite my own fantasies with the reality of you."

I lay my hand on her thigh, wishing she had her usual shorts on so I could feel the soft warmth of her skin, but telling myself that I'll have her entire body laid over mine soon. Or under, whatever she needs. "I want to taste you, drink you down, giving you more pleasure than you think is possible as I use my lips and tongue for more than just words for your ears. I want to feel your warm heat surround me as you take me, slow and easy at first, and then hard and fast as I take us higher and higher. I want you to fall apart in my arms, trusting that I'll hold you together until you come back to your body, changed for the better. Knowing that you can have it all again, anytime you want."

"That actually sounds terrifying," she says quietly. A slow, seductive smile grows across her face. "But I think I want to try it anyway."

I whisper against her lips, on the verge of kissing her. "Because you're a brave badass, Briar."

She laughs, her breath hot. "No, I'm not."

I should argue further, until she agrees with me, certain of her own bravery. But the need to kiss her wins out.

Cupping her jaw, I finally kiss Briar the way I've wanted to all day—intimately, passionately. As I feel her anxiety melt away and she turns to putty in my hands, a sense of power and peace fills me. This is what I'm meant to do. The thought ghosts through my mind, writing itself at the forefront as my new guiding force. For Briar. For Harley. For us.

She breaks the kiss, putting a few inches between us. Panting, she says, "Let's go inside."

As she walks backward toward the door, excitement is written all over her face. It's in her smile, the sparkle in her eyes, the flush on her cheeks. And fuck, I want more of it. More of her. Need riding me hard, I urge her to hurry, taking her hand and running with her to the door.

"Open it, Briar," I murmur low. My hands are all over her. If any neighbors are peeking out their windows, they're gonna see me ripping her clothes off if she doesn't get the door unlocked soon.

The door finally bursts open and we're inside. I slam it shut with a kick and wrap my arms around her, finding her mouth again.

"Down the hall," she murmurs against me, and I dance us that way.

She doesn't reach for the switch as we enter her darkened bedroom, so I do it, flipping the light on. "I want to see you," I tell her.

"I—"

"Don't let him in here with us." I don't want to say Tyler's name in this moment between us, but he's in her head, and I swear to fuck that I will kill that asshole for making her ever question herself. "I want to see you, Briar. Want to worship you . . . love your body . . . fuck you."

Her fingers slowly lift to her shirt and she undoes a button. Then another, revealing a plain white bra beneath. "I couldn't exactly wear sexy lingerie under this," she says.

I don't care about lacy this or sheer that. I just want to see Briar. Naked, for me. "Exactly how you are, that's what I want."

Each button reveals slightly more of her chest . . . her stomach . . . until finally, she pulls it off. Reaching behind her back, she undoes her bra, dropping it down her arms to stand before me. "Fucking beautiful," I whisper, dropping to my knees in front of her.

I take her breasts into my hands, weighing them in my palms and teasing my thumbs over her nipples. Light brown with the barest hint of pink, I think, memorizing the shade exactly. I look up to find her staring at me and her breath catches, lifting her breasts closer. Keeping our gazes locked, I lick a slow circle around one nipple before taking the whole thing into my mouth. I tease my tongue over it, mimicking the move with my thumb on the other one. Briar's eyes flutter closed as she moans and I can't hide the smile that steals across my face. I wouldn't even if I could.

Briar might be nervous, but I'm not. She's so responsive for me, not hiding anything, and I'm going to use that to make her feel good. No, to make her feel great.

As I suck at her breasts, I move down to her waist, undoing the button and zipper. She doesn't hesitate this time, helping me remove her boots, pants, and then panties—also white, but with a tiny bit of lace along the legs that makes me think she chose them knowing our plan for tonight. That's Briar's version of sexy lingerie and it does darkly dangerous things to my psyche, especially as she lowers them down her legs and stands completely nude.

"Fuck, I need to taste you," I grunt, guiding her toward the bed. I try to steady myself, reminding the beast inside me to give her time to adjust, but it's rattling, eager to break free, wanting to be unleashed upon the beauty before me. There's a piece of me that wants to throw her on the bed, rip my clothes off, and fuck her hard and bare right now. But I force myself to go slow, for her sake.

Still, as she lies back on the bed's surface, I rise to stand over her. Bending forward, I take her mouth again, promising her that I'll take care of her with every breath. She undoes the buttons of my shirt and I mindlessly toss it off with no care as to where it ends up. I move down . . . kissing here . . . there . . . leaving a trail of sucking, nibbling kisses over her skin, wanting to write myself onto her body. Sinking to my knees at the bed's edge, I spread her legs wide, getting my first real look at Briar's pussy. She's so pretty, pink and wet, and ready.

"You don't have to—"

"I want to. I get to. I'm fucking honored to," I rumble, and I remind myself to teach Briar that a man wanting to eat her pussy is not a chore, but a gift from her and a requirement to be allowed more. My cock aches in my slacks, desperate to get inside her, and I can feel precum leaking out of the tip. Soon, I tell myself. Because first, I want to give Briar the pleasure she deserves. The pleasure I don't think she's ever really had.

Except maybe at her own hand. That image pops into my head, sending another rush of urgent need through me. I channel it into her.

I lick a long line up through her center, dipping my tongue inside to taste her. She's as sweet as I knew she'd be, and I instantly, desperately want more of her. I want her juices to cover my face, my body, my cock. Putting her legs over my shoulders, I bury my face against her, licking and sucking as I figure out what she responds to best.

Focusing my attentions on her clit, I start to tease one finger inside her, curling it up to rub her front wall. "Oh!" she gasps, clawing the comforter. "What—"

An evil smile twists my lips. I don't know if Briar has ever been touched like this given her surprised reaction. I want to show her what her body is capable of. I want to be the man who gives her this pleasure, who does this for her. With a growl, I slide another finger into her, petting that same spot, as I press my other hand on her lower abdomen, right above where I'm licking across her clit. Briar's cries get higher pitched, more desperate, and I can feel her entire body going tight.

"Come, Briar. You deserve it."

Everything freezes, the moment stretches, and then she goes wild beneath me, her hips bucking. But I stay with her, drawing out her pleasure as much as possible while she soaks my hand.

"Fuck yes," I hiss, licking up the sweet juices.

"Dom . . . Dom . . ." She's panting my name like it's a prayer, her eyes closed and thighs quivering. "What did you . . . how did you . . ."

I feel like a fucking god. No, I feel like *the* fucking god right now as she peels her eyes open and stares at me in blissed-out relief.

I can't wait any longer. I need her too badly.

I stand, ripping the rest of my clothes off. Crawling onto the bed, I lower some of my weight onto her, my cock pressed between us. I can feel her warmth, her juices already coating me. "Briar, you with me?" I ask. My voice is gravel, my instincts animalistic, but I don't want her to regret this later. This is a big deal for her. For me too.

She nods rapidly. "Yes, yes, please. I'm . . . safe."

The revelation urges me on as her nails dig into my hips, guiding me to where she wants me. I pull back slightly, lining up with her entrance, and then slowly, I press my way into her. Not wanting to overwhelm her with the depth of my hunger, I have to grit my teeth to maintain some semblance of control. But somehow, I do it as every inch she takes of me is wrapped in heavenly, hot, liquid velvet. Once I'm fully seated in her, I grind a little deeper, wanting to imprint myself there inside her.

I try to be gentle, going slow to give her time to adjust to my cock and to what we're doing, but she's just as desperate as I am, and in moments, she's squirming beneath me, lifting her hips up to try and take more of me inside her. She whimpers my name in this needy tone that is my undoing.

"Damn it," I hiss as I lose any remaining grip on my sanity, and then finally, I get to fuck Briar the way I've been desperate to for weeks.

I thrust into her hard and deep, her body not only welcoming me, but taking me with tight little spasms of her walls that put me dangerously close to the point of no return in an embarrassingly short time. Desperately wanting to prolong this, I flip us over so that she's on top of me.

*"Whooo—"* she calls out at the sudden change in position.

"Ride me, Briar. Take what you need, give me what you can," I tell her.

She blinks, new uncertainty coming back into the depths of her blue eyes, and wanting to reassure her, I take her cheek in my hand, pulling her in for another kiss. Against her mouth, into our kiss, I whisper, "You can do it. You can do anything, brave badass. You've got me about to come already."

I feel the effect my words have on her—the rush of fresh heat that covers me down to my balls, the vise grip of her inner walls. I groan and move my hands to her hips, gripping her so hard that I feel her skin dimpling beneath my fingertips. "Fuck me, Briar."

I'm the one begging now as I try to guide her.

She lifts her hips slowly, then lowers back down, testing herself . . . or testing me? I groan in pained pleasure and watch her eyes dilate. There it is—the moment she realizes the power she wields over me. Her hands find my chest, one planted right over the commemorative tattoo of the Cup in a hawk's claw and the other over my heart, and she begins to move her pussy up and down my cock more confidently.

And that's the sexiest thing I've ever seen. I fight to keep my eyes open, wanting to witness this transformation of Briar as she discovers what she's capable of, explores the command she holds, and finally—finally!—takes for herself with no regard for selflessness.

She rises, sitting tall as she rides me, and I lick my thumb, coating it in saliva. Slipping it between us, I flick it over her clit as she impales herself on my cock.

"Oh!" she cries out, her head falling back. I let my eyes drop to her breasts, which are bouncing with every thrust . . . her stomach, clenching with pleasure . . . to the point where we're joined.

"Fuck, Briar. I'm gonna come. Where do you . . . where?" I want to give her a choice, even though the thought of filling her with my cum sends me dangerously closer to the edge. I want to paint her insides with it. I want it to leak out of her later, marking her thighs and reminding her of what we've done.

I might be evolved, but I'm still a caveman at my core.

"Do it," she gasps, her movements never pausing. "Please."

I roar, snatching her from over me and pulling her against my chest, stilling her with my arms wrapped around her like vises. I thrust into her, I grunt into her hair, I feel her pussy milking me, and I don't stop.

I might never stop.

My cock jerks, hot cum spilling forth as blackness and stars overtake my vision. I keep fucking her even as my cock softens, as cum leaks out over me because Briar is making these hot, needy sounds like she's close again. Wanting to give that to her, I force myself to pull out and toss her back to the bed. I follow her, shoving my fingers inside her and thrusting them in, over and over again as I cover her mouth with mine, swallowing those sexy noises.

I won't deny that the idea that I'm pushing my own cum back into her, filling her with it again, forcing it back inside her body is Neanderthal-esque. But I can't care right now. All I care about is Briar coming one more time.

Her pleasure.

Her needs.

Her wants.

Her.

"You look so fucking pretty right now," I murmur. "Eyes wild, cheeks pink, pussy covered with our cum." Her eyes jerk to mine, her mouth falling open like she's going to argue. Or maybe like no one has ever spoken to her like that. I pet that spot again, more intensely as I say firmly, "So fucking pretty, Briar."

And she shatters again, her whole body contracting and spasming as she calls out my name.

And it is, indeed, the prettiest I've ever seen her.

Crickets are chirping in the dark outside, but here in Briar's bed, it's amazingly quiet. Even her loud thoughts are quiet as we lay together, our legs entwined.

"Are we going to do your cricket thing?" I murmur as I twirl a piece of her hair around my fingertips.

She lifts up, confusion-filled eyes finding me. "How do you know about that?"

Grinning, I admit, "Harley showed me. It's a good bedtime routine."

Her smile is sweet but hesitant. "You don't think it's silly?"

I shrug. "Maybe being silly is what makes it great. Close your eyes and count with me," I tell her, pulling her back down to settle against my chest.

"One, two, three . . ."

We count together and I wait for her to go first. "The best part of my day was raising money for the zoo and Hadiah getting such a perfect name." I feel her cheek lift against my chest as she smiles.

Nodding, I agree, "That's a good one."

"Let me guess, your best part is the sex," she jokes. But there's a question threaded through the teasing words. A reassurance she needs but doesn't want to admit to.

"Sex with you was amazing, but the best part of my day is this right here, lying with you in my arms. This is the best." I press a tender kiss to her forehead.

"Not sure what that says about my sex skills," she grumbles, not sounding too disappointed in my words.

I chuckle. "No worries there. You're good. Fucking phenomenal there, Briar. But the *why*, and the now? Those are even better."

She cuddles into me a bit more. Even after everything, after making me see stars and coming twice, she's not fully convinced that she's enough. I hate that her past demons haunt her.

But I'm going to take particular pleasure in destroying every single one of them, until she knows without a doubt just how amazing she is.

# Chapter 21

## Briar

"I feel like I'm leading you into the slaughterhouse." I stare out the window at the passing trees, unable to look at Dominic as I whisper the confession that makes me feel weaker than I have in years. My anxiety is through the roof, practically vibrating from my body, and I've already done the breathing exercises I haven't had to call on in years.

Luckily, he's driving, so his eyes are mostly on the road. But he reaches over to take my hand in his, setting them on the console between us. His thumb rubs tiny circles over the back of my hand like he's trying to soothe my nerves, but I don't think that's possible.

"Two things," Dom says.

Why does he sound so casual, like this isn't the big deal that it is?

When he squeezes my hand, I force myself to drag my eyes his direction. Instantly, I realize my mistake. Dominic is not casual at all. He's primed and ready for war, but where my battle preparedness is akin to a hyperactive squirrel trying to burrow into a hidey hole, his is that of a panther—cold, calculated, not wasting a bit of energy before the pounce. This isn't the sweet, kind, thoughtful man who made breakfast with me this morning, then made me his second and third breakfast. Or would that be considered lunch? I'm not sure, and it doesn't matter now. What matters is Harley.

"One, we don't have to do this. If you'd rather pick up Harley on your own, you can. You've been successfully doing this exchange for years and don't need me to step in and fight a fight you've got handled." He lifts our entwined hands to his lips, pressing a kiss to my knuckles. His acknowledgment of what I've had to handle on my own is appreciated. Not necessary, but appreciated.

"Two, I am more than happy to go with you. I'm not scared of Tyler. And you don't need to be scared of how I will react. I'm steady. I'm good. I'm there for you and for Harley, not to measure dicks with Tyler and see whose is bigger."

Dominic's is. But I get his point.

I sigh, letting myself sink back into the headrest and stare at the truck ceiling. "You might be steady, but Tyler won't be." That's the understatement of the century. Tyler has mentioned Dominic at every handover since the hospital, and even superficial things like the size of their trucks is going to stick in Tyler's craw, so I hesitate to imagine what will happen when Harley happily greets Dominic, climbs in his truck, and we head off to his hockey game tonight. "Please don't let him provoke you into doing something stupid."

"Me? Do something stupid? I would never." Dominic sounds like the hockey bro he sometimes is, which gives me second, third, and fourth thoughts.

As he comes to the last stoplight before our turn into the park, my brain is spinning out with all the possibilities. "Maybe this is a bad idea," I say, nibbling on my bottom lip.

"Or maybe you're letting Tyler determine your peace."

The reminder hurts. I have done that for too long, so long that I thought I was being mature and smart by not setting Tyler off, but I have given him too much control, for way longer than I should've.

Dominic lets go of my hand and reaches up, his hand going around the nape of my neck, where he massages the stress away. "I'm not fighting you on this. Or on anything. We're not against each other here. I'm following your lead. You're in control. So I won't go if you don't want me to. But don't decide that based on Tyler. Decide based on you . . . and me . . . and us."

And that's what makes up my mind for me.

Dominic isn't trying to substitute his authority for mine. He's supporting me, something no one—and especially no man—in my life has ever done. His ability to stand quietly behind me, staunchly beside me, and protectively in front of me at any given time is reassuring in a way I can't explain.

Safety.

Surprisingly, that's it. This big feeling working through me actually can be summed up in one little word. Dominic makes me feel safe to rage, safe to fight, safe to disengage, safe to be happy, safe to be . . . me. And that's a precious treasure to a woman who has felt disposable her whole life.

"Let's do it."

This could not have gone worse if I'd imagined the absolute worst-case scenario. And to be clear, I did. Several times, in fact. Still, an actual fistfight with bloodshed and police might've been preferable to this.

But, because this is my life and Tyler will do anything he can to screw me over, here we are.

He no-showed at the park. At first, I thought he was doing his usual power move of being late, and I expected him to eventually roll in with Amber in tow, trying to rub her existence in my face (as if I care). But when I finally called Harley, asking if they were close by, Tyler had him put the call on speaker and said he'd meet me at Harley's game.

The game that started at six thirty p.m. The game Harley is currently on the ice playing. The game where me, Dominic, Tyler, and of course Amber are sitting in the bleachers like we're some happily blended coparenting group.

Except Tyler keeps sniping at me and Dominic with cutting remarks. Meanwhile, Dominic greeted Amber politely, shook Harley's coach's hand, saying he'd heard great things about him, offered to sign autographs for the kids, and has been generally completely chill. The only sign that he's not being totally casual about all of this has been the honestly reassuring constant visual check-ins with me.

Oh, I know he's not as cool, calm, and collected as he's making himself out to be, but his restraint is attractive as hell, especially given that I'm dangerously close to breaking my own gray rock decree and responding to one of Tyler's scathing comments. That will only serve his purposes, I remind myself.

"Why are you here? You're not his dad."

Completely ignoring Tyler, Dominic cheers as Harley moves the puck down the ice and attempts a shot on the net. "Good hustle!"

"Hey! I'm talking to you," Tyler rumbles, pushing Dom's shoulder. "You're not his dad, so quit fucking acting like it."

"Language," one of the other moms chastises. But Tyler waves her off with a grunt about minding her own business.

"Neither are you," Dominic says, casual as you please. His voice is smooth and calm, he might as well have said it's going to be sunny tomorrow. But the words themselves are dynamite, and I inhale sharply. The fireworks show is starting.

My first instinct is to tell Dominic to let it go, that engaging with Tyler is what he wants. But then, for the first time in my whole life, I decide . . . fuck it. I have sat back for years and let Tyler walk all over me in some misguided attempt to maintain peace with a man who doesn't want peace. He wants power . . . over me, over Harley, over everything.

I should fight this battle myself, and maybe one day, I'll be able to. But for now, it's enough that I don't say a word to Dominic. I let him go to war for me. I feel nauseated and powerful, all at the same time, as my body and mind argue with each other about this decision.

"What?" Tyler seethes, outraged. "Yes, I am. She tell you that?"

Dominic turns his attention to Tyler, the first time he's truly taken his eyes off the game since the puck dropped. "No. She never said that. She rarely talks about you to be honest. But a father wouldn't use a child against his mother. A father wouldn't ignore the very important game his son is playing in order to make childish comments about his *ex*-wife's new friend." Dominic pointedly looks back to the ice, his eyes finding Harley instantly. "Teamwork makes the dream work."

Is he quoting motivational posters at a time like this?

No, I think he's truly cheering the kids on, throwing out tidbits to encourage them while never coaching from the sideline.

Tyler shuts up temporarily, but inwardly, his anger's growing like a volcano ready to erupt. I can still sense it just as acutely as I could when we were married. I don't think that skill set ever goes away. Back then, I could hear his truck coming and know if he'd had a bad day or a good one, I could tell by his steps down the hall if he was looking for an argument, and I could feel his moods as accurately as I felt my own.

"You think you know?" he spits back after a moment. "You're not even a dad."

"Nope. But I have one. A great one, so I know it when I see it." Dominic dramatically looks around. "All I see is a weak man who gets his rocks off trying to control a woman who already demonstrated that she's strong enough to not only leave your sorry butt, but be better without you."

Is that how Dominic sees me? I'm actually pretty sure that's accurate, at least in his mind. And maybe in mine, too, I'm starting to realize.

"She didn't . . . I left—"

Tyler tries to speak, but Dominic keeps talking right over him, flat and emotionless as if reciting the weather forecast. "And it pisses you off because it highlights that the only thing holding her back from greatness was the worthless anchor dragging her down—you." A hint of a cocky smirk lifts one side of his lips. "You fumbled the best thing to ever happen to you. Trust me, I won't make that mistake."

Tyler's had enough, and explodes, "Who the fuck do you think you are?"

The woman who scolded Tyler about his language doesn't say a word this time. No, she's leaning in closer to make sure she doesn't miss a bit of the action, and I'm not talking about the Squirts' game. I quickly glance around, realizing that other people are watching too. I don't want this. Harley doesn't need this. This is what I've fought to prevent, yet here I am, not only letting it happen, but egging it on with my silence.

"I'm Dominic Lee," he replies evenly, the difference in the two men's temperaments highlighted by the ease with which Dom speaks. "And I know exactly who I am, which is why I'm not at all concerned with who you think I am."

"You can't just come in here and take my family, my wife."

Dom chuckles like that's the funniest thing he's ever heard. "Not your family, not your wife. And there's no competition here. Respectfully, you can never be me. Disrespectfully, I would never want to be you." He gives Tyler a sneering up and down glance, making it obvious he finds him lacking. "And you already have someone else, remember?"

Tyler completely misses the reference to Amber, who is watching the whole exchange with a confused look on her face, and focuses on me. "Babe, are you gonna let him talk to me like this?"

He's not getting anywhere with Dominic and the loss is obvious. Tyler isn't successfully riling him up to make him seem out of control, nor inciting him to become the violent aggressor he wants to make him out to be. Dominic is sitting still, his hand on my knee, breathing steadily, and he has not raised his voice a bit. On the other hand, Tyler is red-faced, panting, sweating, and looks ready to explode. I don't know if he's ever actually gone up against someone like Dominic.

I don't know if there is anyone like Dominic.

I certainly wasn't like this. In the early days, I'd beg and plead for Tyler to pay attention, cry when my feelings were ignored or misrepresented, and eventually, do anything to prove my own affection, while he sat back and gloated. Later, it just became easier to not put up a fight to begin with. I functioned around Tyler, creating my own pockets of happiness where I could.

But now, without him, my happiness has grown exponentially. So has my spine. I just wasn't using it to its full capabilities. That ends now.

"I am not your babe," I say, keeping my voice as close to an approximation of Dom's even dismissiveness as I can. "And Dominic can speak to you any way he'd like. He's a grown man. I trust him to handle himself appropriately."

And isn't that an amazing thing to say about a partner? The freedom of trusting Dominic rushes through me, healing so many years of hurt.

Tyler scoffs. "I get it. Gotta play it cool for your new man. But we know the truth. You still love me." He makes it sound like we're having a secret conversation that Dominic and Amber can't hear. In fact, despite Dom's reminder, I think Tyler has truly forgotten that his girlfriend is on his other side, listening to every word he says. Or maybe he thinks he has her sufficiently tricked into submission with his manipulative ways. Hell, maybe he does? I don't know.

"I never loved you," I say, the truth coming to me even now. "I loved who you pretended to be. But you can't pretend for long before the real you starts to come out." I glance past Tyler to Amber, hoping she hears me too.

Tyler recoils, and I think for the first time ever, he's actually surprised by me. Like he didn't accurately predict what I was going to say or do. It's the only explanation I have for why he shifts focus back to Dominic, who by all accounts is the more dangerous target. Except . . . maybe Tyler is scared of me. At least a teeny tiny bit. I press my lips together, hiding the joy that brings me.

"She probably told you I'm a narcissist or some psychobabble BS like that, right?"

Dominic nods. "She did actually. But I think she's wrong." That draws both me and Tyler up short. I didn't know Dom didn't agree with me, but

I'm open to hearing his thoughts. He's damn perceptive, obviously, and has fixed some of my damage quicker than any therapist did. "I think you're a nihilist. You don't love anything, not even yourself, and you want everyone to feel the same emptiness you do, see the same bleakness you do." He gives Tyler a chilling grin that borders on maniacal. "But we don't. We feel happiness and sadness, joy and sorrow, and are better off for all the ups and downs. Definitely better off because of the love we experience."

Dominic turns his dark eyes to me, his face going soft in a heartbeat. Is he saying? Could he mean? My heart jumps in my chest as I search for any sign I'm misunderstanding, but there's none. He's an open book and shares everything he's feeling and thinking in his gaze.

I once had a man I thought was rescuing me from a lifetime of daddy issues, but he turned out to be a wolf in sheep's clothing. But Dominic? I think he's a sheep in wolf's clothing. He plays this violent, aggressive sport, and has this image as a brute, but inside, he's perceptive and insightful, honest and genuine, and comes with zero-point-zero baggage, unlike me. That should be terrifying, but it's so reassuring.

Safe.

It whispers through my mind again. I've finally found the peace I've been searching for. In a package I would've never considered. But I'm so glad I did. He's the man I've been looking for my whole life.

I lean into Dominic, pressing the tiniest, chastest kiss to his lips, and feel the lift of his smile against my own.

In the background of the celebration happening in my mind, I hear Tyler mutter, "Fuck you, Briar," before he gets up and stomps away. Amber leaves with him, but I can't worry about her. She has her own journey to get away from Tyler's toxicity. I just hope the seeds I planted will eventually bloom into some hard-to-ignore truths in her mind, too, the same way they did in mine.

I stood up to Tyler. I did that. Finally. And it feels . . . amazing.

The relief is immense, like the young woman I used to be, the one with issues that Tyler exploited . . . that bit her tongue so many times . . .

that barely made it out . . . that woman finally has her day in the sun, and the lightness of her spirit is returning, filling me with freedom.

I don't know that I could've done it without Dominic, but the most important thing is . . . I did it. When it came down to it, I didn't hide behind him. I stood in the storm of Tyler, and blew back like the category 5 hurricane I always wanted to be.

Dominic wraps an arm around my shoulder and drags me in, pressing a kiss to my head. When he pulls back, his gaze is full of something that looks suspiciously like pride.

"Feel better?" he whispers.

I nod and tell him, "Thank you."

With them gone, Dominic and I watch the rest of Harley's game together, cheering and having a good time. The team loses, but he shows real focus and hard work, which is what I want him to get out of playing anyway. I don't need him to be some hockey protégé. I want him to have fun doing something he enjoys and have a way to process emotions that are too big for his little body.

"Where's Dad?" he asks when Dom and I walk up.

"He left," I say evenly.

"Probably because he saw you and Dom kissing," Harley teases, his eyes wide and his smile growing. "But you're friends. Right?"

"The best kind of friends," Dom tells him, ruffling his sweaty hair.

I bend down, getting on my son's level. "Is this okay with you?"

"You dating Dominic Lee? Yeah, Mom. It's kinda the coolest thing ever." He grins, glancing back at his teammates, who are watching Harley with newfound awe. I guess having a professional hockey player show up to your game is pretty cool to nine-year-olds. *Hell, to twenty-eight-year-olds,* I think with a tingle.

I stood up to Tyler. Dominic stood up to Tyler.

I'm happy. Harley is happy.

And finally—finally—I breathe freely.

# Chapter 22

## Dominic

"She's off-limits," Kipson declares before I even sit down.

"Sofia, you mean?" I respond pointedly as I fall into the booth across from him.

He glares at me so hard that I begin to measure the distance between us, making plans in case he throws hands. "Yes," he grits out.

"Fine," I agree. "That's your fuckup to deal with. For now. So why are we here?"

Here is O'Neal's, where, much to my surprise, Kipson invited me today. So either he's going to kill me or he has a friendship bracelet kit in his hoodie pocket. One or the other for sure. And let's just say I still don't think he's the "BFF4EVR" type. This has trap written all over it and my guard is up.

"Tell me about the Hawks," he orders after the waitress sets two beers down in front of us.

"You gotta sweet-talk me first." I lift my brows, taunting him and risking my life in the process. I like to live dangerously, and I think Kipson appreciates my irreverence for his grumpy attitude. Or at least that's what I'm telling myself that tick below his eye means.

"Tell me about the Hawks . . . please." I think it actually pained him to have some manners, and I decide that's as sweet as he's capable of in his current state.

"What do you want to know? We won the Cup last year, probably gonna win again this year barring injury. Stupidly traded their greatest defenseman, so they're down one of the best players this season. You can look their stats up yourself."

He growls. "Tell me about the team."

I take a drink of my beer, thinking before I answer. I could just tell him what he wants to know, but that's too easy. For us both. And ultimately, that doesn't serve my purpose, which is to fix him. "To start, they had the best defense in the league—"

"Because of Mahoney."

"He is pretty good," I say agreeably, "almost as good as me."

He grunts out a bare laugh. "Neither of you are as good as me."

I grin, letting him have that one because a joke, even a snarky one, is a step in the right direction and the tiniest start of what could grow into a camaraderie between us. "I'd rank us one, two, and three. Me, best. Griffin, great. You . . . mostly alright." I wave my hand in a so-so gesture.

It's a test. He could stand and leave at the hint of an insult, even if it's meant as a good-natured tease. He could also stay and tell me why the sudden interest in my old team.

Old team?

As much as I hate to admit it, I'm not a Hawk. Not anymore. I'm not entirely sure I'm truly a Blizzard, either, though.

I've been talking to the guys a bunch. Our group chat pings nearly constantly as guys share pics of their lunches, their PRs on treadmills and weight bars, and general updates about their days. We've done meals out that have nothing to do with pregame prep, but rather, with friendship. I've hit the gym with several of the guys, most notably Pacholek and Sabine. And we've gotten to know each other better, as men, not just the stick in the next locker.

I'm not saying we're a true brotherhood yet, but we're closer than we were a few short weeks ago.

"What about the rest of them? Howe, Krivosky, Jack Off?" He throws out players' names like he's reading from a roster, but I think the most important one is the one he listed first—Howe, who happens to be the Hawks' goalie.

"Howe is like that mean old bull on the verge of being put out to pasture. He's mostly chill, but occasionally grumpy as hell, so you don't fuck with him too much because you're pretty sure he could still mow you down before you made it to the fence. Goalies tend to set the tone for a team. Like how Anderson does for the Blizzard." I add that little tidbit as a teaser, jerking the line I've got Kipson hooked on.

Two steps forward, one step back. It's a dance, getting me closer to figuring out exactly what he wants to know. But he doesn't so much as blink at the comparison. Is his lack of reaction, a reaction? Or does he truly not care?

"Krivosky is the comic relief of the locker room, annoying the fuck out of everyone. But make no mistake, any one of them would go to bat for him. I would too. Jacofovich isn't only the captain on the ice. He's Coach's right hand and keeps the rest of the motley crew in line. And if you want any more insider information, you have to tell me why the fuck you're suddenly interested in the Hawks. You looking for a team trade?"

"No," he answers quickly. Too quickly.

"They've got their right defense handled, so you're shit out of luck there." I give him a sideways glance. "But that's not why you're asking anyway, is it?"

He's quiet for a long minute. Long enough that I consider that I might've pushed too hard, too fast. But nah, that's not like me. Maybe he's just not ready to face the ugly truths I'm shining a too-bright spotlight on.

"You said we're not a team."

It's not a question, so I don't answer and instead, wait him out.

"How did they become a team?"

And there it is. Finally. I don't feel victorious because it's not about me. I feel proud of him for realizing there's a problem.

"Honestly? I have no fucking idea," I reply smoothly. "They were a well-oiled machine when I got there. It's been a generational thing with the Hawks, one group passing on the culture as rookies become veterans, and new rookies come into the nest."

"Motherfucker," he spits at me, then takes a healthy swallow of his beer.

"Buuut," I drawl out, "I saw how it worked, how it got passed down. I was that baby bird once, and I know that the culture is reproducible. Or at least I think it is." I nod, pretty sure.

"And that's what you've been doing here?" he asks, seeming not altogether sure of my motives or intentions despite me being crystal clear since the beginning.

"Yep. And I think it's working. The pregame dinners have been great. Minus Anderson, but I'm calling him a phase two project. The zoo event had zero bloodshed and significant teamwork. As far as I can tell, we're this close to having our periods synced up." I cross my fingers and close my eyes like I'm hoping it happens soon.

Kipson nods slowly, like he's thinking over my assessment of our progress, but I stand by it. We're eons away from where we started. Bill even divulged a secret that he swore he was going to take to the grave since he knows Coach's rules. What's more, we're all hiding that secret with him now and Coach has no idea, nor will he.

"Where does Briar Johns fit into this plan of yours?"

My heart stops beating in my chest, drops down to my ass, and then climbs back up to my throat. "What do you mean?"

He looks at me like I'm stupider than he thought I was. "I know you're fucking Coach's daughter."

"You don't know shit," I snap.

I am not fucking Briar. I'm falling in love with her. Not that I'm going to tell Kipson anything of the sort.

"I know that you were navigating all over that zoo like you could lead a damn tour," Kipson tosses back easily. "Yet you've only been here a couple of months?"

"I've been exploring the city, tourist style," I counter. "Especially since I didn't have any friends to hang out with." I try to make it sound like a jab, but it deflects off him with zero reaction.

"Or you've been going there to see Coach's daughter. Playing, animal-style." I really hate that he's calling her "Coach's daughter" like that's all she is. Even worse, I hate that he makes what Briar and I are doing sound dirty, and not in the good way. No, he makes it sound like . . . the Blizzard way.

I grit my teeth, refusing to answer even though it wasn't a question in the first place. I was expecting a trap about team dynamics, not about my personal life, and I'm feeling unprepared, a sensation I don't particularly enjoy.

Reading people is what I do, but as I stare at Kipson, I can't tell what he's thinking at all. Is this the gotcha moment? Is Coach about to jump out from the next booth and fire me? Or is Kipson going to use this intel to blackmail me into leaving him alone? That seems more likely, I think. At this point, I'm not sure what his angle is, but I need to suss it out . . . quick.

"I know that she was making eyes at you the whole time we were at that fundraiser shindig. I know that every time Anderson spoke to her, you looked like you wanted to murder him with your bare hands." He chuckles, admitting, "Though if Anderson had said one word to Sofia, I would've done the same. Still might." There's truth in the words. Even now, he's one too-sharp verbal barb away from attacking Anderson.

Maybe I can use that?

"Did he ever try anything with her?" I ask like I care, and on some level, I do. But that concern is far down on my priority list, way beneath "protect Briar."

Kipson doesn't let me redirect us. "Nuh-uh, I said she was off-limits."

"So you expect me to pour my guts out while not returning the favor? Got it. Seems fair." I roll my eyes as I tip my head back, taking a long drink of my beer.

"There are guts to be spilled?" he says, one brow arched in victory over a stupidly cocky smirk.

Score: *Kipson 1, Lee 0.*

I drop my beer to the table, locking my gaze on him with my mouth firmly closed.

He shrugs. "Yeah, Anderson tried flirting with Sofia. She told him off, which hurt his feelings. And I didn't have her back like I should've. Told her he was just fucking around, not being serious. In way-too-late hindsight, he was testing limits. Hers, mine, the team's."

Damn. That's some shitty behavior from a friend. From a teammate. "That motherfucker."

"Your turn," Kipson says flatly. "I shared. Now you."

I could tell him the whole story—of talking to Briar that first night, of connecting over hockey drills with Harley, of how beautiful and strong and resilient she is, of how I'm falling for her faster than sanity should allow. Instead, I ask, "What do you want from me here?"

He leans forward, elbows on the table, and hands crossed in front of him. "You want everyone to get on board with your team-building tactics, right?" I nod. "Yet you're not being entirely forthcoming with us."

He has a point. But we're barely past two truths and a lie territory with the group, definitely not entering the realm of deepest, darkest secrets. Well, other than Bill.

"So you're testing me? My willingness to be honest?" I say, the pieces coming together slowly. "Scoring my teammate compatibility, if you will?"

He frowns, inclining his head. "You could say that. Or you could call it dedication to the cause."

He's framing it as the team or Briar. Both are important to me, but there's no decision here. I will protect Briar first and foremost. Especially since I don't trust Kipson yet. He's been hurt, and wounded animals are likely to lash out at a rescuer. Briar told me that as animal trivia, but I already knew it from the most dangerous animal of all—humans. It's what we do.

"Let me ask you a question before I answer yours."

Kipson sits back in his chair, by all appearances open to whatever I'm going to ask, but that painful wound in the middle of his chest . . . yeah, I'm about to poke it with a stick. A sharp one. "Do you blame the team for what went down with you and Sofia?"

His jaw goes tight as he clenches and unclenches his teeth. "Why?"

"Relevant to the topic at hand." It's the most I can give until he answers.

He spins his beer on the coaster, eyes going vacant as the past replays in his mind. "Yes and no. They shouldn't have said the shit they did. It put thoughts in my head that wouldn't have been there otherwise. But that's on me. I said what I said, I did what I did, instead of seeing what was happening and fixing it. They fucked me up, but I fucked up my marriage. I pushed her away with my own bullshit." His voice is flat and emotionless, but the heaviness of his guilt settles over him like a weighted cloak. Coming back to the present, he glances at me. "Joke's on them, though. They thought that without Sofia, I'd hyperfocus on hockey and become one of them. Instead, I want to destroy everything and I've never cared less about hockey than I do now."

Wow. Kipson not only bared his heart, he ripped the whole bloody thing wide open and dared me to judge the shredded pieces. It's an honor I don't take lightly, especially from a man like him.

I want to return the share, but I hesitate. "How destructive are you?"

"I mean, I'm not a danger to myself or others if that's what you're asking," Kipson scoffs.

I'm glad to hear it, but I shake my head. "Are you angry enough with the team—and with me specifically"—I arch a brow meaningfully—"to let an innocent woman be collateral damage of your destructiveness? One who has already been hurt too many times in her life?"

He recoils, disgusted. "No, of course not."

This could go horribly wrong. I know that down to my soul. But if I have any chance at saving Kipson—for his own good, not because it's supposed to be some team directive—I have to be honest with him. This isn't team building. This is brotherhood building. And whether he likes it or not, Kipson is my brother. Or he's gonna be.

I take a big breath, praying I'm doing the right thing. "I'm not fucking Briar Johns."

It's technically the truth. I'm not *merely* fucking her. I've fallen for her, but even so, it feels like a lie. A lie told for a good cause is still a lie. My mom gave me that nugget of wisdom as a kid and it's stuck with me. It echoes in my mind again now.

"Fuck you, Lee." We're back to that old favorite.

"I'm not done," I say, pinning him with a look. "I'm not fucking her. I'm in love with her."

"You're what?" he barks, jerking forward and leaning across the table. But he looks left and right like someone might've overheard me. I glance around, too, but don't see anyone of importance. Notably Coach.

Seeing the shocked look on his face . . . hell, feeling the shock in my chest . . . I start to smile. "I haven't actually said that aloud yet. But yeah, I'm in love with Briar."

"Stop saying that," he orders. Rolling his eyes to the ceiling like he's hoping to find divine intervention there, he finally declares, "You are so much stupider than I thought."

"What?"

"I thought you were fucking her. For fun or to get back at Coach or some shit. I didn't know you were . . ." The words come as one stream of consciousness until he runs a hand over his mouth, stopping them. "Coach is going to murder you. Literally. Or at the minimum, your career is over. Up in flames, poof, never taking the ice again. There's no way he's going to let you date Briar. And this isn't his usual 'hockey first' thing. It's his daughter, man." He's glaring at me as if I don't know that.

"Not sure he has any room to say shit to anyone about priorities," I snap back. "He might be a good coach, but he's an awful father. He basically neglected her for her entire life."

"She's still his daughter. Automatically makes her off-limits." Kipson shakes his head. "He's going to cut your fucking hamstring with a skate and beat you senseless with a stick when he finds out."

Graphic, but also, likely accurate given Coach's leadership style.

"I know," I finally reply. "Still won't change my mind."

I've been avoiding this, even in my own mind. At first, I didn't care because the Blizzard wasn't really my team anyway. I was here to fix Kipson and get the hell out of Dodge. But as the guys have become my friends, my brothers, I do care about them, and I've set a ticking time bomb in the middle of everything. When Coach finds out, he'll be the one to light the fuse, but it'll be my fault all the same. I'll be the reason that everything I've worked to build here is brought to ruins again. I hate that, but I love Briar more.

"Damn, Lee," Kipson groans as he sits back. "You sure know how to fuck things up, don't you?" He says it as though it's a compliment, and under normal circumstances, I'd take it as one. But I feel like I'm on the edge of a black void, inching my toes closer with every decision I make, but this time, I'm not the only one who'll fall in. I'll take Briar and Harley with me.

"Guess so." I shrug.

"You really love her?"

"Yep, I really do. You gonna tell Coach?" I pause, beer poised at my mouth.

His brows knit together. "To what end?"

"Destruction?" I suggest, reminding him that he said that's what he wants. "Could be fun, you know? Shake things up, get everyone arguing and fighting again, a little drama for the 'gram?" I don't want any of that. I want the good-natured taunts, the text check-ins, the friendship the guys and I have built. But does Kipson?

He sighs heavily. "I went to the gym with Pacholek and Sabine the other day," he says out of nowhere, which is news to me but I'm glad to hear it. "We were talking about how things used to be." He tilts his head and adds, "How much better things are now. They say that's you and I think they're right."

I feel like that's the biggest compliment he could've given me. "Next time, shoot me an invite and I'll go with you. I'm a damn good spotter and the best cheerleader you've ever seen. I even know a couple of Penny's routines." I do a few arm movements and shimmy my shoulders in my best approximation of dancing. "Gooo, Mikey!"

"Never call me that again." But obviously impressed with my stellar skills, he chuckles. "That's your sister, right? She's a cheerleader for the Hawks?"

I nod, glad he remembered.

"If I noticed you and Briar eye-fucking, other people probably did too." His tone is ice hard, warning while at the same time almost . . . protective? If I'm not mistaken, he almost sounds captain-esque. "And not everyone is on board with your whole brotherhood agenda. There's one particular holdout I'd be concerned about if I were you."

Fuck. Fuck. Fuck.

He's right. "You think Anderson noticed? Think he'll spill to Coach?"

Kipson snorts a bitter laugh. "I'm sure he noticed that Briar wasn't fawning over him, as per usual, so he might've written that off. But I'd bet he also saw how much attention she was giving you because that woman couldn't keep her eyes off of you." He lifts one shoulder in a careless shrug. "I think he'll have a go at you first. But if he can't beat you fair and square, he'll sell you out. No doubt."

I agree with his assessment of Anderson. The goalie is loudmouthed and brash by nature, and taking me down a notch or two would be justice served in his estimation.

"You want to save him, too, don't you?" Kipson asks after a moment, and I nod, not denying it. Kipson's been angry, not stupid, and he's a perceptive man. "Not everyone can be saved. Hell, not everyone deserves it," he cautions.

"Seems like I was told the same thing about you, yet here we are, shooting the shit, drinking beer, and sharing secrets." I take a slow sip, my eyes locked on him. "Next thing you know, we'll be getting matching tattoos. What do you think? Blizzard polar bears? Could be a team outing," I joke.

"Sure thing, Lee. You go first," he quips, a grin slowly developing.

"If I thought for one second you were serious, I'd do it. I bet a bunch of the other guys would too," I say with certainty.

"Fuck, maybe I would," he says, laughing. "Ask me again after the season ends."

"You and me? Tattoo buddies." I point between us. "It's gonna happen. I'm manifesting it, as my sister would say."

# Chapter 23

## Briar

"I spy, with my little eye, something blue," Harley says around a mouthful of cotton candy.

"Your face." I point at the blue ring around his lips.

He shakes his head, grinning. His teeth are blue, too, and I make a mental note to have him double-brush tonight before bed, while simultaneously giving myself credit for the vegetables I got him to eat before his one sweet treat of the night.

"No fair. There must be a million things in here that are blue." I hold my hands out, gesturing to the entire arena, which is a sea of Blizzard baby blue. We're not sitting on the center glass tonight, but rather, halfway up the lower bowl, not that Harley has minded a bit. Truth be told, I think he's slightly more interested in the junk food selection than the action on the ice, though he's been watching that as closely as he has the wandering snack vendors.

Getting in on the fun, Penny says, "Your mom's jersey."

I meet her eyes, seeing the teasing light dancing in their brown depths as she points at my shirt, which is indeed a Dominic Lee jersey that I paired with red pom-pom earrings to match my tennis shoes.

Dominic's sister is sitting with us tonight as the Blizzard takes on the Hawks, which means Dom is playing against his old team, teammates, and most especially, his "brother from another mother" Griffin. This has the makings of a Shakespearean tragedy, but so far, the game has been pretty evenly matched with a score of 0–0 at the end of the first period. The teams are playing hard, but clean.

Meeting Penny tonight had made my entire belly flip-flop with nerves, but she'd instantly set me at ease by running up and hugging me like we were long-lost sisters. A second after that, she'd become friends with Harley by giving him a signed Griffin Mahoney card, though she'd also required him to raise his right hand and vow to tell Dominic that Honey is the best defenseman in the league, which he'd laughingly done but he'd also held up crossed fingers. Then, as we went to find our seats, she accidentally tumbled up the metal stairs—yes, going up them—and we'd bonded over my handy-dandy, mom-approved Band-Aids, which I'd whipped out of my bag. She's now sporting one on each knee, neon orange on the left and neon green on the right, neither of which match her hunter-green Hawks jersey or black tennis skirt.

In short, we're basically besties now.

"Nope, not a jersey," Harley answers. "Want a hint?"

Yes, definitely. But before I can answer, Penny does. "Not yet. What about the logo on the ice?"

Harley looks down to where she's pointing but shakes his head again. "No, but that was a good guess. You're warmer."

He's giving hints anyway, realizing he really has set forth an impossible task. But it takes several more rounds before we finally figure out that the something blue is the top lip of the wall surrounding the ice.

As the second period starts and Harley loses interest in I Spy in favor of locking in on the game, Penny sits back in her seat and leans my way. "On a scale of one to ten, how much of an asshole has my brother been since moving out here?"

"Is ten a complete asshole or not at all?" I clarify.

"Complete." She winces, one eye closed like she's afraid to hear the answer.

"Then, I'd say . . . a one?"

"What?" she balks. Then she waves a hand, like she's negating what I just said. "You've got it backward. One is not at all."

I nod, sticking by my rating. "I'm sure the guys would feel differently, but he's been great with me. Patient and kind and sweet. He's really thoughtful and has helped me figure some stuff out that I should've seen a long time ago." I hope I don't sound too psycho-chick obsessed, but the truth is, I've fallen hard for Dom.

Her brows knit together, and she smiles wonderingly. "Dominic Lee. Number sixteen. That guy?" She points at the ice like I might be confused. "He's not all grunty and bossy, telling you what to do and what not to do all the time like you'd lose your head if it wasn't attached?" She taps her temple, obviously talking about herself.

"No," I laugh, shaking my head. "That must be just you."

"Well, don't I feel special?" she says dryly. But she instantly perks up. "You should hear the things he says about you."

"He talks about me?" It's none of my business, but a girl can't help but be nosy when she's dangling the intel out so enticingly.

"Oh yeah," she says, her smile wide. "Nonstop. Well—" She pauses, tilting her head, reconsidering. "When he's not complaining about the guys, his apartment, or his new coach. That's your dad, right?"

*Nifty little sidestep there,* I think. I see where Dom gets his verbal skills from.

"Yeah. He takes some getting used to," I say diplomatically.

"Dom called him a pickle juice enema," she confides.

Harley hasn't been paying us any attention, but of course he hears that. "Mom, what's an enema?"

"Uh—"

"Enemy," Penny rushes to say, fixing her fuckup as smoothly as she can. "Pickle juice enemy. You know, makes you pucker like this." She purses her lips and squints her eyes like she's tasting something sour and Harley nods with a quiet "oh" before turning his focus back to the game. To me, Penny wipes her brow and mouths, *Whoo, close one. Sorry.*

I can't help but laugh. Penny has been welcoming and witty, and I feel like even if we'd met under different circumstances, we would've been friends. She hasn't tried to make me feel like I don't belong with her brother—because of my past, my son, or because I'm not one of the puck bunny types. In fact, she stuck her tongue out at one woman who was wearing a Mahoney jersey and not much else, informing me that she "licked it so it's mine," which I'd thought was hilarious.

"By the way," she tells me, "he says you're—and I quote, because I have literally never heard my brother wax poetic before—" She shakes her head like she's still baffled by the concept. "Walking sunshine in a smoking hot body." She drops glee-filled eyes over me, looking like she agrees, even though I'm just wearing jeans and a jersey tonight, nothing particularly hot. Though I did take the ten extra minutes to curl my hair in honor of meeting Penny.

That's what Dominic said about me? How he described me to his own flesh and blood? I feel heat starting to rush to my face and I press my cool hands to my cheeks, feeling how puffed up they are from the size of my smile.

"Oh, and he said that when he makes you nervous, you start spouting out animal facts, which he thinks is adorable. Apparently, he's your albatross?" She peers at me questioningly. "I told him that's a bad thing." She lays her head over and sticks her tongue out, miming a heavy albatross hanging around her neck like the old story. "But he said it's a good thing?"

I press my lips together but can't hide my grin. "A very good thing," I tell her, and she shrugs.

"Hey, you two be weird birds together if you want to be. I'm just glad Dom isn't trying to run my life from afar the way I expected him to. I've already got Griffin doing that, up close and personal." She lowers her voice to a false baritone, in what I'm guessing is an approximation of Griffin Mahoney, "Don't go on a hike by yourself. Don't dance with the soldering gun in your hand. No mafia boss lunches." She rolls her eyes in annoyance, though those sound like somewhat reasonable requests to me, especially the last one. I have so many questions about that, but I decide to save them for Dominic.

"Does he usually try to run your life?"

That doesn't sound like the Dominic I know. Sure, he's told me some hard truths, but in the same breath, he's let me decide what I want to do—with him, with Tyler, with my dad.

Penny scoffs. "Uh, yeah. You could say that. Basically, he's spent my whole life trying to protect me. From what? Literally everything." She rolls her eyes like he's ridiculous, but then, seeing my face, she backpedals. "In his defense, I kinda needed it. I'm a bit . . . accident-prone." She gestures vaguely toward her knees like that's a normal occurrence. "He handed responsibility for me over to Griffin, and I take special delight in making his life as difficult as I can." She winks playfully.

"Mom?" Harley says, tapping me on the knee. When I glance at him, he points toward the Blizzard defensive zone. "Are Dom and Kipson okay?"

Brows furrowed, I look at them. They're in position, eyes locked on the play, and all seems to be fine. "Yeah, I think so. Why?"

Harley frowns. "They're not being as aggressive with blocks. Not how they usually are. Anderson is fielding a bunch more shots than usual."

"Maybe Dom's taking it easy on his old teammates?" Penny suggests.

I meet her eyes, both of us saying simultaneously, "Naaah."

We go quiet, all watching closely, and I begin to see exactly what Harley is talking about. It's not that they're missing the action. They're where they need to be, doing what they should be, but the tension that typically threads through their every move is missing. There's no fight in their play. If I didn't know better, I *would* actually think they're taking it easy on the Hawks.

The next play has Jack Off beelining down the ice. He makes a quick pass to Krivosky and, working together, they send the puck forward. Dominic meets Jacofovich, and they scuffle, vying for control of the puck.

"Get it out of there," I mutter under my breath as they get closer and closer to the crease. But Dom is barely fighting and he's giving up inches of ice too easily. Suddenly, Jacofovich shoots. Anderson drops, legs butterfly split to protect as much net as possible, but the puck gets through. The red light comes on and the horn sounds as the crowd goes wild.

"Score, Jacofovich! *Hawks 1, Blizzard 0!*" the announcer calls.

"Uh-oh," I whisper.

"See?" Harley says. "What are they doing?"

"You don't think . . . ?" I trail off, not wanting to give breath to what I'm thinking. Dom is a pro, but maybe in some twisty-turny universe, he's feeling conflicted about playing his old team? He didn't say anything. In fact, he was downright excited to see everyone, claiming he was going to wipe the ice with them and show Coach Leverson what he lost, which sounds more like the Dom I know.

"Okay, wait," Penny says, her palm held out. Leaning into me and lowering her voice, she says, "Considering Dom possesses exactly 0.0 percent sentimentality, let's go the other way. If they're not playing like that because of the Hawks, could it be because of the Blizzard?"

I blink, thinking that through. If Dominic and Kipson aren't playing to give the Hawks an advantage, that would mean they're playing to put the Blizzard at a disadvantage? Which also makes no sense, but then I scan the ice again.

Another puck goes sailing toward Anderson. And then, another one.

"He's under siege," Penny states.

Harley corrects her. "They're putting him under siege."

I see it. That's exactly what Dominic and Kipson are doing, but why? Why in the world would they let the Hawks make that many shots on goal, when each one is a potential score?

When the clock sounds the end of the second period, the teams disappear into the locker rooms and the Zamboni drives out. Harley is normally rapt with attention anytime the Zamboni appears, but tonight, he's glancing from me to Penny with eyes wide with confusion. But we don't have answers about what's going on either.

# Chapter 24

## Dominic

"That was some fucking bullshit out there, Lee, and you know it! Go suck your boys' dicks if you want, but don't screw us over in the process!" Anderson yells from the other side of the locker room as he throws his helmet at the wall. It hits the cinder block and bounces back, sporting a large crack that'll mean Anderson's going to be wearing a new helmet come gametime tomorrow.

Final score: *Hawks 2, Blizzard 1.*

"Check your fucking tongue, Anderson. They're number one in the league for a reason," Kipson informs Anderson. He's sitting on the bench closest to his locker, but he might as well be standing in front of me protectively for the effect his statement has.

"Oh, so you two are all buddy-buddy now?" Anderson sneers, pointing from Kipson to me.

"Teammates," Kipson says with a shrug before wiping his face down with a towel. But he shoots me a sideways glance, wordlessly asking, *You gonna help with this shit show or not?*

This game was a loss before we ever hit the ice.

From the moment we arrived, Anderson was on a rampage, sounding like a testosterone-addled rager with repetitive roars of "Let's fucking gooooo!" that echoed through the whole locker room and chest thumping on par with the worst of Tarzan theatrics. I was surprised our sports medicine team didn't try to stop him before his heart spasmed. Then he spent Coach's pregame prep time shit-talking about knocking the high and mighty Hawks down a peg or two. As his coup de grâce, he got in my face, declaring that I'd better do my fucking job before boldly suggesting to Coach that maybe I should sit this one out on account of me being "he-motional." When Kipson had told Anderson to shut the fuck up, he'd reared up at Kipson, too, going so far as to say that it was high time he started pulling his weight again, too, because the whole team had been carrying his dead weight since last year.

And while Sabine had tried to get Anderson in check, Kipson and I had silently decided we were going to do our jobs, and nothing more. Anderson could field his own damn shots. And he tried. Bless his cold, empty heart, he did. But the Hawks beat him, flat out, every time. Jacofovich especially, who has always been a beast on the ice and scored both of the Hawks' points tonight.

"You should've stopped that five-hole shot, ya fucking sieve," I snap at Anderson.

"Jack Off shouldn't have been that close in the first place!" he barks back. "But I didn't have any fucking defensive support. You left me hanging out there while they were crashing the net."

"Thought you didn't need any help. Remember?" I sneer. Throwing my voice into an approximation of his, I remind him of his pregame brags, "They won't get shit past me. I'm gonna show 'em what it feels like to get shut out. Jack Off's gonna get the worst edging of his life." In my own voice, I ask, "So which is it? You're so good you don't need us or you suck so badly that you need us to do your job while you stand around and sip fucking tea?" I hold my hands out, weighing both options for him, though it's a lose-lose proposition. There's no way Anderson could've fended off every shot alone, and to be honest, I'm not sure all three of us playing our hardest on defense would've been enough. The Hawks are that good. As much as I hate to admit it, they're even better than they were last year. Offensively, of course, not defensively.

"Where's your rah-rah team bullshit now? Huh, Lee?" he spits out, actual spittle flying from his lip. "Is this what you call a brotherhood?"

"Oh, now you want a party invite?"

It's a low blow. I know it as the words come out of my mouth, but I'm fucking pissed.

We had a real shot tonight. The entire team minus one player came to dinner last night. Twenty-two guys plus some of the sports med and support staff crowded into Big Boy Bowls—where I made a reservation!—and had a great meal. We talked strategy, we shared thoughts, and we hyped each other up. We were ready to go, ready to win. And it'd all gone to hell because Anderson showed up like the rottenest apple in the barrel. His tirade had set everyone on edge, and when his negativity continued on the ice with him chirping at us more than our opponents, he ruined everyone's mental game. Including mine.

Scrubbing my hands through my hair, I growl, "Fuck."

I take a deep breath, forcing air into my lungs to settle my mind. Calmer, I say to everyone, "Look, tonight sucked. Losing always does, but we lost in here"—I tap my temple, then point at the floor of the locker room—"and in here, before we ever hit that ice."

I see faint nods around the room.

"I let you get to me," I acknowledge to Anderson. "And it affected my play."

"You're admitting you suck?" he jabs, chuckling bitterly. "Shocker."

"I'm admitting I could've played better if I'd given a shit about the man behind me. But I didn't." I shrug carelessly. "I don't." I look around at the rest of the team, who is listening closely, watching even closer. "Every other guy in this room? I'd slam my damn brother up against the boards for them. You?" I huff out a humorless laugh. "I might throw you to Honey and pop some popcorn to snack on while he fucks your shit up. That says something about us both."

"Good to know where I stand with you," he declares, bowing up with his hands fisted at his sides.

We're standing chest to chest, our eyes locked, and I try to decide if he's actually going to hit me. I'd put odds at sixty-forty in favor of him at least attempting. But while I have cold strategy on my side, he has desperation, and sometimes that's more dangerous.

I hear feet shuffling as the guys close ranks around us.

"Come on, man, settle down," Sabine says, trying to de-escalate the tension.

Anderson's lip lifts the tiniest bit, triumph in the flare of his eyes. He assumes Sabine is calling me off of him, as in Sabine is on his side. His team against me.

And then Sabine's hand lands on Anderson's shoulder. "We'll get them tomorrow night."

I watch the realization click in his mind. I see him glance around at the guys, noticing for the first time that they're all eyes on him. They're on my side. *My* team against him.

We have created a brotherhood here. And not for lack of trying, but we've done it without him and he's become the odd man out.

Anderson jerks his shoulder, throwing Sabine's hand off, as he shoots a death glare at every man that he once called a teammate. But that was before any of them knew what the word meant. It's not simply signing a contract to play under the same umbrella, or wearing matching jerseys, or taking the ice together. It's giving a shit about each other, on the ice and off.

"If you want to circle jerk each other, go for it. I'm out of here," Anderson snipes. With a growl, he snatches a towel from his locker and heads back to the trainer's room, where hopefully a dip in the cold plunge tub will do him some good.

I look around the room, seeing questions in my brothers' eyes. "I'm sorry I didn't give my all tonight. I owe you that and I let petty shit affect me. It won't happen again," I vow.

"We all have off nights," Kipson grunts. "Apparently, I've been dead weight for over six months. I guess you're allowed to be half-assed for sixty minutes."

Uncertain laughter breaks the silence, but slowly, everyone goes back to their postgame routines with chatter about making things up tomorrow. Because we've got the Hawks again, and we all want our get back.

Just between us, Kipson says quietly, "Hope you know what the fuck you're doing, because that was a hell of a lot of kerosene to throw on that bonfire." He cuts his eyes toward sports med, toward Anderson.

"I'd love to say it's all part of my master plan, but I'm more of a master-baiter than planner." I mime casting a line and reeling Anderson back in.

He doesn't laugh, just raises his brows nearly to his hairline. "Well, I'd say you chummed the waters pretty well. Just look out for sharks."

"Honey, I'm home," I singsong as I walk through my front door, dropping my bag to the bench there.

"In here, fucker," Griffin's deep voice answers. I don't even make it fully into the living room before he attacks me in a bear hug. As he slaps me on the back hard enough to knock the breath out of me, I do the same to him. "Good to see you, man."

"You too."

Penny's next, though we hug much more gently. She whispers in my ear, "I love her for you." I don't need my sister's approval, but our family is close and her endorsement of Briar means a lot to me.

Briar stands from the couch and I sweep her into my arms for a kiss. Nothing too passionate since Harley's lying on the floor, watching highlights from tonight's game on television, but enough to say *hello*, *hey*, and *how're you doing* all at once.

Harley holds up his fist and I bump it with a grin.

"There's food on the counter," Penny tells me, pointing to my kitchen.

This isn't my usual postgame routine, but Griffin and Penny being here changes everything. I grab the huge bowl of diced sweet potatoes, steak cubes, and spinach, digging in as I step back to the living room.

Briar and Penny are curled up in blanket nests on opposite ends of the couch, Harley is still locked in on the television, and Griffin is manspreading in an armchair with his head thrown back and eyes closed. He's probably as exhausted as I am after the game.

I'm struck by how much I like seeing them all here, Briar and Harley especially. It's not home, not really. But it's where my Ninja blender is, which is about as homey as I get. With the people I love being here, it definitely feels warmer and cozier, though.

I drop to the couch next to Briar. Well, nearly on top of her, and when she giggles and shifts, I pull her legs into my lap. Once she's comfortable, I rest my bowl on her thighs to resume refueling.

"Congrats on the win tonight," I tell Griffin. "Don't expect more of the same tomorrow. We're gonna kick your ass."

He lifts his head but only opens one eye. "Why? You gonna actually play tomorrow?"

I could argue that I played tonight, but we both know the truth. Actually, as I look around the room, I realize everyone here knows. Even Harley is looking at me like, *What the hell, Dom?*

I sigh and hold up a finger. I shovel in one more big bite, barely chew, and swallow, before diving in, telling them about the Blizzard locker room battle royale, both pre- and postgame.

"I thought things were better after the zoo fundraiser?" Briar says.

I shrug. "They are, for most of us. Anderson's just a—" I catch myself, glance at Harley, and finish, "Jerk." He's a lot more than that. He's an asshole, a motherfucker, and worse, he's steadily becoming even more of a danger to what I'm building here.

"Sounds like you've successfully completed your mission," Griffin offers. "Kipson's doing better."

I chuckle and then say with a smirk, "Of course. Did anyone expect anything different? I mean, we're talking about me? Dominic Lee, the therapy whisperer."

"Oh God, I forgot how insufferable you are," Penny moans, rolling her eyes. But she's smiling. We give each other a hard time, but it's all in love. Our particular love language is just a bit "affection through shit-talking." Don't be fooled into thinking that either of us would let anyone else say the same things about our sibling, though. Penny would snap right back if someone had something to say about me, and I'd go even further for my little sister if necessary.

"What about next season?" Griffin asks, his tone merely curious, but there's a million inherent factors at play to answer that question.

I came here with every intention of fixing Kipson's shit and going home. To Griffin and Penny. To the brothers on my team, the Hawks. It was supposed to be a one-season side quest, a quick in and out, just an asterisk on my career before I returned to the life I'd carefully built. But now? I've built an entirely different life, here . . . with the Blizzard and more importantly, with Briar and Harley. I have a family here, a brotherhood, and a home. Not in this short-term rental, but at Briar's side. Wherever she is, that's home now.

I look at the woman who has changed everything for me, seeing the doubts trying to bloom in her eyes. She would never ask me to stay. Hell, she probably expects me to leave. So I pin her fidgeting hands with my own, stare deep into her soul, and never look away as I answer Griffin, "I'm not going anywhere. I'm staying right here."

Briar's smile spreads slowly, the hopeful belief gradually drowning out any remaining demon whispers.

Griffin's reaction is much louder. "Thank fuck," he rumbles. "I was so afraid I'd need to physically yank your head out of your ass."

Laughing, I finally turn to him. "What?"

He holds his hands up toward me and then Briar, exclaiming, "I mean, I would've done it. I'd have to return the favor since you did it for me once." Sounding much more relieved, he adds, "But I really hoped it wasn't gonna be necessary and that you could see what a good thing you have going." He lifts his chin toward Briar, then glances toward Harley.

I nod, running my thumb over Briar's hand. "I see it."

"Probably need to put out an announcement to the league, though—Dominic Lee, asshole whisperer, is out of the business of fixing your screwed-up players," Penny suggests, waving a hand through the air like she's writing that on a marquee. She probably would literally do that. Or send out an email newsletter or make a social media post about it. She's good at that stuff since she does marketing for her own business.

Griffin groans, telling my sister, "He's gonna be even more stubborn and arrogant now."

"Well, can you blame me?" I joke. "I fixed you, Kipson, a whole damn team . . ." I count them off on my fingers proudly.

"And me," Briar whispers.

I freeze and catch her eye. "Nah, you fixed you. I just helped you knock the dust off the shine so that you could see how much you'd already done," I say with a wink. "Made the reward worth the risk too." My voice is filled with sexy promises, but I mean it so much more deeply than that. Briar broke every rule she had for herself for me, and I intend to make that gamble pay off in every way I can.

"Dom," she whispers, a pink blush coloring her cheeks as she dips her chin. I see her check on Harley, to make sure he didn't hear us, but he's passed out asleep on the floor in a post–sugar rush crash.

"You two are so cute," Penny coos.

"Not as cute as us," Griffin corrects.

I cut my eyes his way. "You are not cute. You fucked my sister behind my back," I remind him. I don't care anymore. That ship has long since sailed, but it's a nice screw to twist every once in a while. Again, affection through shit-talking.

He grins wolfishly. "Yeah, I did," he says unapologetically. "And you wanna know something?"

Before I can ask, Penny finishes for him. "We *lovvvvvvvvvved* it."

# Chapter 25

## Briar

"Are you sure about this? I understand that you have a game tomorrow," I tell Dominic as he closes the door behind Griffin and Penny. They're headed back to the team hotel for the night, but we've had a great evening of talking and laughing.

I was nervous about meeting Penny and downright terrified of meeting Griffin Mahoney given his reputation, but they were both welcoming and friendly and had made it easy and comfortable. I think seeing them was also good for Dominic. He seems more relaxed, steadier somehow.

"I'm sure," Dominic says quietly. He's watching me, though, checking if I'm okay.

I have never spent the night at a man's house before. I've certainly never tucked Harley into bed in a guest room and then gone to sleep with the guy I'm dating in another room. But I'm doing it tonight. It's probably a minor thing to most people, but to me, it feels like a huge step. Especially after meeting Dominic's family.

"Okay, I'm gonna check on Harley one more time, then I'm ready."

Ready for bed. Ready to see where this all goes. Tonight and beyond.

I peek through a crack in the door and see Harley curled up in the bed, snoring lightly. He's a good sleeper. He never even stirred when

Dominic carried him in here, though my ovaries were stirring enough for us both. I will never forget the image of Harley's head on Dominic's shoulder and him laid out across his arms like a sleeping prince. I blow a kiss Harley's way with a happy smile. Back in the living room, Dominic is folding the blankets Penny and I used, dropping them into their basket home.

"Think that'll be enough light?" Dom gestures to a dim lamp. "Just in case he wakes up and doesn't remember where he's at. The guest bathroom has a nightlight too." That he's aware and cares that a young boy might wake up in the middle of the night and need a light to safely find his way in a sleep-addled state is downright sexy to me.

"It's perfect," I assure him.

With a sexy smirk, he takes my hand, guiding me to his bedroom. I'm trying not to get my hopes up too much. He's had an exhausting day, both physically and mentally, and has to do it all again tomorrow. He needs rest, needs to fall into bed and sleep soundly. But the idea of curling up with his hard body, constant heat, and gentle heart is such a turn-on, so while my mind is saying *let the man rest, Briar,* my body is saying something completely different.

I glance at the bedroom, getting a sense of bland luxury, with everything white and wood, before he directs me to the bathroom. I find that he's already set my overnight bag on the counter, and make quick work of washing my face and changing into my pajamas, which I chose very intentionally. As I enter the bedroom, Dom is leaning back against the headboard, propped against a stack of pillows, waiting for me.

When he sees me, he pauses for a split second and then busts out laughing. "Oh my god, that is just as fucking hot as I knew it'd be."

I strike a pose in the nightshirt I rush-ordered to be here for tonight. It has a giraffe printed on it, the neck ending right below my own neck, and also came with knee-high giraffe leg socks. "So sexy, right?" I point my toes, putting one hoof forward and then the other in a little giraffe ballet.

Dom is nearly crying with laughter. "The sexiest thing I've ever seen."

His laughter stops instantly when I do a pirouette that sends the short gown twirling out slightly. "Oh shit, do that again," he growls, his mood changing in a blink. With a teasing glance, I spin. I know what he's seeing . . . the tiniest hint of what I'm not wearing beneath the silly pajamas—panties. "Come here."

I step closer and he throws the blanket back, revealing that he's wearing only black boxer briefs. I can see the thick ridge of his erection through the fabric. "Giraffes, huh?" I purr teasingly.

"You," he answers, pulling me into his lap to straddle him. I shift, settling my core right over his hardness, and he makes a rumbling sound deep in his chest. "We have to be quiet so we don't wake up Harley."

It's not a question. He's telling me that he understands that even here, in this private moment between us, he knows my son is my first priority. Always.

I nod. "He's a deep sleeper, but yeah."

A wicked grin steals across his lips. "Challenge accepted. Be quiet for me, Briar. No matter what, 'kay?" Before I can answer, he cups my jaw and covers my mouth with his, the kiss instantly heated.

We've wanted this. For too long.

God, I went years without sex, so busy and distracted by my life that I didn't even masturbate for months at a time. But one time with Dominic and I'm a sex-starved lunatic for him. I want to feel what he does to me. I want to make him crazy for me. I want us both to experience that rush again.

My hands find his chest, where I trace the hard planes of his muscles before moving lower, over the solid expanse of his abdomen. Dom's body is made for violent power, and I love the feel of him beneath my fingertips, especially the way he clenches in response to my touch. Despite the intense, barely restrained need I sense in him, his touch is pure, gentle reverence as he runs his hands over me, exploring my curves and leaving heat in his wake.

He snakes his hands under the gown to find my breasts and massages them, plucking at my hardened nipples. Wanting to be helpful, I move to take the shirt off but he stops me. The devil in his eyes, he shakes his head. "I'm gonna fuck you with it on."

Uhm, what?

But the playful look he gives me has me nodding like a robot. "Oh, okay."

With a dark chuckle, he lifts his hips and sends me flying. I land on the bed on my back with my legs askew. He catches one calf, holding it in the air and tells me, "The socks too."

I giggle, thinking he can't be serious. But he is. So very serious.

He presses kisses up my leg, the first one on top of the socks, but very quickly finding my bare skin. Who knew kisses on the inner bit of my knees could be so hot? Not me, obviously. But then his mouth moves higher . . . making his way up my thigh, moving from one leg to the other while pressing them open, wider and wider to make space for his broad shoulders between them. The room's cool air blows over my bare, wet center, chilling me, and goose bumps break out over my flesh.

"Cold?" Dom murmurs.

Yes, but also no. I'm cold and hot. Every sensation feels overwhelming in the best way. I shake my head. "Just need . . ."

I don't want to say it. I've never once asked for anything in the bedroom. Ever. In my life. It wouldn't have mattered if I had asked. But now, everything is different. Dom will care. He'll want to give me what I want. I writhe unconsciously, unable to stop it even if I wanted to. My body is searching for Dom's—his fingers, his mouth, his dick. Anything to relieve this ache at my core.

"Yes?"

Hesitantly, I whisper, "You. Touch me, please."

"It'd be a damn honor," he replies before his hands splay me open even more, exposing my most vulnerable of parts to his gaze. He groans quietly before laying a soft kiss right over my clit. It feels like a greeting of sorts, a promise to take care of me, a vow to give me pleasure, but it's not enough. I'm so aroused, I need more . . . now.

I whimper, my hips lifting of their own volition, searching . . . searching. After a yearning, torturous trio of heartbeats, Dominic finally licks my clit with a long, slow stroke that drags the full length of his tongue. I cry out as a shudder works through my whole body from just the singular lick.

"Shh," Dominic reminds me.

Was I loud? I glance at the closed door, but hear nothing outside. When I look back at Dominic, he has hunger in his eyes and, keeping them locked on me, he licks me again. Okay, feeling him do that is one thing. Watching him, watch me while he does it? Another thing entirely. It's a different type of vulnerability. A different type of sexy.

I let my head fall back to the bed, my eyes fluttering closed as he overwhelms my entire being with the magic he's doing. His mouth and tongue worship my clit, one finger and then two sliding inside me, petting that spot he found, and his other hand works its way up to my breast, where he plucks at my nipple.

The pulsing, throbbing pleasure coursing through my body is immense and all-encompassing. I lose all sanity. All respect for what is polite and proper flies out the window. I grip Dominic's head, my fingers threaded into his hair, and I hold him to me. Not that he's trying to get away. In fact, he's pinned one of my legs beneath his arm, not letting me move except to buck my hips against his evil tongue. But I'm chasing the release he promised with that first sweet kiss.

I want it. I want him. I want this.

I feel it building inside me, like I'm pulling the entirety of the universe to a pinpoint somewhere inside my body right behind my clit, holding every bit of the cosmos tight for one . . . more . . . second.

And with a single heartbeat, a single touch of his tongue on just the right nerve ending, everything flies apart. Or maybe I fly apart? Either way, the tension inside me shatters into a million pieces. Quickly, Dominic's hand is over my mouth, pressing against the noises and forcing them back inside me. Not so tight that I can't breathe, but muffling the sounds I'm making. My eyes flutter open and I see his question if that's okay. I nod, trying to be quieter, but he's thrusting his fingers in and out of me, hitting that spot over and over. In the end, I hold his hand even tighter over my mouth because I can't keep quiet. It's too good. He's too good. What he does to me is too good.

When I finally sag, he pulls his fingers from me and with his eyes locked on mine, he lifts them to his mouth, sucking them clean. His dark brow arches and I blink in shock. That is so hot.

I think I've missed out on a lot. Like a lot. And I can't wait to discover everything with Dominic. In fact . . .

I move to sit up and he sits back. "You okay?"

I lick my lips. I swallow. This is harder than I thought it'd be. "Do you like . . . doing that?" I wave a hand in the general direction of my center.

Dom chuckles. "Fucking love it. Anything that makes you come like that is a win in my book."

Heat rushes to my cheeks. "I want to do that to you too."

Dom's face goes comically slack, his jaw hanging open and eyes wide. He blinks slowly, his eyes narrowing. "You want to suck me off?"

The embarrassment too great, I almost say no. I've only done this a handful of times, and Tyler always said I wasn't good at it. But he never did to me what Dominic does either. Maybe it wasn't that I was bad, it was that I didn't know how, which means I can learn.

I swallow again and nod. "I won't be good at it. But I want to try."

"Fuck," Dom hisses, his hand going to his erection. He still has on his boxer briefs, but he squeezes himself hard. "I'm gonna come just with how you're looking at me."

I didn't even realize I was looking at him, but I do have to lift my eyes to his. When I see the truth there, the pained desire for what I'm suggesting, I get . . . excited. My nerves evaporate. I can do this. I move a hand to the waistband of his boxer briefs to take them off, but he's quicker and in an instant, he's sitting up on the bed, leaned back against the headboard with his legs spread on either side of me.

"You don't have to, Briar," he offers. "But if you want to—"

He doesn't finish the sentence because I'm already running my hands up his thighs the same way he did to me. I press a kiss there, mimicking what he did, too, moving higher and higher. When I get to the top of his thigh, I nuzzle the length of his penis with my nose, letting my tongue sneak out to lick him a bit. Testing me . . . testing him. He groans deep in his chest, his abs clenching tightly.

I like this. This sense of power, this sense of giving pleasure.

It takes me a minute of uncertain licking here and there, but I figure out that Dominic likes it when I swirl my tongue over his tip. He tastes salty and sweet on my tongue and I want more of him. Slowly, I begin to take him into my mouth, bit by bit, deeper and deeper. He stays still, letting me be in control, letting me explore. Letting me play and learn.

When I get all of him into my mouth, he hisses my name and I feel like I've accomplished something great. Smiling around him, I look up his body to find him watching me again.

"Fuck, you look so pretty right now," he praises with a soft smile of his own. I swallow reflexively and he grunts. I'd think it was in pain, but I taste a rush of his precum on my tongue. He likes it.

So I do it again. Slip him almost out of my mouth, then all the way in, and swallow. He makes another noise. Feeling a bit evil myself, I remind him, "Shh."

And then I do it again and again, getting faster as I gain confidence.

Dominic's body tenses, his dick growing even harder in my mouth, and he's starting to make noises every time I swallow. I begin to panic, knowing he's about to come in my mouth, but the doubt-filled, scared woman is drowned out by the excited, confident one that wants to experience this.

I want to give Dominic this pleasure. I want to taste him, feel him come because of what I'm doing, so I keep going. I glance up once and see that his jaw is clenched tightly, his teeth bared, and his eyes unblinkingly locked on me as I suck him off. "Briar," he whispers as I feel him start to jerk. Hot jets of cum spurt deep in my mouth and I gulp them down over and over. I choke a bit but all I feel is pride.

I did that. I gave Dominic so much pleasure that he came.

He rips me off of him, pulling me up and taking my mouth in a kiss. "Oh!" I exclaim, surprised he wants to do that when I taste like him, but he kisses me deeply, his tongue in my mouth without hesitation.

"Fuck, we taste good together," he moans against my lips.

We do, I realize. I taste like him and he tastes like me. I smile, shocked but pleased.

He pulls me, rolling me beneath him on the bed, and my breath catches again. I feel his fingers at my core, testing to see if I'm still wet, and I make an embarrassing squelching sound when he slips his fingers into me a few times. He licks them with another one of those sexy smirks before lining himself up with my entrance. I'm surprised he's still hard . . . hard again? But I don't have time to question it because he slides into me with one deep, driving thrust.

I automatically cry out over how good he feels inside me, and rush to cover my own mouth this time, knowing I won't be able to stay quiet. It's like I walk around, living my daily life not recognizing that this important piece is missing from me until Dominic is inside me. Kinda how I didn't realize he was missing from my life, either, until he inserted himself right into that too.

He strokes into me a few times, letting me adjust to him, before rising to his knees and sitting back on his heels. Bringing my legs to his shoulders, he caresses me over the silly giraffe socks, which are half fallen down now, with a teasing grin. I expect him to gently slide into me again. Instead, he lays an arm over my thighs, keeping us locked together and then begins slamming into me harder, deeper, faster, shaking the whole bed in the process.

Oh my god.

Yes.

This is what has been missing. Dominic, with his ability to let me feel strong and weak, free and safe, in control and out of control . . . all at the same time. Wanting to scream my joy and my pleasure to the sky, I fight to stay quiet, but the best I can do is muffle my whimpers against my palm. When even that gets to be too much, Dominic falls forward, catching himself with his hands on either side of my head, effectively folding me in half despite having never done yoga in my life.

"You okay?" he asks. His voice is gravel, low and gritty.

I try to nod, but it comes out more like a desperate jerk. "More," I mumble, and he smiles.

"Good."

It's all the warning I get before Dominic resumes slamming into me. This new position makes me feel it even deeper. I swear he's hitting my lungs. Or maybe I just can't breathe because I'm folded up like an Auntie Anne's pretzel. But he gives me the oxygen I need, kissing me to muffle our sounds. Okay, mostly my sounds.

In moments, I'm on the edge again. "Dom?" I try to warn him. I don't want to wake up Harley. I have to be quiet, but I don't know if I can be.

"I've got you," he vows.

I think he's still kissing me, swallowing any noise I make. I feel him over me, but my entire soul is floating through black space as my body shakes and spasms. As I return, I realize Dominic is struggling to stay quiet and I return the same favor, sealing my mouth over his to muffle him as he fills me with jet after jet of hot cum.

"Jesus fuck, Briar," he gasps, blinking dramatically when we're done, and I release his mouth so we can both breathe again.

I smile, high on hormones and release and bliss and pride. I did that to him. Little ol' me, Briar Johns. With my silly nightgown and even sillier socks. I do a weird finger wave. "Hi."

"Hey," Dominic answers, grinning. Then with a chuckle, he says, "Stay there. I'll get a washcloth."

Once we're cleaned up and situated back in the bed—to actually sleep this time—Dominic pulls me to his side. With my head on his chest, I can hear the steady thud of his heartbeat. It feels reassuring and comfortable, a song I could listen to forever.

"You awake?" he whispers. "I need to tell you something."

I don't move. I don't let my breath hitch. I try really hard to not let fear grow. That last one is the hardest. "Yeah?" I answer.

"Okay, don't freak out—"

"Saying that makes me freak out."

"Briar . . ." His heart thuds faster against my cheek. "I love you."

I lift up, barely able to see him in the darkened room. But I see his smile. To be sure, I poke his cheek to make sure it's one of the good ones and not a "gotcha, just kidding" one. It's real. "You do?"

He huffs out a laugh. "Yeah, I do. And I know it's fast and I know you might need time, so I'll do the albatross thing and wait forever if that's what you need. But I needed to tell you." He's rambling, which is about the most adorable thing I've ever heard. Confident, cocky Dominic is nervous about sharing his feelings with me?

"Dom?"

"Yeah?" he says, his voice tight.

"I love you too."

Time stops, at least in this room. And in the moment, I think we both realize the hugeness of what we've just said. Or at least I do.

Dominic pulls me back into him, and with our lips close enough that I feel the brush of his, he says, "Of course you do. I'm Dominic Lee, what's not to love?"

I'm still laughing when he kisses me. Even though he's absolutely right.

# Chapter 26

## Dominic

Getting called into the coach's office is never a good thing in my experience. At least once in my career, it's resulted in me getting sent to a new team. I'm reasonably sure that's not going to happen today, but you never know. I would've said the same thing a few months ago too.

My knock on Coach Boothe's door is answered with a curt, "Come in."

Coach is sitting at his desk, looking a little worse for wear than usual. His eyes are bloodshot, his usually clean-shaven jaw has a shadow of gray hair, and his hair is mussed like he's been running his hands through it. On the wall next to him, his screens are filled with stats and plays, and one has a game paused like he was watching before I knocked.

"You wanted to see me after warm-ups?"

The team and I just finished our morning skate and check-ins with sports medicine. Some of the guys are still in the locker room, taking cold plunge dips or getting massages, and some have already headed home for a nap or food in preparation for tonight's second game against the Hawks.

"Sit down." He doesn't indicate where, but I pick the chair in front of his desk that's closest to the door as a strategic move. "I think you know why I've called you in here today."

Honestly? No, I don't. There are so many things it could be related to . . .

To thank me because Kipson is actually doing better, on and off the ice.

To discuss the changing team dynamics.

To dissect Anderson's latest temper tantrum outburst.

To ensure Kipson and I are prepared to play our asses off tonight the way we should've last night.

Or you know, the obvious . . . that I'm in love with his daughter.

Playing it safe, I ask, "What's on your mind?"

He glares at me, narrow-eyed and cold, silently waiting for me to break. I'm pretty sure it's an interrogation technique I've seen in at least a few dozen movies. When I stay respectfully quiet, simply looking back at him, he exhales loudly and stands.

In front of his wall of screens, he points to one. "Know what this is?"

I look at the list of names. "Seems like tonight's team roster."

He arches a brow. "Notice anything unusual?"

I really wish he'd skip all this bullshit and get to the yelling. He's angry, that much is obvious, but I'd like to know why so I can adjust accordingly. But I play along for now and read down the roster. Wait . . .

"I'm an alternate? You're starting Tomville as left d-man?"

"Smarter than you look, aren't you?" he quips snidely. "That's my plan. Could be for tonight. Could be for the rest of the season. That all depends on you."

I have a bad feeling in the pit of my stomach. "On me doing what?"

Coach deliberately steps back behind his desk and sits down. The whole time his eyes, which are filled with fury, stay locked on me. He takes a deep breath in and lets it out slowly. All moves designed to demonstrate the power dynamic in the room.

"Playing hockey for me requires a player's full commitment," he says evenly, but there's a threat already developing his tone. "It's come to my attention that you've been particularly distracted as of late."

He says the word as though I've been drunk or high, or out committing felonies as a part-time side gig, but at least we're getting somewhere. Though, in theory, he could still mean the whole team dynamic or Briar. Testing that, I hum, "Huh. I thought our pregame get-togethers were helping, but I can cancel if you want." I hold my phone up, thumb poised like I'm going to text the group chat right now.

Coach slams his palms to the desk, the noise jarringly loud in the quiet office, and stands, looming over me, though the desk is thankfully still between us. "You are sneaking around with my daughter, Lee. My daughter!" he roars. Digging his fingertip into a stack of papers, he asserts, "That. Stops. Now."

I don't so much as flinch. My face stays perfectly stoic, though inside I'm raging at this asshole who has neglected Briar for her whole fucking life and now wants to demand things like he has any right.

I lift my brows, cockily challenging, "Or what?"

I know the answer. That's what his whole showboating thing with the roster was about. If I kowtow to him, he'll put me back as a starter. If not, he's going to play Tomville. But he doesn't want to do that. Not really. I love the kid and he's damn good, probably even going to be great one day, but he's not me. And I don't mean that arrogantly; there's just no comparison between me and Tomville at this point in our respective careers.

"Or you can sit your ass on the bench tonight. Or all fucking season, for all I care. Or you could never play again. How about that?" He's ramping up, each threat worse than the last, and louder too. "Make your choice."

Choice? He thinks there's a choice here? That's what's wrong with him in the first place, because I don't see a decision to be made. Not at all.

"I'd still get paid, though, right?" I say with a shit-eating smirk.

He blinks, not expecting that response to his nuclear meltdown, which is exactly what I hoped for.

It's time for me to tell Coach how I see this going down.

I stand, meeting his eyes as I plant my hands on his desk and lean in closer. My voice hard, I tell him, "You can control what I do on the ice. You can control my position on this team. What you can't do is control what I do outside this arena." I point toward the door, then drive my finger into his chest. "And what you've never done is give a single, solitary shit about what Briar wants or needs. You left her when she was seven years old and never looked back, so don't start acting like you give a fuck about her now."

I step back . . . move away . . . toward the door. I need to get out of here before I do something I can't take back. I have listened to Briar talk about how she felt when her father basically abandoned her. I heard the tears in her voice, understand the damage he did, not only with his own actions, but by leaving her vulnerable to a man like Tyler because as far as I'm concerned, Coach Boothe carries some responsibility for that too. I have seen how alone she's been since her divorce, without a bit of support from the man in front of me.

He is not a dad. He's not a father. He's the worst kind of man: a leaver.

Every protective instinct inside me is surging up, urging me to punish him for the ways he hurt her. To make him bleed for every time his daughter needed him and he wasn't fucking there.

"Lee."

I don't stop, the doorknob in my hand. "See ya later, Coach." I sneer the honorary label I have said to many men that I've respected to varying degrees over the years, but none I've respected less than Coach Boothe. "Guess I'll be riding the pine."

"You will not see her again!" he bellows.

Glancing over my shoulder, I see how red-faced and furious he is. "See, that's the difference between you and me. You picked hockey. I'll pick Briar every. Single. Time."

He flinches at the dig, but it's only for an instant before his face hardens and he opens his mouth to give some anger-fueled, snappy reply. Probably that I don't know the whole story, or I don't understand what he was going through, or whatever justifications he's spoon-fed himself over the years. Repeating them over and over, so many times until he started to believe his own bullshit.

Not wanting to hear any of it, I cut him off. "Fuck this." I mutter it under my breath, but intentionally still loud enough for him to hear. "Bye."

With that, I walk out into the locker room. There's at least a dozen guys standing there, eyes wide in shock, having heard every word. Sabine recovers first. "Dom?"

"Apparently, Coach is pretty serious about his 'no distractions' rule," I spit out.

"Probably has something to do with the fact that you're in love with his daughter," Kipson offers dryly. I meet his eyes. He warned me. He knew this would happen. And we both know exactly who sold me out. I give him a nod, trusting that he'll handle things appropriately.

Spying Tomville looking shell-shocked in front of his locker, I point at him. "Team call is five. Be here at three thirty so we can get you ready. You're debuting in the first line tonight, brother."

I might not be starting tonight, but I'm not abandoning my team. That's not the kind of man I am.

I'm supposed to be heading home for my pregame routine of fuel and nap. Instead, I send Briar a text that simply reads: Incoming. Don't talk to your dad, before driving to her house as fast as I can.

In front of her cute little house, I take a deep breath. This is going to suck. She thought her dad was finally coming around with the zoo thing, especially when he named Hadiah for her. But he hasn't changed a bit.

Hockey first, last, always, and only.

But I don't play like that. I don't live like that.

Well, to be fair, I used to. Hockey has been my priority for my entire life. I have missed school events, birthday parties, family dinners, and more because I was on the ice, for either a practice or a game. But for all I've given to hockey, it has given me back an entire life filled with celebrations and sorrows, skills and lessons, teammates and brothers.

The most important thing I've learned is: It's a game. On my deathbed, I will look back on hockey fondly, but what I will want to see and feel and experience again and again is . . . a life with Briar and Harley.

I don't have to knock. Briar is already opening the door, as though she was listening for my truck. "What's wrong?" she asks instantly.

"Let's go inside," I say, ushering her back into the house. "Sit down," I tell her, guiding her to the couch.

"You're scaring me," she whispers. "Is Dad okay?"

I huff a humorless laugh. "Depends on your definition." She pales and I quickly say, "Sorry. He's fine. Just . . . your father."

I see the moment she understands in real time—her shoulders round, her perpetual smile evaporates to be replaced with a frown, and her eyes cloud over. "He knows about us."

Nodding, I tell her, "Yep. And he told me that if I want to play hockey, I have to leave you alone." I shake my head, still not able to believe his bullshit.

"Oh." Her chin falls to her chest and she fidgets with her fingers. Swallowing thickly, she says hollowly, "I understand. I knew this would happen. Hockey isn't just what you do. It's who you are. Hockey first, no distractions."

I can see every time Coach Boothe told her that. It's not only a pall over her, but rather, it's woven through her, in her very DNA. And she apparently thinks I'm just like him.

A leaver.

"What the fuck?" I hiss. "Has a single thing you've learned about me given you any indication that I would do that to you? That I would respond well to an ultimatum like that?" I shouldn't talk to her like that, but I'm pissed that she would think so little of me.

Her eyes lift, hope trying to blossom but being tamped down by her demons. "What?"

"I told him to fuck off," I snort. "That I'd ride the pine tonight because I wasn't gonna stop seeing you."

"What?" she repeats. "You chose me? Why?" She seems legitimately confused by the idea.

My heart breaks for her. She truly thought I was going to choose hockey over her when I would never choose anything over her. She's my first priority.

I drop to my knees in front of her, cupping her face in my hands and dragging her eyes to mine. Nose to nose, I tell her, "Briar, I love you. I'm not going anywhere. Ever."

"You're not?" she says softly.

I shake my head. "Woman, you couldn't get rid of me even if you wanted to. I'm a teeny bit stubborn, in case you hadn't noticed."

"I don't want to get rid of you. You're my albatross."

All the tension that's been inside me since Coach's bullshit decree melts away. He can fight this if he wants to, he can punish me, he can yell and scream in useless rage, but Briar and I are a team.

Us. Me, Briar, and Harley. And he can't do a fucking thing about it.

"I'm your albatross," I echo, laughing at how that somehow became our thing, but I will wait for this woman as long as she needs me to. Now, tomorrow, the day after that, forever. I can be patient for her. It'll be worth it to have a forever with her.

I press a kiss to her lips, promising a lifetime of never-leaving and demon-slaying for this sweet, silly woman who brings so much sunshine to my life. When I finally feel the beast in my chest subside, I put our foreheads together. "So you don't have to come tonight if you don't want to. I'm gonna be benched."

She pulls away, meeting my eyes with a surprising flintiness in her blue ones. "Agree to disagree. I'll be there, proudly wearing *your* jersey. I have a few things I'd like to say to my dad too."

# Chapter 27

## BRIAR

"Where's the little guy?" Penny asks, leaning in my direction.

I don't have to glance at the seat next to me to know it's empty. Harley was supposed to come with me tonight, but I asked Trina to come over and babysit him because I'm expecting a showdown with my dad. Harley had been disappointed at first, but when I told him that I had something to handle, he'd settled quickly. I suspect he might've heard some of the conversation between me and Dom this morning.

"Stayed home," I bite out.

Narrowing my eyes, I stare at my dad from our seats halfway up the lower bowl. He doesn't know I'm here and likely doesn't feel my glare amid the packed arena, but it makes me feel better to shoot some laser beams of anger his way.

"Ohh-kay, Grumpypants," Penny drawls. "Leaving that alone, are we gonna talk about why some kid I've never heard of is warming up with Dom? Or is that gonna be a no too?"

I sigh, turning to her. "I'm sorry. I'm mad at my dad, but I shouldn't take that out on you."

She holds up her hands in surrender, smiling. "We're good. Just tell me why we're mad so I can hex him correctly too. Are we talking 'hope you accidentally fill up your gas tank with diesel every time you go to the gas station' or 'feel the pain of a thousand needles pricking your asshole 24-7'? Ooh, or maybe the crowd favorite, 'his dick falls off and chases him'?" She makes a wormlike scrunch and unscrunch motion with her hand. "You know, like the snail that kills you if he catches you?"

I can't help but laugh the tiniest bit at her level of unhinged creativity. "Thanks, I think I needed that." She wiggles her shoulders, happy to be of assistance. "Okay, so here's the deal . . ."

I go through what Dominic told me earlier today about my dad's ultimatum, finishing with Dom telling Dad to fuck off.

Penny pales. "He did not!"

Nodding, I say, "Oh yes, he did. Hence, riding the pine." I point at Dominic, who has taken a spot on the bench far, far, far away from my dad. There's at least five guys between them acting as buffers, but even they seem unsure how this is going to go, their eyes occasionally bouncing from their coach to Dom, back and forth.

Everyone stands for announcements and the national anthem, and then the announcer shouts, "Let's play hockey!" As the crowd cheers and players take their positions, Penny and I watch one particular player.

"I haven't seen him on a bench in ages. Probably since his rookie year. Even when his line's not in the rotation, he's the sort of guy who stands the whole time, for goodness' sake," Penny says in disgusted wonder. She tilts her head. "Well, unless you count the penalty box bench. He's in the sin bin often enough, he needs that theme song—"

I don't say a word as Penny sings a line from "You Wish" by Flyana Boss. She isn't half bad honestly. I'm just staring at Dominic, his jaw is clenched and his eyes locked on Tomville, who's on first line tonight. When the rookie glances at Dominic for assurance, Dom gives him a curt head nod. Even with things going astray, Dom is supporting his teammate.

The puck drops and play starts.

Well, in theory it does. But if Dominic and Kipson were going easy on the Hawks last night, tonight's play is downright . . . mild. I think Harley could get past Pacholek and Sabine, and I wouldn't be surprised if Kipson went so far as to accidentally fall down on the ice so Harley could attempt a shot with how he's playing. The only Blizzard player . . . and I do mean only one . . . who seems to be playing hard is Anderson, who is blocking more shots in the first half of this period than he typically blocks in an entire game.

"What're they doing?" a guy shouts from a few seats away. He's almost ripping his thinning hairline out by the roots as he stares at the ice in confusion.

"Fuck if I know," another guy responds. "Come on, Blizzard! Get it together!"

Penny and I watch in horrified awe. We know how good these guys are and how hard they've worked to get to this level. Why would they throw it away?

"Look," Penny whispers, pointing at the team bench.

There are two men absolutely losing their shit. One, my dad, who is yelling loudly at the guys on the ice, and two, Dominic, who is doing the same thing, but seems to be mostly focused on Tomville. Reading his lips, I think he's telling him, "This is your shot! Don't fuck it up!"

Dad calls something and the lines rotate out, some coming to the bench and others hitting the ice. But it seems that *every* line is doing the same thing, no matter what rotation tinkering Dad tries. The Blizzard are just . . . existing, not playing.

By the end of the first period, the score is *Hawks 2, Blizzard 0.*

As the players go back to the locker room, Penny and I lock eyes. "What is happening?"

A guy in front of us turns around, answering the question that we didn't ask him. "They're choking. That's what's happening. Fucking losers." He looks back at the ice—the empty ice, mind you—and jeers loudly. "Booooo! Blizzard sucks!" He grins back at us like he did something cool.

Penny leans forward, her face filled with anger as she demands, "You think you could do any better?" The guy tries to scoff out a yes, but Penny doesn't let him speak. "Let me guess, you're a big shot in the late-night beer league you play in. Talking shit about how you could've gone pro if you'd wanted to while drinking way too many brews with your bros every week. Am I right?" She points at the stack of already-empty plastic cups in front of him.

The guy's grin falls, replaced with pain from the too-on-target shot Penny took. "Fuck you, bitch."

"You wish," she snipes. When the guy turns back to the ice, she looks at me innocently. "What?"

"Now I understand why Dom says you need protection," I note, amused and impressed. She's definitely Dom's sister. "You're gonna get yourself beat up in here."

She shrugs with a cocky smirk that looks shockingly reminiscent of her brother's. "I have two monstrous defensemen and an actual mob boss in my phone contacts. What's Kyle gonna do?" She cuts her eyes to the guy in front of us, who definitely seems to be not-listening to us and definitely not-interjecting into our conversation now.

"What are *we* going to do?" I ask, not sure there's anything we can do. This is the Blizzard's fight and we're stuck in the bleachers.

"This," she says, holding up a hand. "Popcorn, please."

Which is how we end up watching the second period—anxiously shoveling popcorn into our mouths by the handful as the game devolves even further.

Every time the jumbotron screen shows a close-up of Dad, he looks on the verge of a heart attack, his face tomato red and a vein bulging in his forehead. Tomville is actually playing now so Dominic has quit shouting at him, but the rest of the team is playing in slow motion and is completely unaggressive. Even Anderson is slowing down, though I think his speed is related to exhaustion, not any team solidarity. They might as well be renamed the Sloths.

With two minutes remaining in the second period and the Blizzard down 4–1 now, I turn to Penny. "We have to do something."

"Whatcha got in mind?" she asks, her eyes bright with excitement.

"Come on." I grab her hand and pull her from her seat.

"Think this will work?" she whispers a few minutes later.

It took some slippery maneuvers past a few security guards, and a little bit of tossing our names in people's faces, but we've managed to get down to the lower hallways where the locker room area is. There's just one more guard to get past.

"Hey . . ." I glance at the guard's left chest, hoping to see his name tag, but there's just an embroidered label that says "Security." "You," I drawl with a smile. "I'm Briar Johns, Coach Boothe's daughter."

He chuckles, unconvinced. "Coach Boothe doesn't have kids. Think he's on his fifth or sixth wife."

"Fourth," I correct. "Vanessa."

He snaps his fingers, nodding. "Oh yeah. That one's sticking around longer than usual. But he'll be on wifey five before long. He always is." But he pins me with a stare. "No kids, though, so move along," he orders, pointing back down the hallway we came from.

"Did you know Griffin Mahoney signs autographs again?" Penny asks casually. She turns, moving her hair to show the guard the signature on her jersey. Griffin didn't sign autographs for years, so anything he has signed is an extremely valuable collector's item.

"Damn," he whistles. "How'd you get that?"

"I'm Penny Lee. Dominic Lee's sister and Griffin Mahoney's wife. You might've seen them fighting on the ice last season because of little ol' me?" She frames her face with her hands like she was the one on the jumbotron.

He eyes her a bit more carefully. "Yeah, yeah . . . I did see that. I think everyone saw that," he laughs. "I think your brother won that one."

"How about a little trade? I'll give you this jersey if you let her in the locker room." She rushes to add, "No psycho puck bunnies here, I promise. She really is Coach Boothe's daughter. She's also Dominic Lee's girlfriend."

"Wait, wait . . . what? Is that what all the yelling in there's been about?" he asks, leaning toward us. Gossip is apparently the great unifier. "I heard something about that. Walls aren't that thick, you know?"

Nodding, I spill the tea right back. "I'm Robert Boothe's daughter. I'm dating Dominic Lee. Look." I hold up my phone, showing him a picture of me and Dad. I'm about thirteen or fourteen, but it's still obviously us. And then I swipe to show him a picture of me, Harley, and Dominic.

He seems convinced, but shakes his head. "Still can't let you in. Sorry."

"Hey!" Penny shouts suddenly.

The guard and I both look at her, but her jersey hits the guard square in the face. She shoos me with a wave, telling me to go through the door. Quickly, I do, letting it shut behind me. On the other side of the door, I hear loud footsteps as the guard chases Penny down the hallway. "Come back here!"

I get it. I absolutely understand why Dom and Griffin think she needs protection. But goodness, I love her and appreciate her self-sacrifice to get me in here.

This part, I'll have to do alone.

# Chapter 28

## Dominic

Coach is yelling. Again.

Ranting really, about how we're going to pay for this and he's going to punish us for that. It's all blah, blah, blah to me, the same thing he did during the first intermission, only ramped up even more because we're going to lose this game. I don't even mind. The guys having my back means more than anything Coach could do to me, or us.

It's not just me either. No one in the locker room is listening to him.

From what I can tell, Kipson had a little chatty-chat with the guys, explaining the backstory of what's going down with me and Briar, and therefore, with me and Coach. They've chosen their side. It just happens to be mine, not Coach's. And I think he's finally beginning to realize how much he's lost. Let's just say it's a helluva lot more than one game. It's the respect of nearly every player in this room.

"Getchur asses back out there and play the way we all know you can or—"

"Ahem. Excuse me." The soft female voice shouldn't grab anyone's attention. It's only because it's so out of place that it does. But it grabs mine, and my eyes automatically swing toward it, toward *her*.

"Briar!" I exclaim, standing up in surprise.

She's wearing my jersey again, this time with a cute little flippy skirt I've never seen before. And fuck me, knee socks. The woman has on baby-blue knee socks that match the jersey.

She gives me a little wave with a bright smile. "Hi, Albie. But I'm not here to see you."

What? Who's Albie? I swear I almost look around for some other guy, and then I realize that she means me. Apparently, we have pet names now. Albatross, Albie. Okay, I like it. I want to crow . . . *Caw-caw, motherfuckers.* I don't even know if that's what albatrosses—albatrossi?—sound like. I should look that up or ask Briar. But maybe later because . . .

She holds up one finger, telling me to wait before turning suddenly hard eyes to her father, who's vibrating with unyelled words stuck in his throat. "Dad, a minute?"

"What are you doing here?" he blurts out finally, looking like he's choking on each syllable.

He probably means in the locker room, but just as easily could mean at the game because he had no idea Briar was in attendance tonight. Why would he know? He's never invited her. But I did. I got her seats, made sure she had a parking pass, and confirmed that she had money for the concession stand. I took care of everything for her. Unlike him.

Apparently, though, it doesn't matter as he shakes his head, getting his wits. "It's not a good time. We're in the middle of a game, in case you hadn't noticed." He holds a hand out wide, gesturing to the team around him.

Briar arches a brow. "Trust me, I know. It's not a game, it's an ass-whipping. I also know that, for you, it's hockey over everything, but that doesn't seem to be working this time, does it?" She points at the countdown clock over the door that still reads eight minutes. "Two minutes. Can you spare that for your daughter, Dad?"

I see Coach frown as her words land center-mass, hurting him.

Good. He deserves to hurt for every single time he left a young Briar behind, wondering why she wasn't worth his time and attention.

"Briar," he starts, his tone softening for her more than it ever does for us, but it feels more like exasperation than affection.

"I love Dominic and he loves me." Briar's announcement is crystal clear and loud, undeniable.

There's a bit of muffled surprise from the team, and even an uncomfortable chuckle or two, but everyone falls silent quickly at the hard glare Coach shoots at the team.

"I'm sure you think that. I'm sure he's led you to think that," Coach says, cutting an accusing glare my way. "But you know how hockey players are. How men are. You don't need that. I'm trying to protect you."

"Protect her?" I balk. "From me? You're the one she needs protection from." I move to Briar's side, ready to destroy the man who hobbled the very foundation she built her life on. I'll gladly destroy him for her, for her future. For our future. And to hell with my hockey career.

Briar places a steadying hand on my chest and meets my eyes. I see the strength in hers that I've always known was there. She doesn't need me to fight this battle for her. She's ready to do it on her own.

I give her a supportive nod. "Say what you need to say. I've got you."

"I know how you are," she tells her father. "I know how Tyler is. But not all men are like that. Not even all hockey players are like that," she declares, waving a hand around the room. "Dominic certainly isn't. He's better than that."

"You only know what he wants you to know," Coach protests. "He didn't want to come here, doesn't want to be here, but I'm sure he played a good game to get my own daughter on his side. Against me. Probably thinks I'll trade him back where he wants to go, just to be rid of him. Not a bad idea, actually." He arches a brow, giving the threat serious consideration.

"This isn't about hockey!" Briar yells. God help her, she even stomps her foot. The pain of her childhood is breaking loose, free of every restraint she's had it under for so long. "This isn't even about you. For once in my whole life, it's about ME!"

Everything stops. I don't think anyone even breathes. I'm reasonably certain, no one has ever spoken to Coach Boothe like that.

"And if you try to stop us from being together"—Briar wraps an arm around my waist and I automatically lay one over her shoulders—"you're going to destroy the team you've given your life to and everything will have been for nothing, because this is all you have." She glances around, not at the people, but at the mural-covered walls. The ones with awards and championship rankings, the team's logo, and not much else.

"Briar, I'm trying to protect you," he says again.

But my girl's not done. She's got an entire lifetime of thoughts and feelings and pain pent up and she's letting it all fly, collateral damage be damned.

"You are the only thing I ever needed protecting from," she states bluntly. If she'd yelled it, I think it would've hurt less. The flat statement makes it that much more impactful. "You hurt me when I was still figuring me out and it ruined me in a lot of ways—how I see the world, what I expect, and most importantly, what I accept. Dominic is doing his damnedest to fix what you broke and show me what love is supposed to be like."

She counts on her fingers. "It's not disappearing the way you did. It's not treating Mom and me like we were disposable. It's not showing up only when it's convenient for you. It's not never picking up the phone or coming to your grandson's hockey games. It's not . . . you. I have never once felt love from you, so don't stand there and say you are trying to protect me from the one man I've never needed protecting from."

She's breathless, panting as tears stream down her face. With my hands on her shoulders, I wait, making sure she's finished. I want her to get it all out—every shred of rage, every pinprick of hurt, every scar ripped open to freshly bleed so that she can truly start to heal. When she's quiet, I spin her, burying her face against my chest where she sobs openly.

"This is what your 'no distractions' rule leads to. A shitty father and a shittier team," I tell Coach harshly. "I won't be a part of that." I look around the locker room at the men I've come to think of as brothers. "I'm sorry, guys. Truly, I am. I have loved being a part of the team we've built this season. But I have more at play than just hockey. I have a family." I press a kiss to Briar's head.

"I'm married," Bill blurts out. Eyes turn his way, not in surprise at the fact, but that he's saying it here in front of Coach. "And I'm staying that way. If that's a problem, I can ride the pine too."

"Well, fuck," Lavoie hisses. "I'm dating someone too. Met her in New York. It's still new, but yeah, I'm dating someone. And if need be, I'll ride too. Yeehaw, motherfuckers."

"I talked to Sofia," Kipson says quietly. "Made my apologies and she accepted." He sighs heavily. "It was good. Not get-back-together good, but good."

Rodney holds his hand up. "I have a girl back home, hopefully waiting on me. She just started her engineering program at school. And I really don't want to sit out, because this is my chance, but I want to play for a team that gives a crap about each other."

Briar pulls away from my chest, her arm snaking back around my waist. "Dad, you picked hockey over me every time the choice came up. Now is your last chance. Either Dominic plays, or this time, it'll be me choosing to leave you behind. You'll never see or hear from me again." Her voice quakes a little, and I feel the shiver run through her as she delivers her own ultimatum, but she stands unyielding, demanding more than the bare minimum for the first fucking time in her life.

I couldn't be prouder of her.

Ironically, her ultimatum is similar to her father's—hockey or her. I know what I chose, and I'd do it again, as many times as necessary, but I'm honestly not sure what Coach will choose. And so help me, if he hurts Briar again, I'm going to beat the shit out of him. Given the hard-set jaws and cold eyes around the room, I won't be the only one.

We've all given up so much for our sport, dedicating our lives to it. But it can't be to the detriment of a life outside the ice at all.

"I was a shitty father," Coach says stiffly, his back ramrod straight and eyes unblinking like a guilty defendant awaiting Briar's verdict. She doesn't absolve him, doesn't disagree in the slightest because he's right—he was. "But in a twisted way, I was protecting you . . . from me. You didn't need me around. I was building something all-consuming back then—"

He looks at the locker room around him, but he's gone, seeing the ghosts of his past. Or maybe his mistakes haunting him? He shakes his head, his eyes clearing. "Your mom was doing right by you, and gave me what-for when I tried to drop in and out of your life." For a moment, he sounds salty about that, but then he admits, "She was right, and I didn't want to mess up the good life she was making for you with my own hockey-focused single-mindedness. You standing here, telling me what's gonna happen on the ice, as though you have any right to, is testament to your mother's influence."

He chuckles like he's remembering something about Briar's mom, and when he looks at Briar again, he seems shocked. Vaguely, I wonder if Briar and her mother look alike because the way Coach is peering at her, it's like he's truly seeing his daughter for the first time. He takes a deep breath, and slowly, an affectionate smile starts to stretch his lips, until he finally declares, "You're a good woman, a great mother, and if you think Dominic is worth all this, then I guess I'll have to trust your instincts."

It's not an apology, but the acknowledgment of his past sins and Briar's current awesomeness seems to satisfy her because she covers her mouth with her hands and gasps, "Really?"

Coach nods, his smile growing. "Kinda like that kid you said was good, the one on that trip to Toronto? I was ready to go, but you saw something in him I couldn't see. Now, he's a pro. You see good in people, look for it even. Lee has good inside him?" He shoots me a warning glare that says I'd better be fucking good to my core if I'm in love with his daughter.

"He's full of it."

I joke with a cocky grin, "That's what my mom says too. Full of shit. Full of good. You know, same-same."

"Okay then, let's see if we can salvage this fucking game," Coach announces, ignoring me but thankfully listening to Briar. "Tomville, pine. Lee, on the ice. Rest of you assholes, start fucking playing."

"Yes, Coach!" sounds out from around the room.

"Are we all supposed to sing 'Kumbaya' now?" Anderson sneers as he slams his helmet against his locker. I think it's his new one so he really should be more careful with it.

He's pissed. He made a big move, selling me out to Coach and expecting everyone to turn against me, especially Coach. It was a good plan, and it almost worked. Except, the guys and me? We're brothers . . . we're teammates . . . we're family, and family looks out for each other. Them having my back and effectively refusing to play without me is something I will never forget.

Anderson's move backfired spectacularly, and now he's even further out on a limb alone.

"We can sing a different song if you want?" I offer with a shit-eating grin. Loudly, I start singing "Don't Stop Believin'."

Several guys instantly chime in.

"Fuck my life," Anderson spits out. He pushes past me, knocking my shoulder, and luckily for him, not touching Briar or else he'd be a dead man walking as he clumps in his skates into the bathroom.

"He's gonna have to be a phase two project," I tell Coach. "One per season and I already did Kipson." I draw a checkmark in the air. Mission complete.

"Fuck you, Lee," Kipson growls, but I hear the smile beneath his gruff demeanor. I'm almost certain I see the corners of his lips turning up a little bit too. They're a full two-thirds less glowering than usual this time. That's not just mission complete, that for sure deserves an "exceeds expectations" on my performance review. Maybe even a bonus.

"Okay, you guys go play your best and have fun," Briar tells us, sounding like we're Harley's teammates, not pro athletes. "I'm going to go find Penny and see if she's been arrested."

"What?" I snap. My sister's in on this?

"What?" she answers, trying and failing to look innocent. "She helped me get in here, which wasn't exactly easy." She lowers her voice and leans in, "She's fast, right? Like could-outrun-a-security guard fast?"

"I'm gonna kill her," I groan.

"I've got her. Just don't tell Griffin. I don't want to get on his bad side," she says, waving her hands like that's the worst thing she can think of.

I can think of something way worse than my best friend: me.

I press a quick, hard kiss to Briar's lips and then move to her ear. "Go find my sister. And you are in trouble, young lady."

She makes a squeaking sound and when I move back, already smirking at her, she's blushing a bright pink. Fuck, this woman is going to be the death of me.

No, the life of me.

"Blizzard on three," I shout as I grab my stick and turn back to the guys. "One, two . . ."

"BLIZZARD!" a chorus yells with me. I think Briar even says it.

The guys file out in front of me, but I hang back, not wanting to leave her with Coach. He said the right things, but I don't trust him yet. He's got a lot of making up to do and even more learning to do. But he approaches her slowly, his mouth set in a hard line. "I'm sorry, Briar. For so much."

"Me too, Dad. I should've said something a long time ago," she says. And miraculously, she opens her arms. He wraps her up, the hug they share one that she's needed for a long time. For a lifetime. They stand there for a moment, swaying with each other, healing things in each other's souls.

And finally, it's time to kick some Hawk ass. I've been waiting for this.

# Chapter 29

## Briar

"To the best team in the league!" Sabine shouts, holding up a beer.

The guys around him lift their drinks in response. "Blizzard!"

This postgame outing is a celebration. Not of a win against the Hawks—the final score was a 4–3 loss—but rather, of the building of a team.

O'Neal's is awash in a sea of blue, but that's just the fans. The players are mostly wearing the athletic gear they planned to wear home after the game. No one expected this party. No one expected anything that happened tonight.

Least of all, Dominic. Which is one more reason why I've fallen so completely for him. He moves through his days, creating community by showing how much he cares for people. He thinks I add sunshine here, there, and everywhere, but he opens his heart and changes lives. He's certainly changed mine.

I take a sip of my piña colada, smiling around the straw as I look across the bar. I wish Penny were here to see how this all played out, but she decided it was in her best interest to skip the third period and head back to the hotel before security found her. We stayed in touch via texts, though, so she knows exactly how hard the Blizzard played for those last twenty minutes to make some headway against the Hawks' lead from the first two periods. Her last text came with a picture showing that she's safely at the hotel, tucked into a fluffy nest of pillows and blankets, in her pj's.

"Is this seat taken?"

"Oh, uh . . . no?" I tell Vanessa. "Please, sit down."

She sits beside me, adjusting her short dress and hooking her stilettos on the barstool's lower rung. One lift of her hand has the bartender rushing over, and with a smile, she orders a white wine. Less than fifteen seconds later, he's setting the glass in front of her with a wink.

"Let me know if you need anything," he murmurs, looking directly at her cleavage.

"Will do," she purrs. When the bartender disappears, she rolls her eyes and sighs. "God, is a wine without the visual assault too much to ask?"

"What?" I ask, thinking I must've misheard her. She wasn't flirting—that'd be the bartender doing that—but she's not exactly demure with her curled hair, smoky eyes and glossy lips, and pushed-up décolletage.

She takes a sip of her wine and laughs. "I'm a married woman, remember?" she teases. "And even if I wasn't, bartenders who graduated high school in the last decade are not exactly my type." She tilts her head, leaning toward me as she raises her hand. "Daddy issues, party of one." She arches a brow. "Or maybe two."

"Ah, I guess you heard what happened?"

"Want to talk about it?"

With her? My dad's wife? Absolutely not. She's going to be on his side, no matter what. I'm sure whatever version Dad told her was filled with inaccuracies that make him out to be a misunderstood hero, not the villain in my origin story.

"No thanks," I say, stirring my piña colada instead.

"Can we pretend that we're friends for a minute then?" Vanessa counters, undeterred. "I want to tell you a story about my husband, and maybe you can forget that he's your dad while I do?"

I'm intrigued. And maybe I want to hear Dad's version, just to see how different it is from mine. "I can't make any promises, but . . ." I hold up a finger, take a long swallow of my drink, and finish, "I'll try."

She smiles, and for the first time, I think I see behind her facade to the real Vanessa. Or maybe the piña colada has a bit too much rum?

"When I met Robbie, I was in a bad place mentally. I was taking care of my sister, working three jobs, and trying to make ends meet. It was hard, and then I met this nice guy. He came into the café where I waitressed for coffee every morning and we'd talk." She shrugs like it was nothing, but it must've been something because this story ends with a giant rock of a diamond on her left hand. "He didn't treat me like I was beneath him, even though he had his life together and I was barely beginning to figure mine out. He even helped me. My sister got into a rehab because Robbie pulled some strings. She's doing great now, been clean for three years," she says proudly. "And I took a few online classes to learn how to day trade. Robbie spotted me the funds at first, giving me one hundred dollars to play the stock market and later, one thousand dollars to manage. Now, I make more before ten a.m. most days than I made in a month back then."

I stare at her, gobsmacked. I had no idea. Of course, I also never asked. I thought she was Dad's arm candy, nothing more, and there was no reason to delve any deeper because I figured she'd be gone soon enough anyway. That's Dad's MO.

Seeing my shock, she winks with a bright grin. "I'm more than just a pretty face."

"I'm sorry. I didn't know—" I say, but she waves a hand dismissively.

"Not the point of the story," she tells me. "Point is, Robbie was kind to me . . . *is* kind to me. Because he loves me, and I love him, which means I know that under his tough guy exterior, his heart has been broken for a long time. Broken because of the daughter he left behind." She looks at me pointedly.

It's not that I don't believe her, but . . . I don't believe her. "He could've called me, could've said something, could've done a hundred things to repair our relationship."

"You're right," she agrees with a nod. "But for all his good traits, he's also a stupid old man, who's ashamed of the ways he messed up and didn't know how to fix things without making them worse." She rolls her eyes. "Believe me, we talked about it at least a million times, but he thought trying to be a part of your life now would inevitably come with some painful trips down memory lane, and the one thing he didn't want to do was further hurt you to ease his own guilt."

"He hurt me every time he didn't call. Every time he wasn't there when I needed him. Whether that was fifteen years ago or fifteen days ago."

Behind us, a loud cheer goes up and we glance back to see what's happening. The guys have Tomville hoisted in the air, Kipson under one leg and Dom under the other, holding him up. It sounds like they're congratulating him on his league debut and mostly successful second period. Or at least I think that's what the "you didn't suck too bad" chant is about.

The team is doing well. The thread of brotherhood is nearly visible through them as they revel in . . . well, not a game well played, but at least a period, which, given the roller coaster of tonight, seems worthy of celebration.

Vanessa takes a drink of her wine before asking, "Do you know why he drives the 'no distractions' thing so hard?"

I have my guesses, none of them complimentary.

Seeing my curt answers to the question written in my expression, she says, "It's because he doesn't want any of the guys on his team to hurt their wives or kids the way he hurt you. It's to prevent another you from happening."

I snort out a disbelieving laugh. "You're making him sound noble, but the reality is, he created an entire legacy of assholes who treat women like they're two degrees above a Kleenex and bottle of lotion," I say bluntly.

"Definitely an unforeseen and unintended side effect," she grants, "but ultimately, it was effective. Players' divorce rate in the league is nearly three-quarters. The Blizzard has had none, until Kipson. And Robbie wasn't going to let Kipson ruin his life over it. He takes responsibility for his guys seriously, so he fought hard to get Lee here to save him."

"Which also had some unforeseen side effects," I tease, using her words with a much different meaning as I suck on my straw, thinking about things from Dad's side, something I've never done.

She laughs and for a moment, it feels like we actually are two friends gossiping about our boyfriends. It's kinda nice.

"When you called Robbie about the zoo thing? He called me as soon as you hung up. I thought he was going to come through the phone when he was telling me about it. He was so excited that you'd reached out." I eye her doubtfully, but she nods insistently. "Did you know we had other plans that day? We canceled them because nothing was keeping him away from you and that fundraiser." She smiles brightly. "And he warned me that whatever the highest bid was, he was bidding over it so that you would get naming rights for your favorite monkey."

"Gibbon," I correct automatically.

Vanessa shrugs it off. "How is Hadiah?"

"She's good. Really good. Standing with support and starting to nibble on solid foods," I answer, but my mind is spinning. "Dad . . ."

"I'm not saying he's perfect. Far from it," she admits. "But if you have the heart to give him another chance, he won't waste it this time."

I believe her. After what Dad said earlier today, acknowledging that he's been shitty in the past and apologizing for his choices, and now learning that maybe there were things that I hadn't known, I believe her.

"I think I can do that," I offer with a smile. "Maybe we could go to dinner . . . all four of us?"

Her eyes light up. "Really? We would love that."

With a smile, I tell her, "I think we would too."

A bit later, I'm coming back from the bathroom when I'm cornered again. But this time, it's not by Vanessa. It's by Anderson.

"You're a stupid bitch, you know that?" he slurs, pointing at me with the neck of his beer bottle. I can see that he's peeled the label off, bit by bit. He must've been doing that instead of celebrating with the rest of the team.

Once upon a time, being called names like that made me shrink and hide, but with repetition, they lose their impact. The person using them makes a difference too. Where I might still wince if Tyler said that, past experience telling me to be fearful of the potentially worse thing that might be coming, with Anderson, I don't react at all. I simply try to walk past him. "Excuse me."

He cuts me off, leaning down to get in my face. His breath smells like beer as he mutters, "I can't believe you're actually buying his bullshit."

Narrowing my eyes, I ask, "Whose?"

Is he talking about Dad? Or Dominic? Either way, I seriously doubt he knows what he's talking about at all given the hazy, unfocused look in his eyes.

"That first night, we told Lee to pick three women—one to fuck, one to marry, and one to kill." He obviously thinks this is some great reveal. I can see him mentally doing a ta-da wave of his magic wand.

Rolling my eyes, I'm already dismissing him. "I know. Dom told me."

Anderson's brows furrow together as he frowns deeply. He definitely wasn't ready for that response. "So . . . what? You're just playing along with him? Do you hate your dad that much?"

"My dad? What are you talking about?"

"Lee picked you to marry," he says, sounding puzzled by my question. Scoffing, he says, "I can't believe he's actually going through with it. He's gonna marry Coach's daughter over some bar game because he's pissed he got dragged out here away from his beloved Hawks. Sounds like a surefire way to fuck with the man you hate." He shrugs as a snide smirk tilts up his lips. "Maybe for both of you to fuck with Coach."

My breath catches in my chest as I look from Anderson's right eye to his left. I can see the glee hiding there behind the drunkenness. He wants to hurt me, wants to hurt Dominic, and maybe even Dad.

*He wants to hurt everyone,* I think. Sounds like someone else I know.

Once upon a time, I might've believed him. Or at least let him plant seeds of doubt in my mind. Because, in my experience, men lie. They cheat and manipulate. They leave and shirk their responsibilities. They hurt and cause chaos, not caring about the people who are left behind to pick up the pieces.

Dad did that.

Tyler did, too, and so much worse.

But now? I have no doubts about Dominic.

He's a different animal altogether. He heals, he protects, he cares, and I trust him. I love him. And he loves me, which has nothing to do with a stupid bar bet.

Something clicks inside me and I realize that I don't have to listen to this. Anderson doesn't deserve one second of my time, energy, and attention. I've walked away from scarier men than Wayne Anderson. So I laugh in his face.

"I wasn't the 'marry' option in your silly little game. He picked me to fuck, and you know what?" I lean in a little, wanting to be sure he hears me clearly. "He did. Guess he won. Maybe I should thank you?" I say rhetorically, not meaning it in the slightest. "Because we're going to play it again and again and again. I'm pretty sure that makes me the winner," I say brightly.

His eyes flare with disappointment. He thought I was weak and wanted to exploit the vulnerability he perceived in me. But he was wrong. I'm not fragile. I'm not broken. Yes, I've got some scars on my heart, but they're just a part of my story. Signs of the battles I've fought and survived. Part of the experiences that made me who I am.

"He didn't win anything," he spits out harshly.

I look past Anderson, to the group of guys all having a great time together. And to the man I'm going to join. As a smile naturally blooms on my face, I say, "Really? I think he won everything."

With that, I leave Anderson sputtering impotently and walk over to Dominic, curling into his side comfortably. He looks down at me, his arm already instinctively wrapped around my shoulders. "You okay?"

I look up at him and nod. "Yeah, I'm great, Albie."

The smile that lights up his face tells me everything I need to know. About this man and about his motivations.

He's a helper. He's a stayer. He's a fixer.

And he's all mine.

I wasn't looking for him. In fact, I was actively not-looking for a man. I wasn't ready to take that leap of faith again. Honestly, I might've never taken it, if it hadn't been for Dominic slipping through my defenses, not with aggressive hits to the tall and thick walls I'd built around my heart, but with his patience and kindness. Even then, he could've settled in and made himself a comfy little home in me, not pushing too hard or challenging too much, just fitting into my life like a puzzle piece I didn't know I was missing. That would've been easier for us both.

But then we wouldn't be here.

Instead of easy, he made me grow. He made me look hard truths in the face and gave me the courage to speak my piece. He asked questions that made me look deeper inside than I ever had. And somehow, he did it all with a cocky smirk and who-me charm that I never saw coming.

He made me evolve into a better woman, a better mom, a better me.

"Hey," I say and his eyes are instantly mine again. I lift to my toes and give him a kiss, right there in front of everyone.

And like the immature boys that they are, the team breaks out into a chorus of *"Ooooh!"*

Instead of being embarrassed, I laugh right along with them. With Dom's brothers. With his team.

# Chapter 30

## Dominic

"I wish I didn't have to go," Harley sighs, slouching even deeper into the bench in front of his school.

Briar meets my eyes over his head, the look of worry that I hate growing in her gaze. But she presses a reassuring kiss to the top of his head. "I know, honey." She's presenting a calm front to her son, who's spending the weekend with Tyler. "But he's your father."

The fallout of that showdown at Harley's hockey game has been a roller coaster. Tyler retreated to lick his wounds, but as expected, came back raging and lashing out about stupid shit. He went so far as threatening to take Briar to court, vowing to make it so that I couldn't be around Harley.

Of course, I'd immediately offered to pay the legal fees if he'd been stupid enough to actually file the lawsuit, and he tucked tail as soon as he heard that. Tyler was just trying to intimidate, bully, and scare Briar back into submission any way he could.

When it hadn't worked, he'd skipped his next visit, claiming to be heartbroken because Amber left him. That wasn't unexpected, after she saw through his bullshit, but he blamed Briar for that too.

And while Briar did her best to protect Harley, making sure he didn't feel a bit of the tension from all of that, he's a smart kid and quickly figured out that his dad was causing more drama than usual, which has him reluctant to go with Tyler today.

"Maybe he won't come and I can stay with you and Dom," Harley says hopefully.

Honestly, there's a part of me that prays he's right and that Tyler doesn't show up. Briar and I have the whole weekend planned, mostly with activities to distract her from missing her baby, but I would love to do those same fun outings with him. As a family.

But every time Tyler bails, it hurts Harley, and I would never want that. Tyler may be a shit father, but I won't be the one to drive a wedge between them. I'm going to be the one who'll stand up for Harley and help get him back together. I won't ever claim to be Harley's father . . . but I'll do my best to be there for him, mentor him, and show him how a real man acts and behaves.

That'll be good enough.

"I don't know, kid. That arcade thing sounds pretty fun. I'd hate for you to miss out on that," I remind him. He glances up at me, torn. He's been excited ever since Tyler told him they were going to a nickel arcade, but anticipation comes at the risk of disappointment. Is his dad going to come? Is he actually going to take him to the arcade? Is he going to remember the promise of an entire bucketful of nickels and a whole day of vintage video games? Or will it be another broken promise? I give him a sad smile. "You'll be alright, and if you end up not going to the arcade for some reason, maybe we can go next week?"

It's not about the arcade. Not really. I'm learning that parenthood is about showing up, following through, and making it clear that you prioritize the kid. His feelings, his thoughts, his spirit. I mean, I knew that thanks to Mom and Dad's stellar parenting, but I'm getting a quick trial-by-fire lesson with Harley. And I will not fail him. Or his mother.

"Thanks, Dom." His lower lip quivers a bit, so I pat his shoulder comfortingly and he sucks up his tears before they can fall.

I hear Tyler's truck in the distance a moment before Briar and Harley do, so I see the resignation on both of their faces when they recognize its loud rumble. The white truck turns the corner and pulls to a stop in front of the school, blocking the carpool pickup line, but there's no one here so I guess it doesn't matter.

Tyler climbs out and comes around the front of the truck, pointedly not looking at me or Briar. "Hey, Harley! You ready?"

Zero mention that he's twenty-three minutes late. No cares that the after-school program workers have already left. Not a fuck given that Briar has arranged her work schedule to always be here for handoffs because Tyler is so unreliable.

"Yeah," Harley answers almost morosely, slinging his backpack over his shoulder as we all stand. He gives Briar a hug, tells her he loves her, and then turns to me. He doesn't hesitate. He gives me the same hug and says, "Love you, Dom."

My heart stops. Or maybe it flies out of my chest. Either one would explain the sharp pain that hits me. "Love you, too, Harley. See you Sunday at four at the park." I say the last bit loud enough for Tyler to hear, though, given the sour look on his face, he heard the whole exchange anyway.

"Get in," Tyler tells Harley a little too harshly. He clears his throat, and with a bit of fake enthusiasm, he adds, "We're picking up pizza for dinner."

"Pepperoni extreme?" Harley questions.

"Yeah, whatever," Tyler says, although clearly he knows it doesn't fucking matter. He wanted to be Mr. Big Dad . . . and now he's not. When all he had to do had nothing to do with pizza, and everything to do with just being a man.

In seconds, they're pulling out of the school parking lot. Tyler takes the corner a little fast for my taste considering the precious cargo he's carrying, and I growl under my breath. "I hate this."

Briar chuckles. "Me too. Every time."

"You mean it doesn't get easier?" She shakes her head and I hiss, "Fuck."

She laughs even harder. "Actually, this is the 'easier,' because we can lean on each other. Before, I would say goodbye and they'd leave me here by myself. I'd drive home in silence and then sit in an empty house until Sunday afternoon. Not my best days." She says it so matter-of-factly, like it was just her life, which I guess it was. But the thought of her alone and lonely, worrying about her son, guts me. Even though it's an old hurt, I wrap my arms around her and pull her into me, doing my best to soothe it away.

"I wish I could tell you that it'll never be like that again." I sigh, finishing, "But I can't."

It's the reality of the situation. I played two games this week already and got home late last night, which gave me the opportunity to be here for this handover and for this weekend with Briar. But there will inevitably be times that Tyler has visitation and I'll already be at the arena or out of town for an away game.

"It's okay. It's not as bad as it used to be."

"Because of me?" I nod with a cocky little tilt to my chin, but I'm only teasing, trying to fill the space Harley left with lighthearted humor.

Her soft smile is stunning, like sunshine peeking over the horizon in the morning. "Partially," she allows, "but mostly because of me. I'm pretty badass, you know?" She tries to give me a dramatic wink, but accidentally closes both eyes. Laughing, she says, "That was supposed to be slick and cool, so pretend it was, 'kay?"

"I don't know what you're talking about," I say through a smile of my own. "That was the coolest shit I've ever seen." I copy her double-eyed wink, doing it even worse than she did, and she laughs harder.

I am so proud of this woman. For what she's been through, what she's still going through, and the way she tackles every moment of every day with silliness and turns every bad into something good.

"Come on, let's go home. I'm hungry."

"Oh, we have long chicken nuggets, or I could make pasta?" she offers in perpetual mom-mode.

Catching her around the waist, I rumble in her ear, "For you, Briar. I'm hungry for you." She squeaks in surprise, and I don't have to see her face to know that pink blush is blooming on her cheeks. It gets me every time.

I rush her toward my truck, running and laughing with her the whole way. I hate that Harley has to go to Tyler's, but I intend on making every moment alone with Briar count.

First, by having her for dinner. And tomorrow, we'll sleep in, make breakfast together, and go to the zoo. Not Briar's zoo, but another one that's a couple of hours away. Briar wants to see the cheetah exhibit they have. And I plan on buying her a new zoo shirt . . . an oversize one that she can wear to bed, with nothing else. Except maybe some knee socks.

And Sunday, we'll pick up Harley at the park. Together.

He told me he loves me!

And for the first time this season, I feel like I'm home . . . with this woman, with this boy, with our family. Here, where I never thought I'd be in the first place, but am so glad I ended up.

Thankfully, her house isn't far and I make the drive extra quick. Briar is first to the front door, not because she's particularly fast, but because I like the view from behind as I chase her . . . her hair flying around, her arms pumping, her ass bouncing with every step. In fact, I slow down a little more, tilting my head to get a better view.

"Beat ya!" she shouts, slapping her palm to the door. She whirls back with a bright grin of triumph, but her laughter dies off when she sees the dark look on my face.

"Open the door unless you want me to fuck you on the front porch for everyone to see your pretty face when you come," I growl, letting the slightest hint of a tease arch one brow.

I see the moment she hesitates, not because she wants it out here where her neighbors could see, but because she's deciding if she wants to play more . . . tease me more . . . or if she's done with games too. Decision made, she fumbles with the doorknob and promptly drops the keys. "Oops!"

Given the way she reaches down to pick up the keys, with her ass high in the air, I don't think dropping the keys was an accident at all. I step up behind her, gripping her hips and grinding my achingly hard cock against her. "You drive me crazy," I groan.

"Me?" she purrs, rising to stand with her back to my chest. Letting go of her hips, I wrap my arms around her, pulling her tighter, and she lets her head fall back on my shoulder.

Plucking the keys from her hand, I open the door myself and dance her inside. Kicking the door shut behind us, I reach down to her thighs and scoop her up. Instinctively, her legs wrap around my waist.

I could march down the hallway with her in my arms. Throw her to the bed and follow her down, pinning her beneath me. Fuck her in the comfort of her bed . . . no, our bed. That's what it is now, because I let my short-term lease go and moved my couple of suitcases of stuff into Briar's cute little house a few weeks ago.

But I don't do that.

As I've learned, kids make having a sex life challenging. Rushed make-outs while Harley takes a too-short shower become treasured touchpoints. Quiet time in the privacy of the bedroom behind a locked door is the norm. My travel schedule doesn't help either. I've introduced Briar to the naughty fun of FaceTime masturbation sessions, but having the entire house to ourselves is a luxury we don't take for granted.

So I don't go anywhere. I spin, pinning her back against the front door, right here in the living room. I steal her mouth, kissing her hard and deep as I grind against her core. She moans, not needing to be quiet for once, and I move to her neck so her noises can be the musical soundtrack to our lovemaking.

God, I want to hear her saying my name. Not because I'm insecure, but because it's what she does when she's on the verge of coming, and in that moment of uncertainty, with her pleasure right on the cutting edge of flying or falling, she trusts that I'm there to catch her either way. And her trust is a gift I treasure. Whether she whispers my name, or yells it out . . . like a prayer, like I'm her savior . . . I get to be the lucky man who not only sees her at her most vulnerable, but that she chose to give her the pleasure she's always deserved but never received. Fuck, I feel like the best version of me . . . because of her.

I let her legs lower reluctantly, a positional necessity so I can get her sweater and jeans off, but thankfully, she takes over, stripping herself while I do the same. Quickly nude, I press into her again, sandwiching her between the hard door and my unyielding body. Her skin is warm silk that I want to touch everywhere, but that will have to be for the next round. Now, I need to feel her surround me with her wet heat. I need to feel her pussy clamp down on me as she comes. I need to fill her . . . with my cock, my cum, my love.

"Fuck, Briar. I can't wait," I warn her.

"Then don't." She lifts a leg to my hip as she takes me in hand, trying to angle us to get what we both want, and I lift her once again, using the door as leverage.

This time, when I grind against her, I can feel the slick juices of her pussy covering me. I should take the time to enjoy it, but they make it too easy to slip inside her. She hisses loudly at the invasion, her nails digging into my shoulders, and she cries out, "Dom!"

Yes. Fucking yes.

Again. Louder.

My face buried into her neck and breathing the faint smell of her shampoo, I hold her ass in my tight grip, thrusting into her like the wild animal she makes me become. We've been careful, even gentle as she learns what she likes, what she enjoys, what she wants, but lately, she's been particularly receptive to rougher fucking. With it backed by love, she's discovering not only that she can take it, but that she loves it. And I'm happy to fuck Briar however she wants it. Slow, fast, hard, soft, missionary, face down, cowgirl, and now . . . up against the front door that I will never look at the same way again after this.

Her panted breaths become whimpering cries of pleasure while mine become grunts of need. Shit, I'm going to come before she does. I try to make sure she's first every time, but I'm already there, hitting that point of no return. "Briar," I groan.

"Me too," she answers, gasping.

Oh, thank fuck. She's coming with me. We're coming together.

I fight it off for a few more strokes until I feel her whole body go tight, and as she starts shuddering in my arms, I release my hold on my own orgasm and crash over the edge with her. My eyes slam shut as my entire focus becomes the sensation of her pulsating around me as jet after jet of cum shoots from my cock. Distantly, I hear her cry out my name once more.

My legs shaking bring me back to reality and carefully, I let Briar down. She thumps her head back against the door, holding on to the doorknob for dear life as she breathes out a satisfied sigh. "Wow."

"You can say that again."

"Wow." She gives me a sly look, questioning if I'll get the silly joke.

I chuckle. I can't help it—she cracks me up. She drives me wild. It's like the best of everything in one Briar-shaped package. "C'mon, let's get cleaned up, and then I need to feed you before round two."

"Ooh, I like that plan!"

Later, after we've eaten long chicken nuggets (because they were fast) and had a more luxurious, loud lovemaking session in the bed (because it's comfortable), we're lying in the dim lamplight. Wrapped in each other's arms, with Briar snuggled into my chest, I relax. Tonight was great, tomorrow is going to be even greater, and Sunday will be the greatest because Harley comes home.

"I love you," I murmur, pressing a kiss to the top of her head. She wiggles happily, snuggling in even closer.

"I like hearing you say that," she admits, "but what I like even more is feeling how much you mean that."

Thinking she's complimenting my sexual prowess, I curl my hips toward her. "Oh, I'll make sure you feel it." Even spent and soft, my dick perks up at the smallest hint of a tease that it might get another chance to be inside her.

She giggles, patting my chest. "No, seriously." Lifting up so she can meet my eyes, I see that she's gone thoughtful. "I didn't think this kind of life, this kind of love, was real. Until you." Her voice goes quiet as she adds, "Thank you. For everything."

After all we've been through, on some deep level, I think she still isn't sure quite how she ended up here, with me, like this. She worries, she overthinks, she hurts, but she also smiles, makes the mundane a bit extra special, and loves hard and deep, throwing herself full throttle into me, trusting that I'll catch her every time. And I will.

Because while she thinks I changed things for her, the truth is, she changed everything for me. I was floating through life, dedicated to hockey and not much else, but one conversation with Briar had me changing course quickly. To whatever road led me to her.

I push her hair out of her face, wanting to see her pretty eyes. "Briar, I knew this was real. I've seen it my whole life and knew I would never settle for anything less. So thank you for making what we have possible. For making life more than hockey. For giving me a home and a family." Cupping her cheek, I say, "For giving me your heart and taking mine."

Her smile blooms slowly and gradually, growing brighter until her eyes are lit up from within with her happiness. I feel like a god for being able to do that for her. I want to be the reason she smiles every single day for the rest of her life, because she will certainly be the reason I do.

"No take-backsies, though," she teases. She surprises me and leans down, licking my chest. "I licked you so you're mine."

I laugh out loud. I have no idea where that came from, but I like it. And I will never want my heart back from this woman anyway. It's hers, forever. We might be lying here, naked and postsex, but that's the true intimacy we share . . . in sharing our pasts, ugly as they have sometimes been; in opening our hearts, damaged as they may be; and planning our futures, as weird and silly and wonderful as we can make them.

As long as they involve knee socks. And maybe some cargo shorts.

"You can lick me anytime, Briar. Anywhere too." I catch her eye with a quirk of my brow. "Same goes for you. I'll lick you anytime, anywhere."

She squeaks in embarrassment, burying her face against my chest again. But I can nearly hear her thinking . . . about licking me, about me licking her.

Once upon a time, this woman accepted less than the bare minimum as her fate. With me, she'll never know less than all I can give her. The sun, the moon, the stars, maybe a fucking planet or two. And all of me. Every single bit.

And that's a pretty good deal. After all, I'm Dominic Motherfucking Lee.

Literally.

# Epilogue

## Dominic

"Who's gonna kick the Hawks' asses this time?" Sabine calls out through the locker room.

"We are!" the chorus of guys answers.

"Especially Honey's," Pacholek says, holding up a fist to Sabine. They bump, ready to hit the ice with power, focus, and aggression.

Tonight is a redemption game for us all. Last time we played the Hawks, we were still figuring our shit out. Now, we're solid. Well, I'll say 90 percent solid, with that last bit being Anderson. He's still getting on board with the whole brotherhood thing, but he's a work in progress.

Now that Coach is growing and the team dynamic is shifting to something healthier, better, and fuller . . . Anderson is finally shifting too. It's a gradual process, especially since he's not prone to sharing his feelings, claiming he doesn't have any—other than annoyance with me when I start up the team's theme song, "Don't Stop Believin'." But I've seen him bobbing his head a little, so I think he secretly likes it, though he'd never admit it. Or maybe it's just that it's a catchy tune?

He might be a tougher nut to crack than Kipson was, but I'll do it eventually. One day soon, we're gonna be trading friendship bracelets, I just know it. He'll probably give me one that says "Fuck Off," but I'll know he means *Love you, bro.*

"Hey, Lavoie," Bill says, "your girl is sitting with my wife, right?"

Lavoie nods. "Yeah, Rozalnie put everyone together, I think."

Rozalnie is one of the team's interns, whose unofficial job description includes the superfun duty of acting as WAG coordinator. It became a necessity when guys wanted their wives and girlfriends to come to games. We've had parents and kids too. Well, Harley. So far, I'm the only Blizzard player with a kid that comes to games.

"Briar, Harley, Penny, and my parents are with them too," I interject as I wrap fresh tape around my stick. The thought of all my favorite people sitting together in the stands, watching me play, is a big motivator. We're gonna crush this game.

We're gonna beat the Hawks, I can feel it.

"Bring it in, guys," Coach shouts. He's still a yeller. It's how he motivates and how he hypes us up, so we are very familiar with his red-faced, vein-popping pep talks. But now, he's just as likely to spit out *good hustle* as he is *What the fuck was that?* The balance is appreciated.

We crowd around him, ready to hear him out.

"Tonight's game is a big one," he starts. "I've asked you to play your guts out every single time you take the ice, but tonight, I'm asking for something more. I want you to play your heart out. Leave it all out there."

"No regerts!" Kipson adds, and we all chuckle.

He's doing well now too. He and Sofia didn't get back together, but they've had a couple of good conversations and finally have some closure on what went wrong for them. For now, she's staying in Nebraska, and ironically, he's focusing more on hockey. He's not ready to date again, and probably won't be for a while, but he's better, which is all we can hope for. He's definitely a mission complete, and I've decided I'm out of the business of saving idiot hockey players from themselves.

Coach turns hard eyes to Kipson. "You can't joke your way into winning against a team like the Hawks, so get serious."

"Yes, Coach," Kipson barks, instantly sobering.

Glaring around the room, Coach meets each of our eyes, one by one. "Tonight's going to be hard. There's no doubt about it. But you are harder. You're tougher. You're rougher. You're winners, so get out there and fucking win!"

"Yes, Coach," we yell back, amped up.

Grabbing our gear, we're lining up to hit the ice for warm-ups and Anderson hangs back. "Lee."

Rolling my eyes, I tell him, "Don't worry. Kipson and I will help protect the house this time." Last time we played the Hawks, Anderson was left out to dry and nearly tanked himself out blocking dozens of shots with minimal defensive assistance.

"You'd better," he orders harshly. He glances past me and I look back, not seeing anyone. For a second, I wonder if he's about to sneak attack me, but then he says, "Uh, that's not what I was gonna say."

I look at him expectantly, waiting for him to spit it out.

He sighs heavily. "Everyone going to O'Neal's after the game?"

I blink, surprised he's even aware of that despite it being in the team group chat. "Yeah."

"You think I could come?" he asks hesitantly. "I want to apologize to Briar for the shit I tried to start."

I cock my head, my jaw tight. "What. Shit?"

His eyes widen, looking at me like he hopes to hell that I'm kidding. When I don't laugh, he hisses, "Fuck. She really didn't tell you?"

I shake my head slowly. Whatever Anderson said, I already don't like it.

"First, I'm sorry." I arch a brow, needing him to get to the rest of it faster. "Second, it was a while ago. I told her about the fuck-marry-kill thing."

"Oh. She already knew about that. I told her."

He laughs, nodding meaningfully. "I know. She told me that too. Right after I told her that you picked her to marry and your whole thing was a ploy to get back at Coach."

"You told her WHAT?"

He holds his hands out, stopping me, when I didn't even realize that I'd taken a step his direction. "She didn't believe me. Not a bit. Said you picked her to fuck and that you did, so you won the game anyway. And so did she." He frowns distastefully, like Briar liking fucking me irritates him.

I grin, thinking that doesn't exactly sound like Briar. But in some ways, it does sound just like her. "So you're telling me that you learned nothing from fucking up Kipson's marriage and tried to follow that by fucking up my relationship with Briar?" I clarify, my voice low and on the edge of threatening.

He sighs. "Yeah, and I want to apologize. So can I come tonight?"

I eye him carefully, but I see nothing but regret and genuine sorrow on his face. "Yeah, man. You're welcome to come. You're always welcome to come. Just don't fuck with Briar or Harley. Or Penny or Griffin. Or my parents. Or probably any of the guys' women." I pause, thinking to make sure I covered everyone. "But yeah, you can come."

He swallows as though asking was the hardest thing he's ever done. Fuck, it might be.

"Thanks."

I feel it—the official start of phase two of my work here. Which will have to continue after we beat the Hawks.

And later, I'm gonna ask Briar why she didn't tell me about Anderson's cruel play. Though I already know the answer—she didn't believe him.

She trusted me because she loves me. And I love her.

As I skate around, warming up, I find her and Harley sitting with the rest of my family. "Hey!" I shout, but her eyes are already mine. She waves both hands at me, her smile wide. "I love you!"

"Love you, too, Albie!"

"Who's Albie?" I see my mom ask, her brows wrinkled in confusion.

Penny laughs, telling Mom, "I'll explain later."

They don't get it, but that doesn't matter. What matters is that Briar and I understand the importance of patience. And most of all, we understand how precious our love is, how special our family is.

This is my home now, here with Briar and Harley and with the Blizzard, and I couldn't be happier.

# ABOUT THE AUTHOR

Lauren Landish is a *Wall Street Journal* and *USA Today* bestselling author who captivates readers with irresistibly steamy contemporary romance. Her stories feature alpha heroes who meet their match in bold, unforgettable heroines, delivering all the swoon-worthy tension romance readers crave. Whether crafting tales of grumpy billionaires, protective bad boys, or dominant athletes with a secret soft side, Lauren's stories always promise heat, heart, and a satisfying happily ever after.

Her sexy contemporary romances have garnered a legion of devoted readers who know that when they pick up a Lauren Landish book, they're in for a wild, wickedly fun ride. When she's not writing steamy scenes or dreaming up new book boyfriends, Lauren can be found enjoying oversize mugs of coffee and plotting fresh ways to make readers blush.

For updates on upcoming books, visit www.LaurenLandish.com, or follow her on TikTok (@laurenlandish), Instagram (@Lauren_Landish), and Facebook (@Lauren.Landish).